Restless Souls

Susie

a Happy good
Sweet Soul

Love,
PJ

Restless Souls

Patricia Brunson

Library of Congress Control Number:		2014914961
ISBN:	Hardcover	978-1-4990-6111-6
	Softcover	978-1-4990-6113-0
	eBook	978-1-4990-6112-3

This is a work of fiction. Names, characters, places and incidents either are the product of the author's imagination or are used fictitiously, and any resemblance to any actual persons, living or dead, events, or locales is entirely coincidental.

This book was printed in the United States of America.

Rev. date: 08/08/2014

To order additional copies of this book, contact:
Xlibris LLC
1-888-795-4274
www.Xlibris.com
Orders@Xlibris.com
661290

Contents

Acknowledgments

First I would like to thank those of my friends and family that didn't laugh, nudge each other in the ribs or exchange meaningful glances when I announced that I was writing a book. As a lifelong avid reader, it had always been a secret goal of mine to attempt this project, but it wasn't until I reached my late fifties that I developed the confidence to begin work with the expectation that I would actually complete the book.

Although my goal was to produce a finished product, I never believed that my book would be published in any form other than that which my home printer or the copy machine at office depot would provide. The fact that you are reading this now is due to two factors. The first is the emergence of E-books which makes self-publishing affordable. The second factor is the total support and encouragement given me by my loving husband who, although he is very intelligent and insightful, has a blind spot when it comes to the depth of my abilities.

My friend, Christina Crawford, read a small portion of my original draft and gave me two pieces of advice: Just keep writing and don't join a writers group. I never asked her to read my completed manuscript because she doesn't read fiction, although her own book, Mommy Dearest, has as much drama as any novel. I followed her advice and interpreted it as encouragement since Christina is not given to insincere feedback.

There were many others who pushed me toward publishing including Sheryl Manchester, who listened to some of the stories in this book, offered suggestions and told me I would be an idiot if I didn't publish after all the work I had put into the writing. Sheryl always gets right to the point.

The first person to read the book in its entirety was my friend Sandy Atkinson, another avid reader and one whose opinion I greatly respect. She gave me an unconditional "thumbs up" and the gentle nudges I needed to follow through.

Melinda Hallmark, herself an author, volunteered a great deal of time and much sound input at a time when her energy and efforts were needed elsewhere.

Zandra Evans, a dear friend with a heart as big as her imagination, offered many helpful insights and her unwavering enthusiasm carried me forward. Zandra makes everything fun.

My dear Aunt Mary undertook the task of proofreading my manuscript and was helpful in pointing out areas that were unclear (or just plain nonsensical). Aunt Mary is the kindest person I have ever known so her willingness to help came as no surprise to me.

My sister, Lorrie, deserves mention because she is the kind of person who admires and supports any effort to express a thought or idea. She is that blend of sweet, yet strong womanhood. There is a lot of Lorrie in some of my characters.

Thanks also to my brother Mark who filled in some of the blanks in my computer skills and the many others who expressed interest and offered support over the years. I hope that, in reading my book, they will not feel their encouragement misspent.

Finally, thanks to everyone I have ever known since it is from all of you that I have developed the characters I hope my readers will come to love.

Chapter One

POOR DEAD BERNIE

SAM

Bernie Rauch was officially pronounced dead by the Island County coroner. We all suspected as much since poor Bernie had demonstrated no sign of breathing or heartbeat for three hours prior to the coroner's arrival, making this pronouncement a bit anticlimactic.

What was shocking as I looked around the room was the lack of bereavement on the faces of my fellow inhabitants and probably my own as well if I could step outside myself for a view. The atmosphere in the room was less than somber, but not disrespectful, more like complacent. Almost everyone seemed resigned, if not totally comfortable that, though Bernie's death was a bit of a mystery, no real tragedy had occurred. I confess that I reluctantly shared that view. Yet how can the passing of a man we have spent day and night with for several weeks leave us so unmoved?

Appalled as I was by my reaction to Bernie's death, I found some relief in knowing that my feelings seemed to be mirrored by the most remarkable people one could hope to meet. Though ordinary in their physical appearance and capabilities, these people are cosmic superheroes to me. Bernie could have been one of them, but instead he chose to make his existence a larger than life trash-heap of the seven deadly sins peppered with a profound bitterness that turned his special gift into a curse. I guess under these circumstances, real grief was out of the question. Our main source of discomfort was that no one knew how Bernie had died. There was no sign of violence and his facial expression didn't indicate physical distress or pain. He actually appeared almost serene.

Having given up on appearing grief stricken, I was wondering how long this unfortunate disturbance would interrupt our exploration. Predictably, there would be a number of distractions over the next few days as we tried to find even one human being willing to take responsibility for seeing that Bernie arrived at a final resting place. Even more distressing was that we had been informed that we would all be interrogated as to our whereabouts during the night Bernie died. The sheriff said that he was sure it would be determined that Bernie died of natural causes, but the coroner had not ruled out foul play so he wanted no one to leave the area for a few days as he completed his investigation.

Meanwhile, I was trying to activate all my Christian values to understand in some small way how or if God would welcome his troubled soul. In the end I resigned myself to the belief that some things can only be understood by our maker. Bernie was a wrecking ball to our pursuit of knowledge as we were often distracted from those efforts to figure out how and why he came to be this fractured creature. Yet, looking back at the last few days of his life, I had seen a change in Bernie that made me wonder if he might bring something of value to this planet after all. How sad that he died just as he might have been beginning to live.

Chapter Two

A VISIT FROM BERNIE

BERNIE

Yup. I'm dead alright. I'm not going to go into the details right now. This is Sam's story and, except for those times when I jump in to insert my two cents, I'll let Sam and the others do the telling. Besides, I'm dead so I really shouldn't be speaking out at all, but here's the deal. When we die we are required to review our life and face our failures as well as our victories. So here I am, forced to watch these people try to drum up some grief over my passing. Sam is going to go back and tell you all about how we arrived at this point and you aren't going to get a true picture of my role in this unless I jump in and tell you what was really going on in my head. It's not a pretty picture, but it's part of the price I must pay in order to move on.

Things are a little "up in the air" right now as to my future so, I'll have to get back to you on that later. You are going to find out a lot about me in the course of this story and you probably aren't going to like me one bit. I won't blame you. There wasn't much to admire, but I'd like to believe that in the end, I offered something of value to make up for some of the garbage I brought to the world.

I just want to let you in on one little secret. Maybe some of you already have figured this out, but it has taken me several lifetimes to get there and I suspect the same is true for most of you. It's about eternity. You're already in it! Eternal means just that, always and forever. I'm here to report that eternity doesn't start when you die. It never started at all. It always has been. That means that you are living part of your eternity right now. Do you see where I am going with this? Every thought and deed you have ever had plus those you are having and doing now are part of your eternity. So, you people who are looking forward to an afterlife should pay close attention to every moment. This should be a relief to you because it releases you from the petty cares and worries in your current life. It reduces their importance to where they should be and elevates the truly important things, like love and courage, to the status they deserve. It means you should be living and loving fully and fearlessly every minute because everything you do goes into the soup with everything you have done and everything you will do. Eternity doesn't have an end result because it never ends. It evolves forever based on what you bring to the table, past, present and future. It means that we might get do-overs, possibly giving us a chance to average out some of the bad with good, better, or best. I finally learned that from Sam and these incredible people you are about to meet. I hope it isn't too late for me. I'm going to have to do some A+ work for a long time to bring my average up - if I am given the chance.

I'll turn you back to Sam now. He is probably thinking that he may have bitten off more than he can chew, but I have learned that that is exactly how we should live as long as we never give up.

Chapter Three

SAM WANTS A DO-OVER

My name is Sam Merrick and I do not count myself as one of the "remarkables" I spoke of earlier. My only raison d'être was my willingness and my unearned opportunity to bring the group together. I am not an intellectual and certainly no scholar. My motives were somewhat self-serving and I brought nothing but my financial capability to this sumptuous banquet of humanity, but I believe I created an environment that enabled this group to share the experiences of many lifetimes and these I will pass on to you with the help of my friends.

I will introduce you to astounding people, places and events that richly deserve the attention of an audience such as yourself. You will hear stories that have never been told, spoken by people that have never been heard. These people are composites of every vice and virtue known to man, yet they continue to renew their innocence. They have plunged to the depths of despair and soared to the summits of hope. They have cavorted with evil and bathed in the light of God. They exemplify every extreme you and I can imagine, yet we can see part of ourselves mirrored in each of them. By sharing with you the memories of their many past lives, you will be given a tour of humanity. But first I should give you a little background so that you will understand the forces that drove me to bring the group together in the first place.

Although I am the founder of this expedition, I am not the catalyst. That title goes to one who is truly remarkable. Her name is Samantha Merrick. She is my granddaughter and she is glorious. It was my honor to be present at the moment of her birth, and like any other man at such an event, I was nothing but a shrub, green in color and totally useless except for whatever shade I could provide her tender eyes from the harsh lighting. Those eyes! I swear that the minute she was expelled from her screaming mother she looked directly at me and I felt her reading my soul.

She emerged calmly and peacefully as if her arrival was an everyday occurrence. After a few moments, the physician did what was necessary to elicit the obligatory wail after which she relapsed into her calm and peaceful mode. From that moment on she has been a focal point in my life. I won't expound on her beauty and talents, subjecting myself to the accusations of bias levied at all proud grandparents. You will see her persona evolve as my story progresses and arrive at your own totally objective conclusions. It is my love for her and Amanda, her grandmother and my ex-wife and the other love of my life, that has driven me to spend whatever time and treasure it takes to understand and appreciate the gift they share; their memories of past lives. I will not make the same mistake with Samantha that I did with Amanda.

Even my love and devotion to Samantha has selfish undertones. By virtue of her existence I am granted more time to spend with Amanda. She is equally devoted to Samantha rendering it tolerable for her to be in the same room with me for the sake of our granddaughter. Our son Alexander and his wife Tiffany are both adamant that we have equal access to their child and would tolerate no attempt from either of us to limit the contact of the other, although Amanda would never be that selfish anyway and I welcome the opportunities created by this arrangement. There have been many times that the three of us have shared an afternoon in the park or an evening at a movie with Amanda's presence adding to my joy and my presence seemingly a matter of indifference if not a slight annoyance to her.

For me, having these two women in the same room creates an environment similar to that which plants enjoy during an electrical storm. I am energized, charged and actually experience a sort of metamorphosis that makes me more sensitive and alert to the world around me. I even become more interesting to myself! Of course most of this heightened awareness quickly fades when deprived of their presence, but still, each time a small inkling remains and seems to build on itself creating an addictive reaction.

To keep things in perspective, you should know that I was born and raised in Texas, and it is the Texan in me that tends to put women on a pedestal. They possess virtues and abilities not commonly found in men and I am truly in awe of most of the women in my life. I can't help it and I have never tried to conceal it. This is a heritage passed down to me through my father and re-enforced by my sixth generation Texan mother. Having four brothers and no sisters deprived me of the opportunity to observe females close up, flaws and all, so I am hopelessly at the mercy of the female mystique. Many people find this endearing, but there are a number of women who have taken an instant and strenuous dislike to me. They have no trust in the purity of my motives and often mistake the courtesies I extend as unwelcome advances. This is confusing but causes me little concern, since on the whole those particular women would be of no interest to me in the first place. They usually display all the traits that act as a repellent to any man who is not self-destructive or doesn't believe he deserves to be punished just for being a man. I waste no time worrying about this type of woman and focus all my attention on those other fabulous creatures. Yes, I love women, but I also believe men must be admired for their courage and tenacity in facing the world without the aid of the finer intuitions and sensitivities women possess. Men are amazing beings too.

My search for an understanding of that which made Amanda the woman she is should have begun thirty-two years ago, but sadly, it was delayed by my lack of imagination and courage to seek the truth. I could have spent those years with her witnessing the wonders of her gift, helping her with the burdens and sharing the joys that came with her memories of the other lives she has lived. Instead, I left her alone in her struggles and chose the safer path for myself.

Chapter Four

BOY MEETS GIRL

It was opening day of boating season in Seattle, the first Sunday in May thirty two years ago. Each year I celebrated this event to its fullest with my friends, fellow live-aboards, and business associates. The high point is the boat parade which always has a theme. Those who wish to join the parade decorate their boats along this theme and others participate as spectators. Our group had made it a tradition to position our boats along the parade route days in advance. We would tie our boats together creating a floating neighborhood making it possible to move from one boat to another with ease, sharing food, drink and good times while awaiting the main event. I had been there since the preceding Friday.

Like any true Texan, I consider myself a master of the barbecue and had equipped myself with a huge, custom built barbecue/smoker on the top deck of my boat. Each year I set out to bring my smoky, spicy delight to a few dozen of my closest friends and fellow boaters. I would cook about sixty pounds of ribs, brisket, chicken and sausage resulting in an unusually high level of popularity among my peers for about two hours. I was always able to supply myself with a date who, along with some other friends, would round out the meal with an assortment of salads, breads and special dishes of their own. That day my femme du jour sported only one name, Tulaine, no surname. This should have been an indication to me that she might have some special needs. Tulaine was a manicurist and truly believed that she had some mysterious and elusive quality that drove men wild. In reality she could drive a man wild, but not through her charms. You may have guessed that Tulaine had successfully evaded my pedestal, but don't we all settle for less than perfect from time to time?

People were moving from boat to boat enjoying the sun, snacks and libations. The barbecue was smoking and I had everything under control so I felt I could relax for a couple of hours until after the parade when I would serve dinner. One small glitch; the mysterious Tulaine had locked herself in the head (boat talk for bathroom) with her sister. They were quite close, being the only members of their family that communicated with one another. It was their practice whenever they got together to guzzle several alcoholic beverages in rapid succession followed by a couple of hours of gut-wrenching remembrances of their parched, broken lives. Over the two-month period of our sub-standard relationship I had endured a number of these encounters. It always ended up in a toss-up as to who had failed them the most, their seriously flawed parents or their combined total of five ex-husbands, all of whom were branded as cruel and insensitive. Knowing that this noisy and tearful process could take hours, I set upon the task of re-routing my guests in need of physical relief to neighboring boats. This was accomplished by posting a sign on the door "CONTENTS DYSFUNCTIONAL—PLEASE USE NEIGHBORING FACILITIES". I was then able to resume my period of relaxation and it was then that I spotted the future Mrs. Sam Merrick.

She was attractive, not what one would consider beautiful, but she possessed all the physical traits I cherish in a woman, namely blonde hair, blue eyes and slender legs. Add to that an ample bosom, small waist and pleasing derriere and all my superficial preferences were fulfilled allowing me to concentrate on her more intellectual properties. Her smile indicated pure personal pleasure and confidence. She spoke and listened with her entire body paying complete attention to what she was hearing as well as what she said.

She was a guest on Tom Carlson's boat, which was tied to John Bannon's boat, which was tied to mine. From my top deck I had a clear, but unobserved view and I spent several minutes absorbing her. She was talking with another woman whom I assumed was either her sister or a close friend as they seemed to be sharing a number of private jokes in that intimidating way that women who are close with one another never fail to do. I watched anxiously to see if there was a man about who might possibly have a claim on her. Spotting no one, I strained to see if there was a ring on her finger, even though I could never remember which hand would bear a wedding ring. Bingo!!! No ring on either finger. As a matter of fact, she wore no jewelry at all! What kind of woman was this? I was overcome by a sense of urgency. If she was unclaimed, I knew it wouldn't be for long.

As I pondered various ways I could capture her attention, I saw her purposefully steal a martini Tom had made for his date, not Amanda. He had reached into a secret compartment where he stored the expensive vodka to make the special drink and was momentarily distracted by another guest. Amanda seized the opportunity, crossing the deck as skillfully as any sneak thief, and without spilling a drop, positioned herself in a far corner to enjoy her plunder. Her self-satisfied smile confirmed that she was operating with full criminal intent. That little scene only intensified my desire.

My opening was to board Tom's boat and make certain she knew that all of his guests were invited for barbecue aboard my boat. I crossed over John's stern and, leaping onto Tom's boat, I walked coolly over to Tom making sure she would see me talking to him. You see, this way my invitation to her would seem like a courtesy or afterthought rather than a come-on. Talking to Tom, I could see her out of the corner of my eye, but I couldn't tell if she had noticed me. I would steal glances at her from time to time, but it was spooky. Every time I glanced at her, she was turned away and I found myself looking straight into the cold, steely blue eyes of her female companion. This woman was not an easy person to look at. She wasn't unattractive, quite the contrary, but she was incredibly intimidating. Each time she caught my eye, I felt as if two years were being added to my time in Purgatory. I didn't know how I was going to get past her to reach the object of my desire and I found myself wondering if anyone would notice if I knocked her overboard and held her under the water with a boat hook. I was moderately troubled that I was capable of such thoughts. But then, wild random thoughts are my trademark.

Just about the time I was going to retreat to my boat, beaten and heartsick, the she-devil companion walked over to me and, smiling in a flirtatious, but clearly phony way said, "I see that you are drinking a margarita. Do you think you could find one for me and my friend?" Tom only has beer aboard." (My angel had obviously not shared the secret of the stolen martini.) The first miracle was that I was not immediately turned to stone at the sound of her voice as I feared would be the case. The second miracle was that the minute she uttered the word "margarita", my angel spun around and looked directly at me, her expression a mixture of anticipation and delight. Though in no way did I flatter myself into believing that there was a trace of interest in me besides my ability to produce the desired cocktail, I wasted no time in inviting them to accompany me to my boat, promising them the best margarita they ever had followed by some great Texas barbecue. My angel looked me squarely in the eye and smiled warmly leaving me a bit heady and weak in the knees as I guided them to my floating bachelor pad. Could one man's life change so quickly? Was this the beginning of a grand adventure or merely a temporary and ill-fated social exchange? Was my fly zipped?

That day made me a believer in "love at first sight". Prior to that, I had always believed that "lust at first sight "was a more appropriate term for those who were instantly smitten. Don't get me wrong, there was plenty of that too, but I swear that my intentions were pure and honorable from that first moment.

Introductions were made and I learned that my angel had a name-Amanda. I was glad to learn her name so I could stop thinking of her as my angel. Having witnessed the pleasure she took in her earlier thievery, I sensed that she was slightly less than angelic. Her companion was her lifelong friend, appropriately named Thelma. Amanda and her opportunistic conspirator made themselves at home, finding a prime vantage point from which they would be able to view the parade and have easy access to my makeshift bar from whence the margaritas flowed. I positioned myself as close to Amanda as possible while still being able to tend my barbecue.

At this point, you might be wondering how I was going to manipulate the situation when my femme du jour, Tulaine, vacated the counseling room. Well, that was miracle number three. It seems she and her sister had left the chamber and my boat during my absence having made the acquaintance of another man, one who had a larger and more luxurious vessel than mine. I vowed to seek him out and give Tulaine a glowing recommendation at my first opportunity.

I took little notice of the parade, but used that distraction to observe Amanda's every movement, hoping for some nuance or window of opportunity to infuse myself into her life. Meanwhile, the insatiable Thelma kept me busy replenishing her margarita. All signs of her phony flirtations had disappeared as she treated me like a eunuch at the feet of two goddesses. She had clearly guessed my poorly kept secret and behaved as if she held the power to open the door to my dream world or slam it in my face, locking me out forever. I know this makes me sound like a fool, but in fact I am normally a pretty savvy guy. I knew at that point that if I didn't recover my senses and make a plan my hopes were doomed. Time was running out along with the tequila.

The parade was over and some forty or fifty people had filed through my buffet showering me with compliments and expressions of gratitude. That day all the praise fell on deaf ears. I could think of nothing but how I was going to get some time alone with Amanda. Aside from a few pleasantries, we hadn't shared much conversation. My contact had been mostly with her warden and I was afraid they were getting ready to abandon ship when miracle number four occurred. Greedy Thelma helped herself to another margarita and engaged in, or rather dominated, a conversation with one of my forty new-best-friend dinner guests. At the same time, Amanda rose and began tidying up. She had spotted one of the large trash bags I had strategically planted around the lower and upper deck and was actually collecting used paper plates, plastic glasses and other assorted trash. I was thunderstruck by the intimacy of her actions. She was cleaning my boat, my home, as if we were a couple, or at the very least, acquainted. I pretended not to notice for a while so as not to break the spell. Besides, I was kind of tired and appreciated the help and she was the only one who took my subtle trash bag hint. Finally, I grabbed a bag and started working my way toward her, trying to ignore the fact that we were picking up chewed bones and refuse instead of running toward each other in slow motion through a field of daisies.

She worked quickly and methodically and within a few minutes there were four large bags neatly tied and sitting on the back deck. She then proceeded to the ravaged buffet table and began to deal with leftover food while I cleaned the barbecue. About that time sloppy drunk Thelma and her unfortunate captive crawled over the railings to return to Tom's boat, but not before Amanda informed them that she was riding back with me and would meet them later at the dock. It never entered my mind that she was being a bit presumptuous. I was floating, face up, in a sea of joy.

We were just finishing our "trash bonding" when the usual commotion occurred with everyone firing up their engines and departing for their respective slips. In a panic, I was wondering if Tulaine and her sister would be returning to my boat having already worn out their welcome and/or the liquor cabinet aboard the luxury yacht. Not to worry, I spotted her in the distance waving at me from the back of the other boat and yelling something that I could not make out. I was just happy to see her waving goodbye. Meanwhile, Tom's boat was also departing and I could see nasty Thelma peering at us disapprovingly. As they pulled away, I was struck with the realization that Amanda and I were totally alone for at least an hour, two if I could convince her that it was safer to wait until the crowd had dispersed before making our way home.

I heated water to make gourmet coffee in my previously unused French press. Sensing that I would want to know, she informed me that she loved good coffee and took hers strong and black. Although I had never really been a coffee connoisseur, I became one at that moment. The French press had been a gift from Tulaine along with a tin of gourmet coffee from a country I had no desire to visit. I had been using them as paperweights for my unpaid bills until that moment. I remember thinking that even a relationship as shallow as I had shared with Tulaine had some place in the overall scheme of things as I proudly produced two mugs of liquid love.

Amanda had worked so feverishly that it came as a bit of a surprise to see her relax with the same fervor. She simply melted into the settee. I followed suit, putting my feet up on the coffee table, cradling my cup as I experienced a sense of well-being so profound that all I could do was sit there grinning. She returned my idiot grin with a sunburst smile of her own. I gave her the history of opening day and she listened attentively, seeming to make mental notes as if I were giving her driving instructions to the local mall. After babbling on for several minutes, I finally ceased my chatter as she turned to me and said, "You know, you have refrigerator eyes." Of course I jumped to the conclusion that she saw some James Bond-like quality in my gaze, when she blurted out "They are exactly the color of the green stuff that grows on the food in my refrigerator." My reaction was delayed by a few seconds but then I started laughing and I finally began to relax.

From that day on for twenty-three years we were together. Thelma did everything possible to discourage our union and Tulaine became so angry at being replaced that she boarded my boat while I was on a date with Amanda and threw everything she could get her hands on overboard. We didn't care. We were in love and nothing could change that-not even a couple of crazy ladies.

Fast forwarding to the present, Amanda and I have been divorced for over nine years. Lest you wonder what went wrong with such a great love, let me say that I started taking miracles for granted. But this, along with the usual outside forces such as jobs, kids, in-laws and money that plague all marriages would not have torn us apart. At the heart of it all was my unwillingness to explore that which should have been embraced---Amanda's special gift of memories of her past lives, a gift shared by our granddaughter. A belated exploration of this gift and the adventure this journey has provided is the story I am offering you now.

Chapter Five

AMANDA STEPS IN

AMANDA

OK!!! Stop!! Sam is being maudlin again as most men are when they believe events are out of their control. I need to jump in here to set the record straight. There are two sides to every misery and I certainly made my contribution. From the day I met Sam, I too was charmed. The cool woman he describes bears no resemblance to what I was actually experiencing. In truth, I was half drunk from my stolen martini and the margaritas and therefore oblivious to his attentions until after dinner when I began to sober up. He was a gracious host and none of his guests were lifting a finger to help clean up. I didn't consider collecting trash an intimate gesture as Sam implied. It was merely a job that must be done and I truly had enjoyed the afternoon and wanted to show my appreciation. Also, Thelma was driving me nuts and I was looking for a way to get away from her for a while. It was during his speech about how selective he was about the coffee he drank while I had clearly seen a jar of Folgers Instant in his cupboard that I realized he may have at least a passing interest in me. Prior to that, I had just considered him another free-living bachelor who chose to live on a boat indicating that he rejected a traditional lifestyle. There was something about his effort to establish some kind of common ground via the coffee that struck me as sweetly pathetic and caused me to see him for the kind and gentle man that he was/is. I don't know where the remark about his green eyes came from. Probably it was some remaining vestige of the margaritas.

Sam is correct in his evaluation of the problems in our marriage, but he left out one major contributing factor. You see I possess that one trait that is common to most strong women; our inability or unwillingness to share our deepest fears and needs. We jealously guard these secrets and then blame others for not recognizing them. We set ourselves apart and then lament that we feel lonely. Find a devoted male and a strong woman and observe their dance. It's like a tango with her in the lead, but he will always blame himself when they crash into a wall. This is not deliberate on the part of the woman, it just happens and both seem unaware of the why and the how. As time passes, the man perceives himself to be less necessary to her and seeks solace in work, family and friends or in some cases, not Sam's, some less desirable diversions. The woman doesn't understand why the closeness is waning and blames him for his departure from her. She is left even more alone to face her demons. She feels he has abandoned her with her fears; fears that he never even knew she had. Over time the only thing that is left is love-and love is not enough.

Sam is an adorable man. He is handsome and strong in a poignantly special way. He aspires to all the attributes of an eagle scout, coming very close to reaching his goals, but mercifully falling a little short, which keeps the little boy in him alive. He never quits trying and his struggle is often painful to observe. He has that special kind of courage that allows him to display his tenderness without camouflage. He worships his father and idealizes his mother. He has elevated his granddaughter and me to a level previously unheard of outside of heaven. In short, he wears his heart on his sleeve. On the other hand, he has certain peculiarities that need explaining so I hope you don't mind if I jump in once in a while to clarify things that he says and does.

He suffers from what I call "dyslexia of the mouth" in that quite often things come out of his mouth that are the opposite of what he is thinking. Somewhere in the path between brain and mouth, his thoughts take a shortcut and he will delete one key word or scramble the word order replacing a perfectly designed thought with a derelict sentence. This usually occurs when he is nervous or trying to impress someone or put them at ease. One result is what is often referred to as the left-handed compliment, which he hands out in total sincerity and usually doesn't even realize what he has done. As an example, spoken to an attractive but portly female friend of mine, "A lot of men might think you are chubby, but I think you look great just the way you are." Fortunately, I wouldn't have a friend that didn't have a sense of humor.

Do you think I ever lost my love for him? I had always trusted and respected him. I guess I really did want a hero and he was the only person I had ever come close to connecting with, but we never really had been able to make that connection complete. That couldn't happen due to his refusal to learn about and accept my past lives. That part of me had always come between us, first because I kept them a secret, then later because he refused to accept their existence. Maybe I should have fought harder, but I was afraid he couldn't make that leap. I didn't want to face my fears and demons alone and I was tired of feeling lonely and isolated. I longed for a traveling companion through this life but I feared that Sam may not be up to the task. I let my disappointment fester until it infected every part of our lives. I knew that it wasn't all his fault and I didn't want to hurt him and make him feel like a failure so I ended our marriage before we caused each other more pain.

I encourage you to continue on this journey with Sam. He is a great host and would not invite you to anything that wouldn't prove to be a rewarding experience. I too am a participant, but Sam is the brave one and I am determined to let him lead for once.

By the way, Sam's worries about his reaction to Bernie's death are groundless. There is no great loss to the world. It takes no special courage to die and I am still not sure he didn't do it on purpose just to put a damper on our adventure. Although I am no fan of suicide, if this turns out to be the case, I might even be able to see something heroic in his passing. I was certain that when the investigation was completed, we would find that Bernie's death was a result of some fluke indicating that even God got sick of watching him make His beautiful world a darker place. That man sure made a lot of people mad, especially me. As you may have guessed, I have no intention of granting Bernie compliments in death that he did not earn in life. I have never understood why people do that, except maybe they hope others will do the same for them when they pass on.

SAM

I learned a lot in the years since the breakup, not just about myself, but Amanda too. I knew she will never love me again until I could show her that I understood what went wrong. I had reached several conclusions about strong women.

They don't want our help. They want to face their fears alone. It appeals to their sense of drama. They treasure their privacy. They don't want that intimacy that occurs when two people lie next to each other in the dead of night and spill their guts. They are never lonely and they don't feel isolated like the rest of us do at times.

You can see that I had really applied myself to understanding this woman and I was quite proud of the progress I had made. I believed I just needed to find a way to demonstrate my newfound insights to her so that she could trust me again. That is when I landed on this plan. I was convinced I had found a way to be her hero and increase my understanding of my granddaughter, who shares Amanda's gift, at the same time.

Amanda would probably tell you to drop this journey or at least lower your expectations of my being able to lead you to any lasting insights. She would say that, although I am a good man, I am not capable of provoking thoughts of a higher nature without getting them scrambled. Knowing her, she probably even has some insights into Bernie's character that would help us to be compassionate and understanding of his conflicted life, providing some reason to mourn his death. She is much more brave, generous and inquisitive than I.

Chapter Six

THE HAPPY COUPLE

SAM

Well, Amanda and I met in May and were married on the twenty eighth of December that same year. We had planned our wedding for January but there is a surprisingly practical side to Amanda. She discovered that, through some fluke in the way our incomes were arranged, if we were wed before December thirty first, we could file our taxes jointly and save enough money to pay for a modest wedding and an even more modest honeymoon.

It was a great wedding! We rented a condo overlooking Shilshoe Bay in Seattle. The condo belonged to Stuart Anderson, the owner of Black Angus Restaurants. We invited about one hundred friends and family for a gala party and we took a few minutes out early in the evening to pledge our troth. The condo was already decorated with dozens of white poinsettias and white lights, saving us a bundle on flowers. Amanda and I catered the entire event ourselves, hiring staff to serve and clean up only. We created a feast for our guests, (Did I mention Amanda is a fabulous cook?) saving another bundle in catering costs. It was a splendid party and it lasted until three in the morning. Thelma succeeded in putting a slight damper on the event by whispering some negative comments in Amanda's ear about some nasty remark I supposedly made to her, causing a "discussion" after everyone finally left. Amanda spent most of what was left of the night alone in the Jacuzzi. I had to promise her that we would have the marriage annulled the next day if she would just let me get some sleep. The end result was confirmation of my theory that no one ever has sex on their wedding night. The next morning all difficulties were resolved as we proceeded to open the gifts. Amanda gave me one of those looks and stated that we might as well stay married since we hadn't kept an accurate record of who gave us which gift and it would be embarrassing to try to return them without this knowledge.

Those months between May and our December wedding had done nothing to improve my image in Thelma's eyes. To this day I have no idea why she reacted to me so negatively. She didn't trust me and believed me capable of unspeakable acts. There was no convincing her otherwise since she also believes that she is singularly intuitive and can see things that others can't. Not to be unkind, but I kept hoping that her continual drinking of wine and spirits would dull her memory, wiping the slate clean and that she would come to know me for the sincere and devoted guy I am.

Our son, Alexander, was born on January 2nd, one year after our wedding. Amanda was so absolutely certain that he would be the first baby born at midnight of the new year that she convinced me as well. I found myself staring at her huge belly all New Year's Eve, expecting it to erupt at any moment, but when the hours passed uneventfully I fell asleep just a few minutes shy of midnight. Amanda remained glued to the TV set until two AM when the local news station aired the story of a Seattle woman giving birth to a baby girl. She woke me to witness the fact that the happy couple were two of the homeliest people ever to burden a TV screen and that their interview suggested they were slight of mind as well. Her lapse in charity lasted only a couple of minutes as it was revealed that this was their fifth child and Amanda decided they probably needed all the freebies given the first baby worse than we did. Twenty hours later our son entered the world. He seemed staggeringly tiny at 6 pounds and 2 ounces and he looked like an alien. We were both ecstatic and petrified with fear at the immense responsibility we had created for ourselves. We were so happy.

All was well as we brought him home, but over the next few weeks Alex seemed to be losing energy and was not becoming plump and pink as we expected. He vomited violently after every feeding. The doctor changed his formula and feeding schedule believing the Similac was too rich for his system. Nothing worked. He had no fever or other symptoms and our worry grew as he continued to lose ounces. Finally and belatedly, he was diagnosed with a condition not terribly uncommon in boys-pyloric stenosis. In lay terms, the pyloris, which is the opening to the stomach, closed off leaving his food in the esophagus rather than being processed, thus the projectile vomiting. He was literally starving to death. Surgery was required and, due to the fact that the diagnosis was so slow in coming, reflecting the technology of the day as well as a certain level of complacency on the part of the doctor, the process was quite dangerous. Alex was perilously weak at the time of surgery and we were warned that he was in considerable danger. We were again numb with fear, but this time the source was real. Alex survived the surgery only to develop an infection a week later requiring another procedure with an even more unpredictable outcome.

To make a long story short, Alex survived both surgeries and many subsequent bouts with pneumonia and other complications due to his weakened condition. He definitely had his mother's stamina and will. Through all those hours, days and weeks of crisis, I came to know Amanda better, but understood her less. I can only describe her as stoic. Spending days and nights at his bedside, she never cried or lamented our tragic situation. She simply managed. She knew how many drops per minute should be coming out of the ever-present IV's. She knew his medication schedule and grilled the doctors mercilessly for details about his condition and treatment. She appeared clinical in her care of him and, for me this seemed unnatural. I found myself wondering if she had normal maternal feelings or if this was more like a research project for her. There were times when I wanted us to lie down together and hold each other and weep for our poor suffering child, but she would have none of that. Over those long weeks, I came to realize that all her energy was to be spent on keeping him alive and planning our future. What could be the source of such strength?

It was on one of those grim days that I got my first glimpse of Amanda's secret. Alex was hospitalized for the third time in three months with a very high fever and pneumonia. He was thin and frail. The oxygen mask was so big for his little face. He was being given antibiotics through an IV attached to a vein in the top of his head, this being the only vein large enough to accommodate a needle. It was evening and we were by his bedside and hadn't spoken for over an hour when Amanda blurted out "I've lost children before and it isn't going to happen this time!" I was stunned into silence. I knew Amanda had never been married or even in a long-term relationship before. I didn't respond as I mentally chalked her remark up to fatigue and worry, or maybe by living in proximity to me, she was beginning to develop the same brain-to-mouth dysfunction that I suffer. Nevertheless, I was plagued by her revelation and the vehemence of her delivery. Alex woke at that moment and I was relieved of the necessity of a response, but I knew that it wasn't the end. Amanda needed to tell me something that I wasn't prepared to hear.

It was several weeks after that episode that I worked up the courage to ask her what she meant. We were on our boat cruising the San Juan Islands in the Puget Sound. Alex was doing extremely well and was in the capable hands of Amanda's mother, Margaret, as we took a much-deserved three-day weekend together. Margaret had been a source of strength and comfort to us throughout our ordeal. She was much more than Alex's grandmother, she was his guardian angel. It was easy to see where Amanda got her strength as we watched grandma manage doctors, nurses and medications in much the same way as Amanda. Nothing got past her and we had no qualms about leaving Alex in her care.

We were anchored in a deserted cove, basking in the sun on the top deck of our boat. Amanda was wearing nothing but a suntan, and I was vigilantly keeping watch for intruders. For the first time since Alex's birth, Amanda was in her totally relaxed mode and seemed glued to the deck in such a way that I wasn't sure I would ever get her to move again. I was totally content myself, with no responsibility save that of protecting my wife's modesty should another boat drift into our paradise. Without much forethought I blurted out the question, "What did you mean when you said you had lost children before?" She responded with a question of her own. "What took you so long to ask?"

Her question annoyed me slightly since we both knew the answer was that I had been afraid to ask. I covered with some rambling excuse about not wanting to trouble her when we were going through so much with Alex's illness and I pressed on for an explanation partly because I wanted to know and partly because I wanted to show her that I wasn't afraid of the answer. I also sensed that she wanted and needed me to know.

Chapter Seven

AMANDA'S STORY

AMANDA

I was the second child and the oldest girl in a family of eight children. My older brother, David and I divided our parent's attention for four years before my sister Rachael appeared. Then came Alice when I was six, Vanessa when I was eight, nine with Marcus, 11 with Hope and 12 with Stephen. (My mother named the six youngest children after her favorite soap opera characters.)

The first vivid experience happened when I was about four years old. It must have been then because mother had a big belly and my sister, Rachael, was born when I was four. Mom, dad, my brother David and I were camping in a tent. I was inside the tent having just woken from a nap and they were outside. I could hear them laughing, talking and moving around. Suddenly I knew something was missing. There should be more noise and there should be a smell like something burning. Within minutes the smell was there and I emerged from the tent with a clear mental picture of what I would see, but nothing was as I expected. There should have been many people and several fires, horses and a river, but it was just the four of us, one fire, one tent. I was confused and a little frightened. Real confusion set in when my mother called me Amanda. She should have been calling me Lily. I knew and loved these people, yet I felt strange and uneasy. I wanted to go back to sleep and wake up in one place or another, not feeling like I didn't belong where I was. This feeling of displacement lasted through dinner and then we all went to sleep and the next morning everything must have been back to normal because I don't recall feeling that way for another year or so.

When I was five years old my mother was making me a new dress. The fabric was a greenish yellow, chartreuse I suppose, and it had ugly black designs on it that reminded me of spiders. I hated it and thought it was scary looking so I found her scissors and cut several slashes in the skirt. I remember knowing that it was the wrong thing to do but I believed I would not get in trouble because they would think that I was too young to understand. I was wrong and I got one of the few spankings I received as a child. My mother informed me that she was throwing the dress away and that I wouldn't get another for a very long time. Mission accomplished, but I hated having my parents mad at me. I kept thinking they would leave me behind and I was frightened at the thought. I started having the same feeling as that day in the tent. I wasn't myself. I was someone else but still me. I was older and bigger, not really a child, and I was somewhere I didn't recognize, alone and abandoned. I was crying and screaming much more violently than my current situation with my parents warranted. It was confusing and frightening, but it passed in a few minutes and I felt safe and loved again as my dad came into my room and hugged me, telling me he thought the dress was ugly too, but that I shouldn't have cut it up. I felt like myself again and very glad that I would never have to wear that awful dress.

There were many more instances where I was transferred and transformed and, as I got older, they were more vivid in detail and lasted longer. They scared me less and less as I came to view them as my little adventures. In a way I think I actually looked forward to them. I tried to explain them to my mother one day when I was about eleven years old, but by that time she had a huge family to look after and she said she didn't have time to indulge my flair for drama and that they were probably just very vivid dreams. I knew they weren't just dreams because they happened at various times of the day and were triggered by events, scenes, smells, sounds and colors that surrounded me in my current life.

All in all, I guess I felt pretty lucky to live in so many times and places at once. I liked my memories even though they were often troubling or frightening. For a long time I believed everyone had them and they were just something that were taken for granted like dreams or growing pains where only the scariest or most painful were mentioned. As the scenarios became more vivid, I started sharing them with my sisters, but I noticed that they were not sharing theirs with me. The realization slowly dawned on me that there were some strange goings-on in my head. I think my stories, coupled with the fact that I was mommy's little helper and their constant caretaker, afforded me some measure of awe or fear in the minds of my brothers and sisters, although not enough to exempt me from the constant teasing and baiting that goes on in all large families.

As time passed my mother became more tolerant of my stories, possibly even entertained, but she still attributed them to an overactive imagination. Her life was pretty mundane, centering mostly on getting enough food on the table day by day and keeping us clean and warm. I think she found some pleasant diversion in listening to my tales and I found myself telling her only the nice ones. She was a very bright woman who had little time or opportunity to indulge herself with pursuits that did not involve survival. I suppose my stories took the place of the leisure time other women her age spent reading, shopping or visiting friends.

For the first few years she and my father were married, things were pretty simple and pleasant. There were only my older brother and me to care for and we lived like most families in the 1950's. It appeared we might even prosper over time and achieve the American dream of owning a home with a few creature comforts thrown in such as having reliable transportation, enough to eat and possibly even a vacation every year or two. My parents made an attractive and congenial couple with two seemingly normal children and they enjoyed a modest, but satisfying, social life with friends, family, church and community. There is ample evidence that they also enjoyed a healthy physical relationship.

As the family grew in number, it became more difficult for my father to maintain even our modest lifestyle. As the challenge of providing for his ever-swelling brood increased, so did my father's wanderlust. He was a good man with good dreams, but he had little education and no insights regarding the motives of others more worldly than he. We began a lifetime of seeking greener pastures. He would land the family in some new place where he knew he could find success. My mother would work doggedly to transform dilapidated surroundings into something livable. Both she and my father were very talented and resourceful in this regard. About the time we progressed to the point where we could begin to enjoy the fruits of their labors with little luxuries like indoor plumbing and/or hot water, dad would release his grip on that dream and adopt another.

I believe my father knew that he wasn't in touch with the modern world that was changing so rapidly after the war. This made him vulnerable to others who presented themselves as movers and shakers in touch with the times. There was a constant stream of "good-fellows" who would provide the vision and dad was to provide the work-all of the work for very little money. We would be uprooted time after time, property disposed of to the first and lowest bidder, and away we would travel to the land of new beginnings-so many beginnings, never finishing anything. Mother adapted as best she could. She would argue that we should stay put and continue building on what we had, but dad was convinced we were destined for greater things.

Life was different for women even as late as the 1950's and 60's. They were to follow their providers, not question them. Little did the women of that time know that in the near future they would be called upon to do both - follow and provide. As more women were forced into or chose to enter the workplace, their duties at home were not diminished. Those, such as my mother, who had been slaves to their husbands' whims before, were now slaves to two masters. They now had bosses as well. For those who could afford them, there were modern conveniences such as ranges, washers and dryers that made their home duties easier or quicker, but this did not offset the time and energy they expended on their dead-end "careers". In most cases the men still retained the title of head of household and masters of their domain at home and in the workplace and it took years for the public at-large to accept the fact that this should change if the women were expected to share in the responsibility for the financial survival of the family. Of course that was a difficult argument to put forth since women were paid a mere pittance for performing the duties that men were unwilling or unable to accept, leaving the man as the primary breadwinner and the little woman providing the "extras" through her lowly wages. Of course in my mother's case, those little "extras" were things like food and clothing.

As we continued to move about, my mother did her best to provide some semblance of a stable lifestyle for her family. Needless to say, this was a pretty tough existence for my brothers and sisters. It was different for me because I was older and had enjoyed some measure of comfort and security in my early life as well as the fact that I was more like my father than I would like to admit. I understood his restlessness. I adored my mom and dad. I wanted to help dad with his dreams and mom with her toils and I had this sense that I could do all of the above and still have energy left over to pursue my own dreams.

The years passed with my mother creating home after home in some pretty unlikely surroundings. At one time we even lived in a garage with dirt floors and two electric outlets. Sometimes we would be comfortable. Sometimes we had enough to eat. Sometimes we had furniture and sometimes we got to know our neighbors, although a family with eight energetic children was not usually viewed as a welcome addition to the neighborhood. Through it all, our mother sewed and kept us clean and clothed. I kept the house clean and delegated duties to the younger children, or as we called them, the "little kids".

Hardship was like a season to us. Even in the "summer" times of our lives when everything was warm and blooming, we always knew that there would be another "winter" possibly even colder than the last as my father drifted aimlessly into his world, leaving us behind. He was like a prospector going further and further into the hills to find the gold that would rescue him from his confusion and disillusion. He became a master of self-delusion, never giving up on his dreams. Unfortunately, the only way to keep his dreams alive was to shun the reality of coming home to a wife and eight mouths to feed, so he stopped doing that. He was neither a cruel nor selfish man. He truly believed that someday there would be a payoff for his efforts and he would bring his family to the world he envisioned for us. As his failures mounted, he gave up the ghost of ever being able to derive joy from his children because he lived in fear and guilt. He knew that other men cherished and enjoyed their sons and daughters and he remembered what it was like when life was manageable, when he shared his dreams with our mother and cared for my brother and me, when he had friends instead of drinking buddies. But those days were gone and so was my father. He left us with no money, no food no heat and we were about to be evicted.

By this time I was nineteen years old and my mother was slightly beaten-down, but still strong and beautiful. We were living in Missoula Montana and our goal (not our dream) was to move to Great Falls where the job prospects were better and we could be near my mother's wonderful sister, Maxine.

Between us we raised about fifty dollars which wouldn't get us anywhere near our goal, nor insure our survival where we were, so my mother decided that we would buy enough food for a few days and she would take some of the money and go play BINGO at the Moose Lodge in the hope of leveraging that money into enough to get us moved and settled. I stayed with the kids and she departed with the plan to call me if she won anything so I could join her and double our chances. I remember encouraging her to hurry and call because they were about to turn off our phone service. We laughed at my sick little joke as we always did. Dark humor has always been a specialty in our family.

God intervened, and my mother called saying that she had won two hundred and fifty dollars, a goodly amount in those days, but still not enough to get us where we needed to be. It was decided that we would take one hundred dollars of that money and try again to increase the moving fund. I remember telling God that I was not being greedy, but asking for his help. We won more that night and our winning streak continued for two more days. All in all we amassed a grand total of over fifteen hundred dollars that weekend, which was just enough to get us moved and settled into a large, unattractive house in Great Falls. With the little that was left over, mother was able to purchase some functional, but well-worn furniture at an auction to replace that which had been confiscated by creditors. We both found work immediately and we were off and running. My father dropped in a few times and I think there was a modest attempt at reconciliation, but in the end he asked for a divorce to marry another woman, one that hadn't seen all his failures.

Through it all, or because of it all, I perfected my method of converting fear and anguish into a dark sort of humor which manifested itself in a sarcastic and somewhat cynical approach to life mingled incongruously with unassailable optimism (my legacy from my father). This followed me for many years and, though diminished, has never really left me. Because I knew how quickly life can turn on you, it was difficult to attach myself to anything. I always had a plan B lurking in the back of my mind. For that reason, and with the added input of my "memories" which became more intense during that period, it was a constant struggle for me to be truly present in my life. It was only a year or so before I met Sam that my humor became less dark and I began to live in the moment and trust myself enough to participate in my life instead of dreading outside forces. This was such liberation for me that I even began to take some things for granted, such as my ability to give and receive friendship. I was pleasantly surprised to find that most people liked and respected me. I had never doubted my intellectual abilities. I knew I was no genius, but I do have a good mind and the ability to think things through when I let myself relax. I actually began to make plans and I discovered that we can become what we think about and started to make use of the ability we all have to visualize.

My aspirations in life have never been grandiose in terms of the world at large, but they were huge compared to my starting point. Mostly I sought a peaceful, comfortable, productive, caring and interesting life. Yes, I wanted to see the world, but I didn't crave a life of constant adventure. More, I learned to see the adventure in whatever I was doing. My memories taught me much about happiness. I learned that it wasn't something floating out in space that would hopefully land on my shoulder by finding the right man, or the right job, or the right home. It is a decision we make within ourselves rather than a random event brought about by being in the right place at the right time. Comfort is found in being flexible and enjoying what is available to us each day. Being productive was not hard as I followed the work ethic of my mother and father. Caring and loving is an automatic response in most of us. The hard part is accepting the heartache that often accompanies love as we fail others or they fail us. To do this we must accept that we are flawed as are those we love and be willing to expose ourselves to the risks. I look to my father who lost a lifetime of joy and love through his children because he couldn't accept his limitations and face his own failures.

I still struggled to find the peace in my life that would only come by truly trusting God and being connected with my surroundings and the people in my life. This is hard to do when you find yourself bouncing back and forth between the present and the past. I had memories of people that I had loved, but they weren't with me anymore and there was no one to show me how to live with that sense of loss. How do you make lasting connections, when you see how they disappear? It is very hard to attach yourself to anyone or anything when you know that you will have to begin again in another place and time without those you have grown to love, yet how can you find peace in this life if you feel so alone? Perhaps having God as a companion should have been enough, but it never had been for me. God expects us to share our world with others, not live in isolation. Having the memories should have made that easier, but it didn't. I still had much to learn.

I made a conscious decision to live with the things I knew to be true and hope the rest would work itself out. I knew that we were put on this earth to enjoy God's wonders and love each other as best we could. One cannot live, die and return again, time after time, without developing some faith that God has a plan. Learning from each life is our job, perfecting our soul is our goal. Our souls are placed in mortal bodies that can either nourish or damage that soul depending on how we face the challenges put before us. We are allowed to flourish or fail and we are accountable for our progress or lack thereof. Our emotions are a gift from God that can move us to do great things or we can succumb to our darker side and cause injury to our soul and to those around us. We are put here to grow and help others to do the same. I hoped that I would find a soul-mate to help me with my struggles, but if not, I would continue on alone and try to enjoy the ride. These were my thoughts and beliefs at the time I met Sam.

He did not rock my world, he enhanced it. I never questioned whether I loved him. We simply molded into each other's lives. There were no anxious moments of doubt, there were no anxious moments at all. We respected and enjoyed each other and there were no games. There was, however, that one secret I didn't share for some time, that of my memories.

So many times I wanted to share them with Sam, but it was always easy to find a reason not to. Too often, as a child or teenager, I had related my experiences to friends, boyfriends, even a teacher with a variety of unsatisfactory results. There were those who thought I was a little deranged and chose to avoid me. Others thought I was just a story-teller and I chose to avoid them. These varying responses were disheartening but the one that was the most hurtful was when a teacher, whom I admired and respected, accused me of just trying to get attention. I decided that I wouldn't share my memories with Sam unless he asked to be included. I would offer subtle hints and wait for the day when he would open his mind and love me enough to hear and embrace the whole truth.

Finally, that day came when we were lying on the deck of our boat relaxing after the many stressful months of Alexander's illness. Sam brought up my remark about having lost children in the past. I was both excited and frightened at the onset of this conversation, yet strangely, I had done nothing to prepare myself for what I would say to him. One would think I would have rehearsed some sort of organized response to the questions that I knew would follow my many hints. Not so. I believed that whatever I confided to Sam, he would listen with love and acceptance. I trusted him to know that my stories were real and that he might even have a few of his own to share with me. I was convinced that Sam would not challenge or disregard my revelations once he was ready to hear about them.

I began to tell Sam my story, just as I have told you, except that as I reached the part about Lily and the campfires, Sam interrupted me. He adopted an unmistakably condescending tone and proceeded to tell me about an experience he had had as a child which left him convinced for some time that he had been abducted by aliens. Apparently, he had been playing in his room with his younger brother, Bruce, who suddenly burst into the living room where his parents were entertaining guests and announced that strange little men had come into their room, squeezed Sam's head and taken him away with them. Of course the parents laughed and marveled at Bruce's imagination and upon checking, found Sam safely in his room. Sam admitted that in the years since, he had occasionally wondered if Bruce's account had some substance. So have some of us who know Sam.

His point, which he made in an annoyingly condescending way, was that we all let our imaginations get ahead of us at times. He went on to tell me about some dreams that seemed so real that he truly believed they had happened until he tried to put them in a context of time and place and found that he couldn't do so. That was it! He asked no questions and did not encourage any further revelations. I could see that he was uncomfortable with our conversation and he gave no indication that he took me seriously. I tried to defend my memories against the dream theory but to no avail. Subject closed and Sam went below to make a pitcher of margaritas.

I had never felt such a sense of disappointment, no betrayal, not even when my father left home. I spent the rest of the afternoon reminding myself that I had had a lifetime with the knowledge of my memories and that Sam deserved some time to get used to the idea. I knew that in time he would come to understand that they were real and, by virtue of his love for me, he would make every effort to know and believe that I was telling him the truth and that he would share in that part of my life.

Over the years there were other times when I tried to confide in him but he always had the same reaction, aversion. In the end it became sort of a joke between us, but the joke was enjoyable only to Sam. We would be watching a movie about the old west or some other time in history and Sam would turn to me grinning and ask "Was that the way it really happened?". Sometimes I would laugh with him, other times I would leave the room, but always it was a reminder that I might never have anyone share my thoughts and experiences. I loved Sam so I found ways to forgive him and at times I even wondered if it was better that he didn't understand. After all, if he believed my memories were real we, as a couple, might feel encouraged to share our knowledge with others and that could complicate our personal and business relationships.

There were times that Sam pointed out that my perceptions and thought processes seemed different than most people's, but in the long run he decided it was because I was left-handed, as was his father and my father, and that being right brained accounted for my different approach to life. Sam puts a lot of stock in being left handed and believes that there are many advantages in that trait. If there are any, I haven't found them.

As each year passed, I became more cautious about sharing my thoughts with Sam or anyone else, and though I tried, I could never really accept his rejection of that part of my life. I became more inward in other ways as well because my memories were becoming more vivid and permeated my life. It is hard to discuss our innermost thoughts and feelings when part of them are shaped by experiences we cannot share. Over time it is always a challenge to keep a relationship fresh and meaningful, but more so when there is so much you cannot talk about openly. Our relationship became stagnant and with that came indifference and resentment, mostly on my part. I still loved him so very much and I knew he loved me, at least most of me, but my trust in him had eroded.

A turning point occurred one day about a year before our divorce. We were walking in downtown Seattle heading for the Metropolitan Grill, our favorite place for happy hour. We went there about once a month to enjoy a great Manhattan and some fresh oysters on the half-shell. It was always a special event for us and I was feeling content and romantic. As we approached the entrance, I noticed a well-dressed couple entering ahead of us. The man was very handsome and they were both exquisitely groomed, but the woman was seriously overweight, not just plump, but obese. The man was solicitous and charming to her and I was intrigued by them as a couple. As it turned out, we ended up sitting at a table next to them and I took every opportunity to eavesdrop on their conversation, that being a skill I had developed over many lifetimes which has provided me a great deal of enjoyment and insights. As I had originally guessed, they were a married couple and they spoke lovingly to one another about their children and their plans for the future. The man looked at her as if she was a goddess and indeed she was if one looked closely enough to see the beauty in her countenance and manner. I was struck by his total acceptance of her. She couldn't hide the pounds that our society often sees as an unforgivable flaw, yet he walked her into that room as if she was everyman's dream. I think this was the only time in my life that I have ever felt jealous of another woman. If this man could accept a trait in his wife that others might find repugnant, why couldn't Sam appreciate my "differentness". This man was proud of his wife and because of that she glowed while I felt I had to hide part of myself.

Fair or not, I felt resentment building in me toward Sam that I was not able to overcome or ignore. I had less and less to say to him as time passed. We loved each other, but it just wasn't enough. I wanted to glow like that woman. I couldn't tell him how I felt because I believed he wouldn't listen. I know now that I was unfair to him and I underestimated him and myself. I should have overcome my fears and fought to make him listen and believe in me. I gave up on him and blamed him for feelings he didn't know existed.

Chapter Eight

SAM AND SAMANTHA

SAM

Since our divorce Amanda and I had maintained a respectful, but cautious relationship. I never fully understood the reasons for Amanda's resentment of me, but I knew that I had failed her in some gigantic way. I guess I just never took the time to realize the impact of her memories or that they existed at all. I believed there had to be something more that was causing us to drift apart and I was pretty sure it was my fault. I thought that she wasn't telling me everything in an effort to spare my feelings. It's amazing how couples will often fail to address the issues that are the most important in each of their lives.

Samantha was the common thread that brought us together and I have exploited that circumstance to its fullest. I was the first to hear of Samantha's memories, not Amanda. Even when she was just a young child Samantha would make little comments alluding to incidents that I knew for sure she couldn't possibly have experienced and the frequency of these confidences increased over time. I recognized the pattern as the same as I had experienced with Amanda. I asked her if she had told her grandma her stories and she said no, but she didn't explain why she hadn't. She said she just liked to talk to me. I was flattered and proud so I didn't encourage her to tell her grandma. Although I don't like to admit it, I guess that might have been my revenge for being shut out of Amanda's life.

Over time, Samantha and I spoke repeatedly about her experiences and I came to believe her stories were for real because no child could invent such detail. It was through Samantha's memories that I realized that what Amanda had tried to share with me was real. I began to understand how I had failed her, but I still didn't grasp the full impact the memories had on her life and the loneliness she must have felt at times.

I didn't share Samantha's stories with Amanda nor did I tell Samantha about her grandmother's memories. I didn't feel it was my place and I was concerned about how Tiffany and Alex would respond, so I just let her talk and took pleasure in the fact that she would open up to me. It was painful in a way as I realized that the comfort and attention I was affording my granddaughter was that which I had denied my wife.

Finally, one day Amanda called me and asked me to meet her for coffee at one of the million or so Starbucks Coffee houses in downtown Seattle. I arrived early in freshly pressed tan chinos and a long sleeve white shirt open at the collar with the cuffs rolled twice. Amanda had always said that any man dressed in this manner would be at his most attractive to women, so I decided it was worth a try. I also spent twenty five dollars to have my hair styled and even considered having dark streaks put in to cover some of the gray. I discarded the latter idea knowing that Amanda would spot my deception right away and arrive at the obvious conclusion that I was trying to woo her, which of course I was.

Amanda entered through a side door just as I finished erasing a coffee stain from my fresh white shirt. I had borrowed a wet towel from the barista and, though the stain had disappeared, my shirt was soaked on one side. Spotting her, I pretended to be using the towel to clean a spot on the table left by the last patron while positioning one arm over my chest to block the view of the wet spot. By the amused expression on her face, I could see that Amanda had sized the situation up very quickly, but she allowed the deception to pass. My rising body heat dissipated the wet spot within minutes enabling me to sit like a normal human being again.

Amanda looked fantastic. She was wearing one of her signature outfits. (Did I mention that Amanda is a bit of a clothes horse?) The outfit consisted of a deep brown velvet skirt worn mid-calf with brown boots. She had a wide belt with a gold clasp, a silky, ivory colored blouse with a lacy thing underneath and a short jacket. This was topped off by a brown velvet hat with a wide brim and large gold hoopy earrings. This was vintage Amanda. I knew from experience that all the pieces were likely purchased separately from one consignment shop or another at a ridiculously low price. Amanda took great pleasure in her thrift and, when complimented on her attire, would never fail to let the listener in on her secret. She liked to point out that on a very small scale this made her the natural enemy of Nordstrom's. That penchant for making something out of nothing is her heritage from her clever and talented mother whose skill was born of necessity rather than choice, but a useful skill nevertheless.

Never one for small talk, Amanda unloaded on me right away demanding to know how long Samantha had been confiding in me about her memories and why I had not seen fit to inform her. Her feelings were hurt and I felt bad for her, but at the same time there was still a small section of the worst part of me that found some pleasure in being Samantha's first choice. This disappeared quickly as I saw how distressed she was. I offered the simple explanation that it was not my secret to share, but that I was glad that she was now included as I had greater confidence in her ability to counsel Samantha than in my own. I added that from that point forward, I would not withhold anything from her. It worked. She calmed down.

Amanda had not shared her memories with Samantha fearing an adverse reaction from Alex and Tiffany. This was the reason she had asked me to meet with her. In a word, she wanted me to go to them to find out if they had any inkling of what Samantha was experiencing, inform them of Samantha's revelations and ask them if Amanda could discuss her experiences with Samantha. To her surprise, I agreed that it just might make sense for me to be the one to have that conversation. I had not experienced my financial windfall at that time, but even then I was trying to think of ways to help Samantha and Amanda understand and be enriched by their gift, though not at the expense of usurping the parental rights of Alex and Tiffany. I also didn't want to encourage Samantha to withhold such important information from her parents. Therefore, Amanda's request came at a time when I was considering just such a move anyway. Of course, I didn't share those thoughts with Amanda, but rather allowed her to believe that I was willing to make this move solely at her request. We men take our points however we can get them when it comes to pleasing the women we love.

As a child, Alex had not been aware of Amanda's memories, but as he reached his teen years he picked up on some of our conversations and spoke with his mother about this on several occasions. His attitude reflected my own in that he couldn't bring himself to believe her memories were real, yet he had enough respect for his mother to treat them with indifference and skepticism rather than simply telling her she was crazy. Tiffany totally ignored the discussions and it was clear that her belief system would never allow that these were anything but vivid dreams. They had mentioned to me from time to time that Samantha was a great story teller and had an incredible imagination for one her age, but they did not seem to make the connection between Amanda and Samantha's memories and it was clear that they had no intention of going there. I knew that I would be treading on thin ice, but I decided to go forward anyway. Samantha was so open and comfortable with her stories and I didn't want to see that destroyed and have her be hurt as Amanda had been.

As it turned out, the conversation I had so carefully planned was a lot easier than I had anticipated. It seems Samantha had experienced a particularly vivid event that she shared with them and, just as had been my experience, they realized that no child could have manufactured or dreamed such a story. Consequently, that evening as I prepared to make my case, they actually brought the subject up, or at least Alex did. He had made the connection with some of the conversations he had shared with his mother and I could see that he was concerned and more than a little agitated. Tiffany came right out and accused Amanda of telling Samantha her stories and that this is where she was coming up with these detailed accounts. I assured her that this was not the case and that Amanda had carefully avoided talking to Samantha about her memories. When I told them why I had asked to meet with them that evening in the first place, they were both shocked at how much information I had and that Samantha had opened up to me instead of them. I had no answer for that, but stayed on track toward getting them to allow Amanda and Samantha to share experiences.

Alex was somewhat open to the arrangement, but Tiffany was dead-set against it. I made the case that if they didn't allow her some freedom they would run the risk of losing her trust. I argued that even if her memories are not real, she believes they are and would need some help to sort things out. Otherwise, she might withdraw into herself as Amanda had for so long. They both seemed to respond to this argument and eventually it was agreed that Samantha would be allowed to speak freely with her parents, myself and Amanda. The hope was that if she had us to talk to, she wouldn't feel the need to share her stories with outsiders or other members of the family causing her discomfort or exposing her to ridicule.

I don't have to tell you I was pretty pleased with myself when I left our son's home that evening. It was agreed that Alex would call his mother and let her know that she could discuss her memories with Samantha provided that she keep the conversations as low key as possible and use her influence with Samantha to convince her to limit her discussions to the four of us. Amanda called to thank me immediately after that conversation. She was very excited and I could tell by her voice that her emotions were running wild. She was relieved and grateful and the evil side of my brain wanted to pop right over there and try to collect whatever rewards she might make available to me. Fortunately, my good side won over.

SAMANTHA

I love my grandpa Sam. Who wouldn't? I'm glad I'm named after him. Thank God my parents didn't jazz up my grandma's name and call me Amandarissa or one of those long names like some of my friends have. I'm just Sam. Or they could have named me Tiffanica after my mother as Thelma wanted. I think she thought that up after drinking a bottle of wine. It would have been OK if they had named me Alexis after my dad, but I think they are saving Alex in case they have a boy sometime. If they are going to have a boy, I hope they hurry. It would be great to have a little brother and I am old enough to babysit. I wouldn't even charge them money for it, although I don't think they would pay me anyway because I'm kind of expensive to have around with all my sports and my dance classes.

I sometimes wish my dad was more like grandpa, but I know he can't be because he has to be a dad. Anyhow, grandpa is cool and fun and he loves me even though I am weird. On my ninth birthday grandpa took me out for dinner at a fancy restaurant. It was called the Metropolitan Grill and I could order anything I wanted but I didn't know what most things were so I got up and walked around to the other tables and looked at people's food until I saw something that looked good and then I asked the people what they ordered so I could order it too. Grandpa laughed and said that was exactly what grandma used to do. I had a veal chop and I liked it a lot, but it wasn't really any better than the burgers they sell at the Sonic Drive-In. The waiter told me that they didn't make milkshakes, so I had a virgin strawberry daiquiri with tons of whipped cream instead. That was great. I had on a new dress that grandma bought me and it was really fun although at times grandpa seemed a little sad. I think it was because he used to go there with grandma back when they were married. I wonder why people decide not to be in love.

Anyway, we started talking about things and grandpa asked me about my "adventures". It was really nice to talk to him about them. That was before everyone decided I could talk about my memories. I told him about some of the places and times I have lived in, but that my favorite was when I was named Corinne and I lived on a big farm with my parents. We had lots of horses and I had a horse of my own that I named Tony The Pony but I just called him Tony for short. I don't remember too much about that time, but I do know that my dad was famous for his horses and we lived in Tennessee. I think we had a lot of money because we had a big house and a swimming pool. Grandpa and I talked for a very long time that night and a couple of times it looked like he was going to cry, or laugh, I don't know which, but there were tears in his eyes. Grandma always makes a joke about grandpa's eyes and one time she showed me some cheese that had been in the refrigerator too long and said that it had turned the exact color of his eyes and then she laughed so hard she got tears in her eyes too.

Grandma and grandpa don't live together anymore. They got a divorce, which I think is really dumb. Now grandma has her own condo downtown which is really cool and grandpa lives on his boat on Lake Union, just a few blocks away. The three of us do a lot of things together and I take turns staying overnight with them. I like staying with grandma best because we can just take the elevator down and we are in the middle of the Pike Place Market and we can go to this really neat bakery and get whatever we want. Grandma also lets me order a latte, but I can't tell my parents about that. I love coffee, especially when they make it into a latte. Sometimes when I am at grandmas we sit in the morning and drink coffee mixed with hazelnut cream and talk about our adventures. That's another thing I don't tell my parents about. It's not like a lie or anything, they just never ask.

It's also fun to stay with my grandpa on the boat. I have a little tiny room of my own and grandpa is teaching me to cook on his barbecue. There is another small boat hooked on the back of his big one that grandpa says I can take out by myself when I am older, but I'm not really looking forward to that. I haven't told him this, but I am afraid of the water because I drowned once when I was someone else. That was in our pool when I was Corinne. I didn't tell him about that because I only like to remember Tony The Pony, not the bad parts. Grandma knows though and she is giving me swimming lessons in the pool at her condo so that I can get over being afraid of the water.

I wish grandma and grandpa were still married. It is always so much fun when we do things together. I'm lucky because my parents aren't divorced like so many of my friend's parents. My parents and I do a lot of things together and sometimes they spoil me but not as much as my grandpa and grandma do. I wish when I grow up I could just be a grandma and I wouldn't have to be a mom first. Moms have to do all the work and they have to make you do all the right things at the right time. Grandma buys me fun things and my mom has to buy me underpants and socks.

Grandpa has a lot of money because a couple of years ago he won the lottery. I remember that day really well because I was staying with grandma in her old apartment for a couple of days while my parents were on a trip. He called us on the phone and at first Grandma didn't believe him, but then she realized he was telling the truth because, as she put it, "Your grandpa is not a good liar even though he is from Texas". We were all very excited and grandpa came over with a bottle of champagne and they even gave me a glass. I didn't like it at all and grandma said it was because it was expensive and that she likes cheap champagne better, although she did drink most of the bottle herself, including my glass. I think her remark about the champagne hurt grandpa's feelings, but I know she didn't mean to. Sometimes grandma doesn't realize how hard he tries to get her attention. After her second glass grandma started to laugh and hugged grandpa's head to her chest. I think he liked that because I could see wet spots from where his teeth were pushed against her blouse so I knew he was smiling. She thought it was funny because all her life she had been the one that liked to gamble and grandpa hardly ever even bought a lottery ticket, yet he was the one that ended up winning big-time.

After grandpa won all those millions of dollars, he bought the huge new boat he lives on for himself and a condo for my grandma. She told him she didn't want it, but he kept bugging her and she finally gave in. I know she wanted it all along. Grandpa told me she had been a wonderful wife and she should share in his good fortune. Everyone agreed she should accept it and Thelma told grandma he owed it to her for putting up with him all those years. Grandma didn't agree with Thelma but she finally gave in. I think that was terrific of grandpa and I know grandma loves living right downtown in the middle of things and I think she likes having him nearby. I think she feels safe and I know he likes that.

Chapter Nine

SAM'S GREAT PLAN

SAM

Well, you have met some of the characters so it is time to get on with the story. Samantha told you about my good fortune in winning the lottery. That piece of luck is what has enabled me to launch this adventure. The idea came to me that there must be plenty of others that have the memories and that it might prove meaningful to pull a group together and see what similarities and differences emerge from their experiences and what, if any, conclusions can be drawn. I never intended this to be an academic study and so far I can see that we are in little danger of that becoming an accidental outcome. My goals were, and still are, to prove to Amanda and Samantha that I believe and accept their past lives and to give them an outlet to share with others. I realized early on that I was also going to be privy to some pretty interesting tales, but I never dreamed the scope of the world that would be brought to my door. I had no clue as to what I was getting myself into.

My methods were somewhat unscientific, but in the long run effective I think. I simply went on the internet and Googled reincarnation and followed it from there. I read about dozens of experiences. Some were fairly lame as Samantha would put it, but others piqued my interest. There was also plenty of information about various studies on the subject and a great deal was written about the religious aspects. I had never realized that nearly every religion in the world, including the Christian faith had, at some time if not currently, incorporated the belief in reincarnation into their doctrines. What had always seemed to me as a wild delusion shared by a few, is in reality a widespread belief that is simply not a part of the culture I grew up in. It is estimated through studies that nearly one-third of Americans believe in reincarnation, but it is our Christian background that has kept the idea out of the mainstream. Many people who believe in reincarnation do not see a conflict between Christianity and their beliefs, but most Christians do and certainly most members of the clergy cannot wrap their arms around the idea. Much is written on both sides and I am glad I read through so many of the articles, because as it turns out, this debate is at the heart of much of the internal conflict for those who have the memories and has contributed hugely to their discomfort in sharing their discoveries and memories with others.

After about a week of studying the information on the internet I had a pretty good idea of how I wanted to proceed and the type of person I wanted to attract. I wanted those whose memories had begun when they were children and continued and intensified throughout their lives as had Amanda and Samantha's. From the research I learned that these people had the most vivid experiences and the best retention of facts and details. I also wanted people who remembered several lives, rather than just one or two. They also needed to be free to spend a month or two away from home and family to be part of my study group. I was willing to pay them a stipend each week to compensate for lost wages and other expenses, but even so, I thought it would be difficult to get people to take that much time out of their daily lives. Not a problem! Those who responded seemed eager to make any necessary sacrifice to meet others that shared their experiences.

I hired a friend of mine to design a very simple website. I wanted it to appear as an opportunity that I was offering and less like an advertisement. I wanted people that were trying to learn and benefit from the experience itself, not just have a free vacation with a bunch of like-minded old souls. I hoped to find people that yearned to share their discoveries and beliefs. I wanted intelligent and sincere individuals who came from diverse backgrounds. I guess I also wanted people who would appreciate me for my efforts as a fellow human being rather than viewing me as some sort of voyeur peeking into their lives. I didn't want them to feel like experimental rats in a cage, or a control group for a pharmaceutical company. I wanted to be part of the group even though I didn't share their gift. I secretly felt that their acceptance of me would increase my standing in Amanda's eyes, although I honestly did want to be part of the whole picture for their sake. My friend set up the website and Amanda helped me word the invitation.

I have another friend, Patrick O'Neill, who has a huge and luxurious home on an Island in the San Juans. I felt this would be a perfect venue since it was remote enough to provide seclusion, yet was close to Seattle and offered some fabulous amenities to keep my guests entertained and comfortable. The home itself has four bedrooms plus a guest house with two more bedrooms, a living room, bathroom and small kitchen and it has the same fabulous view as the main house. I have spent many restful weeks in that guest house with my boat moored at the dock in the village nearby. My guests could go fishing, crabbing, hiking, biking, beachcombing, or just relax and watch the ever changing weather patterns and animal life. The nearby village has an excellent used book store and a homey restaurant called the Sandcastle that makes everything, including the bread, from scratch and features a pleasant little lounge that evolves into a real bar for the locals later in the evening. I had discovered more than once that the relaxed and pleasant atmosphere of the bar during the day deteriorates after nine p.m. into something less than enjoyable as the year-round inhabitants of the island take over, bringing all the petty jealousies and intrigues of island life to light. For the most part, our group has avoided the after nine scene, but a few have sought out this limited night life with mixed results.

Patrick was only too happy to rent his home to me during the off-season months of September, October and November as he was seldom able to free his schedule at that time to enjoy his retreat. I was also able to hire Serena, the daughter of still another friend, Ed Shook, to act as housekeeper and cook. Ed has not been fortunate in his life in terms of love or money, yet in spite of this he is widely admired among our group of friends for his good humor and unyielding optimism. Nowhere was his optimism more evident than in the choice of name for his daughter. Serena's mother, who abandoned them both shortly after Serena's birth to follow her secret lover and drug dealer to greener pastures, had nothing of any value to add to Serena's genetic makeup, and Ed, though attractive as a person, had none of the physical attributes that would adapt themselves to the gentler sex. Consequently, I remembered Serena as slightly homely, very clumsy, outrageously noisy and incredibly kind and funny. Thus neither in manner nor appearance does she reflect the gentleness of her name yet one only has to be around her for a few minutes to realize how gifted she is in every way that counts. People are just drawn to her and she responds to them with genuine interest, understanding and a tenderness that one usually learns from one's mother but must have been implanted in her nature from a higher source. She is too mischievous to be called angelic, yet an angel she is and we all feel privileged to have in our midst. She creates a spirited environment that is fun and involves everyone. Even Bernie liked Serena and sought out her company regularly. I can honestly say that when he was relating to her he seemed almost pleasant, at least as long as he had her full attention. If he had to share her with anyone he would revert to his usual disagreeable self.

For the first two weeks my website received very few responses that fit our criteria. Many were from people who had repeatedly experienced some intense déjà vu but had few actual memories. There were several hits from people that Amanda labeled as "crackpots" and these were quickly eliminated.

The first that held her attention was from a young man in Toronto Canada named Etienne. His letter was so open, genuine and fearless that Amanda just knew he had to be for real. He also fit our criteria to the letter in terms of how his memories started and his willingness to share them. I responded by e-mail to his inquiry with details of my plan and he expressed a firm desire to be included. I asked for some personal information and references so that I could check him out as best I could. His reply was sketchy but he gave me the priest at his church as a reference. I called the priest first in the guise of wanting to offer the young man a responsible position within my fictitious company. He seemed surprised and very suspicious of me and demanded to know details of the company I had just invented. As it turned out, I proved to myself once again that I am a terrible liar and ended up telling him the truth. I felt like a kid going to confession and he treated me that way as well. He suggested that instead of calling around lying to people in order to get the information I required, I should just call the boy's mother and ask her permission. Etienne was only fourteen years old! I apologized once again for my attempt at deception and informed the priest that I was not aware of his age. Our conversation continued with the priest informing me that Etienne had confided in him regarding his special gift and that he had often counseled the boy and his mother, both devout Catholics, on the church's stand on the subject. Obviously, Etienne's claims violated church dogma, yet the priest seemed very sympathetic toward him. I asked what his advice had been to Etienne regarding this matter and he suggested that I ask him myself as Etienne was very clear about his feelings and his beliefs and was quite comfortable in both areas. It was obvious that the priest thought a great deal of Etienne and I was wondering how he was able to reconcile his knowledge of the boy's memories to the teachings of the church and not be critical or try to make him believe he was a great sinner. I guess the church has changed a lot since I was a boy. Perhaps the recent publicity surrounding the behavior of so many priests has injected a little humility into the hierarchy and caused them to be more open minded, or maybe they just have bigger battles to fight than one little boy with memories. A third possibility is that this priest is just a very good man who believes in a good and generous God and does not pretend to have all the answers.

I decided to take the priest's advice and speak with Etienne's mother. I called the number and a young voice, sounding neither male nor female answered with a slight French accent. I identified myself and the voice became excited and thanked me for calling. I explained that I had spoken with the priest and was surprised to discover that he was so young and that it would be difficult to imagine that his mother would allow him to go to a foreign country with a perfect stranger to hang out for a couple of months with ten other strangers. The next thing that happened astounded me. He called his mother to the phone and she flatly stated that she would have no problem with my plan. She had known about Etienne's response on the website all along and considered it to be a grand opportunity for him. I was flabbergasted that in today's world, a mother could be so cavalier about her son's safety. From the impression I got from the priest, this was not some selfish woman that just wanted someone to take her kid off her hands for a few weeks so that she could party. I questioned her further as to what assurances she would require of me and she said there were none. I was beginning to feel very uncomfortable about this until she informed me that the reason she wasn't worried about him was because she would be accompanying him. That was part of the deal. Etienne would not be allowed to accept any payment from me for his attendance, but I would have to allow her to accompany him. I would pay for their transportation to and fro and provide meals and accommodations, but they would be free to leave at any time with no further obligation. Her accent was French, but her meaning was clear. Take it or leave it! I took it without a moment's hesitation. There was something about the two of them that made me afraid to say no or even hesitate for fear I would miss a great opportunity.

Amanda was also enthusiastic about Etienne, but was less so about the mother. This surprised me since I couldn't imagine the boy coming unaccompanied and I would have thought Amanda would be the first to recognize that. Basically, we couldn't have one without the other. Big deal. We had plenty of room and the mother sounded like an interesting person. Amanda wasn't adamant, but reluctant. I'll never understand women.

I informed Etienne that our target date was the first Friday after Labor Day, which meant nothing to him since he isn't an American. For me it meant that I only had another month to line up the other participants, but fortunately new applicants were pouring in. It was like a dam broke and suddenly there were a couple dozen attractive candidates. I began to work diligently at screening responders and, with Amanda's help we whittled the number down to twelve. We began with an initial telephone interview with the both of us on the speaker phone. We had to first ascertain whether they would be able to work within our time slot and our financial offering. This eliminated three of the candidates immediately, leaving nine who could make the necessary arrangements. This is where a striking similarity manifested itself. Of the nine remaining, none seemed particularly concerned about the financial arrangements. True, most had obligations that must be met, but their concern did not go beyond meeting the minimum requirements and they were modest in their needs. Only one, Bernie Rausch asked for some kind of reassurance that they would be paid as promised. In fact I had already decided to arrange regular automatic deposits into their bank accounts. This satisfied Bernie as he could call on the appointed day and make sure that the funds had arrived. I didn't blame him for his concern. I just found it surprising the rest of the group didn't ask more questions. I wondered at the time if this was due to a shared personality trait or if it just that they were so excited about being included that they were throwing caution to the wind.

Amanda took over for the second interviews to identify those who would likely have the most input and would represent a cross section of the candidates. She eliminated three more because they seemed reluctant to share some of their memories with others. This was one stipulation that must be met and, even though they didn't outright refuse, Amanda felt that they would not be forthcoming with all details and that would not be fair to the other participants or true to the spirit of the endeavor.

I took over for the third and final round of interviews of the six remaining candidates. Amanda was satisfied that any or all would fit the bill for our purposes, yet somehow she didn't seem as enthusiastic about the whole scene as I thought she would be. I was beginning to wonder if this was such a good idea after all. Samantha, on the other hand was so wildly excited, I couldn't have backed out if I wanted to. Alex and Tiffany would not allow her to be a part of the study which is why I was able to schedule it for the autumn months instead of summer when she was out of school. They did say that she could come for a weekend or two, but not until we had acquainted ourselves with the other attendees and made sure that the environment was safe and appropriate. This seemed more than reasonable to me and a bit surprising.

In recent months Alex had taken more interest in Amanda's memories, possibly because he had seen indicators that Samantha's were becoming more frequent and vivid. The relationship between Amanda and Tiffany had always been a little disappointing to Amanda. She had long looked forward to being close to her daughter-in-law but it was hard when the younger woman perceived her as strange and possibly even a little scary. Although Alex concealed his growing interest from Tiffany, she sensed it and that furthered the distance between her and Amanda. I think she felt that Amanda was growing closer to her daughter than she and that understandably created some uncomfortable emotions in her.

To make matters worse, Tiffany's relationship with Thelma was closer than that with Amanda. Thelma took great pride in this and never failed to make Amanda aware of the special moments she shared with Tiffany. Thelma also claimed to be like a grandma in Samantha's eyes and liked to compete with Amanda for her time. I have often wondered what Amanda gets out of her friendship with Thelma. Maybe Thelma is just a bad habit. She has gone to great pains to keep her standing as an unofficial member of the family and I hoped I would be able to keep her nose out of the study.

I decided that for the duration of the meeting, I would stay on my boat which was moored at the marina in the village just a quarter of a mile away. This would allow me privacy and help the participants to get comfortable with one another on a personal level without me looking on. Even more compelling was my hope that Amanda might break down and sneak off to the boat with me and rekindle our passion. This had not happened since our divorce, but I never gave up hope that I would once again be irresistible to her. Men are like that. We never give up in that department. Go into any retirement village and you will see at least one eighty year old stud that still believes he is the Casanova of the neighborhood. I regularly see old men in restaurants, bars and even grocery stores flirting, groping up and engaging in other shameless behavior with women the age of their granddaughters, never realizing that the only reason these girls are letting them take liberties is because they consider them old and harmless. No matter how old they are, they think they've still "got it" in spite of all physical evidence to the contrary. These men are idiots and I have promised myself never to become one of them. I want to be a gentleman like my father. Besides, I didn't want anyone but Amanda, although I had often tried to fool myself into believing that there might be someone else out there for me. I missed the passionate and intimate relationship we shared and I didn't believe it was over. Amanda is still beautiful to me. She has retained all the physical attributes that attracted my attention in the first place, although she would argue that I am just going blind and fail to see the emerging flaws. Additionally, she has become softer and smoother in her persona while her natural wit and ability to see the humor in most things has sharpened.

As I spoke with each of the six remaining applicants, it became clear to me that it was going to be difficult to eliminate even one of them. My original plan was to limit the number to six, not counting myself and Amanda. However, taking stock of the available space, I decided that we could accommodate everyone if I put two people in the master suite, which had a small retreat room attached and if I could get Etienne to bunk in the living room of the guest house and have his mother and one other female take the two bedrooms. This would leave three bedrooms in the main house to accommodate the other four people. One of the rooms had a set of bunk beds, obviously intended for Patrick's grandkids, so I had to get two of the attendees to agree to share that room. As it turned out, this was not a problem. Since all were so eager to come, I had two volunteers immediately. Only Bernie Rausch flatly objected to the arrangement. He insisted on having his own room and, in retrospect, I can see that as being a very wise move. In the end, most of us didn't want to share the same planet with Bernie, let alone a room.

I won't go into the history of each guest at this point because I am going to let them introduce themselves later. I want this experience to be as real for you as possible so I am willing to give up the spotlight to anyone who wants to jump in.

AMANDA

Thank you! I've been waiting patiently for my opportunity to step in again. First of all, let me say that my enthusiasm for the project had not waned as Sam indicated. I was simply becoming a bit overwhelmed by the magnitude of what he was doing. As much as I had always wanted to meet others that shared this gift, I was getting nervous about what would or wouldn't be discovered in this study and I was still not used to being able to openly discuss my memories with Samantha, Sam and the rest of the family. I kept waiting for some kind of explosion or rejection. I was nervous and a bit in awe of what Sam was putting together. I felt like a jittery hostess that didn't know if anyone would have a good time at her party. I had adopted responsibility for the success or failure of the event because I knew Sam was doing this for me and Samantha. I couldn't imagine being in the same room with others like me, laughing, talking and crying about our experiences without feeling self-conscious or dreading repercussions. The mixture of anticipation and trepidation was overwhelming and I was only too happy to turn the third interviews over to Sam and kick back to take a deep breath. At the same time I was relieved that Samantha would be involved but only to a limited and well monitored degree. I didn't really know what to expect myself and I didn't want anything to upset her or cause her to feel uncomfortable.

Sam made all the arrangements for the transportation of his guests and Serena and I worked together to make the necessary provisions for food and other necessities. Serena is a fabulous cook, and a very organized person, so my role in this was largely advisory. For the next month I did little except think about the coming event and help Sam with the logistics of getting everyone to the island on the right day.

For the first evening Serena and I planned a barbecue on the deck overlooking the water, complete with appetizers, a full bar and a fabulous selection of desserts. Of course, Sam would preside over the barbecue to keep him busy so he wouldn't have time to make any of those backward comments which are his signature when he is nervous. The idea was to introduce everyone to each other and get them as relaxed as possible. The formal introductions would take place the next morning, with everyone giving a short narrative about themselves and a statement about why they wanted to participate. There was no time limit placed on this in the hope that we could get people to open up right from the beginning. With this in mind, I was elected to get the ball rolling by being the first to speak. I spent a lot of time deliberating on my approach. I didn't want to go so far with my own introduction that I would intimidate anyone else who might not want to open up so early in the meeting, yet I wanted to make it clear that this was going to be an event like no other they had ever experienced in any life. I have spoken publicly in front of audiences of all sizes, but never have I felt so nervous nor prepared as carefully as I did for this.

Sam could see the strain in me and was constantly telling me to relax and enjoy myself. He repeatedly pointed out that this was not a test or experiment, it was just meant to be an enriching experience that might prove helpful and informative to everyone. I knew he was right, but it wasn't until about one week before we were to leave for the island that I finally relaxed and started looking forward to the coming weeks. Samantha was the one that really turned the tide for me. She had been moping about and pouting for weeks that she would not be allowed to be part of the "real scene" as she put it. She has always been very sensitive to my moods and emotions and she could see how stressed I was making myself. She began by telling me that I would have to tell her absolutely everything about what was said and that she wanted to hear the real version. She argued that if I was stressed, I might miss out on some details and that I definitely wouldn't be able to tell her the stories in a funny way as I usually would. She also pointed out that grandpa Sam would be disappointed that all his effort and a great deal of money would be wasted if I couldn't enjoy myself. Samantha loves Sam and would do anything to protect him from being hurt or disappointed, including chastising me for my self-centered behavior. It worked. I stopped worrying and began to take total enjoyment from all aspects of the adventure. I could hardly wait to meet the other guests and I felt like a youngster counting the days until the trip to Disneyland.

Sam saw the change in me immediately and I could see the excitement in his eyes. I wondered at that time how I ever could have let us drift apart the way we did. I don't know if it was the way he was taking charge and moving forward so confidently or if there was an actual physical change in his appearance, but he was becoming increasingly attractive to me again as he always was in the past. I caught myself fantasizing about various scenarios where we would be thrown together and renew the passion we had denied ourselves for so many years.

I have dated sparingly since our divorce and always with less than satisfactory results. More often than not I found myself wishing I were at home alone watching reruns of some inane sitcom that I had never bothered to watch the first time around, or even better, sitting in my kitchen with Samantha drinking Hazelnut coffees and learning the shorthand of text messaging. These disappointments have driven me to a celibate lifestyle. To some of you that might seem like an obvious circumstance coming from a woman my age, but those of us who have crossed the fifty mark, understand that we still have carnal cravings and, although the efficiency might diminish, our anatomy remains the same. This is especially true for a woman since her performance is not "measurable" as in the case of a man. I speak from my own limited experience and what I have gleaned from many conversations with friends in my age group. Many men over fifty suffer greatly from diminished capacity and in some cases I am not referring to their intellect. I cannot say for sure, but I am almost certain that Sam has not suffered such a fate. At any rate, I was not at all upset that he was staying on his boat during our event since that would provide an element of privacy should the situation arise. No pun intended.

Chapter Ten

THE BIG DAY

SAM

Finally the big day arrived. Amanda and Serena were already at the house to put everything in order. The pantry, freezer and both refrigerators were stocked with food and drink requiring only a weekly trip to the market in Port Townsend for fresh produce. I had installed a long trestle-style table in the spacious dining area that could easily accommodate up to fourteen people if necessary so that our meals could be taken together in what I hoped would be a relaxed environment. This room was perfectly situated to take advantage of fabulous sunsets and the ever-changing weather patterns that engulf the area. Patrick is a great fan of unusual lamps, a hobby shared by Amanda. Everywhere you look there is an illuminated animal, human or some other form that is not usually found connected to an electrical outlet. This gives the main house a very warm and comfortable glow which is especially enjoyable on those dark cloudy days that frequent the island. Amanda still has a large collection of these lamps at her small condo. Most of them I have given to her and I can't tell you what a relief it was to have the question of birthday and Christmas gifts covered by a visit to an upscale gift shop that carries a good selection.

Nearly every room in the house takes advantage of the view as would be expected in a home like this. Only two guest bathrooms and two bedrooms are toward the back of the house along with the utility room and a four car garage. The house itself would have to be categorized as "rustic Italian". Its architecture features the wood and glass arrangements so typical of the Pacific Northwest, yet the interior has touches of the Mediterranean in style, color and texture providing a very pleasant shock as one leaves the woodsy, glassy exterior and enters what slightly resembles Italian villa. It's an interesting combination.

The master suite is another world unto itself, resembling an accommodation suitable for a sultan. The colors are a variety of blues ranging from the palest sunny sky blue to a deep sapphire. The floors are sand colored tile and the furniture is of a wood that I am not familiar with, but looks a little like bamboo. There is a huge pedestal style bed with a blue comforter so thick and fluffy that you could put it on the floor and use it as a mattress. The bed has a canopy with mosquito netting hanging in tiers creating a snug little room around this massive structure. The effect is strange, elegant, airy and very sexy. There is a walk-in closet the size of my boat and French doors leading to a retreat that is similarly decorated and features a wardrobe, two overstuffed chairs and something called a daybed with huge fluffy pillows and another one of those thick comforters. The master bathroom adjoins both rooms and the theme is carried out with the sand colored tile floor and gigantic spa. There is a huge mirror over double sinks in a tiled counter and a shower that is eight feet square with eight showerheads at varying levels. This room was definitely suitable for sharing and I wondered if its future occupants would be a bit overwhelmed. I also wondered if I had made a mistake in deciding to stay on my boat. It was hard to look around that whole scene without picturing myself cavorting about with Amanda. Oh yes! In my thoughts I did use the word "cavorting" which illustrates the sorry state of my sex life at that time.

The other bedrooms are large and very comfortably furnished. All of the beds had the finest feather mattresses. I knew that my guests would be in for a great experience and would have no cause to complain about the accommodations. Even Bernie had trouble finding something to criticize, although he never stopped trying.

The living room is open to the dining room and kitchen with a large conversation area in the center where we hold our sessions. Directly off the living room, through French doors, is a comfortable study that contains every state of the art electronic device available and certainly more than I can name. Even so, it is a snug and inviting room. It's obvious that Patrick has spent a great deal of time there by the worn appearance of the leather chairs and the disarray of the bookshelves. Though Serena and Amanda had dusted and cleaned, that little bit of disarray and the cigar burn on one of his end tables give the room just the right look. I was looking forward to spending a lot of time there reading and enjoying some quiet time. I was wrong.

The house sits on a promontory over one-hundred feet above the water and a footpath winds down the hill to the right of the house to a beach area below. There are also 192 rock steps that give a more direct, but riskier access to the beach. The beach itself is a small cul-de-sac surrounded by rock formations with small trees growing out of every crevice. Patrick has built a fire pit in the center of the beach with long wooden benches on each side and four Adirondack chairs facing the water. Off to the left is a small shed containing folding chairs, coolers and wet weather gear. On the opposite side is a long picnic table constructed from the halved trunk of a cedar tree. Here we could enjoy our own private campground and I pictured us sitting around the campfire eating s'mores and telling the ultimate ghost stories.

On this arrival day I was to stay in Seattle and shuttle our guests between SeaTac Airport and Lake Union Air Service, located coincidently, on Lake Union in downtown Seattle. They would travel by seaplane and would be met by Serena or Amanda and transported the short distance to the house. I was glad to have Amanda meet the guests before I arrived to avoid any initial discomfort by having me around. Amanda is a very outgoing person and I had full confidence that she would be better off by herself for the first meeting.

Since our guests were coming from all over the country and arriving at different times, I knew it was going to be a long day for me, making several trips back and forth to the airport and then the seaplane trip to the island in the evening, but I welcomed the day with child-like anticipation and a very adult Irish coffee. I was staying at a hotel near the airport as my boat had been moved to the island two days earlier. Amanda and Serena had cleaned and stocked my boat as well as the house and I looked forward to the nice little touches I was certain they would provide.

I will postpone sharing the details of my first impressions of each guest as I picked them up at the baggage claim area. They had been informed that I would be driving my black Cadillac Escalade (a recent purchase that I justified by telling myself that I deserved some compensation for all those years of driving older vehicles and doing my own repairs to save money) and that I would have a magnetic sign on the door panel reading "Sam Merrick Excursions" (my attempt at humor). This worked very well as each flagged me down. I made a game of trying to identify who among the many passengers flooding the pickup area might be my guests. I was wrong every time except on my last run at four PM when I easily identified Etienne and his mother, Antoinette. They stood out like a sore thumb as Etienne, despite his youth, was wearing pressed slacks that rested on his slender hips but did not show even one inch of his butt-crack. His hair was dark brown, a color that is sometimes found on human beings his age, and was worn slightly longish, but well cut. His mother is every bit as exquisite as I had visualized her from the sound of her voice. Her hair is reddish-blonde, slightly darker than Amanda's and was styled very simply in what I think is called a chignon, loosely framing a beautiful face with fine features and glorious green eyes. She is very petite and appeared more so standing next to her four huge pieces of luggage. She was wearing a bronze colored trench coat that made her appear even slighter and more helpless. I guess only a man would use the word "helpless" as a description. A woman would say delicate, although I knew from our discussions on the phone that she is neither.

I pulled to the curb before she even had a chance to signal me. We exchanged introductions and I hurried to load their monstrous luggage into the back of my vehicle before one of the endless number of airport security personnel could accuse me of loitering. Once out of the airport, I explained that we would be dropping my vehicle off at a friend's house and he would drive us to catch our chartered flight.

I regretted that I had not paid a few extra bucks to charter a larger plane as I considered the size and weight of their luggage, but I figured the pilot would be used to this since they frequently flew celebrities with their entourages to the

San Juan's for rest and relaxation. I reasoned that those people probably brought half the merchandise on Rodeo Drive with them. I was wrong again. The pilot took one look at the three of us and the bags and stated that there would be too much weight aboard and that he would have to come back for a second run with the luggage. He took me aside and apologized for the added expense, but said that this looked more like cargo than luggage, chuckling at his little joke. Other bad news included the fact that he couldn't bring the luggage until morning because he wouldn't fly after dark. I relayed this to Antoinette with my apologies, but she just looked at me as if I was lacking in intellect and pointed to the smallest of the bags,(which was still bigger than any I had ever owned), and informed me that that bag had been packed to get them through a day or two in case such an emergency arose. The pilot loaded the one bag, locked the others in his van and we took off right on time.

The plane was noisy and the views were spectacular so we had little conversation during the flight. I did find out from Etienne that his mother was very excited about this opportunity for both of them; for him because he would get to meet others with his gift and for her to give her a break from her normal routine. It hadn't occurred to me when I first spoke with him, but I and Amanda had both wondered since how Etienne could get away during the school months. Etienne explained that his schooling was directed through a private tutor with whom specials arrangements had been made to accommodate this trip. Actually, part of their luggage included his computer and a few books as most of his education was online. This had been the arrangement since he was ten years old when his mother took him for the first day of the school year. Even though he would have only been in the fifth grade, Antoinette did not like what she saw as she dropped him off and immediately pulled him out of public school and within a few days had made other arrangements to provide him with a more suitable education. Etienne stated that he didn't mind being privately tutored. He claimed that most of the kids he had met were nice people, but he really didn't find much to talk about with them. He did not appear to be regretful or lonely and seemed to agree totally with his mother's decision.

I studied him carefully as we discussed the coming events. He was fair skinned, but had very dark brown eyes and hair. He resembled his mother only in some very subtle ways, that is, certain mannerisms and facial expressions, although I do not mean to imply in any way that he wasn't "all boy". If he was subdued at times, it was because of his training, not his inclination. I had the feeling that when he was released from a confined space, he would run around in crazy circles like any other boy his age. Yet, there was a very serious side to him, not darkly so, just pensive and cerebral while, at the same time, he appeared to be one of the happiest young people I had ever met. In this he reminded me of Samantha. I could not picture either of them ever suffering from that self-centered angst that engulfs most teens. There was too much joy and spirit in them for that.

Looking at him, I found myself missing Samantha and looking forward to her visit in a couple of weeks. I knew those two would hit it off, possibly become lifelong friends or even more. Good lord, I was becoming a real romantic in my old age, or was it just that I wanted Samantha to have what Amanda and I had shared and more. Theirs could be an even greater life since they could share what Amanda and I could not. I had to pull myself back wondering why I would figuratively hand my cherished girl over to a perfect stranger when neither one of them was old enough to drive a car. Etienne was barely old enough to shave, although Samantha confided in me that she was already shaving her legs. Has it always been the case in modern times that girls started shaving before boys? Definitely a question for Amanda.

We arrived at the harbor exactly as scheduled and I could see Serena waving from the landing at the top of the dock. Etienne grabbed their piece of luggage from the pilot and headed up the ramp struggling not at all with the weight of the bag. This young man was a lot stronger than he appeared and he seemed older than his fourteen years. I helped Antoinette up the dock as she was wearing at least three and a half inch spiked heels and they do have a tendency to get caught in the spaces between the boards. I could just see that fine leather being scraped off the heels of what I was sure were a very expensive pair of shoes. I wondered if this woman owned a pair of jeans and sneakers-appropriate wear for this setting, or if she was going to be bound to the house for the entire time due to lack of solid footwear. Certainly neither Amanda nor Serena could offer any shoes that would fit that dainty little foot. By the time we reached the landing Serena and Etienne were already old buddies and Etienne was going on about getting to ride from the airport in a Cadillac Escalade. Apparently, this impressed him more than the flight in the seaplane. I informed him that my friend would be putting the Escalade on the ferry from Seattle in the morning and I would retrieve it for our use during their stay. During the short drive to the house Antoinette informed us that Etienne was enchanted with Cadillacs of all styles and vintages. At home he had dozens of models that he had lovingly built and he could identify every model from every year all the way back to1909. Serena stated this was certainly harmless as opposed to the activities of so many boys his age. Antoinette nodded in agreement and added that it wasn't just the boys, girls were getting to be just as dangerous, which is why she would never put Etienne back in any school, public or private, until it was time for college. Serena looked at Etienne sympathetically. Antoinette saw the look and it was clearly written on her face that she was prepared to do battle should Serena or anyone else express any negative thoughts about her decision. It didn't happen. Serena is much too polite and sensitive to ever show a child that she disagreed with their parents. The moment passed and everyone relaxed.

We pulled into the drive just past dusk and the house was ablaze with lights, and I do mean ablaze. Amanda had gone throughout and turned on every one of Patrick's amazing lamps in addition to the plentiful light the home itself provided. It looked very festive and I was grateful to Amanda and Serena for their efforts.

I could see many of the guests out on the back deck with drinks in their hands and the whole scene looked as festive as I had hoped. Serena had prepared smoked salmon canapés, crab stuffed mushrooms, crudités (meaning veggies with dip although in my opinion "crudite" is an ugly word for such healthy fare even if it is derived from French) and a variety of cheeses and fruits to tide everyone over until I, the master barbecue king, could work my magic on the grill. I had decided upon a mixed grill since I wasn't sure who ate meat, who was allergic to shellfish, who was a vegetarian or who was on a special diet. As it turned out, I needn't have worried. This entire group, with the exception of Antoinette, is made up of champion eaters. Even Amanda, who could consume more than any man or woman I have ever met, was amazed at the appetites. All the meals, breakfast, lunch and dinner have been consumed with energy and enthusiasm. At first I thought it was just the celebratory environment, but after a few days I could see that this was a permanent situation and that provisions would have to be brought in more frequently than planned.

I will only focus on the high points of the evening since I promised to let each guest make his own introduction to you the next morning. The first interesting event occurred when we arrived at the house and I told Antoinette and Etienne that they would share the guest cabin which was connected to the main house by a covered breezeway. I was a little nervous about this but she seemed extremely pleased and asked to be shown to the guest house so that she could freshen up before dinner. The next hurdle was to explain that they would also be sharing the house with Amanda and that Etienne would have to occupy the living room and sleep on the hide-a-bed. I deliberately waited to tell her this part until we had entered the cottage so that she could see how roomy and comfortably furnished it was. Etienne went nuts! Amanda or Serena had thoughtfully lit the gas fireplace in the living room and the entire cabin glowed with warmth. He was ecstatic that he could sleep in this big room and wondered if he could keep the fire going all night. Plopping down on the couch, he announced that it was the perfect size for him and that there was no need to open it into a bed.

The bedrooms upstairs are connected by a shared bathroom so the ladies had their privacy and there is a separate bathroom on the main floor. There is also a large screen TV in the living room and a desk by the window which was perfect for his studies. Antoinette was satisfied with the arrangement and didn't concern herself at all about the fact that they would have a roommate. I think she knew that she was capable of remaining aloof if she found Amanda annoying. She treasures her privacy and this was certainly more private than the main house.

I returned to the main house to greet the other guests and begin my grilling ritual. Serena had everything prepped and ready to go so my part was pretty simple. The meal was a huge success with the fillet mignon wrapped in bacon and grilled to order. The scallop and scampi skewers took on just the perfect touch and were served with a beurre blanc. Fresh grilled asparagus, and Serena's potatoes mornay rounded out the main course. Amanda had prepared her Caesar salad from scratch and served everyone individually and we had fresh breads purchased from the Sandcastle.

While I was manning the grill, Amanda and Serena were busily moving from guest to guest making sure everyone was comfortable and had a beverage. My involvement with the barbecue gave me the opportunity to observe the group dynamics. I had met everyone on their arrival and had some time to get acquainted during the trips from the airport to the seaplane landing. It was clear to me from the beginning that this was a diverse and unique group and I had no idea how it would all play out.

I spotted Bernie Rausch sitting on the couch next to Adrian, the oldest member of our group. She is average in height, but in no other way. She has very long black hair streaked only slightly with gray. In every way she gives a visual interpretation of the word "aristocrat" with her fine, well defined features, smooth complexion and impeccable posture. She exudes strength and breeding and it was clear that she did not lack in charm, intelligence and wit. She strolled over to me shortly after my arrival and announced that prior to his death ten years ago, her husband of fifty years had been the self-proclaimed king of the barbecue, implying that I had to meet some pretty high standards. That challenge would normally grab my full attention but I was distracted by the math, deducing that even if she married at age fifteen, which was unlikely, she would have to be at least 75 and more likely 80 years old. She read my mind and stated that she would be celebrating her 80th birthday here on the island in just two weeks. She took obvious pleasure in my surprise and displayed no discomfort in revealing her age. It occurred to me at that time that only the very young and the nearly old are really concerned with age, though for different reasons. I guess once you are old, you are old and it really doesn't matter how old, especially if you look and carry yourself like Adrian. A fifty year old man or woman might encourage others to believe they are forty, but an eighty year old will freely offer that information and are just proud to still be alive and functioning well. Adrian has a lot to be proud of! She is beautiful and one can easily spot the knockout she must have been in her youth.

Having made her announcements, she drifted off in search of more interesting conversation leaving me to my thoughts and tongs. I couldn't help but wonder what kind of man was the lucky soul who lived with that stunning creature for fifty years. I pictured him as a cross between John Wayne for his masculinity and Anthony Hopkins for his refinement and intelligence. You can see why, when I saw her sitting with Bernie, it seemed totally inappropriate and I was right. It only took a few minutes for her to rise and go outside on the deck leaving him sitting alone on the couch.

Bernie instantly lunged to the bar and fixed himself another very strong drink, the third that I had seen in the short time I had been there. He leaned against the bar taking in the whole scene with an expression that I can only describe as smug and disdainful. His eyes settled on Serena, who was moving about the room tidying up while engaging in lively conversation with another of the male guests. Watching her interact with others, Bernie's face reflected, not jealousy, but rather that "Mom likes you best look" that you might see on the face of a six year old. I remember thinking at that time that Bernie's stay with us might be short lived, but it never occurred to me that he would leave as he did, although I have often wanted to ship him off marked "Return to Sender".

The next event that evening was the arrival, no "entrance", of Antoinette and Etienne. He preceded his mother by a few seconds causing some interest among the guests due to his tender age. As Antoinette appeared and the room went silent. She glistened. That is the only word I can think of. The light in the entry hall was quite bright and it was as if her hair, skin and even her clothes absorbed that light and made it their own. Reddish-gold hair, translucent skin, and the most amazing bronze colored dress I have ever seen were assembled to create this artistic light show. As with any work of art, you inhale the entire image first, then the eyes drift to the individual components. In this case it was the bodice of her gown. Did she or didn't she? No question about it, she didn't. Beneath that elegant fabric were two perfectly formed breasts clearly free of all restrictions. I, for one, admit to being mesmerized and when I regained my senses, it was apparent that all in attendance, male and female, had been captured in much the same way. Antoinette looked sublimely female and goddess-like. As in all cases, Serena was the first to regain her composure. She crossed the room to take Antoinette by the arm and introduce her to the guests one-by-one starting with Amanda. I can honestly say that in all our years together I had rarely seen Amanda at a loss for words but, though she recovered quickly, I could see the awe in her eyes and it took her a few seconds to respond to the introduction. One thing about Amanda, she has never been the type of woman who was jealous of the beauty of another. She has always enjoyed being with others who are comfortable and confident in who they are whether or not they are physically attractive. She is not a competitive person in anything except card games and gambling. I was counting on this when I decided to make her and Antoinette cabin mates. The other introductions were made and the room regained its previous atmosphere with the exception of frequent stolen glances at Antoinette from the men.

From the moment Adrian introduced herself to Etienne they have been inseparable. Aside from their shared fondness for Cadillacs, they enjoy a special bond that is punctuated with a rather sophisticated brand of humor. That first night was the beginning of a relationship that I suspect will last as long as Adrian is still adorning the planet and, considering the unique properties of this group, maybe long after that.

Etienne seemed to enjoy himself thoroughly that evening. He was polite and genuinely interested in everyone and there was no indication that he was bored or felt out of place. Actually, teenagers don't usually act like they feel out of place. They just try to make everyone else feel that way. It was not so with Etienne and within a few minutes I could see that his youth was not going to present a problem. Part of this is due to Antoinette's approach to rearing her son. He was given a great deal of freedom, yet it was obvious that a betrayal of her trust would have severe consequences. He behaved like a gentleman, but was still very much a boy. At dinner he was allowed to sample small amounts of the various wines and actually made some favorable comments regarding their quality, although I did overhear him telling his mother that perhaps she should go with me the next time I made a wine run and help me pick out a better port.

Amanda sought out Antoinette and they engaged in a warm and lively discussion until dinner was served. The table was set beautifully, but not too formally and Serena announced that there were no special seating arrangements. It had never occurred to me that there would be, which demonstrates how many formal dinners I have arranged or attended. When I announced dinner was ready, there was activity just short of a mad dash to the table with Bernie plopping himself strategically in the chair nearest the bar. Others didn't seem to pay any special attention to positioning. The table is wide and long, providing ample room for our guests to sit comfortably, but still allowing for conversation. Serena, it was agreed, would join us for any meals she wished, but she insisted on being seated on the end near the kitchen so that she can perform her serving and replenishing duties. With this group those duties kept her jumping.

The dinner ended up lasting nearly three hours with the wine flowing as freely as the conversation. Serena and Amanda had accomplished such excellent preparation that each course was served with a minimum of interruption and a maximum of appreciation. Dessert was served with coffee and a selection of liqueurs and I announced that anyone who wished could accompany me to the den for a Cuban cigar.

Among those in attendance were Adrian and Amanda. Amanda had enjoyed a good cigar with me from time to time, but Adrian took me by surprise. Etienne and Antoinette had retired to their cabin shortly after dinner. Bernie joined my group, but had little to say and didn't seem to take any real pleasure in the cigar, although he clearly enjoyed the cognac. What a waste of a great cigar!

The party finally broke up about one in the morning and everyone dragged themselves to their respective rooms with the assurance that breakfast would be delayed until ten a.m. to allow them to recoup from their journey and the evening's festivities. I stayed for a while and helped Serena finish cleaning up and then departed for the short walk to my boat.

As I had anticipated, Serena had taken some special pains to make sure I was comfortable. She had even prepared my coffee maker so that all I had to do was push a button in the morning. It was that time of year when the nights get cold and although my boat was snug, I was pleased to find a brand new set of flannel sheets on my bed. I knew this was compliments of Amanda because she knows of my love for flannel as long as I am not wearing it on my back. I also detected a faint scent of her favorite perfume by Georgio and I wondered if this was an accident or some subtle reminder. I decided it was probably just from the contact with her while she was making up the bed, but I enjoyed the sensation anyway.

I slipped into the soft warmth of the new sheets and the matching comforter, confident that I would lie awake half the night thinking about the events of the day and reveling in the apparent success of the evening. I planned to take this time to analyze the different personalities and design my strategy for the next day. Instead, I awoke seven hours later with no memory of closing my eyes. I wondered if the other guests had as foul a taste in their mouths as I did, regretting that I had not taken the time to brush my teeth the night before to remove the residual from the cigar, garlic and the indiscreet blend of several different wines and liquors. I pressed the button on my coffee maker and retired to the head for a hot shower. This and a generous serving of toothpaste followed by two Alka-Seltzer returned me to a world filled with a promise of survival. One cup of coffee, one pair of jeans, a fleecy over-shirt and some footwear and I was ready for an exciting day.

Chapter Eleven

THE STAGE IS SET

I arrived at the house about nine-thirty expecting to find it quiet with Serena and possibly Amanda busily preparing breakfast and the guests drifting in later. Instead I walked into a gathering much like the night before. Everyone was up and about, dressed in comfortable clothing and holding on to their coffee cups as if they were their lifeline. The atmosphere was cheerful and electric. It reminded me of the times Amanda and her group of women friends would escape their work and household duties and go to Las Vegas for a few days of hedonistic pleasure. They would all congregate in the airport lounge an hour or two before their flight and defiantly guzzle bloody Marys or Irish coffees at eight in the morning. The atmosphere would be charged in anticipation of their temporary escape from reality. I don't think I have ever seen males so courageously display their excitement. We tend to camouflage our enthusiasm for fear of being presumed un-cool. There was no such inhibition that morning in our group. Everyone was charged up and if there was any fear or trepidation about the process that was to begin, it wasn't obvious to me.

It had been agreed that most meals would be served buffet style to minimize the fuss and distraction from our real purpose-whatever that was. Amanda had been a caterer in one of her many careers so we had all the necessary equipment to present three meals a day to a large group and, between her and Serena, they certainly had the knowledge and skills to create some fine cuisine.

Breakfast that morning consisted of pork chops, scrambled eggs, leftover potatoes mornay, cornbread with huckleberry jam, and oatmeal with yogurt, fresh fruit, nuts and raisins for the health-conscious. Everyone ate everything within twenty minutes of serving. The only person not present was Antoinette. Etienne fixed her a tray and delivered it to the cabin. Amanda informed me that Antoinette had decided to stay there for the day since she wasn't really involved and she didn't want to make the others feel uncomfortable, but that she would like to attend some of the sessions later. Looking around me I couldn't imagine anyone in this group feeling uncomfortable, but I appreciated her consideration and time would tell if the atmosphere would change.

Breakfast over, we assembled in the living room, thereafter referred to as the "story pit". For the first time that morning the group became silent as each gravitated toward a particular chair or couch. Adrian and Etienne chose to sit on the hearth of the fireplace and, as it turns out, that has remained their permanent vantage point for all sessions. Bernie chose a rather formidable looking straight-backed chair that I would characterize as being more ornamental than functional. I claimed the deep leather chair I had earlier positioned near the fireplace. Serena was quietly working in the kitchen cleaning up from breakfast and beginning lunch preparations. The kitchen was open to the living room but separated by the large dining area so any noise that she created was strictly background and in truth added a comfortable aura to our activities. Besides, it was already obvious to me that this group would not be offended by any distraction that involved food or drink. I wondered if this somewhat bohemian approach to life was one of the commonalities we would discover.

I started with the welcome speech I had carefully prepared over the preceding weeks. It was speckled with humor which no one picked up on causing me to eliminate the pauses I had planned to accommodate their laughter. I abandoned my notes early on because the group was simply not behaving in the manner that I had expected. They were not nervous so I didn't have to calm their fears. They were all strangers, yet they were already at ease with one another with the exception of Bernie, who took great pride in distancing himself not realizing that no one cared whether or not he joined in. It has always been a source of amazement to me that most negative people take great pride and care in informing others that they value their privacy and deliberately lead secluded lives. It never seems to occur to them that no one is really looking for them so they don't need to hide.

I had not intended to go into much detail about my relationship with Amanda and the reason I was sponsoring this event. I only wanted to impart to them my desire to offer everyone present the opportunity to discuss their experiences freely and openly with like-minded people and that, although I wasn't "one of them", I didn't want them to think of me as some sort of voyeur living vicariously through their lives. As it turned out, the group was so responsive and accepting that I ended up spilling my guts for thirty minutes telling them all about our life together and my failure to respond to Amanda's needs and my dedication to ensure that the same thing didn't happen with my granddaughter. In short, in any other circle except this one, it might be considered that I had made an ass of myself. Having bared my soul and destroyed any possible perception that I was a suave and sophisticated rich guy, I turned the floor over to Amanda to begin the proceedings.

AMANDA

"Well, it is obviously not necessary to elaborate on Sam's motives for bringing us together. They are pure and honest. Sam is to be trusted in all ways and he is too hard on himself for not understanding because, as you all well know, his reaction to our stories is perfectly normal. We have all felt the loneliness that goes along with our "expanded memory bank". In reviewing each of your interviews, it is obvious that everyone here has experienced more than just the common déjà vu that many people have encountered once or twice in their lives. We have actual memories of former lives, some more vivid than others, and have lived several lives, some more interesting than others. Perhaps you are like me in that one or more of my lives I would not be anxious to remember. Nevertheless, I will share that story with you as well as others because I truly believe these memories have a tremendous impact on our subsequent lives, including the one we are living.

We will call upon each of you to introduce yourself and give us whatever history you care to share about your current life and a summary of your experience with past life memories. We won't get into the stories today, rather the details of how your memories started and how you have dealt with them in your daily life and relationships. You can go into as much or as little detail as you wish.

All of you are making great sacrifices to be here. You are separated from your friends, families and jobs, possibly postponing some important responsibilities to be present. That tells me that you sincerely want to share your experiences in the hope that we can all learn from each other. As Sam mentioned, we have a granddaughter that has had the memories since early childhood. I want to help her to understand what is happening to her so that she can be enriched by this, not inhibited. I want this for her and in truth, I want it for me. I have come to grips with the knowledge that we will never be fully believed, but I want that road to be easier for her than it was for me. She will be joining us for a couple of weekends and I look forward to introducing her to all of you and especially you, Etienne, as you are close to the same age and you both have tremendous spirit.

I would also like to get feedback from everyone on the subject of Antoinette sitting in on some of our sessions. She feels she can benefit greatly as Etienne's mother, but is reluctant to be present unless you all agree. Does anyone have a problem with this? If so, please come to Sam or me privately and express your concerns?"

SAM

At this point everyone looked at each other and at Etienne and there was a murmur of approval from everyone except Bernie who later told me that he felt she would be too much of a distraction and that, not him, but some of the other men might be reluctant to open up in front of her. I told Bernie that if he himself was not uncomfortable, he should let the others speak for themselves and that I had not heard one other objection. Bernie claimed that he was just trying to be helpful and that I was obviously going to do whatever Amanda wanted me to do anyway since it was clear that I never said "no" to

Amanda. Good God, I wondered how he had ever slipped through the screening process.

Amanda sat down after her opening speech and secreted some note cards into her pocket. She had never consulted the notes so it was obvious to me that she also had not given the introduction she had so carefully prepared. I found that shamefully comforting. Adrian was sitting to my right on the hearth so I asked her to speak next and indicated that we would go around the room from there. She rose gracefully and gave us her beautiful and gracious smile. I felt warmed by that smile. It occurred to me that Bernie, who was missing a couple of front teeth, was probably wondering if she was wearing dentures. Where did that thought come from? Everyone's eyes were glued to her as she spoke.

Chapter Twelve

ADRIAN

"I am not just an old woman, I am an old soul. I told Sam that I would be celebrating my eightieth birthday with all of you in a couple of weeks and, in all my eighty years, I cannot think of a time when I wasn't conscious of my former lives. I was fortunate to have parents that worshipped me and had the financial and social standing that shielded me from ridicule. Clive, my husband of fifty years never once doubted my memories. He would encourage me to tell him stories about the people that I was and the people that I knew and the history I had witnessed. I must admit that every once in a while I would embellish a bit and I think he knew it, but we led a very quiet and peaceful life so my embellishments were forgiven for their story value. I promise you that I will not engage in any such activity here.

Clive and I married when I was twenty. My father was a cattle rancher as was my husband's family. I was an only child and Clive's only brother was killed in World War ll. Being the only heirs, Clive and I merged our properties upon our parents' retirement and enjoyed a prosperous but hard-working lifestyle. In later years we were free to do a lot of traveling and, though it is not always possible for me to remember actual physical locations of earlier lives, we did visit some places that I knew I had been before and I was able to identify buildings or landmarks that still existed or the locality of some that had been erased over time. If my husband had any doubts before, my ability to describe locations prior to our arrival would have certainly convinced him. He loved these excursions as did I and I am happy to have had those memories with him.

We have one son who now runs the ranch with his wife and I have four beautiful grandchildren and six great grandchildren. My son does not have memories but, like Sam and Amanda, I have a granddaughter living in Portland Oregon who writes short stories that I believe are based on personal experiences in past lives, although she claims otherwise. This granddaughter is twenty seven years old and she refers to me affectionately as a spooky old lady. I moved to a condo in downtown Portland to be near her and we spend a great deal of time together. As you can see, there are many similarities between myself and Amanda. My granddaughter is named April which is one of the characters in some of her stories. It was she that found the website on the internet telling about this event and encouraged me to inquire further. I wondered at the time how she happened to be exploring the subject via the internet in the first place, but she claimed she was just doing some research for a story.

At first I was reluctant to come, but after speaking at length with Sam and Amanda, I realized that since my husband's death, I had not shared my memories with anyone, including April, and I was beginning to feel a little isolated. The urge to participate became stronger and my granddaughter was very insistent that I come here. I believe she is close to coming out of the closet, so to speak, with her memories and I think she hopes to gain some understanding through my participation. Sitting in this room with all of you, I am so glad that I made that decision. I have had a number of former lives. To be honest, I'm not sure how many as new memories are still popping up. I can tell you this for sure, I never get tired of living whatever life I am given."

SAM

Adrian's last statement was punctuated with another glorious smile and, as she sat down, Etienne gave her a big hug and she took his hand. The group became animated as they shared instances with persons next to them about having visited places they had lived before. I left them to their discussions for a few minutes before I moved on to introduce Etienne. It was then that Adrian took me aside and said that Etienne wanted to be introduced later rather than next as the rotation would have provided. I could see nothing wrong with that request so I moved on to the chair to the left of him which was occupied by a man named Glen Dresser.

Glen rose with some difficulty to introduce himself. He is quite tall and I knew from our interviews that he is fifty-four years old. From the brief time we had spent together, I had learned that he retired as CEO of a large national company and he also does some motivational speaking for different organizations. It isn't hard to see why he would be sought after for this purpose. He is intelligent, affable and has the mark of a leader about him. He is the type of man that one intuitively wants to get to know. Everything about him seems genuine and he has that easy going manner that accompanies a person that has worked hard at being the best he can be and has achieved success. His interest in others is obviously genuine and when he speaks, you feel as if you are the only person in the room. Glenn is also a double amputee. He smiled as he spoke.

Chapter Thirteen

GLEN

"Well, I have the feeling that all of you are as happy to be here as I am. When I am giving public speeches, I usually begin with a joke to warm the crowd up but I think in this case we can forego that exercise as this is already a pretty warm group and certainly well fed thanks to Amanda and Serena-oh, and you too Sam. You may have noticed that I am a little slower in getting around than most of you. I know that Adrian, at the proud age of eighty, could whip my ass in a footrace, but then I think that she could beat most of us here with the possible exception of Etienne. However, (lifting one pant leg) I have an excuse so the rest of you can just suffer with that knowledge.

I was nineteen years old and working summers for a contractor while attending the University of Indiana when I had a pretty difficult day. The bottom line is that I was electrocuted by some power lines and blew my legs off along with some sustaining other lesser but serious injuries. It took a few months, but I eventually realized that I was fortunate to have doctors that struggled hard enough to save not only my life, but one of my knees. The fact that I still have the use of one knee is what enables me to walk on these prostheses without the aid of canes or a walker. It still is no picnic, but I have always been able to get where I needed to go. Sam tells me that we will have plenty of time to explore the island and enjoy the beaches. I intend to do just that but I must warn everyone that sometimes when I am walking on uneven terrain, I can get into a little trouble. Usually it involves one of my legs falling off. If that happens, just pick it up and hand it to me, I'll do the rest. There is a lot of new technology available for amputees, but I haven't gotten around to exploring the possibilities yet. I guess as we get older, we are a little slower to try out new things or maybe we are simply more content with what we have.

As the CEO of a large company, I was pretty careful to keep my memories of past lives to myself. My first memory occurred later in life than most of yours. It was during that time that I was being treated for my injuries and recovering from the many surgeries and the burns that I began to experience my memories. For a long time I believed it was just the drugs they were giving me that caused what I considered to be "hallucinations". After a year of treatment and rehabilitation, I was taken off medication, yet the images did not disappear. They became even more vivid and frequent. At the same time, I was able to return to school although it was another two years before I could be fitted for my first set of legs. During this time, I was bound to a wheelchair and pretty dependent on others since there weren't a lot of handicapped facilities in those days. God, working through the dean of the school of engineering, sent me a roommate named Aaron. Aaron was huge and as strong as any man I have ever met. He could pull me and my wheelchair up three flights of stairs without getting winded. I weigh considerably less than most men due to my "shortened stature", but nevertheless, it was quite amazing. In addition to his physical size and strength, Aaron was a giant among men in spirit, kindness and intellect. It was as if God one day decided to create a perfect man. Like Sam, I believe he created many perfect women and perhaps he wanted to see if he could do the same with the other side of the species. Aaron was a gifted student as well as a gifted human being. He was my best friend and, if he were alive today he would still occupy that position in my life.

One night, almost three years after my accident, we were getting ready to travel to our respective homes for spring break. Aaron was from a small town about one hundred miles away and was attending on a full academic scholarship. He worked at a local gas station evenings and weekends. He spent little and sent the rest home. He had struggled to save up bus fare to get home for the break and was excited to see his family. We had finished our packing and I had provided us with a six-pack of beer and some cheese and crackers as a special celebration. Neither of us were big drinkers so at three beers each, we were waxing philosophical. I don't remember how the subject came up, but I expressed my growing suspicion that what I thought were drug induced hallucinations might actually be something more than that. I approached the subject of reincarnation with Aaron expecting him to react as if I was crazy, but he didn't react at all. He just looked at me and said "Why not?". Aaron and his family were staunchly religious so even in my semi-drunk state, his question seemed out of place to me. Aaron went on to say that there were a couple of people in his town that claimed to have such memories. One couple for years claimed to have been married to each other in a former life and believed that because the wife had died very young in that life, they were given another chance to be together in their current lives. This couple had just celebrated their sixtieth wedding anniversary and had never been known to be anything but devoted to one another, their family and their community. Aaron said that no one in their town questioned the couple's belief in their former life together, or if they did they never expressed it.

Another woman in his town claimed to have a memory of a former life as a male stagecoach driver. Her credibility was not as solid as the couple's, but her anatomy and general demeanor served to substantiate her claim. She had often been known to do some heavy drinking at the local bar and was prone to starting fights with men and women. Of course few women in the town would allow it to become physical, but neither did most men as it had been proven that she could probably beat the crap out of any of them. The men were able to save face by stating that no gentleman would hit a woman, but a few of these same men were known to make an exception in the case of their wives and children, so the term gentleman didn't apply to them.

Aaron and I discussed the matter often over the next couple of years. I related my memories and he listened eagerly. Until now, Aaron is the only person I have ever confided in and I am more excited than nervous at the prospect of sharing them with this incredible group.

I married a wonderful woman named Peggy when I was thirty years old. She had been married before and brought two beautiful children with her. They were three and five years old at the time and their father, Peggy's first husband, had abandoned them all. It took her four years to track him down and obtain a divorce and we were married shortly thereafter. We never had children together, but her children became my own and I couldn't have asked for a more devoted family.

I achieved some measure of success in the corporate world and our life was as close to perfect as one could hope for over the next eighteen years. I was very busy and happy and, though I still had the visions, as I referred to them, they weren't as frequent nor as vivid. For some reason, I never discussed them with Peggy. I guess my life was so full, I didn't need to. Aaron and I kept in touch over the years and during our frequent visits the subject would come up, but it wasn't important to me then as there were many other things to catch up on.

Aaron died eight years ago of a heart attack and it hit me pretty hard. It was more than just losing my best friend, but I couldn't put it into words at the time. I know now that beyond his kindness and friendship, I had lost the only other person in the world that I could talk to about my experiences. Peggy and I had been together for so long by that time that it might have felt like a betrayal to her if I brought it out then. It was around Christmas five years ago that Peggy died suddenly of an aneurism. Our children are living their own lives now and I am alone. In these recent years the visions have been increasing to the point where I have actually been able to remember entire lives. I know these aren't the delusions of a lonely grief-stricken man. I am simply freer to examine my memories.

I look forward to hearing all of your stories and sharing mine. Like Amanda, I believe it is our responsibility to learn from our pasts-all of them. I believe we were given the ability to recall in order to fulfill some greater purpose. I believe that we must look upon this as a gift and proceed fearlessly to explore our minds and grow our hearts. I believe that everyone is meant to experience great joy in their life, no matter how difficult or how short and that every life has a meaning and purpose. I believe that we are all capable of great good and great evil and that ultimately our eternity will reflect how well we have nurtured the good and defeated the evil. I have had a rich and rewarding life this time around and I hope to take what I have learned to the next life should it be God's will to return me once again to this world. I hope he does chose to send me back because, although I do believe in an eternal afterlife where we blissfully share in God's glory, I also believe that in another life on earth I can spread some of the joy that has been mine - and God knows the world needs joy."

SAM

Glen's speech was met with rousing applause. It was obvious that he had the honesty and charm necessary to hold the attention and command the respect of any audience. Amanda was particularly enthralled by him which makes sense because she has always been drawn to strong, upbeat people. I guess we all are, but in her case, these traits can bring her to an almost rapturous state. I felt a twinge of jealousy as I watched her, sitting motionless for once, devouring his every word and gesture. I wondered if I had created a situation that could bring my own dreams of happiness with Amanda to an end because, throughout his speech, it seemed like Glen had established eye contact with her for long periods of time-much longer than with the others. I felt sick and elated at the same time. Glen was definitely the kind of man that could fill Amanda's dreams and they also had their special gift to share. I decided that what will be, will be, but my heart was not agreeing with my brain.

AMANDA

It is so seldom that we find someone in our lives that we can simply adore. I have never been one to fall in love with movie stars or other public figures. I loved Sam from the beginning, but those feelings were based on his simple goodness, his frailties and foibles, his innocence, his love for me and a great deal of physical attraction. Glenn was different. With Sam I wanted to share everything, even our faults and shortcomings. With Glen I only wanted to see the goodness and greatness. I didn't ever want to see the weaknesses because I wanted so badly to believe that such a great man could exist-without flaws. He remains the closest thing to a perfect man that I have ever met. I thought Sam spotted my infatuation and it bothered him a little and that made me feel good and bad-mostly good.

SAM

We voted to have another introduction before lunch and the next person in line was a young Native American woman named Kate Westar. To this point Kate had been friendly, but not overly communicative. At times she even seemed a little put-off by the immediate "closeness" of the group. It was clear that Kate was part of a culture that had more physical boundaries than others. She seemed aloof, but not offended by all the hugging and eye contact, yet I had no doubt that once she established her relationship with each person, she would become more trusting and open.

Kate is from a Northwest tribe and was raised on a reservation. She is in her mid-thirties and has spent most of her adult life working for her tribe in an effort to bring the other members into the mainstream while retaining their Native American heritage. She is not a small woman, but what I would call pleasantly rounded. Caucasian women cannot carry extra weight as gracefully as darker skinned women.

White women tend to look "doughy" with extra pounds while women who have darker skin look womanly, motherly, exotic, and yes, sexy. Native American women are also free of excess body hair. Their hair is generally thick and glossy and located on the top of their head where it belongs. Kate has a glowing and flawless complexion which, coupled with her other feminine attributes, creates a picture of good health and that special kind of gentle strength that only a mature woman can possess. It comes from within and is not challenging nor is it challengeable. There is a peaceful yet mysterious aura around Kate and though she participates less in the conversations surrounding her, I sense that she knows more about our group than any of us. Her voice is soft, but her speech is clear and she is as easy to listen to as she is to look at.

Chapter Fourteen

KATE

"I am grateful to be included. I find this group interesting and lively and I look forward with pleasure to the next few weeks. For one thing, this setting is fabulous in its natural beauty and I plan to spend a great deal of time exploring outdoors.

My experiences will mirror many of your own, but my beliefs regarding my memories may be different than most of yours. You see, among my people and in most tribes, our memories are a truth, not a belief. Those of us who have adhered to our culture, view the universe as a continuum with ourselves, our ancestors, the earth and our Creator. Our ancestors live within us and we live with the earth not on it and to move away from this bond creates chaos and destruction. We believe that we return to advance this continuum by bonding with and passing on the wisdom of our ancestors. We want to keep returning and do not believe that we are sent back again and again until we "get it right". Our purpose is to earn the honor of returning. In that respect, Glen and I share the same goal.

I was raised in a traditional Native American family, but one whose roots are being severed one by one. As children, we were allowed a great deal of freedom and were encouraged to explore the world of our creator. My life has been divided into many parts. My early years were spent outdoors with my two sisters and my brother-running, playing, fishing, swimming and picking huckleberries. We had many friends of various ages and there was always a game or competition of some kind. Our tribe was very poor in those days so our mothers were busy sewing and cooking or working outside the home. My grandmother lived with us and she was definitely the head of the household. We adored her and feared more than anything, her disapproval. My father was absent a lot. He worked in the lumber mill which was part of the tribal enterprise, and spent a good deal of his off hours at the local bar. Often he would come home late at night drunk and bloody from some fight at the bar. My mother would put him to bed and the next morning there would be a lot of yelling and perhaps even some blows exchanged between them. We didn't let this bother us too much as it was what we were used to and this situation was mirrored in the homes of many of our friends and relatives.

Our tribal school was small and poor, but looking back I can remember the dedication of our teachers. They had so little to work with and so many of the children came from violent and desperately poor homes. The dropout rate in high school was horrendous. As the years passed, some of the businesses in the enterprise began to prosper a little and the quality of life improved to some degree. The added prosperity did not benefit everyone because so many had no idea how to manage the extra money, so much of it went to toys, alcohol and drugs.

I was sent to college by the tribe and graduated with a teaching degree. About that time our tribal leaders had heard about the many successes in other parts of the country of the tribal casinos. There were none in our area and, after much investigation and negotiation with the state legislature, they were able to put together a plan and the money to open a casino of our own. I went to work there right out of college as the marketing person. There were few of us trained in running a successful business, but the time and the territory was ripe for a casino and, to be honest, I think in the beginning it would have been impossible to fail. In just a few short years we prospered and, due to good leadership, we reinvested in our property to expand our casino and build a fabulous resort and golf course to go along with it. Since all tribal members share in the profits, life on the reservation took another turn for the better. Our schools were improved and the dedication of our leaders to health, wellness and education became evident everywhere on the reservation. But to some, that new money brought still more drugs and other temptations and our traditions and values became harder to identify in our daily lives. I left the casino after five years to begin teaching and working with others to protect and enrich our disappearing native culture. I could see that in just one generation we were in danger of losing that which has sustained us for so long and there are many of us who will not let that happen. This is how I will spend the rest of my life and by doing so I believe I will earn the right to return for more lives to continue my work.

I tell you all of this because it is in part my reason for being here. My own memories are becoming somewhat vague and less frequent. This is happening more often among those of my people who share the memories, so for me, this is a retreat to restore and rejuvenate my connection with my ancestors. I debated for a long time as to whether this was the proper forum for my retreat and I finally decided that I have nothing to lose and I do believe I might have some good things to bring to this table."

SAM

Kate made quite an impression on us all and there were a number of questions from the members of the group that led me to be glad that I included her. Hers was a different perspective and she was open and willing to share, yet no one had to feel that they were being recruited to her way of thinking. Only Bernie was skeptical. As others were expressing their sincere interest through intelligent and sensitive questions, Bernie's only response was an occasional snort through a crooked smile indicating that he and he alone was not being taken in. I could see that some in the group were embarrassed and uncomfortable. Others, like me, wanted to knock him off his chair. As we broke for lunch, Amanda whispered to me that she could not envision us being able to tolerate him for the next few weeks. She was very upset and wanted to know what I was going to do about him. She spoke of him in the most severe terms. By that I mean she used words to describe him that one rarely hears outside of a locker room, including a couple of threats and gestures that were definitely less than lady-like.

Amanda despises very few people. She can usually find something to enjoy in everyone she meets, but when someone brings poison to the party she is merciless. Bernie never had a chance in her book as he was pure poison in an ugly bottle. I knew that her opinion was not going to change and I knew there were others that shared her feelings and that those who didn't were not far behind. The situation was going to worsen if I didn't do something about it. I am not a confrontational person and I suspected that confrontation wouldn't be effective with Bernie anyhow, so I resolved to take Bernie on my boat for a little chat at the first opportunity. I thought if we could share a drink or two man to man, I would find a way to neutralize his toxicity. Well, that's a story for a later time.

The group approached the lunch table with their usual vigor and good humor. Serena had whipped up another feast consisting of a variety of sandwiches on fresh baked rolls, an incredible pasta salad and an array of fruits. Huge trays of food disappeared like magic. I found myself remembering some old movie I had seen as a child where swarms of locusts devoured everything in sight. Serena loved it, claiming there is nothing more rewarding than cooking for an appreciative group. Dessert was her own special peanut butter cookies served with pitchers of ice cold milk. Not since kindergarten had I seen a large group sitting around a table dunking their cookies in their milk. Five or six dozen cookies later, we each went our own way for an hour of exercise or leisure. I found myself yearning for a nap, but couldn't pry myself away for fear I would miss something.

Earlier I had sent Etienne in search of his mother to invite her to lunch. She had joined the group making her entrance as inconspicuous as possible. I was relieved to see that she was wearing a pair of casual slacks and elegant, but fairly practical boots. Her long hair was loosely held back by a scarf and her makeup was impeccable but daytime appropriate. She looked a little tired but was in good humor. Etienne brought her up to date on the activities of the morning and wanted her to go for a walk on the beach with him and Adrian. Antoinette declined, stating that she had spent the entire morning on the beach and was ready for a nap. Etienne appeared disappointed, but perked up immediately at the arrival of the cookies and milk. Adrian was studying Antoinette intensely and I felt that she might share my opinion that Antoinette's appearance belied her story of spending the morning on the beach. She was just too fresh and clean and her hair was too well done. Beaches are messy and windy places, very unforgiving, especially to women.

Amanda and I were helping Serena clean up after lunch. Everyone else had dispersed. If my own head was any indicator, most of them were taking a nap to help recover from the lively events of the night before. We had agreed to re-convene for more introductions at two-thirty. From the dining room window, I could see Adrian and Etienne on the beach below us. There are exactly 192 rock stair steps down to that beach and of course the same number coming back up. I was wondering how Adrian would fare on the return trip and regretted that I hadn't told them about the winding path that they could take as an alternative route. The slope is a lot gentler and even though they would be going the longer distance, I believed it would be a lot easier for Adrian. Suddenly, I began to tense up and feel slightly depressed. The sight of the two of them on the beach should have been a good thing, but I found it disturbing. As I turned around, I spotted a figure in the den seeming to hurry to get out of my sight. I crossed the living room quickly and entered the room as nonchalantly as possible. Seeing no one, I turned and left the room. There is only one way in and out of that room so I knew the person was still in there, but I wasn't sure I wanted to know who or why. After all, there isn't a room in this whole house that is off limits so why the concern? Someone needed their privacy and I was glad to let the moment pass. I returned to the kitchen in time for Amanda to hand me two large bags of trash and I was distracted by thoughts about the way we had gathered trash together on that first day on my boat. Was I crazy to hope this would be a new beginning? At least our trash bonding took my mind off my discomfort.

The hour passed quickly and by two-thirty everyone was back in the living room "story pit" for the remainder of the introductions. Happy hour was scheduled to begin a six, with dinner at seven, so it was obvious that we needed to move along a little more swiftly to get everyone introduced.

Etienne and Adrian had returned by way of the steps and neither looked the worse for wear. The temperature was in the high fifties and the wind was blowing at less than twenty MPH, so the conditions had been as ideal as they were likely to get at that time of year for their first exploration. Etienne stated that he wanted to be next to introduce himself and that he had already asked his mother to be present while he did so. I hadn't seen Antoinette since lunch but at that moment she emerged from the den confirming my earlier suspicion that it was she I had spotted watching Etienne and Adrian on the beach. She was composed, but I wondered if she had been crying as her eyes were slightly puffy. When Amanda cries her eyes swell up like crescent rolls. She has always said that the reason she doesn't cry often is because she doesn't cry pretty like some women. I'm guessing that she would say Antoinette was one of the lucky ones. Etienne stood by his spot on the hearth beside Adrian as Glenn made room for Antoinette between him and Kate on one of the sofas. While Etienne spoke, he never took his eyes off his mother for more than a few seconds at a time and she never took her eyes off him at all.

Chapter Fifteen

ETIENNE

"Like Adrian, I don't remember a time when I didn't have the memories. I do remember the first time I realized that they were not part of the present. I guess before that I merged the past and present and didn't know any different. I must have been about five years old when I became aware that the events occurring in my memories were not part of my current life. It was pretty simple really. My mom and I were at the park. We had packed and eaten a huge picnic lunch and we were lying on our blanket. My mother fell asleep but I was looking up through the trees at the sky when I felt myself moving to another place just like so many times before. I was with my brother and sister and we were laughing and playing on the beach beside a river. We had a beach ball and my brother and I were throwing it to one another over the head of my sister. She was running in every direction at once trying to get the ball. We were all laughing and our nanny was sitting in a chair up the beach keeping watch over us. My older brother hit the ball very hard and it landed in the river and began floating slowly downstream. We all ran to retrieve it, with my little sister in the lead. I was trying to catch up with her, but she had a big head start on me. She went running into the water and had the ball in her hands, but it was large and kept getting away from her so she kept going in deeper. She had never been allowed to go in the water past her knees. The river moved slowly, but she was little and the current was pulling at her as she kept running after the ball. I could hear nanny screaming and my brother pushed me down as he ran to rescue our sister. She was giggling and did not know that she was in danger. She had caught the ball and it was pulling her further into the water. Pretty soon she was over her head and my brother was still a few meters from her. I could see a log floating toward her with one limb sticking straight up in the air. I watched helplessly as our sister was hit by the log and disappeared from view. My brother was frantically diving and surfacing looking for her. We were all crying and nanny was up to her waist in the river screaming for help. My brother grabbed the limb of the log trying to pull it out of the way so he could get to the spot where he had seen her go down. At this point the log was perpendicular to the beach. I could see the other side of the log and I spotted another limb just under the surface of the water. For some reason, I swam to it and I spotted the bright blue fabric of my sister's swim dress snagged on that limb. I grabbed the dress and pulled as hard as I could to free it from the limb. It did come free and I pulled my sister to me as I tried to get back to the beach. The log kept bumping me in the head and a couple of times I grabbed onto it for support, but it would spin around and I would lose my grip. My brother could not see all that was happening from his side of the log and my body blocked my sister from nanny's view. I was trying to scream for help, but I kept going under trying to support the weight of both of us. I just kept pulling her and kicking my legs as we drifted further downstream. Finally my legs touched ground and I was able to drag us both out of the water. I was out of breath and bleeding and my sister was unconscious. Nanny came screaming down the riverbank with my brother behind her. I didn't know what to do to help my sister and I was so weak I couldn't stand up. Nanny picked my sister up and hugged her to her chest. Then my brother arrived and grabbed my sister and turned her upside down and pounded on her back. It took a minute or so, but finally, my sister started throwing up water and coughing. My brother kept pounding her back and she kept coughing. Then she started wailing at the top of her lungs and beating at my brother with her little fists. We all fell down laughing hysterically. None of us could move for a long time. Nanny just sat there in the muddy sand, crying and holding on to my sister. I remember thinking that at that moment nanny looked like my grandma had looked when she was in her coffin. Then everything started to fade out.

My mother stirred in her sleep and I looked over, surprised to see her and even more surprised that I wasn't all wet and bruised and then I remembered that I was an only child. I was shaken and confused by the experience and it took a day or two for me to get over it. Young as I was, I was still old enough to realize that you can't be two people at the same time. The experience was too real to be anything other than an actual memory and I knew it wasn't a dream. I told my mother about this and other experiences and she always listened and even suggested that these might be memories from past lives. I liked that idea. I think I am very lucky because my mother has always allowed me to talk about my memories and never doubted me no matter how crazy my stories sounded.

About four years ago we moved from Dijon France to Toronto. I don't remember much about that whole year but I do know it was a very bad time for my mother and I know that I had a lot of memories at that time. My mother was always watching me as if I were going to disappear or something. I didn't want to move to Canada, but she was determined and when my Mom is determined, nothing stops her. At first we were both very sad, but then we met Father Karl and things got better. My mother became more relaxed and encouraged me to talk to Father about my memories. Always before in France she didn't want me to mention them to anyone especially not the sisters or the priest, but we both trusted Father Karl. He explained to me that the church would not approve of my beliefs and that in former times I might have been put to death. I guess that is true because I just finished reading about the crusades and the dark ages. What a bummer!! I'm glad I didn't live back then, or at least I don't have any memories of that time-not yet anyway. Father Karl told me that he didn't like to go against the teachings of the church, but he couldn't see that the idea of reincarnation went against the teachings of Christ. It isn't mentioned in the bible one way or another.

Father Karl and I talked about it many times because and he didn't want me to feel guilty or think I was possessed by the devil. We came to the conclusion that a soul is a soul and a body is just a shell for the soul. I believe that it is the soul that binds us to God and it is the soul that has to progress and earn the right to sit with Him. Jesus Christ healed bodies, but his real mission was to win souls. I don't know how many bodies I will have to go through or how many chances we each get to attain our reward, but I do believe that our bodies might be like BIC lighters and pens, when they wear out we get another one and we start again where we left off. That doesn't mean we should not take care of our bodies because they have to help us fulfill whatever purpose God has in mind for us in each life and a healthy body helps us to live better. I doubt that God even pays attention to our bodies and when he looks down on us with love it is only our souls that he sees.

I think that giving some of us the memories is God's way of making sure that there is some sort of continuity like Kate said. It is a gift we have been given, but we also have the responsibility to learn from our past lives and try as hard as we can to share what we learn and remember the lessons of the past. That doesn't mean that we are special messengers of God or anything that big. I'm so glad I had my mother and Father Karl to help me work through this. They are two of the wisest people in the world and now I got to meet Adrian and you guys so I am really lucky.

I like being home tutored and I really don't miss the social life at school. I have a couple of friends that I hang out with at times. I guess the three of us are kind of nerdy, but we don't care. My mother likes my friends and they think she is the most beautiful woman in the world. So do I. I worry sometimes that she will be lonely when I grow up and move away, but she tells me that is ridiculous and that she loves having me with her, but she will be fine when I go on with my life. She has always told me that she is never bored when she is alone. It is only in the company of stupid people that she wants to escape. Sometimes I think she is a little hard on people and can be a bit rude, but she says that is because she is French and that's the way the French are. I'm only half French, but I know what she means. I've seen some pretty awful people in my lives and I really try hard to avoid them. That's why I feel so fortunate now to be with such great people.

I never met my father. He died before I was born. My mother doesn't like to talk about it. She says it is too painful. I think she loved him a lot or it wouldn't hurt so much. I know his name was Andrew McGill and he was very rich and his family owned a lot of businesses so after he died, they arranged for us to have an income, but we don't have any contact with them. I have only met my grandparents on my father's side once and that was when I was very young so I don't remember them at all. My other grandparents are both dead and my mother has only one sister. She lives in Toronto too and that's why my mother was so anxious to move there. My mom's sister is named Aurelia and she is very artsy and talented like my mom so when we moved to Toronto they started designing jewelry. They don't actually make the jewelry, they just sell their designs to some really ritzy shops and when these shops have some rich customer that wants something really special, they call my mom and Aunt Aurelia. The shops take the credit, but they pay us a lot of money. Mom says she likes it that way. She doesn't like attention.

We live in a really cool house and my mom spends a lot of her time growing plants and flowers. I help her quite a bit. Our house has a huge room full of exotic plants that we tend year-round. My Aunt Aurelia is taking care of them now. In the spring we begin working on our outdoor garden. We have every kind of flower that will grow in our climate and some that aren't supposed to. I really like our garden, which just makes me seem even more nerdy, but I don't care. My favorite hobby is model cars, and my favorite car is a Cadillac. I have built models of every caddy ever made. I can't understand why Americans are so keen on European cars when they can just buy a Cadillac or an Oldsmobile.

People are always telling me that I seem so much older than my age. I guess all of you heard the same thing when you were growing up. How could that not be the case when we have all these visions in our heads of our different lives? Heck, I can even remember being an old man. I can't say that I know all he knew, but there are moments that I have insights that surely do not come from my own mind in this body.

I worry that I won't become the person I am supposed to be and that I won't use this gift to accomplish my purpose, whatever that is. There is a reason that God gave us these memories and I am often afraid that I will miss the point. My mom tells me to quit worrying and just enjoy being a healthy young man. I do enjoy my life.

I'm really glad to be here and to meet all of you. The food is great and there will be a lot to do in my free time. I think Sam is the coolest guy I have ever met and Amanda is really hot for a grandma. She told me all about Samantha and I can't wait to meet her, but I am a little nervous about that too. She is lucky to have grandparents. I want to adopt Adrian as my grandmother, but she says she is old enough to be my great grandmother-whatever!

Oh, I almost forgot. If anyone is interested, there is a big field above the beach that looks perfect for kite flying. I saw a kite shop as we passed through town. Sam and I are going there to buy a couple of kites tomorrow, so let him know if you want to join us.

I guess that's all except that I truly believe this will be an experience that will stay with me all my life and we have Sam to thank."

SAM:

I wish you could see for yourself what an incredible young man he is. As he returned to his seat on the hearth beside Adrian, anyone could see the bond that had already formed between them. She had such a look of pride on her face that one could scarcely believe he wasn't really her grandson. Antoinette was beaming at both of them. I had noticed some slight discomfort on her part when Etienne spoke of his father and that family. She also flinched noticeably when he said she didn't like attention. What a strange and beautiful little family they make. The others in the room, except for Bernie, applauded loudly and it was apparent that Etienne's youth and exuberance would make a significant contribution to our little society. The next thing that happened took us all by surprise. Bernie suddenly jumped from his chair, knocking it over in the process, and declared loudly that he would be next. Once again he reminded me of a little boy, only this time he was like a little kid in school with his hand raised begging "pick me, pick me".

Chapter Sixteen

BERNIE SPILLS HIS GUTS

BERNIE

I finally had the attention of everyone in the room and I was darned determined to make the most of it. I wanted to make everyone see what a miserable time I had had in this and other lives. They all seemed so smug, looking at those damned memories as a gift and acting all brave and superior. I wanted them to admit that they were just as scared as I was. I was certain that when I spoke out with the truth, I would be able to read their fear and anguish on their faces. I wanted them to be honest for once. I jumped right in with the speech I had wanted to give from the moment I arrived.

"Well hello everyone! It seems we all come from different backgrounds yet we are brought together by this common bond. I first want to thank Sam for his hospitality and Serena for her efforts regarding our comfort and some excellent meals. (I turned to Amanda at this point and looked her in the eye for a few seconds to show that I was deliberately excluding her from my praise, Amanda glared right back at me). As a single man, I have had few opportunities to enjoy home cooking and the many niceties the right kind of woman provides. (I spotted Serena rolling her eyes as she set out the hors d oeuvres in the dining room and assumed she was just trying to appear modest.)

I have not had as interesting a life as most of you and that is by design. I was pretty much raised by my mother and grandmother. My father was around but he paid little attention to any of us. He worked, he ate, he drank with his buddies and he slept. I was a sickly child, which made my existence a matter of supreme indifference to him. He was a man's man, a longshoreman, a union guy, not given to nurturing a scrawny, sickly son. He was never cruel to my mother or me-he just wasn't there.

At the age of nineteen, I enlisted in the navy having overcome my childhood illnesses. I remained in the navy for twenty years and had a very unspectacular career. I spent most of my time in clerical positions and a short while in base security. I retired from the navy ten years ago and have worked in private security ever since. For the past five years I have worked the graveyard shift at an office building in downtown Detroit. I spend most of my time alone. I have never had an inclination to marry. Although at times the comforts of home and hearth have had some appeal, I enjoy my solitude too much to endure the chaos that accompanies family life. I guess I am a little like Antoinette in that I am never bored when I am alone. (I noticed that everyone looked at Antoinette when I said that and I thought they were wondering if anything was going on between us. Of course I know now that they were really just nauseous at the thought of Antoinette and I having anything in common). If my life sounds grim to you just know that is exactly the life I have chosen, simple and devoid of pretense, nothing but the bare essentials. I will spare you the misery of delving into my inner psyche just as I am bored by the emotional "discoveries" of others. I only deal with what I know to be true.

We are put on this earth, we live and then we die and are forgotten. That is it. You probably find my attitude a bit strange considering the company I am in, and perhaps you wonder why I agreed to join this group believing as I do. Well, I'll tell you! I am here to debunk any myths regarding what so many of you call our "gift". It is not a gift, more like a curse, but at best an aberration. There is no grand plan, no purpose, no special responsibility and no reward! Our lives today are just lives, we take nothing forward, we gain no perspective and we have no more obligation to the world than anyone else. We still have to just take what comes our way. Our natures are set and we must live with that as best we can. This knowledge dictates how I live. I don't have to worry about my purpose. I referred earlier to my childhood illnesses. There were no physiological causes. The reason I was sickly is that I was tormented by these damn memories. They began when I was about 4 years old. At first I thought they were just bad dreams, as my mother and grandmother said. As I grew older I came to know the truth.

As a child I lived in constant dread. Most of my memories were horrible and they left me sick and weak. I quit talking about them, since my father had no patience with my complaints and my grandmother went along with whatever he said. My mother, on the other hand, seemed to know what was going on. She coached me on how to separate the memories from my reality. I came to view them as movies in my head and I am often able to just turn them off or ignore them. But every once in a while I am overpowered by an especially strong one and I revert to my boyhood fears. When this happens I distract myself by inflicting pain on myself. I usually burn my hand on the stove or ingest something that makes me violently ill. It works pretty well. I am here to learn how to free myself completely if that is possible. I wish I could trick myself into believing there is a reason for all this as you all seem to have done, but I can't. I just want an end to the agony.

I lead a totally selfish life. I give nothing to others and I ask for nothing. I have no desire to share my life and my pain with anyone and I don't want to take part in theirs. You might be wondering why I don't just kill myself and bring an end to it all. The answer is simple. I've done that before a couple of times and it doesn't work. At least in this life I have some measure of control, whereas there is no telling what my next life might be like. I will fight death to the bitter end because in this body I have found a way to give my soul the only rest it has ever had. I make no apologies for what I am as I have had no choice in the matter other than to shield myself as best I can from the past."

SAM

When Bernie finished, the room was silent, no applause and no apparent condemnation. I wondered if Bernie was aware of how transparent he had become to us. I had noticed before that his left hand was somewhat scarred and misshapen. Then I knew why. I can only imagine the pain and fear that would drive someone to such lengths. Or was it self-loathing? He certainly seemed loathsome enough to the rest of us. I found myself pitying him and wanting to help him, but in the end, Bernie was successful in erasing those urges.

AMANDA

At first I thought Sam had really blown it when he allowed Bernie to remain as a member of our group, but after witnessing this display, I changed my mind. He is the poster boy for what we could become if we allow ourselves to fall victim to our fears and disappointments. His speech was a perfect example of negative inspiration, if there is such a thing. He has contempt for life and all the good it can bring. He is faithless. He is unreachable by anyone but God, and he won't accept His help. Looking back, I realized that most of my prayers have always been for myself and those I love. This is the first time I felt compelled to pray for someone that I could never love.

SERENA

I can't imagine what it must be like to live in his skin. It hurt me to listen to him and I am ashamed to admit that I wished he would just go away. He is always seeking me out and wanting to talk, but I can't think of what to say to him. He is pathetic. So much so that it makes it hard to sympathize with him. I once had a friend that had a child that was so disagreeable that I found myself almost hating the poor thing. Bernie reminds me of that child. He is helpless, yet vile and mean. I would like to be his friend, as he desperately needs one, but I can't force myself to want to spend time with him. Please Sam, make him leave.

ADRIAN

What an idiot! I can't feel anything for someone who refuses to learn and grow and then turns around and brags about it.

ETIENNE

My mom kept looking at me all while Bernie was talking as if to warn me to stay away from him. No problem! Everyone in the room looks a little nauseous if you ask me. This is the quietest it has been since we got here. Sam looks kind of funny, like he would look if he put a big dent in his Escalade or something. He keeps looking at Amanda. I think he is afraid she is going to do something embarrassing. They are such a funny couple. I can't imagine either one of them being with anyone else, although I wouldn't mind it if Sam decided he liked my mom. We would have a blast together!

SAM

We took a little break to allow everyone to bring themselves back to life after Bernie's narcotic speech. I would have liked to start happy hour early, but I didn't think we should mix alcohol with the dose of crap he had just administered. The results might not be too pretty. Fortunately, I could turn to our next guest, Jenny, to brighten our spirits.

For the past twenty four hours Jenny had been on spin cycle. She was everywhere with everyone and had brought with her enough energy to power every house on the island. She never passes up a reason to laugh and her laughter is so deep, it infects everyone around her. She is a riot of beauty and joy. Later you will meet her best friend Alfie. They have been friends for fifteen years. They met in college and were drawn to each other by their mutual love of interior design, only to find out later that they shared a lot more than that. The story goes that they had met at some sort of design show and ended up at Alfie's apartment saluting each other's good taste with multiple shots of the finest tequila. It was through that tunnel of truth that so often accompanies tequila that they discovered they both have the memories. The rest is history and it is clear to me that they will likely be best friends forever (BFFs in Samantha's parlance). They escape the danger to their friendship that usually accompanies male-female relationships by virtue of the fact that Alfie is the gayest man I have ever met. He is also one of the happiest and seemingly well- adjusted people on earth. Jenny, on the other hand, is a bundle of neuroses all of which only add to her charm if you can believe that. I have never met anyone who accepts their frailties with such grace and humor. I wonder if there is such a thing as a psychological immune system. She has been exposed to so many emotional ailments, yet with Alfie's help, she is able to overcome them and remain happy and strong. What a stroke of luck to find them both.

When we were doing the telephone interviews with Jenny, she and Amanda spent two hours on the phone with Amanda laughing so hard that she went through half a box of Kleenex tissues. Amanda tears as heavily from laughter as she does from crying with the same effect, swollen, crescent roll eyes and a runny nose. Jenny insisted that if she came, Alfie must be allowed to attend as well. Amanda made the case that anyone as funny and charming as Jenny could not possibly bring anyone to the group that wouldn't be a welcome addition.

I had no idea what to expect when I picked them up at the airport, but they spotted my Escalade and flagged me down. The next thing I knew I had this couple of characters in my back seat laughing and regaling me with stories as if we had known each other for years.

Jenny is six feet tall and built like the proverbial brick shit-house. She is slender and well-toned with curly shiny black hair, stylishly cut to frame her beautiful face and café au lait complexion. She is 38 years old and there is not a line or a soggy spot on her anywhere. Her smile is broad and genuine, exposing a perfect set of teeth. Her voice is melodic and clear and she speaks with a slight southern accent which adds to her charm. She is the most transparent person I have ever met, oozing with joy and energy at one moment and exposing a full range of emotions in the next. Her demeanor and body language give even strangers an easy read as to what is going on in her head and she doesn't seem one bit self-conscious about that. But my description would not be complete if I did not mention her manner of dress. On this day Jenny was wearing an obviously expensive two piece outfit that used less fabric than my pillow case. She wore knee high boots of the softest tan leather with stiletto heels. From the top of her boots to the hem of her tiny skirt stretched an expanse of beautifully formed brown bare thighs. She wore a lacey garment (I think they call it a camisole) under a silk blouse which was tucked into her skirt but unbuttoned to the waist. She looked perfect. Rising to speak with her spike heels augmenting her already grand stature, she dwarfed my five foot ten inch frame, but she looked down on me so kindly as I scurried to my chair and she began her story.

Chapter Seventeen

JENNY AND ALFIE

JENNY

"Have you ever been in such a beautiful place with such wonderful people? I'm happy and astounded that we all found each other. Perhaps even old Bernie will cheer up a bit over time.

I was raised in Atlanta in the tiniest house you have ever seen. For three years before I left home for college I had to stoop to go through our kitchen door. In addition to that, my room was in the attic and there was only one spot in the room where I could stand up straight without bumping my head. I spent most of my time at home bent over. For this reason and others, I practically lived at the gym in our community center or at the neighborhood library. The end result was that I developed a lifelong desire to be physically fit and, due to my time at the library, I graduated at the head of my class and won a full scholarship to the University of Southern California where I studied interior design. It was there that I met my friend Alfie and my life has been perfect ever since.

My first 18 years were not so great, but I had the memories of other lives as an escape from my grim reality. My father was a minister, with all that implies and much more. He married my mother when she was fourteen and he was thirty. It's actually not as bad as it sounds. He rescued her from a very abusive household. The abuse came not from her father, as is often the case, but from her mother, my grandmother. I wish it were possible for me to say that I am incapable of hating anyone, but that is just not the case. I hate my grandmother, so much so that I try very hard not to think of her at all. I don't like the feel of hatred. My mother was tiny and beautiful and my grandmother was convinced that her beauty was a gift from the devil to conceal her wickedness even though my mother never did a wicked or mean thing in her short life. Nevertheless, there were beatings, burns and emotional torture. My grandfather died when my mother was a baby, so there was no one at home to intervene on her behalf. By the time my mother was fourteen years old she had been beaten down so badly that she had no self left other than her desire to please anyone that would give her a kind word. She died ten years ago for no apparent reason. She just went to sleep and never got up again. I don't mourn her because I never really knew her and I believe she is in heaven. By the time I was born, there was little left of her to know.

At the time of their marriage, my dad had built a modestly successful ministry with my grandmother being his most devout, but overzealous follower. I don't know which motive was stronger, his desire to rescue my mother from her torturer or his lust for this woman-child, but he managed to convince my grandmother that he could save my mother from her evil inclinations. Their marriage caused little stir in the congregation even with my mother's tender age, as everyone believed she would be better off. My grandmother's cruelty was no secret, but no one had found the strength to come to my mother's rescue.

I was born less than a year later. For the rest of her life and all the time I was growing up I never heard my mother laugh or cry. She was kind and gentle to me, but never truly with me. I like to think that my mother is an angel watching over and caring for me now in a way that she couldn't when she was imprisoned on this earth.

My father left me pretty much alone as long as I did nothing to embarrass him in front of his congregation. Our house was like a tomb. We rarely spoke to each other, but there were noises. My father didn't seem to care much that my mother had lost her spirit, but he did like to partake of her body and did so at every opportunity. He never cared whether I was aware of his activities and, in our tiny house, I learned about the birds and the bees at a very young age. Fortunately, I learned about love from my books and from so many kind neighbors and members of the congregation, most of them better Christians than my father. I have had no contact with my father since my mother died. This is not out of bitterness or hatred. We just don't exist for one another, never did.

Needless to say, I never shared my memories with either of my parents. I have often wondered if my mother had them as well and possibly told my grandmother. That might explain why my grandmother was so convinced she was an instrument of the devil. We saw my grandmother only in church, never at our home. My father was cordial to her as a member of his flock, but he kept her away from my mother and me and she didn't seem to mind this arrangement. I guess I was afraid of her, but I think I also was curious about how someone who did so much evil could believe they were good in the sight of God. The last I knew, she was still alive but that was several years ago so it is possible she has gone to her just reward. Anyway,

I seemed to know intuitively, even at the age of five to keep my secret to myself.

I can't explain how I interpreted the memories as a child. I guess they served as a substitute for a real life and they were often quite pleasant so I didn't find them troubling. Since I lived in a home that was an emotional vacuum, my memories served to teach me how to connect with others outside my home. They started just before my fifth birthday. My first memory was that of being a white girl living on a farm. I had a bunch of brothers and sisters to play with and we had animals to care for. My mother was a happy woman who sang all the time while she did her chores. My father was a gentle giant who, when he wasn't working in the field, always had three or four children hanging on him. It was a happy and healthy life, but not a long one. I'll tell you more about this at another time. I will tell you now that I was actually able to find that farm two years ago and even met some of my former brothers and sisters and my mother. Of course they have all grown old. That too is a story for another time.

I wanted to join this group because of my experiences with Alfie. He and I agree that our happiest times have been spent sharing our memories with one another, even the painful ones. We both came here hoping to meet others like ourselves and just have a blast, but now I realize we were underestimating the possibilities. Not only are we having the time of our lives, but as we share your experiences I have come to believe that however long we spend here will be the most amazing time in any of our lives. I hope we can contribute to y'all as well.

I'm going to sit down now as Sam seems a little worried that I am going to tip over on him. Isn't he just the sweetest man? I can see why Amanda is just head over heels over him even after all these years."

SAM

Amanda looked fit to be tied at that last comment. She tried to pretend that she didn't hear as she leaned over to whisper some comment to Glen in an effort to cover her embarrassment. This just made matters worse because as she leaned over she placed her hand on his knee. I don't know if it was his real knee or his artificial one, but something didn't feel right and she drew her hand back in astonishment before she had a chance to think. There was an uncomfortable silence until Glen grinned at her and loudly stated "If you think that feels too weird, try the other one, but I must say, you aren't very good at flirting." Everyone laughed and it broke the tension and, as much as I felt a little sorry for Amanda at that moment, I also enjoyed seeing her flustered since that doesn't happen often and it was clear that Glen wasn't at all upset by her reaction. I wondered if incidents like this work against me in Amanda's mind, but I didn't linger long on that thought. It had been many years since I was privy to anything going on in Amanda's mind.

Jenny's speech was short so I decided to let Alfie talk before we adjourned for cocktails and dinner. Not that there was a person left in the room that hadn't met him. Alfie, as I mentioned before, is the gayest man I have ever met in all senses of the word. He is a good eight or nine inches shorter than Jenny when she is wearing her spike heels-and Jenny is always wearing spike heels. He wears his hair in the same style as Jenny's, but with a definitely different effect. Alfie is as fair of skin as Jenny is dark and his hair frames a face that is quite ordinary rather than the masterpiece that is Jenny's. His hair is a golden blonde color with some natural curl, whereas Jenny's is black and lustrous with thick wavy curl. I noticed that their clothing is always color coordinated.

If Jenny is wearing beige and brown, Alfie wears brown and beige. Everything they wear is elegant, expensive and stylish. Even an old Texas boy can see that they know what their way around a clothing store and I can only imagine the wonderful interior design work they do. I suspect they are top-notch at everything, including having fun.

As I mentioned before, due to the fact that I hadn't wanted to eliminate any of the candidates from the group, it would be necessary for two guests to share a room. Jenny and Alfie solved this problem for me. They are inseparable and were perfectly comfortable with the idea. As Jenny told me, they usually spend the night at one or the other's place anyway. Besides the room was large with bunk beds and its own bathroom and I figured this made it easier for them to co-ordinate their wardrobes. They make quite a pair those two, and everyone, even Bernie, seemed to enjoy their exchanges. Alfie sat on the edge of his chair as he told his story.

ALFIE

"This is going to be very short since I have already met and fallen in love with all of you. We need to get on with our happy hour and another of Serena and Amanda's fab dinners. Had I known that the fare and the accommodations were going to be so spectacular, Jenny and I would have brought some special arrangements for the tables but in reality, the food speaks for itself.

So anyway, yes I'm gay. No I haven't always been gay in prior lives. I have been both male and female before and frankly, I prefer the female side because it is more exciting and dangerous. I have enjoyed every moment of this life and I expect it will remain that way until the end. I have had the memories since before I can remember if that makes any sense. I feel like I came into my life somewhere in the middle, like walking into a play in the second act. I can't explain it any better than that. When Jenny entered my life, everything fell into place and I have never looked back. Prior to that, I had derived the most pleasure from my work. Even as a young boy I was interested in design and how things fit together. I didn't have many friends, but I was active and well liked in school. From the moment I met Jenny I knew I wanted her as my partner in life for as long as she would permit it. I know there will be a day when she marries and starts a family and when that happens I will adjust my role in her life to the appropriate level, but for now she is my best friend. We share every detail of our lives, including our hair and skin products.

I grew up the middle child with three brothers and two sisters. My two older brothers were very close in age and interests. Then came my two sisters with me in between and finally my youngest brother. My older brothers are very gregarious and heavy into sports, which pleases my dad greatly. My sisters have bounced back and forth between being tomboys and fairy princesses. My youngest brother was mama's little boy, and I was quietly content in the middle. I had a great childhood because I could be invisible and live in my own world. My parents were good and fair people who gave all their time and efforts to their children and each other. They still do. My entire family, except for me, lives within 20 miles of each other. My parents revel in their many grandchildren and that takes all the pressure off me. Thank God I am not an only child or the only son. I don't have to be anyone but myself. I have sort of a celebrity status in my family. They all know I am gay and that doesn't seem to bother anyone. They live pretty traditional lifestyles so I bring a certain notoriety to the fold. I go home at least once a year during the holiday season and I get the reception of a rock star.

The first time I brought Jenny home with me for a holiday, you should have seen the looks on their faces. It took a while for them to recognize the non-sexual nature of our relationship. In the meantime, Jenny was endearing herself to everyone. At first my brothers just stared at her with their mouths open until they realized that behind that gorgeous façade lurked a real athlete. From that time on I had to compete with them for her attention. Touch football, shooting hoops, and tennis are tough competition so I spent most of my time with my mom cooking and redecorating. My sisters took their share of Jenny's time as well as they enlist her in their quest for the perfect "look".

My past lives are many and varied so I won't go into any at this point. Just let me say that I came here because I go everywhere Jenny goes and because I wondered when she brought it up to me if this wasn't a little "dangerous". For both reasons I didn't want her to come without me. Now that I have met everyone, I know that, as usual, Jenny's instincts were right on. This is going to be the experience of a lifetime."

Chapter Eighteen

SAM RECALLS THE DAY

Well, the introductions were over and I have to confess, I was glad. It was time for a cocktail, some good food and mindless chatter, if such a thing was possible with this group. In spite of the fact that I considered the day a tremendous success, I was experiencing some free floating anxiety and I had no clue as to the source. As everyone adjourned to the dining room and the deck for cocktails, I spotted Amanda sitting alone on the hearth staring into the fire apparently experiencing emotions similar to mine.

Alfie had taken the position of bartender and was whipping up some cosmopolitans for the ladies. Bernie had been first in line at the bar and I noticed that Alfie had the foresight to make his drink tall and strong, I suppose to postpone Bernie's next visit for as long as possible. Serena had dinner well under control and the aroma of her Yankee pot roast and fresh baked bread created heaven within those walls.

Amanda and I were free to spend a few quiet moments by ourselves, or together if I discerned any welcoming signals on her part. The fact that she was sitting off to one side rather than in the middle of the hearth, leaving plenty of room for another was enough of an opening for me. I pride myself on my ability to read signals from the opposite sex. I sat down facing the room rather than the fire to avoid forcing her into conversation if she was not so inclined. That positioning would make it easier to make a graceful escape should she seem reluctant to engage. We sat quietly for a minute or two and, against my better judgment I was the first to speak.

"I think that today went very well" said I. She nodded in agreement and remained silent. "Great bunch of people" I added. Again a nod and silence.

"Alfie is making cosmopolitans for the ladies, shall I get you one?"

She turned to me and I could see doubt and anxiety in her eyes. "I guess so. I don't mean to be a downer, but I can't help wishing everything could stay just like it is now. Everyone is so perfect. Even Bernie is a perfect pain in the ass and plays true to his part. I am not looking forward to the warts".

Bingo! She hit it right on. That was what was bothering me. I knew that as time wore on, the frailties and scars of each of our guests would emerge and tarnish our perfect picture. Even superheroes have weak spots and I didn't want to see them any more than Amanda did. I realized then that I was letting my ego get involved. Instead of creating a learning environment, I was hoping to form a perfect society. That's not what this exercise was all about. Instead of just sharing that thought with her, I put on a false front as if I were immune to my own weakness and blurted out a little too loudly, "Bring on the warts". As often happens when I am making a ridiculous statement, there was a spontaneous moment of silence in the adjoining room and everyone turned to me without a clue as to the context of my exclamation. The silence lasted a few seconds longer with good old Bernie to the rescue saying, "Yeah, I want to see that too". It makes sense that he would be the one person in the room that would understand my outburst, only for different reasons. He was looking forward to the "warts" as confirmation of his dark view of humanity. He never missed a chance to make his case. Amanda just looked at Bernie with a wry smile, shook her head and got up to go claim her cosmopolitan leaving me sitting there relieved that Bernie's response had taken the heat off me. For such a strong, optimistic woman, Amanda certainly had her dark side. I guess that's one of her warts.

I must have looked lost and confused because Antoinette came over to me and put her arm around me comfortingly and said in her beautiful French accent, "Come with me I'll buy you a drink. You deserve better treatment than you are getting". She grabbed my arm and guided me to the bar where I was given a stout Canadian whiskey on the rocks and we preceded, arm in arm, to the deck to join the others.

It was a glorious evening, just slightly chilly, with a fabulous sunset and I was receiving the attentions of a beautiful woman. Better still, Amanda was watching with a curious look on her face, which improved my mood exponentially. Two cocktails, a glass of fine wine and a lovingly prepared dinner and all was well on the western front. Antoinette sat with me through dinner and Etienne hovered around us at frequent intervals extolling the virtues and talents of his mother. Amanda, on the other hand, was being entertained by Jenny and Alfie and, judging by her frequent bursts of laughter, I could see that her mood had improved as well, although I did notice her watching Antoinette and me out of the corner of her eye. At least I hoped she was. Adrian was slightly tipsy since she really isn't much of a drinker, but had succumbed to the charms of Alfie's cosmopolitans. Glen and Kate seemed to be hitting it off well and I noticed that, despite the age difference, they really made a handsome couple. I made a note to remind myself that I wasn't running a dating service, but I was glad to see Glen diverting his attention away from Amanda. Serena sat down to eat with us and was quickly taken over by Bernie. She looked miserable, but he was glowing instead of glowering. I made another note to save her a place by me in the future. As soon as dinner was over, she began cleaning up, clearly relieved to extricate herself from her tormentor. She knew she was safe in this because Bernie, by his own admission, was much too lazy to help out.

The plan was to end the evening fairly early. I just wanted to get back to my boat and relax, maybe sit on the top deck and enjoy what might well be one of the few precipitation free evenings in the near future. Everyone assured me they were going to make it an early evening as well, although Amanda, Jenny and Alfie were still sitting around the table and it appeared that Glen, Kate and Adrian were going to sit by the fire for a while. I thought it was a good idea to leave everyone to their own devices. Kate and Adrian seemed to get along very well, which is good since they were sharing the master suite. Kate had taken the small anteroom and assured me she had all the space and privacy she needed, although she let it slip that Adrian was given to snoring. She was amused, not annoyed, as she couldn't believe that such a racket could come out of that sweet little body. Apparently Kate is a very sound sleeper so she didn't see any problem with the arrangement. Jenny, Alfie and Amanda jumped up and helped Serena finish cleaning up the kitchen, a fairly easy job since, as usual, there were no leftovers to deal with. God this group can eat! I walked Antoinette and Etienne to the guest house and spent a few minutes enjoying a cup of tea with Antoinette secretly hoping that Amanda would walk in on that little scene. No such luck. I returned to the main house with my absence having gone unnoticed.

During our tea session, Antoinette had hinted that she believed Amanda was slightly jealous of her attentions to me that evening and that amused her. Antoinette said that she was very fond of Amanda, but thought she was behaving in a manner that was beneath her with regards to me. She also stated that she found my willingness to appear foolish in order to win back Amanda's affections was really quite endearing and that she believed that it would serve me well in the long run as long as I didn't overdo it. Of course she stated this in a much smoother way, but the message was the same. I thanked her and left the cottage feeling a bit like a schoolboy with a crush on his teacher. What a gift this woman has! It didn't occur to me until later that she told me I was acting like a fool.

As I entered the main house, there was still much revelry going on in the kitchen so I decided to teach them all a lesson for having so much fun without me and I returned to my boat. It was still early so I poured myself another glass of wine and went up to the top deck to enjoy a few minutes of solitude and ponder the day's events. I woke up three hours later, cold and damp in my lounge chair.

Chapter Nineteen

TRAGEDY STRIKES

The next day was Sunday and it had been agreed that Sundays would be free days with no formal gatherings. As I arrived back at the house at nine am, I was greeted by the same scene as the day before. Everyone was carrying either a cup of coffee or a bloody Mary, Amanda being in charge of the latter. Her bloody Mary mix was a secret recipe, with her own special ingredient which I have always believed was simply an extra shot of vodka. At any rate, one was more than enough for me and the group seemed to agree. Breakfast consisted of blackberry crepes, crispy fried bacon, eggs made to order, a fruit tray and assorted rolls and breads with cream cheese and homemade jams and jellies. Glen led the group in prayer and the carnage began. Again, no leftovers except for one crepe which had been dropped on the floor by Etienne, but I saw Bernie eyeing it and I wondered if it would survive. Apparently even Bernie cared to some degree what others thought as he left it untouched on the tray.

At this point everyone began to disperse. Kate, Glen and Adrian were heading to the beach for a walk. I remembered that I had promised to take Etienne into town to the kite shop and then to the fields near the house to try them out. I secretly hoped he had forgotten that promise as I really just wanted to go into the den and read my new Grisham novel. No such luck! He was much too well brought up to insist, but I saw his expectant glances in my direction so I feigned enthusiasm and told him we would leave in half an hour. I thought he was going to do cartwheels throughout the house, but he ran over to Antoinette to make sure it was alright with her. Of course it was and she asked if she could accompany us so she could explore the village. Amanda's ears perked up and she informed Antoinette that there was very little to see and she might be bored. Antoinette's response was to laugh and say that if that happened, she would just buy a kite and come with Etienne and me. Amanda shot me a nasty look leaving me wondering if I should have given her a special invitation. That would have never occurred to me as I couldn't picture Amanda running with a kite without incurring serious injury. Even in her younger days, she was no athlete and was a danger to herself when she tried to be.

Jenny and Alfie also wanted to come with us. Alfie said he enjoyed looking at the elaborate designs in kites and he wanted to be there to untangle the strings when Jenny made a mess of things. Jenny slapped him affectionately on the back of the head. Amanda donned the role of martyr and said she would stay behind and help Serena. Bernie announced he would be taking a long nap. We all endorsed that idea.

The five of us piled into the Escalade and drove the quarter mile to the village. Antoinette spotted the local boutique which also housed a candle shop in the loft above. She agreed to meet us later at the coffee house which was midway between the boutique and the kite shop. The coffee house also served as the village bookstore and I had spent many contented hours there during my frequent visits with Patrick. It was a windy and chilly day so that would have been my destination of choice had I no promises to keep.

The kite shop itself was but a tiny hole in the wall, merchandise covering every space from floor to ceiling. It occurred to me that if we spent enough time picking out kites, perhaps we could delay the actual flying session until another time. Etienne teamed up with Jenny and began the task of sifting through the hundreds of designs to find just the right ones. I picked out a simple model that didn't look too challenging. I didn't want to look like a novice in front of my guests, especially Antoinette should she decide to join us in the flying fields.

Half an hour later we were armed with a respectable sampling of the available inventory and the three of us were standing outside the shop waiting for Alfie, who was still anguishing over his selection. Actually, the kites were of less interest to Alfie than Paul, the owner of the shop and designer of many of the models. I had met Paul before and even had coffee with him a couple of times, but I really hadn't picked up on the fact that he was gay. You see, most island people are transplants rather than indigenous and are a bit different to begin with. They live here because they have moved away from the "courser" elements in our society. Male and female alike are generally more soft-spoken and laid back. Their clothes are carefully selected from expensive catalogs, to give them that special "I choose to be comfortably chic" look. The women generally sport a loose jumper with matching turtleneck and tights, their feet encased in a solidly constructed pair of sandals that are suitable for either gender. The men tend toward jeans or loose fitting corduroy slacks and sweaters or a flannel shirt with a turtleneck underneath. Most do not own a suit, but I have spotted several wide-whale corduroy sport coats with leather elbow patches. That is what

Amanda refers to as "island formal". Brown, tan and moss green are the prevailing colors for clothing.

Paul fit the island mode in dress and demeanor, but apparently there was something about him that attracted Alfie's attention. Jenny was watching them with interest and didn't seem annoyed by the delay. I went back into the shop and told Alfie we were headed to the coffee house and we would meet him there when he finished. For this I received a grateful smile from both men and I was quickly dismissed as they continued their exploration of kite dynamics. They provided a sharp contrast in style, but so do men and women so who can account for what constitutes physical and emotional attraction.

Antoinette was already seated at a table with one of those huge cups that hold a cappuccino. It looked tempting so we all ordered one. She had a small bag from the boutique and another from the book store. Etienne and Jenny showed her their kites. Each had purchased two. I also purchased two, both exactly alike. One was for Antoinette should she decide to join the group. If she didn't show any interest, I was prepared to hide it so that she wouldn't get the impression that I was trying to woo her into accompanying us. Etienne spoiled that little plan. That kid doesn't miss a thing. He told his mother that I had purchased a kite for her and that she just had to come with us or my feelings would be hurt. I made a mental note to strangle him with his kite string.

Alfie joined us as we were finishing our cappuccinos looking flushed and excited. Jenny gave him a big hug and a smile to match. These two were obviously as close of friends as any I have ever seen. Anyone could see that something very special had happened between Alfie and Paul. I guess I like the both of them well enough to respect the moment, but Jenny was glowing in the light of Alfie's excitement, showing no sign of feeling threatened or jealous.

It was a perfect day for kiting, sunny and cool with a steady breeze. Keep in mind that anywhere else this breeze would be categorized as wind, but in the San Juan Islands anything less than thirty miles per hour is considered a breeze. The field lies between the village and Patrick's house. There are about five flat and grassy acres with a few trees around the perimeter and a dirt road running near the ridge on the beach side. The field lies high above the beach atop a severe slope of rocks and grass. In some places there is a straight drop to the rocky beach below. A narrow strip of the field runs between the road and the ridge. It is usually littered with beer cans and wine bottles and, judging from the charred remains of several campfires, I would say that area is a popular gathering place for young people looking for outdoor entertainment after dark.

Jenny and Etienne had assembled their kites in the coffee house so they were ready to go while the rest of us were still working on ours. Antoinette declined my offer to help with hers on the grounds that she really didn't want to participate but she did want to watch. In truth, I really couldn't picture that frail little body running across the field with a kite that just might lift her off the ground if the wind became strong enough.

I was attaching the tail to my kite when I spotted Jenny and Etienne already across the field. Jenny had launched her kite successfully and was running backwards letting out more string and doing a magnificent job of keeping it in the air. Etienne was still running, trying to get the wind to catch his. Suddenly a gust of wind picked up the kite and took it directly over his head and he began running backwards letting out the string as fast as he could. Backwards was straight toward the ridge, but he was still well inside the road so I wasn't too concerned at that point. A few seconds later, he was crossing the road and approaching the edge and still had not looked around to see where he was headed. I started to run, waving at him to stop, but the next thing I knew he had fallen over the side and out of view. Jenny must have seen the danger as well because she was already running toward him, her kite left behind, floating freely over the field. Alfie was detangling his kite string and was oblivious to what was happening. As Etienne slipped out of sight, I looked over my shoulder, hoping that Antoinette wasn't watching and that we would be able to rescue him before she even knew what had happened. It was clear that she had seen it all as she crumpled to the ground and was crawling on her hands and knees trying to find enough strength to get to her feet.

I was running as fast as I could, but I was still quite a distance away and it felt like I was in slow motion. Meanwhile Jenny had reached the edge where Etienne had disappeared and was looking down. I tried to get some clue from her body language as to what she was seeing, but before I knew it she had taken off her full length leather coat and disappeared over the edge as well. By this time Alfie had spotted what was happening and was loping across the field. We arrived at the same moment from different directions and I am ashamed to admit that we both stalled for a second or two before looking over the edge in dread of what we might see. We heard Jenny before we saw her. She was about twenty feet below us, having slid her body down a steep grassy slope while holding on clumps of grass. She was in an area about three feet wide that was free of rocks and although steep, was not as dangerously so as other areas surrounding her. We couldn't see Etienne, but soon realized that he was below her by some four to five feet. He was lying on his stomach and holding on to a large clump of grass with his right hand and his left arm was stretched above his head reaching out to Jenny. He was positioned on an overhang of dirt and grass and beneath him, from his hips on down was nothing but air.

Alfie was calling 911 on his cell phone, but reception is spotty in the islands so I couldn't tell if he was getting through to them and we had no idea how long Etienne could hold on as he was bleeding heavily from a cut above his eye. Jenny dared not go lower for fear of dislodging the overhang and plunging them both to the rocky beach below. She was hollering at Alfie and it took us a few seconds to realize that she was telling him to slide her coat down to her. Her plan was obviously to use her coat as a lifeline to Etienne and then pull him up. Before I knew what was happening, Alfie had crawled over the edge as well and was delivering the coat to her in person. He said that he would be staying there for her to grab onto should the grass she was holding onto give way. His feet were lodged into the soil just above her head, but he himself had nothing to grasp with his hands except the long grass. I had little confidence in his plan, but the deepest admiration for his efforts.

I spotted a fairly large tree root running laterally and partially exposed just below the ridge and a few feet above Alfie. I had brought my Swiss army knife to work on our kites and I used it to clear away enough dirt so I could get a firm grip on the root with my hands. I could hear Jenny talking calmly to Etienne, telling him to grab her coat sleeve with his left hand first and then with his right and that she would pull him up. She mentioned that her coat was real leather of the highest quality and was probably stronger than any rope. She coached him to push with his feet once they got above the overhang and that they would be on top within a minute or two. She reminded him that she was an athlete and incredibly strong and capable of pulling him to safety. Meanwhile, I had positioned myself over the ledge as far as I could go while holding on to the tree root as an anchor. I figured one of us had to have something to hold onto besides grass. Alfie was able to reach my ankles and the hope was that we could supply the support necessary to handle the extra weight as Jenny pulled Etienne up. It would only take a few seconds for Etienne to reach the point where he could help push with his feet and then we could all inch our way to safety. The plan was working except for one thing. Just as Jenny pulled him clear of the overhang, Etienne passed out from pain. I could see that his leg was broken and lying in a sickeningly unnatural position. He had failed to mention that to Jenny or perhaps he didn't know. His entire body was lying on solid ground, but Jenny couldn't be sure how long it would hold and Etienne was not holding on to anything at all. She decided not to wait for an emergency team. Instead she began to lower herself backward, inch by inch until she could get a firm grip on his arm. Alfie and I were holding our breath. There were just a few inches of dirt and the strength of a large clump of grass between them and disaster. I have never prayed so hard in my life. I could see Antoinette running toward us, stumbling and crying

Then, to everyone's amazement, Jenny pulled Etienne to her in one swift movement ending up in a position where she could put her left arm around his back and drag him up inch by inch. Alfie and I were perfectly useless until she could reach out and grab Alfie's hand. I breathed a sigh of relief at that point because, even though Alfie was a small man and not muscular, he loved Jenny and would never let her fall. Jenny pushed and Alfie pulled and finally I was able to grab Alfie's hand and pull him over the top and then, gently as possible, Etienne. Jenny, relieved of her burden, bounded the rest of the way and she and Alfie rolled on the ground half laughing and half crying in relief. I could hear sirens from the emergency vehicles, but they were still some distance away. Etienne was drifting in and out of consciousness as Antoinette arrived at his side. I had seen that woman stumbling, falling, crying hysterically, but when she reached his side she suddenly turned calm and composed. Here it was again, that ability of women to reach inside of themselves for strength when needed for their children. She reminded me of Amanda in those days when Alex was so ill. She might fall completely apart later, but for this time, she was Etienne's rock.

My prayer was that there wasn't too much damage done to the leg that was broken. Jenny was shaking with the fear that she may have caused him additional damage during her rescue. She began to second-guess her decisions and was actually apologizing through her tears to Antoinette and Etienne. She kept saying that she didn't know at the time that his leg was broken or she may have waited for the emergency team. It was perfectly clear to me and Alfie that Etienne may not have been able to hold on that long or that he might have passed out while half of him was hanging in thin air, but Jenny needed some convincing.

Antoinette was holding Etienne's head in her lap as the EMT's arrived. Etienne was awake and watching his mother intently. He was in terrible pain, but I could see his concern for her in his expression. Within minutes those trained professionals had performed their various duties and were loading him into a waiting ambulance for the fifteen mile drive to the hospital on the other side of the island. Antoinette clamored in beside him and away they went. We all made a beeline for the Escalade and followed. We agreed that we would not call and let the others know what had happened until we had more information about Etienne's condition. We were hoping we could bring him home with us, although from the looks of his leg, I doubted that he would be released. The bone had pierced the skin and it was definitely the worst break I had ever seen but the gash above his eye appeared to be fairly minor once the blood was cleaned away. The ride to the hospital was the quietest few minutes since our arrival two days earlier. I was thanking God for saving Etienne and I suspect Jenny and Alfie were doing the same.

We spent the next few hours in the tiny waiting room with Antoinette as the doctors decided what to do about Etienne's injuries. Finally, a doctor emerged that we hadn't seen before and informed us that he was an osteopath and a friend of the local physician. He happened to be here visiting his friend and had volunteered to take a look at Etienne. He was most encouraging as to Etienne's full recovery, but concerned about the possibility of infection and felt that they needed to take care of the wound to his leg before they could apply a cast. This would require Etienne to be hospitalized for the next few days so they could treat the wound, stabilize the leg and keep Etienne sedated for the pain. Antoinette was agreeable, but wanted to know if there was room for her to stay with him. The doctor told her this was impossible in that the hospital itself was very small and she would need to stay at the motel on the edge of town. I interjected that she definitely would not want to stay at that motel and that the house was only a twenty minute drive and I would bring her back and forth anytime she wanted or she could have full and unlimited use of the Escalade. She reluctantly agreed and told me to go home and that she was going to sit by him through this first night and that she would call when she needed me to come and get her.

We were all exhausted, physically and emotionally and I could only guess how Antoinette felt. I do know how she looked, and it wasn't good. There was something else amiss with her, perhaps physical or maybe emotional, but whatever it was, it was serious. Etienne knew it too, but I didn't know if he knew the source of her pain. He was very protective of her. I felt so bad for them both as we left the hospital. Jenny had recovered her composure, but she was totally drained. Alfie just held her hand and kept talking to her in soothing tones. These two are closer than any married couple I have ever met.

By the time we arrived at the house it was almost dark and the lights were lit as before, but the atmosphere was less than festive inside. Remember, we are on an island and news travels fast. Serena is friends with the wife of one of the EMT's so she had been filled in on the events of the afternoon. She had a clear picture of Etienne's medical condition and had reassured everyone, especially Adrian, that he was going to be fine and would rejoin us by the end of the week.

One look at Amanda's puffy eyes told me she had been crying and she wanted to know how Antoinette was holding up. Her compassion for Antoinette was understandable. Any mother that has ever had the life or health of her child threatened will always reach out in a very personal way to the mother of another endangered child.

As if our group hadn't attracted enough curious attention from the inhabitants of this island, the story of Jenny's heroic rescue added fuel to the fire. The phone had been ringing off the hook from the curious seeking confirmation of the various versions of the story that had emerged. As I mentioned before, cell phone reception is notoriously unreliable where we are so we had to depend on the land line for calls from Antoinette, otherwise I would have taken the phone off the hook. The one call that was welcomed came from Paul. I answered the phone and assured him that everything was under control. He was very solicitous and genuinely concerned, but I also knew that he wanted to talk to Alfie and was shy about asking for him so I invited him for dinner. He accepted immediately and I insisted that he come right over for our not-so-happy hour. Jenny perked up immediately when she heard he was coming and Alfie was obviously pleased.

Within minutes Paul arrived and was introduced to the rest of the gang. I made a pitcher of manhattans, which is Amanda's favorite and that seemed to suit everyone else as well. Adrian, proposed a toast to Jenny for her courage and asked if she would tell the story of the rescue. Jenny declined so Alfie chimed in and gave a short and accurate accounting but minimizing his participation. Everyone was silent for a couple of minutes. I imagine pondering how this could have played out. Serena jumped in at that point to lighten things up and give Jenny some relief by announcing that dinner would be served in half an hour so we had best get busy with our cocktails. Adrian visited with Paul and Alfie, asking Paul questions about the locals which brought out the comedian in Paul as he told tales of some of the more colorful characters. He also echoed my warning about going into the local bar after nine PM. As he put it, all the alter egos emerge and it can get ugly.

Jenny sat with Glen and Kate, purposely avoiding the subject of the afternoon events. The only reference was made by Glen regarding her physical strength and his decision to cancel any thoughts he might have had of challenging her to an arm wrestling contest. Jenny laughed for the first time and the atmosphere turned less somber.

Amanda and I ventured out to the deck. She was still upset, but seemed calmer. She told me she wanted to drive to the hospital later and take Antoinette some dinner and just sit with her for a while. I had planned to do just that, but realized that Amanda would be a better companion for her under the circumstances. I was hoping she could convince Antoinette to come home and get some sleep and go back in the morning. In reality I knew that Amanda would probably end up spending the entire night with her at the hospital and that is exactly what happened.

BERNIE

I am ashamed to tell you what my thoughts were at that time, but it is part of the program so I have to do it. Here is what was going on in my mind.

Well, that was a bummer. He seemed like a pretty nice kid, but after all, that's what kids do!! They break things, often their own bones. Although I felt for Etienne and his mom, if this was to become some pity party I was ready to leave. All afternoon I had sat there and listened to those people go on and on, even when it was clear that he was going to be all right. It was impossible for me to understand how someone could get that wrapped up in another's life. That's why I lived the way I did. In truth I had wondered if people really care that much or if it is just an act in most cases. I mean, I was looking at Amanda sitting over in the corner crying her puffy eyes out for some people she has known exactly two days. Adrian acted like the kid was her own grandchild. Ok, you can kind of understand it coming from women, but let me tell you, Sam looked like he'd been to hell and back. Again, how attached can you get to a kid in just two days? Then I thought maybe Sam had the hots for Antoinette and wanted to play up to her through the kid. Even Glen was acting all goofy, although that's nothing compared to Alfie and his new "boyfriend". That's a pair to draw to! And what was Sam doing inviting that Paul guy to dinner? He wasn't part of the group. Who would be next?.

I figured I'd hang in there for a few more days, but after that I wasn't making any promises. I thought the whole bunch of them were a bit strange like they are the stars of some special movie going on in their heads. The only reason I had come in the first place was to get moved out west for free. I had quit my job in Detroit because the city was falling apart.

I told Sam I was taking my vacation time and he believed me and was paying me twice what I had been earning. He never asked for proof of what I made at work so I gave myself a big raise and he didn't even question it. I figured if Sam was dumb enough to believe my story that I wanted to share memories, well so be it! I'd give them a glimpse or two just to string them along, but I didn't think they could take the whole picture if I really laid it out to them. Not if they react like this to a little broken bone.

I thought Amanda was a real bitch. It appeared she had Sam by the balls and frankly, I couldn't see why he was so hung up on her. She's kind of good looking if you like the type, but nothing to write home about. Serena adored her and the whole group just fell all over her and laughed at all her jokes, but I was already sick of her. At first I thought she was coming on to me because she was all gushy when I arrived, but I decided that is just her way of getting attention.

In my opinion, Serena was the only person worth knowing, but she was always busy and didn't have much time to spend with me. Every time I got near her she had to run off and perform some duty. She worked like a slave. I would have offered to help, but that wasn't part of the deal. I didn't come here to be Sam and Amanda's servant. Like I said, I didn't think I would stay much longer, but then again I thought I might stay on just to shake them up when they got too full of themselves. I knew Amanda wished I would drop off the face of the earth and I could forsee some fun in sticking around just to irritate her. Besides, I didn't have anywhere else to go.

Yup. That was me at that time. Not one of my prouder moments. I hope you never have to go back and view yourselves this way.

SAM

Dinner was unusually quiet, but rather pleasant in spite of the events of the day. Amanda ate quickly and then departed, armed with a plate of food for Antoinette and Etienne to share. Serena made the assumption that the hospital food would be inedible so she wanted to make sure Etienne had something good should he be awake enough to eat. She threw in a dozen cookies and some bread pudding that she had baked for the next day's breakfast. I could tell she was upset and it made her feel better to think she might be providing him some comfort.

Alfie and Paul sat across the table from one another and Adrian led the conversation by asking Paul about his background and what brought him to the island. Paul spoke very openly saying that he had moved here from the bay area (this drew a "knowing" grunt from Bernie) where he had earned his living producing educational videos and had even created a few video games, none of which were huge commercial successes as they lacked the violence and gore that seemed to be a prerequisite for real success. "Regretfully", he stated "The video game audience doesn't seem to be interested in self-improvement but would rather play in a world that is darker than the darkest part of reality." At this, Bernie murmured something that sounded like "What do you know about reality?" but he kept his head down and his voice low so his comment didn't beg a response even if any of us cared to offer one. He appeared to be disgusted with the whole scene and I wondered if I would want to know what was going on in his head.

GLEN

After dinner that night everyone seemed a little lost. Sam returned to his boat early and Bernie retired to his room supposedly to get some sleep, but we all knew that he spent a lot of his time playing Dragons and Dungeons or some such video game. That's why I enjoyed Paul's remarks about the video game business so much. I know it irritated Bernie. God, that man brings out the worst in people. Alfie, Paul and Jenny stayed at the table long after dinner was cleared talking, laughing, sharing stories. We helped Serena clean up in the kitchen and then Adrian, Kate and I headed for the living room "story pit" to enjoy the warmth of the fire and relax.

We spent a few minutes discussing the events of the day, a subject conspicuously avoided during dinner. Though we were concerned about Etienne, we all agreed that his youth and exuberance would bring him to full recovery. It came as no surprise to me when Adrian expressed more concern for Antoinette, a view that I shared. Something about Antoinette has triggered a protective response in me since the day we met. It's not just her petite size, she just seems burdened even though she tries to camouflage it.

Kate was her usually quiet self until Adrian expressed her concern for Antoinette. Suddenly her voice became louder than usual and she made the observation that we definitely were all brought together for a reason and that Antoinette's plight was just more obvious that the rest of ours. I didn't see anything that I would call obvious about Antoinette, but I guess Kate did. In the short time I have known Kate, I have grown quite fond of her and I don't mean in a fatherly way, although I am old enough to have played that role. I can't describe her in normal terms. The word that comes to mind is "fullness". She is sensual and warm, but slightly distant. I think she is one of the few people I have ever met that possesses true empathy for her fellow human beings, yet she has little patience with effuse sentimentality. She and Amanda are a lot alike in that last part, although I think Amanda is more sympathetic than empathetic. Amanda feels bad for others, but doesn't really absorb their pain. Kate does, and she carries it as a privilege that accompanies being human.

Wow! I guess I'm getting carried away here. Bernie was right about one thing, we had all grown very close in just two days. I think it was partly the isolated environment and all the meals we shared around the big table. I also believe we were anticipating the many secrets we would learn about one another and recognized the need for trust if we were to experience this opportunity to its fullest. What I did know for sure that night was that I was in it for the long haul and that I had never felt so content in my life. I could have sat there all night talking to the two of them, Adrian for her intelligence, wit and ageless beauty and Kate just for being Kate.

One other thing, I knew that we had to get Sam to accept the fact that he could not control everything. By the time he left for his boat, he looked half sick from the stress of the day. Accidents happen, but Sam seemed determined that nothing was going to go wrong for anyone on his watch. Well, things just don't work out that way. Throughout dinner I could see Amanda stealing glances at him obviously sensing his discomfort. When she left to go to the hospital she gave him a big hug then looked into his refrigerator green eyes and held the gaze for several seconds. It was a very intimate moment and I felt uncomfortable, as if I had invaded their privacy. I remembered what it was like to have those non-verbal exchanges when Peggy was alive. God, I miss that part of being married the most, the knowledge that you can communicate deep emotion without a word being spoken. I remember wondering if I would ever have that again when I looked up and discovered that Kate was looking directly at me, and she didn't look away when I returned the gaze. A warm flush went through my entire body and I wondered if that was what a hot flash felt like in women who were going through menopause. What kind of thought was that? Was I becoming like Sam? I hoped no one could read my mind. That warm flush lessened, but remained in part with me throughout the rest of the evening. I woke up the next morning knowing that I had dreamed of Kate, but couldn't remember what the dream was about. I just knew that I was going to make sure I spent as much time with her as possible while I had the opportunity.

From time to time that evening I would steal a glance at Paul, Jenny and Alfie, still sitting around the dining room table. They had helped Serena finish in the kitchen and as she was preparing to leave, Jenny intercepted her and insisted she join them for a glass of port and some chocolates that she had purchased in the village. Jenny waited on Serena and Paul and Alfie and made a big fuss over the dinner Serena had prepared. Paul seemed completely at ease and spoke openly about what it was like to live on that island as the only gay man. He told some stories of being hit on by several of the island women, some of them old enough to be his mother. He didn't name names, but Serena was familiar enough with the population to put two and two together. He had her in stitches and she could barely speak as she filled in some of the gaps for the others.

It seems one woman whose husband had run off for reasons that were obvious to everyone but her, was especially fond of Paul and she cornered him one night at the Sandcastle where he had gone for a nightcap. Paul had not wanted to embarrass her, but at the same time was not anxious to announce to the island that he was gay. Well, this woman had way too much to drink and proceeded to arrange herself on Paul's lap, facing him with her legs wrapped around him and the chair. She soon began making some very strenuous gyrations that were meant to be sexy. Paul had tried every polite way to remove her, but she wasn't taking the hint. Everyone in the place was laughing so he could see no help coming from friends or the proprietor. The next thing he knew, the chair seemed to explode beneath them and he was flat on his back on the floor. His captor had landed with her legs straddling his ears and his face was completely covered by her very large crotch area. He nearly died of suffocation before some good Samaritan pulled her off and checked to see if Paul was still alive. By this time the whole place was in an uproar. Paul did have a slight wound on his arm where part of the chair had poked him so he went to the men's room on the pretense of cleaning of the wound when in fact, he crawled out the window, circled around the parking lot and headed for his van. He remembered that he hadn't paid his tab, but he didn't care. They knew where to find him. That was the last time Paul was out past nine PM. until his evening with us.

It was after midnight when everyone finally retired that night. Alfie walked Paul to his car and was gone several minutes. When he returned, Jenny ran to him and gave him a big hug. The house was quiet except for muffled sounds we heard coming from Bernie's room as Jenny, Alfie and I were heading toward our respective rooms. Bernie's room is positioned by itself to the left of the foyer, our rooms are down the hall on the right. We assumed the sounds were from one of the video games he so loved, but as we got closer we heard grunts and groans, music and voices and we all realized at the same moment that Bernie was watching porn. Fighting back the mental image of old Bernie whacking off, I just wanted to get as far from that door as I could. Alfie and Jenny were laughing convulsively with their hands over their mouths to muffle their sounds. They stumbled down the hall holding each other up, weak from trying to control their laughter. What a weird guy. I knew he made Serena very uncomfortable and his contempt for Amanda was readily apparent as was hers in return. I found myself wondering if Sam shouldn't intervene and get rid of Bernie. Of course we don't have to worry about him anymore, but I'll be relieved when they find out what killed him-at least I think I will be.

KATE

I had been lonely for a long time and that evening with Glen and Adrian was the first time in many months that I had really enjoyed myself. I just felt like we were all exactly where we should be at that moment in time. I sensed Glen felt that way too. Adrian was the glue that brought us together. She is so bright and true. She is an incubator for trust and open sharing. She reminds me of my grandmother in her honesty and wisdom. My grandmother was dedicated to her children and grandchildren. I was not her favorite. She considered me too worldly. My older sister, LeAnne, was the one my grandmother placed her trust in to preserve the ways of our ancestors. When LeAnne was killed in a car accident at the age of eighteen my grandmother withdrew from the world, but I wouldn't let her shut me out. As a result, over the past few years and until her death three months ago, we shared many spiritual moments for which I am eternally grateful. I mention this because it was my grandmother who helped me recognize my memories for what they are and taught me to embrace them. She encouraged me to come here because she sensed that I was in danger of losing my ability to "return" to the source of my memories and she knew she wasn't going to be around to guide me. Her words held even more importance for me since she had died less than two months before I was drawn to Sam's website. She spoke to me in a dream and I believe she directed me to his website. You see, when we work out in the world, no matter how hard we try to keep in touch with our true natures and our ancestors, we often drift to the material present and lose our way back. Grandmother did not want this to happen to me. I was in danger of losing that connection with my ancestors and my Creator. That evening with Glen and Adrian, I was able to talk about my grandmother and my people and if they didn't understand all that I was saying, at least they understood my need to be here.

Adrian and I talked some more in our room after we retired. She liked Glen a lot and it was obvious that she was trying to point me in his direction. I liked him too. I had never been able to have a satisfying relationship with a man my own age, so the age difference didn't bother me a bit, nor did the fact that he is an amputee. Actually, the only thing that inhibited me is that I will never give up my home and my tribe and it wasn't likely that a man like Glen would want to move to Idaho and live on the reservation. That didn't have to stop us from becoming great friends, but I didn't see much beyond that for me in the future with any man.

SAM

Monday morning ushered in a brilliantly sunny day. I was up by 6 AM and felt so great that I felt guilty remembering poor Etienne in the hospital. I decided to go over to the house early and help Serena with breakfast since I was sure Amanda would be sleeping in if she had even returned from the hospital. I arrived about 7 AM to find Amanda and Antoinette sitting at the kitchen counter eating some of Serena's carefully hoarded canned cherries and the bread pudding she had baked the night before. Both were having tea and both looked like hell. Amanda never has been able to hide fatigue. She normally looks quite youthful for her age, but if she is stressed or tired she looks like she has earned every year. Don't be hard on me. I'm not saying anything she wouldn't say herself. Antoinette, on the other hand, looked like a tired, but beautiful little doll. They had spent the night at the hospital, but Etienne finally sent them home to rest. Their instructions were to eat, sleep and bathe and then and only then would they be allowed to return. I could easily just picture him laying the law down to those two grown women.

Antoinette said that Etienne would probably remain in the hospital until Thursday or Friday, whenever the doctors felt that they could cast the leg without fear of infection from the wound. She seemed relieved and even managed to find humor in the fact that he had to pee in a bedpan. According to her, he was more upset by that than the injury itself.

By 8 AM they were both asleep in the guest house and Serena and I were cooking breakfast for the gang. Jenny and Alfie were the first out and they were laughing and giggling like a couple of teenagers. Next came Bernie, his usual charming self. Jenny was all concern as she asked Bernie if he had had a pleasant night. Both she and Alfie were holding back laughter as Bernie replied that it was the same as every other night. Obviously there was some joke going on that I was not privy to. Bernie looked annoyed but proceeded to ignore them as he loudly slurped his coffee, still another annoying habit of his. When Glen entered the room Alfie and Jenny greeted him with huge smiles and inappropriate glee. Glen just rolled his eyes and moved to the coffee urn, but I spotted him blushing as he turned to face us again. Bernie made some comment to the effect that not everyone is a morning person and it is hard to take people who are so bright and cheery before noon. Jenny asked him if he enjoyed the late night hours the most and both she and Alfie burst out laughing again. Glen was smiling, but avoided looking at Bernie. I decided then and there that I didn't want to get to the bottom of that story.

Since we were a smaller group, Serena was making eggs to order along with Italian sausage. I wanted some of her canned cherries like she had given Amanda and Antoinette, but she refused me saying that they were for special occasions and the way this group eats, they would be gone in one sitting. I was glad Amanda was not there to give me one of her smug smiles. I settled for two eggs over easy, two large sausages and bread pudding with huckleberry syrup. I knew this eating frenzy had to stop. I resolved to skip lunch.

We decided to carry on with the day's plan even though Amanda and Etienne would be missing from the group. This is where it was going to get really interesting as the members would share memories from the past. I wanted it to happen naturally so I suggested we just sit and talk about whatever came to our minds until someone wanted to tell about a past life. I did not want this to feel orchestrated so I really didn't care how long it took to get to the stories. We were talking about the news of the day and somehow ended up on the subject of global warming. Everyone agreed that the weather seemed to be getting colder, not warmer, which surprisingly prompted Kate to be the first to tell a story. This was an important moment and all eyes were on Kate as she rose and moved to stand in front of the fireplace where Adrian was sitting without Etienne.

Chapter Twenty

KATE: BIRD OF LIGHT

"I was alone on a mountain several miles from my village. I had wandered off in the morning to collect some of the last berries of the summer. They were scarce and suitable only for drying, but I was enjoying the solitude and didn't mind the scant harvest. The leaves had already turned on the trees and the nights had been cold, but it was sunny that day and I was determined to absorb all the remaining rays to get me through the cold winter. My grandmother, Eagle Watching had taught me to love all the seasons equally as they performed the functions dictated by the Creator, but I loved autumn above all.

I was to be married soon and, being the only surviving daughter of my father, I was cherished and loved as the one who would provide him with many grandchildren. My father had named me Bird of Light because I was born at dawn and when he looked to the east at the moment of my birth he could see a bird at a great distance flying upward above the rising sun. It appeared to him that the bird was pulling the sun up from behind the mountain, thus my beautiful name.

I was told that my mother hemorrhaged to death giving birth to me, yet I always knew in my heart how she looked, smelled and sounded. I ached for her all my life. Her mother, my grandmother, raised me and taught me the old ways. When I was about six years old she told me that I had a twin sister who died at birth along with my mother. My grandmother believed that I had taken the spirit from my sister along with my own and left her powerless to enter this world. She didn't view me as evil, she said it was just my nature. I yearned for my sister and mother and prayed to the creator that they would forgive me for stealing my sister's spirit. I believed that my mother let herself die so that she could stay with my sister and protect her. I felt ashamed and alone. I loved and respected my grandmother and wanted to do all she and my father asked of me to help ease the pain of their loss. I did not look forward to my marriage as I found no comfort in my future mate's company. I just knew I had to go through with it. There was no one else whose child I wanted to bear so my heart didn't yearn for another. My soul-mate was my dead sister, so it didn't matter who I married.

As the day wore on, I became less and less aware of where I was. By late afternoon I was in an area that was not at all familiar to me, yet I wasn't afraid. The minute the sun began to go down, the temperature dropped dramatically and I was having trouble staying warm even though I was moving furiously trying to find my way home. By the time the moon was high, it was bitterly cold and I wondered if my father would find me. I knew he would have everyone looking for me, but I also knew that I had wandered far. I kept moving through the night, but even though I tried to take direction from the moon and stars, I wasn't able to find a familiar trail. Just before the morning light the wind started to blow and then it began to snow. I was dressed in a cloth dress with what we would refer to as a pinafore made of buckskin over the dress. I had actually been too warm in the afternoon sun, but that morning the cold wind and snow cut right through me. The sun did not come out. The wind kept blowing and the dry powdery snow felt like ants crawling on my skin. I didn't know if I should keep wandering or just sit somewhere sheltered, and wait for my father to find me. Finally in late afternoon, cold and exhausted I collapsed under a clump of bushes to rest. I stayed there only a few minutes and then started moving again to try to get warm. As night surrounded me again I could see that the sky was perfectly clear and there were more stars out than I ever believed possible. I slipped and fell onto a fallen tree and a broken limb pierced the underside of my arm just above the elbow. It ripped the skin and punctured deeply, but I barely felt the pain. There was a lot of blood at first but it soon abated, probably due to the cold. Finally, I laid down on the ground and spoke to my grandmother, telling her that I was sorry to cause her pain. I could see her face in my dream state, but then her face became younger and softer and I knew I was looking at my mother and I could see a young woman standing behind her. I was still cold, but I felt comforted. I stopped shaking and fell into a peaceful sleep.

I have had this memory many times and it is always exactly the same only each time the image of my grandmother becomes more vague and my mother's face more distinct. I don't understand why that happens, but it doesn't disturb me. I do wonder why my mother does not appear a day older than when she died, yet my sister appears to be my age.

I know that I died that night and I dreaded the grief I would cause my grandmother and my father. This is the sad part of having the memories because when you see your own death or that of someone you love, you carry that sorrow forward. You still feel it in your next lives, not just for yourself, but for those that shared that life with you. Once you remember that sadness or joy, it becomes a part of your present life and everything changes in you from that point on. That is why it is so hard to find a way to share your feelings with those around you. They don't understand what the memories are. And that is why this gift can make us feel so lonely. There is one other thing you need to see. Right here, on my arm is a birthmark in exactly the spot of my injury from the fallen tree. Sometimes when I remember that life I can feel the pain in that spot."

SAM

Kate sat down and smiled contentedly looking around at each of us. It was strange behavior and seemed incongruous with her story. We were all deeply touched and here she was smiling like she had just had a delicious meal. It dawned on me then that she hadn't finished her story. There was more and she would tell us in her own time.

My mind was spinning as I realized the full impact of a remembered life. Had Amanda ever tried to explain it this way, or had I just refused to listen? I was ashamed of my lack of imagination and my insensitivity to what she was experiencing. I remembered all the stupid remarks and bad jokes I had made when she tried to talk to me. To have lived and loved before and experienced the pain of losing a child or other loved one, then of course, you would remember that pain as part of the memory, and that pain would follow to your other lives. I was only beginning to see what we were dealing with here. I was grateful that Amanda was not present that morning because I don't think I could have stood the look in her eyes as she saw the realization in mine of how badly I had failed her. Now I could go to her and tell her what I had learned in my own words. The end result is the same, but at least I am spared the humiliation of having her witness the moment that the light went on in my head. Thank you Kate. It was so unlike her to take the spotlight right away like she did. Would it be conceited of me to think that she had chosen that time when Amanda was not present to teach me? If so, she did me a huge favor. If not, she did me a huge favor. Jenny appeared very moved by the story and echoed Kate's observation that one carries forward the emotions experienced in prior lives, but she reminded us that they also bring forward the joys. Jenny and Alfie obviously choose to embrace the joyful and learn compassion from the sad. This seems to be true of everyone but Bernie. He just had to put in his two cents

BERNIE

I couldn't just let it lie. I had to jump in and try to make my case about what a curse the memories are. After all, if I didn't, what would be my excuse for my terrible outlook on life? I stood up and started ranting and frankly, I went too far, but I couldn't control myself.

"Hell yes, we bring it all forward!! That should be obvious. I can remember and relive every bad thing that was ever done to me. Why do you think I keep to myself? I'm not going to give anyone another shot at me. You guys can run around singing the praises of the universe, but some of us don't exactly lead charmed existences like Adrian here. And Glen, in spite of his accident early in life, has been pretty darn lucky if you ask me and, (leering at Kate) I wouldn't be a bit surprised if he is about to get lucky again. Then Amanda has Sam catering to her every whim and of, course we have the dynamic duo of Jenny and Alfie, which looks like it is about to become a threesome with this Paul guy. I can't remember ever being as well off as any of you in any life and, to tell the truth, I think you are all kidding yourselves with your syrupy rhetoric. I wonder if Etienne will come away from this life with a more realistic view than the rest of you have. It is obvious to me from looking at Antoinette that he is about to experience more pain than a broken leg in the near future."

ADRIAN

I admit that I totally lost it at that point. That man is so vile. I jumped up and started screaming like an old fishwife.

"That is enough Bernie!! Just sit down and shut up. For God's sake Sam, can't you do something about him? Bernie, you are a broken human being and I doubt that you are fixable. I have always believed that everyone has own their story and it is worth our while to listen to them. But after eighty years and several other lifetimes, I have found an exception to that rule. I'm a big girl and I can simply ignore you, but I want to warn you to avoid spreading your venom to Etienne and I am sure that Sam will not want you anywhere near his Samantha when she arrives. I know Amanda will not want you breathing the same air. I can't remember ever saying things this horrible to another person and for that I am ashamed of myself, but I do not apologize to you, Bernie. Stay out of my way and stay away from Etienne."

SAM

OK! It was time for a break. Serena was bustling about the kitchen pretending that she hadn't witnessed this. Alfie and

Jenny went for a walk to get some fresh air. Kate went out on the deck by herself. I think Glen would have liked to follow her, but I'm sure he was embarrassed by Bernie's remark. Adrian went into the study and motioned me to accompany her. I did reluctantly, knowing what was coming. Bernie just shrugged his shoulders and went to his room probably to play his stupid video games or whatever he did in there.

When I joined Adrian in the den, she was on the verge of tears and apologized over and over for her outburst. I assured her that if she hadn't spoken up, someone else would have. I also made a promise to take Bernie aside that very evening and have a talk with him. There had to be a way to make him see how destructive his behavior was. I was certain that if we went over to the boat and shared a couple of single malt scotches and a cigar, we could find some common ground and a way to neutralize him.

Looking back, I wonder why I was so stubborn about Bernie. I can't really tell you why I didn't just send him packing. I think I truly believed he had something to contribute about the why and wherefore of those with the memories. I wanted to understand why it seemed like a blessing to so many, and a curse to him.

Although it was still early, no one returned to the story pit that morning. There seemed to be some tacit agreement that we had shared enough and I was grateful to have a couple of hours to plan my strategy with Bernie, although my time alone was less than fruitful, and by lunchtime I still had no idea how I was going to get through to him.

Amanda and Antoinette joined us for lunch; both looking refreshed in spite of their vigil the night before. Antoinette was to take the Escalade back to the hospital to spend the afternoon, but promised to return in time for dinner. We had a light meal of soup and salad and fresh fruit, no cookies, no cake, as if Serena was already starting to take notice of some changes in our collective physique. After lunch, I sauntered over to Bernie and, ever so casually, mentioned that he had not yet seen my boat. He responded that, to his knowledge, no one had. Nothing was ever easy with this guy. I changed my tact and simply stated that we needed to talk and that I hoped he would join me on the boat after dinner so we could chat about a few things. He looked sideways at me and gave me a sly smile, but no response. I followed up by saying that we could head down that way about eight thirty. He grunted agreement and walked off, throwing Amanda a dirty look that none of us could miss. Amanda, having no knowledge of the events of that morning, gave me that "What did I do?" look that people get when they believe they are being unjustly persecuted. Jenny grabbed her by the hand and led her down the hall on the pretense of showing her something in her room.

Serena left for the day informing us that we were having a build your own pizza night and we were on our own until morning. She looked slightly disgusted and I felt like crap for letting things get so out of hand. I had one guest in the hospital and two or three others wanting to drop Bernie off a cliff. I was beginning to doubt my ability to hold this group together. Alfie stepped up to rescue the day. He had a story he wanted to tell and I gladly turned the floor over to him, hoping he would fill the entire afternoon.

As everyone drifted back into the room Alfie was rushing about in his most girlish way handing out cushions and making sure everyone was comfortable. He was obviously enjoying himself immensely in the knowledge that his mannerisms were annoying Bernie. Jennie was sitting next to Amanda and they seemed to be sharing some kind of secret joke. Adrian was in her usual spot on the hearth. She had regained her composure and appeared to be looking forward to Alfie's performance.

Glen and Kate were seated on the couch opposite Amanda and Bernie was sitting at one end in his usual straight backed chair. His head was bowed and he appeared to be sleeping, but we all knew that we wouldn't be that lucky.

As I settled into my usual easy chair, it occurred to me that we might be privy to some insights into the gay phenomenon. The question of gender in past lives had not occurred to me. I had assumed that Amanda was always a woman, but at that moment I realized that she might have been a man at some time. The thought of it made me feel creepy! I have never considered myself a homophobe, but thinking of your wife as a former man would freak any guy out. Alfie had been a woman in other lives and he had told us he liked being female better. I had less trouble picturing him as a woman than seeing Amanda as a man. I tried to cut my thoughts off at that point because I knew that I was ignorant about the subject but my mind kept racing. Good God! Was Bernie ever a woman? That would have to be one ugly broad. I wondered if he would admit it if he had been. Bernie didn't seem too fond of women, or anyone for that matter. I looked over to where he was sitting slumped in his chair and suddenly he raised his head and looked me right in the eye. I hoped he could read my mind, it would serve him right. I forced myself to meet his stare-first one that looks away loses. Damn, I never have been able to win at that game. I was relieved when Alfie finally got everyone settled and began his story.

Chapter Twenty-One

SETH'S GREAT DISCOVERY-A HERO'S LIFE

ALFIE

"Well, it's raining like hell outside so it's a perfect afternoon for doing just what we are doing. I thought I would start by addressing the issue of my gayness. I am not a woman trapped in a man's body. That is something entirely different from being gay. I am a man who is attracted to men instead of women. It's that simple. I also know for sure that I was born that way. The reason I know this is because in past lives I have been a man at least twice and a woman twice for sure, possibly three times. I know how both sexes develop and what are normal feelings at different ages. I know how most eight year old and six year old boys and girls feel about their bodies and it is a lot different than I have felt in this life. I don't know if this holds true for all gay men, but most of my gay friends would tell you that they have always known themselves to be different. I don't know if there are some out there that have "become" gay, perhaps through a seduction or some sort of traumatic experience. I guess it's possible, but I adhere to the nature, not nurture theory.

Another thing I want to make perfectly clear is that being gay does not mean that I am promiscuous and amoral. I do not hang out in the men's room of airports or rest stops in state parks and I do not prey on young boys. There are some who do, it can't be denied, but most of us seek monogamous, fulfilling, relationships with a likeminded partner. I, for one have only had three partners in my life. I say this not to impress you, but to lay the groundwork for what most gay men consider normal within our culture. Heterosexuals, both men and women, have those who deviate from the norm as well. I have many male and female heterosexual friends that have had literally hundreds of sexual partners and engage in some very strange, and often illegal, activities. My point is that I do not consider myself a deviant. I'm just a regular gay guy, except that I am not nearly as good looking as many gay guys. I have been called many names because of my sexual orientation, but never has anyone referred to me as a "pretty boy".

Since I met Jenny, she has filled such a gap in my life that I guess I really haven't cared too much whether I was in a relationship or not. Jenny has been my constant companion and, although we are not romantically involved, it has been a blast and I don't see that changing in the future, even if one or both of us do find a romantic partner. I don't believe I could love anyone that didn't love Jenny. (Jenny smiled and blew him a kiss-everyone around the room was smiling except Bernie who appeared once again to be sleeping.)

This memory came to me in stages. It began when I was twelve years old in this life and my last visit came two years ago.

My name was Seth and in that life I was also 12 years old when the memory first emerged. My family lived in a large frame house, quite ordinary in appearance except for one thing. Although the house had two stories, there were no stairs to the top floor inside or outside. My father rented the place when I was six years old and had finally saved enough money to purchase it from the owner who lived in New York. At least that is what he told us. The main floor had always accommodated our small family quite comfortably and it had never occurred to me that it was unusual to live in a two story house with no stairs.

On this particular day our parents told us to remain at the table after breakfast as they had a surprise for us. It was spring and school had just let out a week or so before, and my older sister Maggie and I had spent our first few days of freedom helping our mother with the spring cleaning. This consisted of tearing the entire house and yard apart and putting it back together. Mother was bragging to our father about what good workers we were and how we deserved a reward. Father teasingly suggested an apple, which grew in abundance in our yard, as a reward. Mother insisted it must be more than that. Father suggested an extra piece of pie for each of us after lunch, but mother held out for more. Of course they were playing a game with us and we knew it, but we played along knowing that they had already agreed on what our reward would be. After a few more ridiculously small offerings and rejections, father reached into his shirt pocket and drew out two folded pieces of paper handing one to each of us. We both just held them in our open palms and stared at them wondering if the game was still on or if the paper contained the real reward. Finally father told us to open them and look inside. They had done a first-rate job of heightening the anticipation so my heart was pounding and I hurriedly opened mine before Maggie so that I would be the first to see the surprise.

I couldn't believe my eyes! It was a ten dollar bill! You have to understand that this was the first time I had ever held more than a nickel in my hand and rarely that. This life took place in the late nineteen thirties. The great depression was in full swing and it was a time when kids were not given an allowance in exchange for chores. It was expected that we would help out as members of the family. One wasn't rewarded for keeping his room clean and bed made. That was part of the training for adulthood, along with mowing the lawn, helping with the laundry, canning, washing dishes, feeding the animals and cleaning out the garage. In addition, we each donated two hours per week to help out at the church. It would never have occurred to either of us to ask to be paid for any of this. It was the same with our friends and classmates, except for James Sanborn, whose father was the president of the bank. He received two dollars per week and it would have been no surprise to any of us if he had glued them to his forehead, so fond was he of letting others know about his status.

Maggie and I stared at our fortune for some time, studying each side as if expecting it to disappear. During this time, our parents were laying down the rules for how this money was to be used. We were forbidden to buy anything of a practical nature. This money was to go for something totally unnecessary and impractical. We were not to use any portion of it to buy gifts for our parents or each other. I remember wondering if my father was dying and this was his last wish, but he looked far too happy and healthy for that and my mother was beaming as she looked from each of us to him and back again. Finally, father explained that our family had come into some good fortune, the origin of which would remain a secret to all but him and my mother. They did ask us not to flaunt our wealth as that would be in poor taste and it was no one's business anyway.

The requirement that we not spend the money on anything practical was totally out of character, causing Maggie to giggle like an idiot. It was nearly impossible for me to think in those terms, but Maggie was having no trouble. She and my mother left the dirty dishes in the sink, something else I had never witnessed before, and headed for the mercantile. I went to my room and laid on my bed engorged with a feeling of power, anticipation, and the seven pancakes and four eggs I had eaten for breakfast. I decided to take my time before spending the money, partly because I wanted to enjoy the sensation of having a little wealth, but mostly because I had no idea of what I wanted to buy. I had stayed busy with school and chores and the normal "boy things", but I had no hobbies or passions at that time.

For the first time in my life, I was alone in our house. My Dad was at work and I knew mother and Maggie would be gone for a long time so I could make as much noise as I wanted and go anywhere in the house, including Maggie's room. I had rarely been allowed to enter that shrine. I crept in and snooped through her closet and drawers and found nothing I could use to torment her. I wandered back to my bed and stared at the ceiling. It was a warm, sunny day and I wanted to do something adventurous. I got up and looked out the window and I could see Mr. Long, our neighbor, standing on a ladder and painting his shutters. Suddenly, I knew what I wanted to do. I wanted to explore that second floor of our house. My dad had always told me that the reason there were no stairs was that the second floor was not finished. It was just open studs with no walls or ceiling. That afternoon I decided to see for myself. I hurried because, even though I had never been told I couldn't climb up there, I knew this was something my parents wouldn't approve.

I grabbed a ladder from the shed and propped it against the back wall where there was a window and I could not be seen from the street. The ladder was a couple of feet shy of reaching the window, but I figured I would be able to pull myself up if I could get the window open. I was surprised to find that it opened quite easily, too easily for a window that supposedly had not been touched for years, but that didn't register with me at the time. I was just barely able to pull myself high enough to get my arms and shoulders through the window and from there, I leveraged myself into the room. Yes, it was a room, all finished and painted a delicate pink with one wall in flowered wallpaper. The room was in perfect condition and I could see other rooms as well, three to be exact, one large room and two smaller ones all surrounding an open square area which would normally be used for a staircase and access hallway. There was also a very small door adjacent to the largest room that looked like it might be for storage. I looked in the other rooms and found them to be much the same as the first, just different colors and sizes. I decided to check out what was behind the little door. Finding nothing but a stuffy little space, I was about to shut the door and leave when I spotted another little door along the back wall. It was no larger than my dad's lunchbox and it was hinged on the bottom and held closed by an ordinary screen door hook at the top. I had to stoop to enter the room and sit on the floor to get to the little door. There was hardly any light, just what came in through the door, and I had to reach into total darkness to explore the area. My hand brushed against something firm and covered in fabric and my heart was racing as I pulled out a carefully wrapped bundle. Something had been hidden all these years and I was about to discover some giant secret or perhaps real treasure. Would this bundle hold any clues as to why the upstairs had been closed off? Why would my dad lie to us, or had he ever even checked this out? Maybe he had just believed the prior owner. That made more sense.

It was about the size of a small book. I thought to myself that it could also be two stacks of money and my heart started to beat wildly, or I thought it could be just a small book and my heart slowed down to normal. I crawled out of the little room to where the light was better and I carefully untied the twine and began to remove the wrapper. The first thing I saw was a tiny face staring directly at me as if to say "What did you expect?".

The wrapper fell away and I found myself holding a bundle of pictures, all black and white of course. Yes I was disappointed, but also curious. The tiny face was that of a girl about six years old. She was rather homely and very poorly dressed and her dirty little face bore a look of defiance. She stood very erect and she had both hands on her hips. In the background was a tiny, run-down shack with a porch running across the front. A woman was sitting on the porch with a baby in her arms and there were three other children varying in ages but younger than the girl. The children were playing in the dirt. Two of them, the younger ones were naked and the third, a boy about four or five was wearing a pair of baggy pants held up by a piece of rope. The whole scene reeked of poverty.

The three smaller children looked at the camera with dull, blank expressions. Only the girl appeared alive and responsive. As I stared at her, I realized that she was not homely at all. What I had mistaken for dirt were bruises, on her face, on her arms and God knows where else. She had huge dark eyes and I could see that one was slightly swollen and bruised. Still, she was, by her stance declaring herself to be definitely in charge and appeared to be demanding that I recognize her authority. She was trying to hold her world together. My young heart grew up a little as I stared at her trying to gain control of her surroundings. I wanted to crawl into the picture and help her. I wanted to be her hero.

Minutes later, I came out of my trance and began to sift through the other pictures. I think I was hoping to find another picture of her, maybe a happier one. There were no more of that family, but each and every picture seemed to have a story to tell that drew me in. I had never been exposed to fine art or great music so this was my first experience with the magic that can be produced by an artist. I knew that these pictures were treasures and I resolved that they would always belong to me.

I wrapped the pictures in the cloth and tied it exactly as I had found it. I wanted to open it again in the privacy of my own room and experience again the sense of discovery. Mainly I wanted to look at the girl's face and memorize it in the hope that I could somehow bring her to life. I crawled back into the little room and reached again through the little door to see if there was more treasure or, perhaps some clue about the origin of the pictures or information about the former tenant. Sure enough, there was another package, larger and quite heavy, but wrapped in the same cloth and tied in the same manner. I was getting nervous about being found there should anyone return so I decided to wait to open it until I was in the safety of my room. I felt a sudden urgency to get out of there- not fear or panic, just a sense that something could be lost if I didn't act quickly. As I returned to the open window, I discovered another door that I hadn't noticed before. By the configuration of the outside wall, I knew that it had to be a very small room, probably a closet. I had to investigate. Who knew when I would have another chance?

I pushed the door open and discovered what originally had been a long narrow closet. There were three sinks installed in a counter, but no plumbing attached and two clotheslines ran the length of the room-nothing else except a bundle of odd looking paper and some empty bottles. It looked like some kind of weird laundry room and I regretted spending the extra time to explore it.

I returned to the window and realized that it would be difficult to lower myself to the ladder with my two bundles. I had to secure them somehow so that both arms would be free. I took off my shirt thinking to use it as a wrap and tie it around my waist, but it was too small. I took off my pants, stuffed the bundles in and tightened my belt. Then I tied the legs around my neck so the package was hanging down my back. I turned on my stomach and lowered myself feet first to the top rung of the ladder and carefully made my way to the ground. It was then that I realized that the window was still open. If my dad saw that he would surely put two and two together and I would be discovered. However, I didn't relish spending any more time than necessary outside in my underpants, so I ran in the back door, placed the bundles under my bed and put my pants back on. I was heading out the back door when I heard mother and Margaret coming in the front door. I drug the ladder to the barn and stashed it just as mother came outside looking for me.

The rest of the day was agony for me as I listened to Margaret go on and on about her new hat, gloves and matching shoes. I spent what seemed like hours lying about what I had done all morning alone in the house and explaining why I wasn't in a hurry to spend my money. I didn't dare go to my room. I had to stay with the family and guard the back yard in case someone decided to enjoy the afternoon shade and notice the open window. I was a nervous wreck by the time dinner was over. I helped with the dishes and finally made it back to my room claiming I was in the middle of a good book. I knew I would be left alone for at least two hours until my dad would pop his head in the door to say goodnight.

I had to deal with the window and that the only time I could do so without getting caught would be in the middle of the night. Even then, it would be risky and I was strangely titillated by the idea. After all, I was twelve years old and this whole thing was the closest thing to an adventure I had ever encountered. My parents went to bed around nine. (You have to remember that these were the days before television, people went to bed early and got up early.). My plan was to wait until midnight when they would be sleeping deeply. The whole thing shouldn't take more than ten minutes and I could be safely back in my room with no one the wiser.

Meanwhile, I had my bundles to explore! I sat on the floor with the bed blocking the view from the door in case one of my parents made an unexpected visit to my room. I re-opened the first bundle and, as before, I saw that little face staring up at me defiantly, yet pleading to be rescued. At least I wanted to believe the part about being rescued because I had already declared myself to be her hero. I stared at her for several minutes before opening the second bundle. I was so hoping that there would be some clue to her identity inside that second bundle, although I knew that was unlikely since there were many other pictures of different people in different locations. My only hope was that the second bundle contained some sort of journal that would explain the circumstances surrounding the picture, although the bundle was not shaped like any journal I had ever seen and it was very heavy.

I loosened the twine and as the fabric fell away I couldn't believe my eyes. There were two objects. The largest I recognized as a camera, a Brownie Hercules to be exact. My uncle Thomas owned one. It was his pride and joy and he made a nuisance of himself at family gatherings, insisting on having us pose over and over again. He was positive that we would all thank him in the long run as he chronicled our lives. My dad always said there was a need for only three pictures in one's life-a wedding, a family photo ten years later and one more after the grandchildren are born. Before I saw those pictures in my bundle I would have agreed with him, but having seen the mastery of the former owner, I realized that, although Uncle Tommy was correct in some ways, he did not have a gift for seeing what the camera can see.

The camera did not belong to me, but what was I to do? I couldn't turn it over to father without confessing my mischief. The owner obviously didn't want it or else he was dead and couldn't claim it. I decided that it was mine and I would make no apologies. The other item was a lot more problematic. It was a gun, a Smith and Wesson 32-20-model 1905 according to the markings. It was a small gun, but a serious weapon, one any boy or man would be proud to own. Hiding a camera and a few pictures was one thing, but hiding a gun was something else. Or was it? Lots of my friends had been given rifles by their dads for hunting and had been taught how to use them. No one thought anything of it. My dad was definitely no hunter so he saw no reason to have a gun in the house. Why did that have to prevent me from having what other kids had? I wasn't going to use it. I didn't even have ammunition. I checked it carefully to make sure it wasn't loaded, wrapped it separately in a pair of old holey underpants, and stuck it under my mattress, way to the middle so that mother wouldn't find it if she changed my sheets. I knew I had to find a better hiding place, but this would do for now. The camera was another matter. It was way too bulky to fit under the mattress. For the time being, both the camera and the pictures would be hidden in my toy chest. No one had looked in there for years. They would be safe among the building blocks, precious rocks collected from our back yard, my Davey Crocket hat, hardened modeling clay and the toy guns of my youth.

My uncle had shown me how to take the film out of his camera without exposing it so I checked to see if there was more film in the camera. It was empty. The thought struck me that I didn't know how long these pictures had remained hidden. The girl in the picture was about six or seven then, but how old would she be now? I knew that the first Brownie Hercules was sold in 1931 and the last was made in 1933, which is when my uncle bought his. That meant that the girl was at least my age. That subject being dealt with, I took her picture out of the bundle and placed it under my pillow to give me courage for what was to come later that night. No matter what, I had to do to protect my secret. No matter how many lies I had to tell, it was worth it. I knew my life was forever changed and I was sure I was the luckiest boy in the world.

That night I struggled to stay awake until midnight, but I fell asleep somewhere around eleven. When I woke, it was nearly dawn. I knew my parents would be getting up soon, but I couldn't take a chance on leaving that window open. It was Sunday and my dad would be home all day and take his nap in the hammock in the back yard as he did every summer Sunday after dinner. The hammock would give him a clear view of the window. I had to do this now and I cursed myself for falling asleep. Some hero I was.

It was easy to get out of the house undetected. I knew every squeaky board in the place and I was soon lugging the ladder to the window again. I also made a note to erase the spots left on the lawn by the ladder. I climbed to the top rung and reached for the window, but pulling it down was harder than pushing up. I adjusted myself as high as possible and grabbed the window. It was stuck so I had to give it a jerk. It came loose suddenly throwing me backwards with nothing to grab for support. I twisted slightly sideways and I could see myself colliding with the 200 gallon drum that held our fuel oil. I grabbed the handle on the end of the drum to break my fall. The drum was mostly empty since it was summer, but very heavy nevertheless. It did break my fall, but it also came down with me. I remember hearing myself screaming with pain and my father yelling for my mother to help him lift the drum off my legs and my father's shocked expression as she ran ahead of him and lifted that drum all by herself. Then I passed out.

I awoke an hour or so later. The pain in my legs was excruciating, but I was drugged to the point that I was too weak to really grasp the source of the pain. The doctor was there and I heard him tell my father that I had a slight concussion but I didn't break my back. The problem was in what to do about my legs. My mother was sitting on the bed applying a cool cloth and much love to my aching head. She saw that I was awake and ordered them out of the room to finish their discussion. I went back to sleep and didn't awake fully again until late that evening. When I did wake up, the pain had lessened but I felt something very bulky on my left leg. It was enclosed in a cast halfway up my thigh. My right leg was not cast, but stabilized with a splint. My mother told me not to move at all for fear of causing further damage. She said I was going to be just fine, but I had much healing to do and must follow the doctor's orders. She looked old and tired. Margaret was out in the hall and I could hear her crying and carrying on as only girls her age can.

My mother fed me some broth and told me that if I felt nauseous I should vomit into the towel she gave me. I remember thinking that I must be in really bad shape because the towel was one of her precious yellow guest towels that none of us had ever been allowed to use to dry our bodies. I started to laugh at the absurdity of this, but the movement triggered such severe pain that I guess I passed out again.

The next morning I awoke to find my father sleeping in the chair beside my bed. I felt more like myself and, though there was still a lot of pain, it was bearable and I was even wondering when I would be able to get up and move around on crutches. I looked forward to the sympathy and attention I would receive from my friends. I wondered if I would still be on crutches when school started again. That would surely get me some extra consideration from my teachers. Either way, I would definitely have the best story when we were asked to tell about our summer vacation. It hit me then that I had some explaining to do and very soon. My dad was going to want to know what the hell I was doing on that ladder. I couldn't tell the truth and risk losing my treasures. I was having trouble thinking clearly, but I had to come up with a story. I decided to pretend like I was asleep until I could think of something. It didn't take long. I knew I didn't want them to know I had been up there before so I had to make it look like I was trying to get in there for the first time. The only thing I could think of was rats. My mom and dad were in my room later that day and dad finally asked me why I was up there. I told him that I woke up in the middle of the night and heard scurrying sounds. I was sure there were rats up there and I explained that I didn't want him to have to deal with the problem on his only day off. I wanted to take care of it myself so that he didn't have to. He bought my story completely. He had tears in his eyes as he leaned over to shake my hand telling me that I was fast becoming a man and that he was proud of me. I felt terrible lying to him and even worse when, looking over his shoulder, I saw the look in my mother's eyes. She wasn't buying my story. She looked confused and a little shocked but she didn't say a word. She just turned around and stared out the window. After a few minutes they left me to rest with dad telling me that we had a lot to talk about but it could wait until morning.

It was then that I remembered the picture of the girl. I had left it under my pillow when I went out to close the window. With some difficulty and a great deal of pain I searched for the picture. It was gone. I knew I had left it there so it must have been found and I knew then who had found it. Why didn't she speak up? There had never been lies in our house, probably because there was nothing to lie about. Our lives had been structured and secure until that morning when my parents gave us the money.

Later that evening my mother brought me some mashed potatoes and gravy and a pork chop cut into tiny pieces like when I was very young. She fed me like a baby and said nothing about the picture. Then she brought in a small table that had previously occupied the entry hall. On this she placed a glass, a pitcher of water, some tissues, some comic books, my reader from school, a lamp, and one of her baking pans. It took me a while to realize what the pan was for, but a few minutes later it came to me that I hadn't relieved myself since the accident. She explained that I wouldn't be able to get out of bed for a long time and the doctor had left instructions as to how I would deal with my bladder and bowels. My dad would be responsible for the task of helping me. I was humiliated and it was just starting to sink in that I was in this situation for the long haul. He came in a few minutes later and we performed the ritual that would be the bane of my existence for the next few months. My mother returned to tuck me in and told me they would leave both our bedroom doors open in case I should need them and she added that the table held everything I would want. She kissed me tenderly on the forehead and left the room looking sadder than I had ever seen her. I felt terrible for what I was putting them through and I was beginning to be aware of the consequences of my actions for my own sake. There was no way I could have known at that point just how severe those consequences would be.

I awoke the next morning before dawn. I knew I had been dreaming all night of the girl and the picture. I couldn't think of anything else. I had to find it, but how? I couldn't ask my mother. I painfully searched again under my pillow and under the edge of my mattress. Then I remembered that the table had one shallow drawer which my dad used to keep all his keys and other items that should not be lost. I remembered my mother's words about everything I would want being on the table. I knew I would find the picture in that drawer. It had been emptied of everything else, but I felt around in the semi-darkness and my hand came to rest on the picture. My mom had to have placed the picture there and for her own reasons had decided to keep my secret, at least for the time being. I fell back into a deep and dreamless sleep for a couple of hours until mom brought me some oatmeal and my dad came in to talk to me about what would happen next.

The news was not good. My left leg would heal, but the rim of the barrel had landed directly on my right ankle crushing it beyond repair. The bottom line was that the doctor would do all he could to piece it together and to make it strong enough to support my weight, but there would be no mobility causing me to walk with a pronounced limp for the rest of my life. That was the good news. The alternative would be if the ankle didn't heal at all, they might have to amputate below the knee. It took a couple of days for me to realize the full impact of what he was saying. I think my mind would only let me take in a little at a time. I prayed as best I knew how, first for a miracle that it would all go away, then just that my ankle would heal in some form and I could keep my leg.

The next few weeks were terrible for me and I didn't make it easy on my family either. I was despondent and unresponsive on some days, on others I was just plain impossible. It was summer, so it was unbearably hot in my room and I couldn't go outside to catch a breeze, let alone a softball. My friends came to visit, but they never stayed long. The outdoors was calling them and they had to respond. I would stare at the picture for hours and wonder how I would ever be able to find the little girl. I constructed many scenarios in my mind as to how we would be united, but all of them involved my being able to move about on my own. To my young impatient mind, that seemed like an eternity away.

Then Ethan moved into our neighborhood and everything changed. Ethan was a scrawny, funny looking kid with huge brown eyes and dirty blond hair that grew in every direction at once. He had a smile that covered the lower half of his face and teeth that looked like they belonged on a large farm animal rather than a twelve year old boy. He also had a healthy sprinkling of pimples that were the curse of so many twelve year olds. It didn't seem fair that such an uncommonly homely young man should also be cursed with such a common affliction. He should have been spared at least that. Needless to say, he wasn't the kind of kid that found friends easily. He was funny and good natured, but kids being what they are, he was an easy target for ridicule. Ethan needed a friend and companion as desperately as I did, and he was generously endowed with all the qualities that make a good friend. I learned plenty from him and I like to believe some of his goodness and joy rubbed off on me. He was the one person that could always make me laugh and my family adored him, especially my mother. Even Margaret, superficial though she was, took him under her wing and never allowed anyone to torment him in her presence.

As Ethan spent the rest of the summer with me and every minute before and after school, I became more hopeful and a lot easier to get along with. By the time school started the doctor was pretty sure my leg could be saved. By Thanksgiving, I was able to get up and move about with crutches. I returned to school but that was all the activity I was allowed. I had to return to my bed the minute I got home. Ethan was always there. About a month after I met Ethan I confided in him about my upstairs adventure. I showed him everything I had collected except the picture of the girl. He was ecstatic with the mystery of it all; the second floor without the stairs, the gun and the camera and pictures. We would spend hours spinning different scenarios of how we could go about solving the mystery of who left these treasures behind.

It was Christmas vacation and I had been forbidden to go outside due the danger of falling in the snow and ice. Ethan spent every day with me, but I was pretty despondent about my imprisonment. Finally, I took out the picture of the girl and showed it to Ethan. He stared at the picture for a minute or two and then looked at me wide-eyed and flatly declared that we had to find her and help her. He had fallen just as I had. The next few hours were spent poring over every detail in the picture. Ethan was a lot more clever than I at finding clues and details that might lead us to her location and when the picture was taken. He pointed to a clump of oak trees in the background and he sifted through the other pictures until he came to one that I had paid little attention to before. There was another angle of what appeared to be the same trees. We counted the tree trunks and could see that there was exactly the same number in both pictures. We could also see in the background the backside of a cabin which looked to be about the same size as the girl's. In the forefront of the picture was a huge red barn, very new and very well kept. Sitting in front of the barn was a brand new tractor, a John Deere. Ethan deduced that if we could find out what year that tractor was made, we would be able to nail down the year the picture was taken as it seemed likely that the pictures were taken on the same day. I was in awe of his skills of observation and deduction and energized by his zeal. Ethan took the picture and ran through the snow to the local farm equipment dealer. He returned an hour later with a grin that covered most of his pimpled face. The tractor was manufactured in 1934 so it was at least that year or the next that the pictures were taken which meant the girl was near our age.

Ethan also came up with the idea that we should give the girl a name. We couldn't keep referring to her as "the girl". I jumped at the idea and secretly chastised myself for not thinking of it myself. It was becoming clear to me that Ethan would be the brains of this outfit. We spent the next two days trying out different names until the afternoon of Christmas Eve. We decided to call her Mary.

The memory ended there and I didn't have another visit from Seth for many years. During that time, I often wondered what happened to him, Ethan and Mary. As time passed, it seemed that I would never find out, but I felt good about Seth's friendship with Ethan and I believed that he was on the road to recovery, at least to the extent that he would be able to get out in the world and possibly fulfill some of his dreams. I never doubted that he and Ethan would find Mary.

The fact that I was the same age as Seth when I first met him stuck with me and I was convinced that we would both have grown to the same age if we met again. I was right.

Shortly after my nineteenth birthday Seth reappeared. I'll have to set the stage for you.

It was my first year in college and I was having a hard time of it. I had just broken up with my first love and I was at a bit of a loss for how I would fill my spare hours. I hadn't met Jenny yet and was feeling adrift as I had no gay friends. There were a number of girls that included me in some of their shopping trips and girl parties. They viewed me as an oddity and there seemed to be a contest among them to see who could be the most open minded. I was entertaining and funny at all events and I played the gay role to the max. Most of them had boyfriends and the girls made them be nice to me, but in reality, I was the butt of many jokes and I was really filling the role of court jester. One Saturday, the girls decided to have a "Gone With The Wind" party in their dorm. It is a four hour movie so they loaded up on snacks and drinks. They insisted I attend.

When it came to the part in the movie where Scarlett O'Hara was lamenting the loss of her seventeen inch waist, the girls decided to measure each other's waistlines. This was not good for some of the chubbier members of the group, but the skinny ones rallied and everyone was forced to comply. I was given the tape and placed in charge of measuring and announcing the results. This I did not like because I knew how hurtful it would be to some of the girls, one in particular. Elaine was built like a fireplug and she had the body type that no matter how much weight she lost, she would never have the shape that has been declared desirable. She was like me in that she knew the role she was to play. She was to be the good-natured hanger-on, smiling through her pain. I wanted no part of this and I was beginning to panic as it came down to the last three girls. One of the skinny girls was named Lucy and she was like one of those bitchy high school girls they make movies about. She kept looking at Elaine with a look of absolute pleasure at what was about to transpire. I was sick with dread so I did the only thing a reasonable person would have done. I pretended to have something important I had to do and I bolted for the door. I started to run down the stairs but in my haste, I tripped and fell down the stairs breaking my ankle in the fall (coincidence?). A couple of students saw my fall and called 911. The sirens brought my whole group outside and I was trying to behave as if I was in shock in order to avoid their questions. While waiting in the emergency room, I looked at the clock. It was 7:15 PM. The next thing I knew it was 8:30 PM and I was still waiting for the doctor. In the interim hour and fifteen minutes, I experienced the rest of Seth's amazing story.

Giving the girl a name gave her more than an identity. It brought her into our lives in a way that might seem unnatural to others-not to me and not to Ethan. Eventually I was able to get around without crutches, but there was no mobility in my ankle and my right leg ended up about two inches shorter than my left leaving me with a definite limp and making it impossible to run or ride a bicycle in a normal manner.

Throughout our high school years Ethan and I remained inseparable and so impervious to the jeers and taunts of our classmates that they eventually left us alone. We did everything together including our studies, which benefited me a lot more than Ethan. We managed to get through high school and Ethan won a full science scholarship to Ohio State University. I did not fare as well, but I didn't want to go on to college anyway. Our plan was for me to move to Columbus and make my living as a photographer while Ethan attended school. In this way we could continue our friendship, but more importantly, we would finally be free to explore our mystery in our spare time.

Our years in high school had not been wasted in that regard. We had made it a point to meet all the older people in our town, people that might be able to give us information about the former inhabitants of our home. The unforeseen consequence was that we quickly became much beloved among the senior community and our parents gave us an inordinate amount of freedom since it was clear that we were not likely to be involved in some of the less desirable activities our peers were pursuing. We would target certain individuals that had lived in our town since the beginning of time and we would track them down and contrive opportunities to engage them in conversation about local history, and gossip was definitely included in their tales.

We finally made the acquaintance of an old widow named Sylvia. She was at least forty years old, and we were amazed that her memory was functioned so well. She was able to fill us in on most of the family histories and we enjoyed listening to her and often visited just to hear her stories and munch on those fabulous sugar cookies that were always available in abundance. From Sylvia we learned that a man named Walter Armstrong had bought our house in 1929 and moved there with his beautiful, but strange wife. That was the year of the stock market crash and the great depression was on its way, yet Walter did not seem to suffer from a lack of money. He paid cash for the house and hired a local carpenter to update the wiring and plumbing and to fix up the second floor. It was rumored that he had some weird special room built up there, but no one seemed to know what it was for. No one really cared because Walter never missed an opportunity to offer work to people in the community. He hired a gardener, a housekeeper, another woman to do their laundry and any number of young people to run errands for him. All of these were paid generously, well beyond the normal rate, and it was rumored that he covered many of the expenses of the two local churches for the years that he lived here.

Incongruous with this generous outreach, Walter had no desire to mingle with others. He was rarely seen in town and his wife was almost invisible. Sylvia learned that her name was Isabelle and she claimed she only saw her up close a couple of times and she spoke to her only once. According to Sylvia, Isabelle was the most beautiful woman she had ever seen and her voice was simply enchanting. On one particular occasion, Sylvia said she was restless and decided to take a drive alone to the country for a change of scene. She went to a place by the river she and her husband often visited and discovered another car. She recognized it as Walter Armstrong's because no one else had a car that nice. It was a 1929 Ford Roadster convertible, yellow and black with spoke wheels. It was stunning. She assumed that it had arrived carrying Walter Armstrong and was about to turn around and leave, not wishing to be subjected to the kind of gossip that could arise from a married lady being seen in a remote area with a man, especially a man as handsome and mysterious as Walter Armstrong. As she backed her car up, she saw Isabelle, not Walter. Isabelle was standing, rather precariously and barefoot, on a high rock at the river's edge, holding something to her eyes. It was clear that she was oblivious to Sylvia's presence and Sylvia did not want to startle her so she brought the car to a stop and just sat there watching her. Isabelle was taking pictures, which seemed strange to Sylvia since at that time, it was rare to see a woman who owned a camera, let alone operate it herself. For the most part, that was something men did, not women, but here she was taking pictures of what appeared to be a beaver dam.

Sylvia admitted that this was one of the few times in her life that she had felt intimidated by another person. She said that Isabelle's beauty accompanied by her obvious rapport with her surroundings left her feeling like she didn't deserve to be there, yet she felt compelled to stay. After a few minutes, Isabelle floated down from the rock and spotted Sylvia. She didn't seem startled or surprised, she just smiled warmly and began to walk toward the car, slowly as she was still barefoot. She was wearing a simple housedress that looked like an evening gown on her perfect form and her long blond hair was held loosely back from her face by a shoestring of all things.

Sylvia just sat in her car as Isabelle approached the driver's window. Isabelle introduced herself and told Sylvia she would be leaving in a minute and that Sylvia could have the place to herself. Sylvia finally found her voice and asked her to stay and visit for a minute or two. She wanted to get to know this astounding creature. Isabelle consented on the condition that Sylvia share some of the lemonade Walter had made for her that morning. The passenger door to Isabelle's car was open and Sylvia was directed to sit there while Isabelle filled the top from the thermos and handed it to her. Isabelle sat on a stump very nearby and proceeded to drink directly from the thermos. That one act, so incongruous with the graceful image Isabelle projected, caused Sylvia to laugh and she instantly found herself at ease. She told Isabelle how much she and her husband enjoyed visiting that very spot. Without warning, Isabelle raised her camera snapped a picture of Sylvia. Then she asked Sylvia to take a picture of her. Sylvia had never operated a camera in her life, but could not bring herself to offer such a frail excuse. Isabelle showed her exactly what to do and Sylvia snapped the picture and then did a very strange thing. She told Isabelle to turn sideways and look at the treetops and she rolled the film as she had seen Isabelle do and snapped another. Then she asked Isabelle if she could have a copy of that picture. Isabelle just smiled and said she had to get going or Walter would be worried about her. Sylvia helped her load her things into the car and Isabelle, still barefoot, drove off with no indication to Sylvia whether they would ever meet again.

About a week later Sylvia went to her mailbox and there was an envelope with no address and no stamp, just her name. Inside was the picture of herself, sitting in Isabelle's car, and the picture of Isabelle sitting on that stump looking off at the treetops. Sylvia brought out an album and turned to the page where she had mounted the pictures. She had not exaggerated. Isabelle was the most beautiful creature either of us had ever seen, but even more surprising was that when we looked at the picture of Sylvia, taken just a few years before that day, we saw an entirely different person, and from that time on, she looked different to us. Not old, not young, just Sylvia. This, I knew, was the gift a camera could bring when in the hands of the right person. I had known before, but that moment convinced me that I would take pictures. I would be an artist. I also knew that they were Isabelle's pictures I had found in our house.

The rest of the story of Walter and Isabelle Armstrong came to us piecemeal through a variety of sources. There were many variations, but the central theme was the same. Isabelle was ill and Walter was beside himself. He indulged her in every way, especially in her hobby of photography, and I finally realized that the strange room I had discovered was actually the darkroom where she developed her wonderful pictures. He did everything he could to keep her happy, probably praying he could keep her alive through his love. In the end, she died and Walter was left alone in that house. At some point, before or after Isabelle's death, he must have hired the very discreet carpenter he had used to build the darkroom to seal off the upstairs and remove the staircase. There were rumors surrounding her death. Some said that she killed herself to spare Walter the horror of watching her die. That theory struck a chord with Ethan and me as it gave a believable explanation for the gun and the pictures being sealed away where Walter would never have to see them again. We had to accept that theory at least for the time being, but we knew that when we were old enough we would be able to investigate further and learn the whole truth - and find Mary.

The summer after we graduated from high school we began our search in earnest. We were armed with the stack of Isabelle's pictures and an old jalopy we had purchased with money we received for graduation and part of the proceeds from odd jobs we had performed over the years. We were ready for battle. The plan was to leave early each morning and just drive in all directions until we found something that we could identify in one of the pictures. Isabelle wouldn't have traveled too far so we were convinced that we would find what we were looking for within a 30 mile radius of our town.

Ethan drove and I rode shotgun. Our first destination was the neighboring county. The farm dealer had told us of a farmer that had bought that exact model in 1934. He remembered because that was the only tractor he sold that year. The depression was in full swing at that time so not many could afford such an expenditure. The farmer's name was Jacob Smith, but that is all he could tell us. We were confident that we could easily find him and we were right. After we crossed the county line, we stopped at every farmhouse we came to, keeping our eyes peeled at all times for a site that would correspond with something in the pictures. At the fourth house we were rewarded with the information we sought. We were told Jacob lived about 15 miles south and to look for a big red barn on the right. Ethan drove slowly and I pierced the landscape with my eyes.

You might be wondering at this point just what it was we were going to do when we found Mary. Would we kidnap her and take her away from her family? Would we track down whoever has caused her bruises and kill him? What about her family? Would we just leave them there to suffer? The truth is, we had no idea what we would do when we found her. We just knew that she was out there waiting for her rescuers and we were not going to let her down. You should also know that under the passenger seat was the gun I had found so many years before and it was loaded with bullets Ethan had stolen from the mercantile. There was one other thing I knew for sure. Isabelle had taken that picture for a reason. She was not just chronicling human suffering. She had a plan, for that picture and that little girl. I was sure of it and I was going to finish that plan for her.

We arrived at the red barn and were able to stand on exactly the spot where Isabelle had stood to take the picture of the tractor. We could see the clump of trees in the background and the back of the shack that might be Mary's.

It is my hope that every man on this earth will at some moment experience the exhilaration, power and fear that I was feeling at that moment. This is how God intends for a man to feel at least once in his life. It creates a standard for all future experience. I had discovered what it meant to be a man and what I experienced at that moment defined me forever. I knew that, gimpy leg or not, I would achieve every dream I could imagine and I would never stop imagining. I felt like my heart would explode with the joy of my future and nothing could ever take that from me. I knew I could perform the mundane duties that would be a part of my life as magnificently as the heroic acts I would be called upon to perform.

It had been some twelve years since the picture was taken and Jacob Smith had purchased the tractor. We had no idea if he was dead or alive or what he knew about the occupants of the neighboring cabin, but we decided to see if we could talk to him before driving directly to the cabin. As we started walking toward the house, the front door opened and a man emerged and walked toward us accompanied by three border collies, all of whom seemed to be attached to him in some way. The four of them moved as one entity and the image they created was one of good health and energy. I felt encouraged and not the least bit hesitant about the prospect of explaining our mission to this man. Some people just inspire trust without even trying, besides which I have always trusted border collies as the best judge of character in humans, and it speaks well of any man who would choose that breed over the more aggressive killer types. As we drew nearer, I could see that the man was probably in his late fifties, but remarkably well built.

Ethan spoke first, asking the man if he could take a few minutes to visit with us and assured him that our mission was personal and we were not there to sell him anything. He laughed and invited us into the house for coffee where we were welcomed by his wife, Elena. She was every bit as wholesome and friendly as Jacob and I thought to myself that I had never seen a couple more suited to each other. Ethan and I had agreed that we would reveal no more than necessary to anyone about the details of our quest, but within minutes I found myself spilling my guts to these strangers and showing them not only the tractor picture, but that of Mary and her family. Ethan added that it was our mission to find Mary and help her if we could. We implored them to tell if they recognized Mary and if the cabin in the distance was her home.

I could hear the air rushing around my ears as Jacob and Elena silently searched each other's face for the way to proceed. Ethan and I knew we had come to the right place.

Finally, Elena spoke and began her story by telling us about Walter and Isabelle. This seemed a strange place to start, but neither Ethan nor I would say a word to interrupt her. She sat at the table folding and refolding a napkin as she spoke.

"First let me say that I feel both free and compelled to tell you this story for three reasons. The first is that I know you will never give up until you learn the truth anyway so I want you to have all the facts so that no one gets hurt. I also know that you would never do anything to hurt your Mary so all secrets will remain safe with the both of you. Most important is that we now know for sure that you are in possession of certain items that need to remain hidden and you need to know why. Besides, all the main players are dead now and have escaped the possible consequences of their actions.

Walter Armstrong and my Jacob had been friends since childhood, much like the two of you. I met them when we were all in college. Jacob and I fell in love and married after we graduated and returned here to run the family farm and care for Jacob's father in his final years. Walter came from a wealthy family and was charged with managing his late father's estate for the benefit of his mother, sister and himself. For this reason he decided to become an investment broker and make his home in New York City. When Jacob's father died he was left a modest sum and Walter managed that for us as well.

In the spring of 1929, Walter came to visit and surprised us by bringing his new wife, Isabelle with him. He also brought all of his family fortune and all of ours as well, in cash. He carried it in two valises and told us to keep our cash at home. He didn't even want us to trust the local bank. We followed his advice, although we thought he was being overly cautious. Months later, we were happy we did as the entire financial system fell apart. You can imagine how grateful we were to

Walter. Shortly thereafter, Walter bought the house in town and moved there with Isabelle.

We had wonderful times together. Every Sunday we would have dinner here at our house usually joined by our friends Frank and Sylvia. Yes, it is the same Sylvia you have known these past years. That is how we know as much about you two as we do. Sylvia is a wonderful woman, but she has not been totally truthful with you, and for good reasons.

Isabel loved to wander off by herself and take her wonderful pictures. Walter worried about her going out alone, but she insisted that other people were a distraction and she was usually gone for only a couple of hours in the afternoon. She would return with stories about her discoveries and we often would be treated to a showing of the photographs she had taken the week before. As you know, Walter had built a special room for her so that she could develop her own photographs at home. Not long after they moved here, Walter and Isabelle confided in the group that Isabelle was very ill and it was unlikely that she would live more than a few months. Frank, Sylvia's husband, had been fighting heart disease for three years prior, so I don't need to tell you there were some poignant moments among our band of six. Walter was devastated, but determined to make the most of whatever time they had and to fight for her life in any way possible. Isabelle worried more about Walter than she did about her own future. Sylvia and Frank were both optimistic about his chances, but faced their future together realistically, living their life fully and with great courage.

One Sunday afternoon, after the announcement of her illness, Isabelle took the car and struck out on her usual photographic excursion. You could see the pain in Walter's face at letting her out alone, but he never complained or tried to stop her. When she returned, she was visibly shaken and angry, but she wouldn't talk about her experience. She just told Walter to take her home with the excuse that she was feeling poorly. The following weekend Jacob and Walter were leaving for a ten day trip to New York City. Walter had some business to take care of and Jacob was going along to visit some old friends and get a look at some new farm equipment that was on display at the agricultural show upstate. It was agreed that Isabelle would stay with me while they were gone and Frank and Sylvia would come out the weekend after and stay until Walter and Jacob returned the following Wednesday.

All went well through the week. Isabelle and I had a wonderful time sewing, playing cards and tending the garden. She had brought the pictures she had taken the week before and I could see what had upset her so much. It was the picture of your Mary, all battered and bruised. Isabelle was determined to do something to help this little girl, but she didn't know what. When Sylvia and Frank arrived on Friday afternoon, Sylvia and Isabelle decided to take the picture to the county sheriff and see what could be done. The results were unsatisfactory as the sheriff was of the belief that a man had a right to anything he saw fit to keep peace and order in his own home. There would be no interference from his office. Isabelle was livid and unable to get the image of this poor family out of her mind.

On Sunday she took the car and left for her usual excursion after promising me that she would not go near that cabin where the girl lived. She even had a little spring in her step and seemed a lot more cheerful so I was pretty sure she was going to give it a rest. When she hadn't returned in over three hours, we became concerned and Frank went to look for her. He saw her car parked on the road leading to the girl's cabin and set out on foot to find her. As he rounded a corner and the cabin came into view, he was not prepared for what he found. Your little Mary and her mother were kneeling on the ground trying to revive Isabelle who was unconscious. Her camera was lying near her, but she had a gun in her hand. It took him a few moments to notice the body of a man a few feet away. He was clearly dead. Mary and her mother were covered with blood and bruises and crying over Isabelle. Frank rushed to her and was satisfied that she was alive, just unconscious. The mother told Frank in a very passive voice what had happened. Her husband had come home in the early hours of the morning, drunk as usual after his Saturday night party. He had passed out and when he awoke after noon, he began to yell and beat on Mary's mother. The younger children had been put down for a nap, as his behavior had a pattern and they had learned to keep the babies out of his way. Mary was trying to keep her father from beating on her mother and the struggle proceeded noisily to the front yard. Mary was getting beaten very badly when Isabelle emerged from the bushes with her camera, screaming at the father that she had pictures to prove his abuse and she would find some way to have him jailed. He chased after Isabelle with a shovel and she ran, but fell with him coming at her, the shovel raised in position to strike her. From her pocket, she pulled the gun and shot him in the head. The mother said Isabelle had started to get up, but then collapsed and had been unconscious for several minutes.

Frank was finally able to bring her around and Isabelle told him that she had been hiding in the bushes for a long time listening to his bellowing and the screams of Mary and her mother. When they brought the fight outside she had tried to distract him with her threats. She had known he was very dangerous, thus the gun and a firm resolve to use it if necessary. She showed no sign of remorse and her only concern was for Mary and her mother. Frank, on the other hand, knew that she was in grave danger of being prosecuted for murder as she was the intruder on private property. The fact that she had already gone to the sheriff and that she had come armed indicated premeditation. In fact, Frank himself was not sure that she hadn't come with the intent to kill him. He told Mary and the mother to go inside and keep the other children from coming out. He and Isabelle decided to bury the father and act like he had just run off abandoning his family. Mary and the mother preferred this story to the truth and promised to stick to it no matter what.

Frank and Isabelle returned that day dirty, sweaty and bloody. It was impossible for them to conceal the details of what had happened even though they wanted to shield us from that horror. They had dragged the body to a place far from the cabin and buried it covering the site with rocks and other debris to prevent it being exposed by scavengers. Isabelle begged us not to tell Walter what had happened as it would just add to his worries. Jacob had to be told because the body was buried on our property in a location scheduled for a new crop. It had to be moved to a spot that would never be tilled.

That was the last time Isabelle was able to visit our home. Her health deteriorated quickly after that. Walter moved her to a room on the first floor and hired that carpenter to seal off the upstairs offering no explanation. To this day we don't know if Isabelle told him about her crime. We knew that Isabelle must have hidden the gun and pictures where they were unlikely to be found. She died two months later and Sylvia's Frank soon after.

When the two of you started visiting Sylvia, she knew that you, Seth, lived in Isabelle's old house and had likely discovered something Isabelle had hidden, but she knew that it would be difficult for you to put all the pieces together. The father and brothers of the dead man made a bit of a fuss about his disappearance, but no one in authority cared to investigate further and the abandonment story was generally accepted.

Frank and Jacob went back to the cabin the following week. It was obvious that Mary's family needed help. Jacob had purchased a small parcel of land from a family in need of money in order to move and join relatives in another state. We hired the carpenter to build them a small cabin. Walter was called upon to help as well and did so as he had aided so many families in the past. He hired the mother to help care for Isabelle and marveled at the tenderness and devotion she showed his dying wife. Mary came to help as well, but refused to let Walter pay her. She spent hours sitting with Isabelle, talking in low tones and holding her hand. Both Mary and her mother were present with Walter at the moment of Isabelle's death.

Now you know the story behind your discovery and you are wondering what happened to your Mary. First you should know that her name actually is Mary. Her mother's name is Laura. Three years after the father's disappearance, Laura was able to obtain a divorce and she married our trusted carpenter. They now have two more children and are living a happy and prosperous life. Laura continued to care for Walter after Isabelle's death until Walter decided to return to New York and leave his pain behind. Jacob visited him several times in the years that followed. Each year it became more obvious that Walter was living the life of a hermit in the middle of the city. His home was in disarray and it was clear that he was not eating and sleeping properly. Clearly he was in jeopardy and something had to be done. Walter finally agreed to let Mary move in and be his caretaker while she attended high school. She has been there for the past four years and she is entering New York University this fall. She intends to become a photographer and journalist. Jacob has seen some of her photographs and is convinced she somehow absorbed Isabelle's gift for capturing life on film. She is an excellent student and has a real aptitude for writing so there is little doubt that she will be successful in her plan."

Jacob had left the room and returned with a picture album. As we looked through the pages there were pictures of he and Walter, then Elena was added and finally Isabelle. Sylvia and Frank came later and then Isabelle and Frank disappeared. The last page had one photo-that of Walter and Mary. Jacob said he had taken the picture less than a month before as the three of them were dressed to go out to dinner and the theater. If Ethan and I each had five pairs of eyes, it wouldn't have been enough so hard were we working to absorb every feature of our dear Mary. She was small standing next to Walter, but she appeared strong and formidable in a very feminine way. The look of determination was still in her eyes, but was softened and there was no hint of fear or anger. She was exquisite and it was abundantly clear that this girl/woman did not need rescuing.

Jacob removed the picture and handed it to me. There was such kindness in this gesture and understanding in his eyes. He understood love and he remembered the ardent desire of a young man to be a hero to one he loves. As I stared at the picture I realized that it was Mary who rescued Ethan and me. It was our joint resolve to find and save her that had taken me through my injury and carried us both through what could have been some lonely years. Ethan and I had been bound together by our quest and that gave us both the strength and support we needed to go beyond our own troubles and live for another. It was because of her that we had developed into young men rather than self-centered adolescents.

Elena wanted to know what we were going to do with our knowledge. Would we find Mary and tell our story bringing her back to those painful times and renewing her fear that the details of that afternoon would be exposed? The gun and the picture were outside in our jalopy. What would we do with them? She knew the answers or she wouldn't have told the story. I retrieved the gun and turned it over to them as well as all the pictures, all but the one I carried with me at all times. I asked her to give the camera to Mary, but she insisted that I keep it even though I had since purchased a new one. Mary had her own memories of Isabelle. The camera would bring her pain.

We found that there was nothing else to be said. After a few awkward moments, we made our way to our vehicle accompanied by Jacob and his band of adoring canines. I felt such joy that Mary had found her way, yet I knew that my dreams had been wiped out at the same time. How would I replace her in my life? Jacob drew me aside and put his arm around me and, in a tone so low I could hardly her him, told me that I would meet her someday. Her name was Mary Collins and she would be a photographer as I was planning to be. Jacob whispered "Isabelle will find a way to bring you together, Mary still needs you".

I drove home while Ethan stared at the picture Jacob had given us. Neither of us spoke until we reached his house. He didn't get out right away. Finally, he looked at me and asked "Does this change our plans?" He was wondering if our friendship had been based on anything beyond our Mary adventure. As looked at him I wondered how I had failed to notice how much he had changed since first entering my life. Ethan was no longer a homely, skinny, freaky looking kid. He was not what anyone would consider handsome, but he had a look all his own that would carry him well. He had a strong jaw and what women (lots of women) later told him were "puppy dog" eyes. His face had grown into his smile and his appearance was what I would later refer to as "arresting". Yes, I knew Ethan had some good years ahead of him and there was no way I was going to let him go his way without me. My response was "Kiss my ass, jerk. You aren't getting rid of me just because I'm a gimp. Are you afraid I'll cramp your style?" He slugged my arm as he got out of the car and left with a huge smile. I was happy and excited to get on with our plans, but there was one more thing to clear up.

I found my mother at home, alone as Margaret was enrolled in secretarial school and dad was still at work. I had never asked her about the picture and what she knew about my accident. She never approached the subject with me either, but it had occurred to me on the drive home that perhaps there was another discovery by another person in our family. My dad had hired that same carpenter to build a staircase and re-open the second floor shortly after my accident. They had purchased the house from Walter and had never explained how they come by the sudden good fortune that had indirectly resulted in my permanent injury. I asked her point blank why she had covered for me all these years when she knew very well I had been upstairs prior to my accident. She answered right away as if she had been expecting the question that very afternoon. Apparently, dad had accepted Walter's story that the upstairs was unfinished and unusable. Mom, on the other hand had her suspicions which were reinforced when she met the sister of the carpenter who claimed that her brother had been hired by Walter Armstrong more than once to work on the second floor. My mother had formed the idea that if there were finished rooms available, she could rent them out to boarders and make some extra money for the family. She had made the same journey up the ladder as I had and she had found a treasure of her own. In the bathroom under the sink she found something wrapped in an old piece of cloth and bound with some twine. It was a stack of money, nearly three thousand dollars. She did not tell my dad about the money because she knew he would make her try to discover the owner, but when her brother was dying a few weeks after her discovery, she went to visit him in the hospital. I remembered her being gone for several days. When she returned, she told my father that her brother had stashed money and told her where to find it. She said he wanted her to have it. She added that he asked her to keep it a secret as there were others in the family that might be angry about his choice of beneficiary. My dad bought the story, contacted Walter and bought the house.

Obviously, Walter had not planted the money there and from mother's description, it was wrapped in the same material as my own treasure. I am convinced that since Walter had converted his wealth to cash before the crash, Isabelle had decided to get some of this money to Mary's family, but was too ill to make the journey. Maybe she forgot it was there or maybe she was waiting for Jacob to come and complete her errand. It is possible that she hid that money right after the incident, but when she saw that the family was being cared for, she planned to return the money to Walter's stash. Walter most likely was so overcome with grief that he never missed the money or thought he had made an error in his accounts. It is doubtful that Walter cared much about anything but Isabelle at that time.

I promised to keep my mother's secret as she had kept mine. I shared Isabelle and Mary's story with her and showed her the picture of Mary and Walter. She cried for an hour, but she told me that forever in her mind, she would be living in Isabelle's house. The idea pleased her very much. Neither of us ever considered discussing the issue with Walter and repaying the money.

My memories of Seth are the most vivid and complete of any that I have experienced, but for a long time, I thought I would never learn more about what happened in Seth's life from that point on. Then about two years ago I was watching a rerun of MASH when Seth visited one more time. He had been earning his living as a freelance photographer for a number of years. He and Ethan were still the best of friends. They had befriended a girl named Sally during Ethan's college years and, as before with Mary, they were both enchanted by the same girl. In the end, Sally married Ethan, he being the most stable of the two, and she bore him three children in four years, thus limiting his ability to share in Seth's life. At no time was there any jealousy or friction between Seth and Ethan regarding Sally and, as time passed and Sally became more the doting mother and housewife and less the adventuresome companion, Seth considered it a blessing that he had dodged that bullet. Ethan was happily working for an engineering firm and performing the role of husband and father exactly as Sally demanded. Seth knew that he was destined for a different life and a different kind of woman.

Over the years, Seth had established relationships with a number of publications that paid handsomely for his freelance photos of world events. He was able to travel to wherever something was happening. The editors he worked with knew that if Seth was there, they would get photos that would connect with their readers and they were willing to pay for them.

The day Seth reappeared to me again, he was in Korea. The war was in full swing and Seth had been traveling about taking photos of the action and trying to put together a real scenario of what was going on for the people back home. In the process, he had been injured in the shoulder by a piece of shrapnel and was transported to a MASH unit for treatment. He had been there about a week and was recovering nicely.

He had managed to befriend some of the doctors and nurses, many of whom had initially resented having to spend their time on a civilian when there were so many injured soldiers to deal with. On this particular day, word had come that a film crew would be arriving to do a story on the brave personnel working under such dire conditions to save lives. No one was particularly impressed with this prospect because it had been done before and nothing had improved. The crew was to arrive by helicopter around three in the afternoon and would be staying overnight and returning to Seoul the next morning.

Just before three o'clock the shelling started in an area not far from the camp. At three o'clock the helicopter came into view and the shelling was following it in. The chopper landed about fifty yards outside of the camp and the shells were falling all around it. It was obvious that it had become a target. The doors opened and several people tumbled out and began running toward the camp and what shelter it could provide. Seth was taking pictures as fast as possible when he saw one of the crew collapse and grab his lower leg. Seth was the closest to the victim and, without thinking twice he dropped his camera and ran to help. Shells were falling everywhere and Seth's bad leg was slowing him down, but he was thinking in those moments that he was exactly where he was supposed to be. He knew that it was he, gimpy leg and all that had to save this man. The reason didn't matter, it just was. He reached the crewman and threw him over his shoulder, surprised at how light he seemed, but then he remembered his mother lifting that oil barrel off his leg all by herself so many years before. He ran for what seemed to be a mile back to safety.

Miraculously he made it to shelter and collapsed on top of the victim. A medic had already reached the spot where he landed and began examining the injury. It was a leg wound, but not severe, at least not by MASH standards. Seth recovered his strength and bent down to tell the victim that he would be Ok. In doing so he found himself looking into a familiar pair of eyes.

He choked back his tears and said "Hello, Mary Collins, my name is Seth."

That's all there is folks, but I can tell you that there is no doubt in my mind that Seth and Mary spent the rest of their lives together- and something else, my right leg is shorter than my left. Although this does not cause me to limp, it does make me run like a girl. Just kidding, I would run that way anyway.

Chapter Twenty-Two

SAM AND BERNIE SHARE AN EVENING

SAM

What a great story and what a relief from Bernie's earlier speech and Adrian's outburst. Everyone kept begging for more details about Seth and Mary once they were united, but Alfie could add nothing except his own belief that they shared their life from that point on. I was sorry that Amanda and Etienne were not there to hear the story. Amanda would have loved it and I was sure that Etienne would have identified with Seth, Bernie had sat with his head down for most of the story. Alfie sat down beside Jenny and Bernie finally looked up and glared at Alfie as if he wanted to do him bodily harm. I couldn't imagine what he could have found offensive in that story, but apparently Bernie sees things differently than everyone else. I dreaded our evening together even more than before. I had not the slightest idea what I was going to say to him to get him to change his behavior and I was getting more nervous by the minute.

My question for the group was whether others had such a detailed memory of another life. The consensus was that in many cases the memories were glimpses of events rather than a life story, but each had at least one particular character that they knew better than the rest. I looked forward to hearing the other stories. I wondered if it was these characters that had the most influence over their current lives. I also wondered what Amanda's story would be and I felt ashamed that I didn't already know.

Alfie's story had taken the better part of the afternoon so we adjourned to get some personal time off before our pizza party. Everyone went their separate ways until five o'clock when we gathered for the happy hour. Amanda and Antoinette returned about that time in good spirits. It seems the wound on Etienne's leg was not quite as bad as initially thought so the doctors felt they could cast the leg on Thursday at which time he could be released. Our island doctor volunteered to make house calls to check on Etienne as necessary. I wondered if his offer had anything to do with the many charms of Antoinette. The doctor was a widower and beautiful single women were not plentiful on this island. It didn't occur to me that Amanda was a very attractive single woman as well since I never really accepted the fact that we were not a couple. On the other hand, the doctor might have been curious about the goings-on up here and viewed it as an opportunity to get the inside scoop. Last on my list was that he was just a dedicated professional.

The pizza party was an unqualified success. Serena had prepared a huge variety of toppings and cheeses and three different sauces which could be combined in an infinite number of ways to suit everyone's taste. She had par-baked three dozen small crusts and we each created our own masterpieces. A vote was taken and Adrian's was voted the best of the best. Hers was a Greek pizza with a creamy pesto sauce, artichokes, Greek olives, spinach, and those white cheeses that I have never been able to identify. My own entry was more traditional-good, but no creativity involved. We had a selection of wines and beer and everyone gorged themselves.

Eight o'clock came much too quickly, but I was determined to get Bernie alone and set him straight. Amanda confided that she was pretty sure I was taking him to the boat as part of a plan to drown him and she volunteered her services to hold him while I tied him up and attached the concrete shoes. I declined her offer but reserved the right to change my mind at a later date. Everyone knew what was going on so there was no need to excuse ourselves when it came time to leave. Bernie had behaved wonderfully during the pizza party, almost charming, and was telling everyone how anxious he was to see my boat. On the short ride he chattered giddily and I found myself relaxing a bit, even congratulating myself on the brilliance of my scheme to turn the unpleasantness around.

I gave Bernie the tour of the boat which didn't take long since it consists of a large aft cabin, a head, a guest cabin and head, and the main salon which is open to the galley. He remarked about the beauty of the teak floors and paneling and declared that he could easily make this his home. When we entered the aft cabin, my bedroom, he went bonkers. I have to admit it is pretty plush, but Bernie went well beyond that. He said he had never seen anything so perfect-truly a man's room. He asked if Amanda liked it and I ignored the question.

I poured us each an eighteen year old single malt scotch and grabbed a couple of cigars, not my finest but acceptable, and we headed for the back deck to enjoy the night air. That lasted for about three minutes because the night air also contained the night mist. It was cold and damp so we went indoors to the salon. Bernie plopped down in my favorite chair and I sat opposite him on the couch. We didn't speak for a while but the silence was not awkward. For a short time it seemed like we were a couple of friends enjoying a quiet moment. Of course, Bernie couldn't leave anything that pleasant alone. He downed his drink and held his glass up for a refill. I guess he didn't understand the basics of sipping fine liquor.

As I was pouring him another drink I asked if he was enjoying his experience so far. He replied that he would not have missed it for the world. He added that he thought he was making a real contribution to the group. I choked on my cigar and asked "How so?" He pointed out that no one else seemed to be able to get the others to show their true selves. He used Adrian as an example and contended that her earlier outburst was more indicative of her true character than all her gushing over Etienne and her older but wiser routine. I asked Bernie if it was just possible that Adrian is just as she seems and that her outburst was a result of his negativity. He offered no response and I was beginning to think that perhaps I was getting through to him. A couple more minutes of silence passed as Bernie stood and moved about the room, the ashes from his cigar falling heedlessly on the teak floor he had so admired. He gulped down his second drink and then asked if I had any plain old bourbon, adding that he didn't have a taste for scotch. He could have fooled me with the way he bolted his drinks and, once again I regretted wasting the good stuff on him.

I handed him a full bottle of the cheapest bourbon I had and a glass of ice. He poured himself an obscenely large drink and set the bottle on the table next to my favorite chair that was once again occupied by his skinny ass. He was still ignoring the ashtray I had provided and the ashes were falling onto his pants. I knew it was too much to hope that the ashes were hot enough to set him on fire so I just decided to ignore his carelessness and clean up the mess later. The situation was deteriorating rapidly. I could feel Bernie staring at me and I wasn't about to let him make me feel uncomfortable so I looked him square in the eye and asked him why he thought it was beneficial to the group to antagonize people. He ignored the question and commented that it must be painful for me to go to all this trouble and expense to bring everyone here only to watch Amanda come on to Glen. He said he felt sorry for me and wondered how long I was going to go on kidding myself that I would ever get her into my fancy bedroom.

I was speechless and amazed at how easy it had been for him to suck me in. I wished to hell I had taken Amanda up on her offer, only drowning would be too easy a death for him. I was determined to control my anger and I was proud and surprised when I spoke to find that my voice sounded calm. I informed Bernie that our arrangement was not working out and that it would be best if he left first thing in the morning. I offered to pay him for three weeks even though it had only been four days. I put it as nicely as possible, but informed him that he was a detriment to the group and there was no benefit whatsoever to continue to include him. I rose and walked to the window to allow him a little privacy with his thoughts. As I gazed at the window, the night was black and all I could see was my own reflection and that of Bernie in my chair. I could see him leaning forward as if to rest his head in his hands, but he never stopped leaning forward. The next thing I knew, he was lying in the floor in the fetal position wailing like a baby. OK, this I did not expect. I turned around and just stood there with no inclination as to what to do. I suppose my normal response would be to offer some sort of comfort, perhaps a hand on the shoulder, but this was repugnant to me after what he had said. Instead I just sat down on the couch and stared at him. The wails became sobs and the sobs finally evolved into a voice.

Bernie began telling me that he had never found a place where he felt welcome. He had never had a best friend and he had begun to believe that I would be that person. He said he knew he had trouble connecting with people and in spite of his words to the contrary, he really did want to have a life that included other people. He had thought that perhaps this group would provide that opportunity. He went on to say that he had not taken vacation time from his job, but had actually quit his job in the belief that he would be moving on to a better life. He had nothing to go back to. He fell into silence, but continued lying on the floor in that same pathetic position. I thought I would give him time to compose himself before I said anything. Several minutes had passed before I got up and looked down at him and discovered he had fallen asleep.

The last thing in the world I wanted to do was wake him up so I grabbed a pillow off the couch and placed it by his head in case he woke up. Then I threw my grandmother's afghan over him and went to my quarters to bed. By morning I had made my decision, Bernie would not be sent packing, at least not yet. I went out to the galley to make coffee and found that he had moved to the couch, which was fine except that he had also removed his clothes and was lying there uncovered and buck naked next to the empty bourbon bottle. The afghan had fallen on the floor so I picked it up and carefully covered him. It was very important to me that he would not know that I had seen him physically naked. Seeing him emotionally naked the night before was bad enough, but the physical spectacle was something I wanted to pretend never happened.

I had nothing there for breakfast since all my meals were taken at the house and I was grateful that we had that as an excuse to leave. Serena wanted us all there by nine a.m. and it was close to that by then. Bernie opened his bloodshot eyes and accepted a cup of coffee. I told him we had to leave in a few minutes and that I would jump through the shower and he could do the same when I had finished. He declined and asked when the next ferry was leaving and how he would get to the airport when he arrived in Seattle. I responded that it didn't matter because he was staying and I told him to get dressed so we could get breakfast. Not another word was spoken about the night before.

When we got to the house, everyone was up and about. Antoinette borrowed the Escalade and left immediately for the hospital. Bernie said he was skipping breakfast and went to his room to shower and change. He did not come out for the rest of the morning. Amanda cornered me and asked how things had gone the night before. I couldn't bring myself to tell her the whole ugly story so I told her that I thought we had reached a meeting of the minds and let it go at that. I guess there is honor among men. I didn't want to tell her about Bernie's tearful breakdown and I sure as hell didn't want to mention the condition I had found him in that morning. She seemed disappointed that I hadn't sent him away, but she didn't appear to hold it against me. Instead she gave me a sly smile as if to confirm my own suspicions that I had been played like a fiddle.

After breakfast Serena announced that she needed to take the ferry to Port Townsend to pick up a few groceries. It seems she had grossly underestimated our capacity for consumption and needed to fill in on some staples. Adrian said that she wanted to make a few phone calls where the cell phone reception was more reliable and that she would enjoy the opportunity to accompany her. Bernie showed no sign of emerging from his room and Etienne was in the hospital so our group was seriously diminished and I saw no point in having a morning session. Glen and Kate hitched a ride with Serena into the village to check out the bookstore and try out the lunch menu at the Sandcastle with a leisurely walk back. Jenny called Paul and he was only too happy to accommodate her request to take her and Alfie for a tour of the island since the kite shop was closed on Mondays. Amanda was going to stay at the house and enjoy some quiet time, but Antoinette begged her to accompany her to the hospital. This was uncharacteristic of Antoinette and I wondered at the time what was on her mind. I had a sense then that something unwelcome was going to happen, but nothing could have prepared me for the revelations that would take place that day.

I was perfectly content to spend my free time in the den with my book. After everyone left, I tiptoed to the kitchen for a cup of coffee to take with me taking great pains not to wake Bernie and spoil my few hours of freedom. With all that had happened with Etienne and the incredible nuisance of Bernie, I was feeling a little apprehensive about the way things were going. The group, as a whole, was getting along famously and I was glad that I had left the time frame open-ended since we were forced to take so much time off from our sessions. Overall, I believed that things would settle down and we would get to the heart of the matter when Etienne was released and we could all be together again. I wondered if I was providing enough leadership to the group, but I also wanted to keep things informal so that everyone would feel comfortable. I finally came to the conclusion that, when all was said and done, my part in the progression of this event was minimal and that I would have little to do with the outcome. On that note, I dug out my Grisham novel and settled into Patrick's overstuffed armchair for a few hours of escapism.

I fell asleep with my coffee cup in my hand and my glasses resting on the tip of my nose. I was having some kind of disturbing dream and awoke with a start to find myself looking into a pair of beautiful green eyes. Antoinette had returned alone and was sitting on the ottoman in front of my chair. I don't know how long she had been there, but I was relieved when I checked my chin and confirmed that I wasn't drooling. My immediate concern was for Etienne, hoping he had not taken a turn for the worse. She assured me he was fine and everything was going according to schedule. She needed to speak with me about a different matter. She looked exhausted and I guess desolate would be the appropriate word. We all knew there was something going on with Antoinette and I had always suspected she had some sort of health issue. I didn't want to hear whatever she was going to tell me, but I wanted to help her if I could.

Chapter Twenty-Three

ANTOINETTE'S SECRET

ANTOINETTE

"Sam, I can tell by the way you look at me at times that you have concerns about my health. You treat me like a porcelain doll, but I can assure you, I am not breakable. I do have problems though and I don't know what to do. I have to enlist your help. You see, I have been lying to my son all these years. His father did die before he was born, but I didn't know that until two weeks ago.

I met Andrew McGill while vacationing in Spain. We had what you Americans would call a whirlwind romance and were married three months later at my home in Dijon, France. I was blissfully happy. My husband was exciting, handsome and very wealthy. For the next six months my life was perfect. We traveled all over Europe and enjoyed all the pleasures available to the young and the rich. I had never had any extra money available to me before and I loved the way I looked in fine clothes. I discovered a vanity in myself that I didn't know existed and Andrew made it possible to feed that vanity. Andrew had great style and was only too happy to dress me up as a complement to him. We wandered from one fashionable resort to another, showing each other off to jealous onlookers. At least we assumed they were jealous. In reality we probably looked like a couple of silly peacocks. After a while, I became bored with that parade and wanted to settle down and begin our real life together.

I finally convinced Andrew to take me to meet his family in Scotland, and there my fragile new world began to fall apart. The family owns a very large import/ export business along with several other smaller enterprises. Andrew's brother, John had taken on the responsibility for running their empire and Andrew had put himself in charge of spending the money. When we returned to Scotland the family believed that Andrew had finally matured and would begin to accept more responsibilities. I assumed we would settle down, set up a home and raise a family.

We moved into the guest house on his parents' estate and it suited me perfectly. It was large enough for the two of us and several children. I had a maid and a gardener, but I did my own cooking and helped expand the gardens. I got along nicely with his family, especially John who was brilliant, kind and committed to the family. Meaghan, his wife was an absolute treasure and I loved spending time with them.

Things were fine for a few months until I became pregnant at which time Andrew began to show just how selfish and immature he really was. He had taken a position in the business and put on as good a face as he could, but I started to suspect that he was too irresponsible to give the business his full attention and too selfish and narcissistic to share the spotlight with a child. He wanted to be the only child in my life. Nevertheless, I felt safe and cared for by the family and believed that Andrew's good cheer and boundless energy would make up for his shortcomings. Our child would have a good home and unlimited opportunities, and I was still charmed and very much in love with my husband despite his character flaws.

As the pregnancy wore on, Andrew became restless and irritable. He certainly did not share in the belief that a woman was at her most beautiful when pregnant. He told me I was repugnant and boring and he couldn't stay in the same room with me, let alone the same bed. I was ashamed, and still am, at my lack of judgment in marrying this man without giving a second thought to the kind of father he would make. I had been drawn in by his good looks, charm and fortune. To this day I find it hard to believe I could have been so superficial. I am so ashamed of my foolishness.

Andrew would disappear for days at a time and when he was home he ranted and raved about how I had misrepresented myself to him and was ruining his life. Finally, he came to me and told me he wanted a divorce and that he wanted nothing more to do with me or our child. I refused to divorce him, at least until our baby was born. I guess I hoped that when he saw his own flesh and blood and my body returned to its former glory, he would want us again.

For several days before Etienne was born, Andrew was nowhere to be found. John and Meaghan sat with me at the hospital through my labor and the delivery. I never saw Andrew again nor did his family. He had disappeared along with a considerable amount of money from the family business. His parents were embarrassed and ashamed and went out of their way to be kind to me, but they displayed very little real interest in me or Etienne. I stayed on for a few months, but I was lonely and felt we were a constant reminder of their son's selfish cruelty.

Finally, I decided to return to Dijon where I had friends and my sister Aurelia was still living there at the time. We had lost our parents in a car accident several years before and Aurelia is my only living relative. John looked into a divorce for me, but it was never finalized since we couldn't find Andrew to sign the papers. I didn't care. I just wanted to be free of him. The family settled on a generous annual stipend for Etienne and me. John has always been responsible for seeing that our needs are met and we have maintained a long-distance friendship over the years. John lost his wife to cancer three years ago. They never were able to have children, which leaves Etienne as the only heir to the family fortune once John passes away.

Two weeks ago John called me to tell me that Andrew was dead. As it turns out, my story to Etienne about his father dying before he was born was not a complete lie. Andrew's body was discovered in a shallow grave not far from the family home. He had been buried there at the time he disappeared. He has been dead all these years. When you called to see if Etienne could join this group, I had just received another call from John informing me that I was a possible suspect in Andrew's murder. In your country I would be called a "person of interest". The police had been to see John to discover my whereabouts. Andrew's parents had told the police that John was responsible for our financial arrangements so he would be the one to talk to. John had been putting them off but I knew it would be a matter of days before the police showed up on my doorstep in Toronto and I needed time to think and a place to go where Etienne wouldn't be involved. Your offer created the perfect opportunity to disappear until I could decide what to do.

I did not kill my husband and I have no clue as to who did, but I can see why I would be a suspect. Too many people had witnessed his cruel treatment of me to allow me to escape suspicion. Andrew's parents might actually believe I am guilty, but John believes in my innocence and has offered to hire the best solicitor available to represent me. As yet, I have not been charged, but he believes I need to get back to Scotland and try to clear myself of suspicion before things get out of hand. John and I agree that the best course would be for me to turn myself in for questioning, but I need to know that Etienne is safe in a place where he cannot be found. My Sister cannot shield him, as she will surely be questioned as to our whereabouts. I haven't told her or anyone except Father Karl where we are and it is doubtful that the authorities would think to question him.

My concern is that Andrew's parents would try to locate Etienne if I were to go to trial and try to get custody since they now know that Andrew is dead and Etienne is the heir to their fortune. John says that is already being discussed. I can't let that happen to Etienne, but I have no one I can trust except you, Amanda and Adrian to protect him. I want to leave immediately for Scotland and I am asking you to keep Etienne safe for me. I have told my story to Amanda and she assured me that you would help. She also helped me tell Etienne the truth. I told him everything except the part about me being a suspect. He thinks I am going to Scotland to deal with the legal issues surrounding the estate. I can't bear to have him worry about me. Father Karl will be the contact person, as I don't want to leave any kind of trail that could allow the family or anyone else to locate Etienne. If I am charged and held for trial, Father Karl will come for him and see that he is placed somewhere safe. He is very fond of Etienne and he seems to have a flair for intrigue. In the meanwhile I hope that Etienne can stay here and continue with the group. I know this is a lot to ask of you, but I don't know what else to do."

SAM

I pushed my Grisham novel aside. There was plenty of drama all around me, I didn't need more. Antoinette looked lost and distraught, and I could see the toll this was taking on her. I was slightly annoyed by Amanda's presumption that I would agree to the plan, but in reality, I couldn't imagine myself saying no. I have to admit that, for a brief moment I wondered if Antoinette had killed Andrew, but even so, how could I refuse to help Etienne? If Antoinette was charged with murdering her husband, it might be in the Toronto papers and, if the family was that wealthy and powerful, it would likely make international news. I couldn't let Etienne be exposed to that kind of notoriety and run the risk of him being sent to live with a family that had shown little concern for him over the years. All this was going through my mind as I looked into her sad face. Etienne would stay and he would be protected.

I asked Antoinette if we could share her story with Adrian, since she would likely be his closest friend during her absence. She agreed wholeheartedly and gave me a weak smile as she added that she couldn't imagine anyone getting past Adrian to get to Etienne.

The next two hours were spent online booking her flights. She would leave from Seattle at noon the next day. I volunteered Amanda to accompany her on the morning ferry and drive her to the airport, adding that I was certain Amanda would want it that way. (It occurred to me then how easy it was to make presumptions.) I drove Antoinette back to the hospital and picked up Amanda so that Antoinette could spend what might be the last evening for a very long time with her son. I promised to return for Antoinette later that night.

I waited in the Escalade while Antoinette entered the hospital and it was less than five minutes later that Amanda emerged. She was a basket case. The scene of Etienne and Antoinette together for what might be the last time was hard enough to witness, but the idea that Antoinette had to go through the next few weeks, alone and friendless, put her over the edge. I reminded her that John would be there for her, but even I was not convinced that a member of Andrew's family could offer the support Antoinette would need. When I informed Amanda that she would be the one to take Antoinette to the airport, she broke down the rest of the way. She was terribly upset at the prospect, but I pointed out that she was the person closest to Antoinette and she would just have to pull herself together. I knew she would, but I wondered if by tomorrow morning her eyes would be too puffy to see to drive. Another stupid thought best left to myself.

Dinner was a quiet event as it was obvious to everyone that something was amiss. Jenny and Alfie gave a lively account of their adventures on their island tour. Paul joined us for dinner, but left shortly after, perhaps a bit uncomfortable with the undercurrent. Bernie never said a word the entire evening which ordinarily would have been cause for celebration, but in this instance, it was barely noticed. Amanda agreed that we should include Serena in our secret as she could be a valuable ally to tip us off should strangers come to the island asking questions about Etienne. We helped Serena clean up after dinner and invited her and Adrian to take a ride with us to the boat. Not a word was spoken from the four of us until we were settled in the salon. Adrian and Serena knew something was up, but waited for us to begin.

I took the lead as Amanda collapsed into my favorite chair so recently occupied by Bernie. (I wondered if she would have chosen that spot if she knew he was the prior occupant.) I told the story as it was told to me. Serena, true to her name, serenely stated that we were doing the right thing and she would help in any way possible. She volunteered her car to Amanda to take Antoinette to the airport so that the Escalade could remain on the island for the hospital visits. Serena had a motorcycle and she assured us she would be happy to ride it to and fro for a couple of days. Adrian was silent for a few minutes, but I could see that her heart was about to leap out of her chest. Her only comment was that anyone trying to get to Etienne would have to go through her. That pretty much ended the conversation and we proceeded to the hospital to collect Antoinette. Adrian suggested that she go in alone to bring her out, keeping the drama to a minimum. I don't think I could have endured the parting of mother and son and I know Amanda couldn't either.

Several minutes passed before they both emerged composed and collected. Once again I was witnessing that strength that women display when facing a crisis with a child. Amanda and Serena followed suit and the drive back to the house was spent attending to the practical matters that needed to be dealt with. Amanda told Antoinette she would help her pack her bags and everyone should get a good night's sleep. I was dismissed and gratefully retreated to the den where I decided to spend the night on the couch in case I was needed.

I awoke at six a.m. with a sore back and a feeling of dread. Serena was already in the kitchen preparing an early breakfast for the girls. She looked terrible and I suspected she hadn't slept a wink. I took my coffee to the deck and was enjoying the cool air when Amanda and Antoinette arrived. I checked out Amanda's eyes to satisfy myself that she would be able to make the trip. They were predictably puffy, but not swollen shut. Antoinette was quiet and distant. She was clearly already on her journey in her mind if not with her body. They left in plenty of time to catch the ferry and that was that. Amanda planned to spend the night in Seattle so she could visit with Samantha and fill her in on the details of our gathering. Samantha had called the house several times to see what we were doing so this was a good opportunity to satisfy her curiosity and to convince Alex and Tiffany that the environment was suitable for a visit from Samantha in a week or two. I guessed that it would not be a good idea to clue them in on Antoinette's problem.

I had a quiet breakfast with Adrian and we decided to tell the rest of the group the same story as Etienne, leaving out the ugly details. I had the distinct impression that they all knew we were holding back, but no one questioned our explanation including Bernie who couldn't have cared less what was going on outside of his nasty little world.

ADRIAN

I couldn't say for sure whether or not Antoinette did her husband in, but I did know that she is an excellent mother and this boy needed to be protected and I intended to do my part. I have been fortunate to be sheltered and protected all my life, first by my father and then by my husband. Antoinette had to face the world alone and if she made mistakes, it isn't for me to judge her. I just prayed that everything would turn out well for her sake as well as Etienne's. In the meanwhile, Etienne was in the right place. There isn't a person here, with the exception of Bernie, that wasn't willing and able to protect him and make this situation easier for him. Speaking of Bernie, he had been silent all morning but I doubted that he had "seen the Light" as a result of his conversation with Sam. His nastiness was too much a part of him to remain submerged. I vowed to keep a sharp eye on him and do bodily harm if he tried to take advantage of Etienne's vulnerability to turn him into a Bernie clone.

I had another issue to bring up with Sam, but that was not the right time. While we were in Port Townsend I called my granddaughter in Portland. As I mentioned before, she writes short stories and I have always believed they were rooted in experiences from her past lives. She was the one who encouraged me to come here. Well, she finally admitted to me yesterday as I was going on and on about this wonderful experience, that she too has the memories and asked if it was too late to join the group. I didn't know how Sam would feel about this. I thought he may have been a little overwhelmed as it was and might be reluctant to add another personality to the mix. I did hope it could be arranged because I believed April would fit in very well and her presence would be mutually beneficial.

April is a bit of an anomaly in today's world. On the one hand, she is capable and independent to the point of being headstrong, reflecting the attitudes and life choices of modern women. Yet, she is also very traditional in her values. She believes in personal responsibility and that the greatest shame lies in not living up to our potential. She abhors those who whine and dwell on the negatives. She believes that God blesses us all, but expects us to use his gifts. Her prayers are for strength and courage to carry out God's purpose for her. She does not believe she deserves more from life than she is willing to earn and she believes that we should thank God for the things that didn't happen to us in our lives as well as the blessings He provides. With her strong beliefs, she also tends to be a little impatient with those who won't accept responsibility for their own lives. She has a nose for irony that sometimes borders on sarcasm, but she is never unkind or cruel. Rather, she uses words in a humorous way to expose the listener to his own inconsistencies and she is just as likely to use this method to expose her own follies as those of others. For this reason, her friends trust her to get her point across while making them laugh at themselves and allowing them to laugh at her. She loves people but hates crowds and her friendships include individuals from a variety of occupations, religions, economic circumstances and political persuasions. Her only requirements for friendship are honesty, a good sense of humor and the ability to have clearly defined values without taking oneself too seriously. As you can tell, I like her a lot. At the age of twenty seven, she demonstrates more understanding of what moves people than many of us will ever have.

April makes a modest, but consistent living from her short stories. This is not a genre that typically generates the big bucks, although she is quick to point out that most novels today are really nothing more than expanded short stories. Many popular novels can be read in one evening and some of the more prolific novelists write the same story over and over with different characters and settings. They build a template and just drop in the variables. April is not critical of these authors as she is a total capitalist and will admire anyone who finds a need and fills it as long as it is legal and ethical. I decided to wait a couple of days until Etienne was back and settled in and then approach Amanda to get her thoughts about April joining the group. I didn't want to put Sam in an uncomfortable position, but I promised April I would ask. Besides, I knew that if Amanda liked the idea, Sam would likely go along with it.

I love watching those two. There is such love and tenderness between them. They do tend to push at each other, but never too hard. I get a kick out of the way they anticipate one another's reactions and volunteer each other's services without asking. It is a little game they play and neither will be the one to disappoint. I suspect that before this experiment has ended they will be sharing more than meals. I got a good look at Sam's cabin on the boat and it is certainly an environment that would have lit my fires a few years back. I hate to brag, but Clive and I could have put that facility to good use in our day.

Chapter Twenty-Four

GAMES, GAMES, AND MORE GAMES

SAM

Adrian left for the hospital to spend the afternoon and evening with Etienne and, with Amanda in Seattle, once again we decided to forego the sessions for the day and occupy ourselves in other ways. Rain had set in so no one felt like going outdoors. Jenny suggested we spend the day playing poker. To my surprise the group responded enthusiastically, including Serena. She provided us with dried pasta to use as currency; macaroni for quarters, rotini for half dollars and fusilli for dollars. Everyone was given a twenty dollar dish of pasta. We had a blast. Serena told everyone to wash their hands before playing because she would have to re-use the pasta for dinner. I knew Serena to be a thrifty person, so it occurred to me that she might not be kidding.

We played all morning, took a break for soup and sandwiches, and continued the games. One would have thought this was a bunch of starving orphans as we fought for those precious victuals. Pasta was borrowed at exorbitant interest rates. Serena was the banker and those whose stake was wiped out were allowed back into the game with fresh funds by signing a note promising to do dishes or laundry. Needless to say, Serena was the big winner in all of this and they were all happy to lighten her burden in exchange for gaining another chance to own the contents of my pantry. There could have been no better way to spend the day. Bernie took the game more seriously than anyone and ended up being the grand winner. I was glad to see him wearing a smile instead of his usual glum expression.

It had been agreed that the game would end at four o'clock and whoever had the most "cash" at that point would be allowed to select the menu for Sunday dinner. Bernie ordered country fried chicken, potatoes and gravy, corn on the cob, biscuits, and apple pie. He glowed as everyone praised his selections and he celebrated his victory with three very large glasses of bourbon. He gloated all the way through dinner, but as obnoxious as he became, it was still an improvement over his usual behavior.

The evening was spent watching a movie from Patrick's extensive collection. Bernie wanted to watch "Braveheart", but Jenny and Kate and Alfie voted for "When Harry Met Sally". Glen said he didn't care so he declined to vote. I think he would have watched a blank screen if he could sit next to Kate. Bernie stated he had no intention of watching some chick flick. Alfie piped up and said that he was under the impression that all the movies Bernie watched had chicks in the starring roles. This sent Jenny into spasms of laughter as Bernie went to his room and slammed the door. So much for Bernie's good mood. I had watched that movie at least twice with Amanda and Samantha, so I opted to spend some time alone on my boat.

I walked the short distance since Adrian had taken the Escalade to the hospital, and I can't remember a time when I enjoyed a walk more. I pictured Amanda in her condo in Seattle with the soft light from all of her little lamps, probably having one of her "special" dinners which often consisted only of a head of steamed cauliflower drizzled with butter. Yes, she would be eating in her reading chair in a long flannel nightgown. She would give a mild curse as some butter escaped and dripped on her gown. As I mentioned, Amanda has big boobs and it is not uncommon for her to adorn them with part of her dinner. I laughed to myself and realized that, for the first time in many years, I was confident that we would be together again. I pictured her lying provocatively on the bed in my cabin, wearing a clingy, white satin sheath, her arms extended as an invitation. The end result of that fantasy made me glad that there was no one around to witness an erection so hard I could hardly move my legs. Walk it off-walk it off, I told myself, but I didn't want to. Instead I sat down on a poor unsuspecting rock and had the best time I have ever had by myself. I regretted that there was no place on the island where I could purchase a white satin gown. It would be great to have it on board just in case.

I slept like a log and awoke refreshed. I was anxious to get to the house and find out for sure whether Etienne would be returning that day as planned. I hate to sound selfish, but I wanted our days to get back to normal, (whatever that meant for this group). I had to keep reminding myself that, even though things were not going as planned, my guests were definitely enjoying themselves for the most part and we would have plenty of time for our discussions. As I walked along, I resolved that from that point on I would walk to and from the boat, rain or shine. I needed the exercise and it was invigorating. As I passed my favorite rock, I gave it a salute and chuckled at my cleverness.

Everyone was up and about when I arrived at the house. Under Serena's careful direction, they were rearranging furniture to accommodate Etienne's wheelchair. Adrian had offered to change the sleeping arrangements so that Etienne could be in the main house, but he objected to that. He loved sleeping on the couch in the guest house and the passageway was paved and covered so it wasn't a big deal to go back and forth in a wheelchair. However, Adrian insisted that she occupy the guest house to take care of Etienne as she had promised so we moved her into Antoinette's room.

Adrian and I left immediately after breakfast and by noon we were back at the house with Etienne, his wheelchair, instructions for his care and a promise from his doctor to stop by and check on him every other day. Serena had a special lunch prepared and Glen made a welcome home sign with a cartoon illustration of a kid hanging off the edge of a cliff. The caption read "Has anyone seen my kite?" Paul came by with a huge bunch of balloons and a model car kit for a 1975 Cadillac Coupe De Ville. It was kind of fake festive, but it got us through the first few hours. Of course it was easier for Etienne because he didn't know the full story. Yes, he was separated from his mother, but he didn't know that she might not be coming back for a long time, if ever. Those of us who knew the full story had to keep reminding ourselves not to let on to the seriousness of the situation. I wondered if I was going to be able to keep the story straight. I have been known to embellish rather wildly at times, but I'm not very good at out and out lies.

Amanda called that afternoon to check up on Etienne and to tell me that she would not be home until the next evening, which was Friday, and that she would be bringing Samantha with her. Somehow Samantha had convinced her parents to allow her to miss school on the following Monday so she could have a little longer to stay with us. I was glad for Etienne's sake as well as happy to see my granddaughter. Most of the afternoon was spent getting Etienne settled. Adrian, with Alfie's help, filled the hours after Antoinette's departure by telling the story of Seth's great discovery to Etienne. Etienne was all over Alfie with questions about Seth and Ethan. He wanted to know everything about them including which was the taller of the two and a complete description of both boys at the time they met. He kept pushing for more details. I had an idea of why he was doing this, but I didn't share it with anyone at the time.

By late afternoon we were all settled in the story pit. Etienne and Adrian reclaimed their normal spot on the hearth. Etienne used the seat of the wheelchair to keep his leg elevated as the doctor ordered and he leaned against Adrian for support. Glen volunteered to be next with a story that he believed would be one of particular interest to Etienne but was short so it would not interfere with happy hour.

Chapter Twenty-Five

THE SUBJECT IS FEAR

GLEN

The boy was small, maybe seven or eight years old. He was playing in a field chasing whatever he could find with his slingshot. He had already taken out a dragonfly at medium range and was hoping to get a shot at a rabbit or some other varmint. He had been practicing for days, ever since his uncle had presented the homemade weapon to him as a birthday present. This was the best of the best, as everyone knew that his uncle was the most skilled whittler and all around carver in the area and the boy was his favorite, so uncle had taken extra time and pains with his gift.

It was very hot and everything, the wildlife, the trees, the grasses, even the insects, seemed unusually restless. The boy felt uneasy, like he should be running home, but there was nothing visibly threatening him. He was taking some pleasure in the nameless danger surrounding him and pride in knowing that he had a weapon with which he could defend himself against any threat except one, a hungry wolf.

But the boy was not worrying about wolves today. He knew that they were in the high country and, being mid-summer, there would be plenty of prey for them to feed on without venturing to the lower lands. The wolves came down in the winter, when food was hard to find and the snow drove them into the valley to take their chances with the humans. The boy had seen them attack chickens, dogs, pigs, even full- sized cattle with a speed that could never be matched by a domestic animal and certainly left little time to draw back and fire off a rock should the wolf come across an unsuspecting boy. Yes, a hungry wolf was the most dangerous demon in this boy's collection of nightmares. He had heard of some wolves that grew to be over two hundred pounds, but he had never personally seen one that big. Most wolf stories had come from uncle who claimed to have wrestled a wolf larger than himself with fangs that were over two inches long. He had killed the wolf with his carving knife, but was unable to take the time to remove the fangs as a souvenir due to the well-known fact that wolves travel in packs and he didn't want to stick around long enough to meet the wolf's relatives.

The boy had taken these stories to heart to the point that he never drifted from his yard during the winter months. He wanted to go sledding and play in the snow, but he was too afraid he might get face to face with a pack of wolves. He had nightmares about wolves and could not bring himself to look at a picture of one. The other boys mocked him and called him a big baby, but he didn't care. He was not going to be a meal for one of those angry beasts.

The boy was thinking about his uncle's wolf story when, within seconds, a huge wind erupted and the sky and all around him had darkened ominously. The boy turned to run home to safety but he was knocked down by the force of the wind and was unable to stand. The wind ripped at his hair and clothes and the grasses around him beat at his face and hands. He tried to crawl on his hands and knees, but he could no longer tell in which direction home would lie. Then he was flying, spinning in a circle, his clothes ripping from his body. He was floating and flying at the same time and there were branches and trees all around him, some with their roots waving in the wind. The boy was beyond fear. He was intoxicated with the feeling of being weightless and moving at a speed never before imagined. He looked toward the ground, but could see nothing but dust and flying objects beneath and above him. He thought about an expression his uncle used about a neighbor who was so stupid he didn't know which way was up. At that moment, the boy wasn't sure himself. His eyes burned, but he managed to keep them open even though he was unable to force his hand to his face to clear away the dust and debris. He was stretched out with his arms above his head and his legs apart and he thought he must look like a kite. His bare skin was being pummeled with dust and pebbles and he could see small amounts of blood oozing from scrapes and scratches all over his body. Surprisingly, he didn't feel much pain. It was if his skin was stretched so tight that nothing could penetrate it far enough to cause serious injury. He was having trouble breathing, and he was coughing, but he didn't feel like he was suffocating. He knew he was caught up in a tornado. He had spent many anxious moments in the storm shelter near their house. He knew that people died in tornados, but he didn't think he was going to die.

All this took place in a matter of minutes and the boy was wondering how long his flight would last when he saw the dark outline of another living thing near him, spinning and flying as he was, but different. This body was moving in a different way. It had four legs and the legs were moving as if swimming in the air. It was some distance away, but it looked as though it was trying to move toward him. As the boy spinned and turned he managed to keep his eyes focused on the animal. He thought it might be his neighbors' dog, but soon he got a glimpse of the eyes. They were yellowish and seemed to glow and they were fastened squarely on the boy. This was no dog, this was a wolf, and the wolf was trying to make his way to him. Now he was crying and trying to scream, but no sound could be heard above the roar of the storm. They were spinning in a circle and seemed to stay in the same relative positions for a long time, but the boy knew that if there was a change in direction or force, the wolf would come to get him. His fear was choking him but he couldn't take his eyes off the wolf. They seemed to be dropping lower, although now the boy really couldn't tell which way was up or down. All the boy could see was that the wolf was getting closer and was still trying to swim through the air toward him. The boy was distracted by the heavy amount of debris floating around him. Now there were doors and broken furniture and the boy thought he recognized one of his grandmother's quilts fly by. He tried to grab it, but it moved too fast. His eyes burned terribly and it was difficult to blink to clear them, but he managed to close them for a brief moment and when he opened them again he was looking straight into the eyes and the open jaws of the wolf, now just a few feet away from him. He could see the fangs and could almost feel them ripping into his flesh. Was that foul smell the wolf's breath? The boy was sure the wolf would soon reach out and snag him with one of his huge paws. He would die in the jaws of this beast. The boy cried from the inside out. He wanted to be safe in the storm shelter with his family. He wanted his uncle to come and kill the wolf. He didn't want to be ripped apart and devoured as he had seen happen to other animals. He wondered if there were other wolves nearby, but decided that this must be the "lone wolf" people were always referring to. The boy tried to "swim" through the air like the wolf appeared to be doing, but he didn't have the strength to move arms or legs. He remained face to face with the wolf and those eyes were riveted on him when suddenly they weren't. There were no eyes, no teeth, nothing. The wolf had exploded. The boy could see a large, bloody sheet of metal, as from a roof. It had cut through the wolf severing the head and torso from the rest of the body. The body parts flew off into the storm and the metal sheet was moving higher and higher away from the boy. He was laughing hysterically and thanking God as he saw an old rusty plow heading straight for him. He didn't feel a thing.

SAM

A few moments of silence and then there were groans from around the room. Bernie laughed and made a remark about the boy going from the fry pan into the fire. Etienne's eyes were as big as saucers as he begged Glen to finish the story. Glen said that he was sorry to report that he had no further memory of the boy and that he had to assume that the life ended there. Adrian and others were looking strangely at him for bringing such a troubling story to the scene, but he seemed unmoved by their reaction and simply stated that we were all here to share these memories and that he was quite sure that many of them would not be pleasant. More moments of silence and then Kate spoke up to say that the episode of the boy points out that often our worst fears are not the ultimate threat. The boy feared wolves above all, never thinking to fear an old plow.

I would have thought she was just sticking up for her friend had she not decided at that point to continue the story of Bird of Light. I had always suspected there was more to that story. Adrian jumped in at this point to bring Etienne up to date on the story so far since he had been in the hospital when Kate had shared that memory. She told the story even better than Kate which made me look forward to hearing her own memories. I suspected that Adrian had some pretty juicy tales to tell and I found myself wondering if we would have to put an R rating on some of them and exclude Etienne, and certainly Samantha, from some sessions. Another random thought that I didn't express aloud.

KATE

"I told you that I thought I died on the mountain that night and I guess I did, but the story of Bird Of Light doesn't end there.

I could see my mother and my sister and I tried to run to them, but only my spirit could drift slowly toward them, leaving my tired, cold body behind as I drew nearer. I could see that my mother was the same age as she was when she gave birth to me yet my sister had grown to be a mirror image of myself. I was happy to be reunited with them and eager to have my mother hold me in her arms, but the closer I got, the more I sensed a cold presence that felt like evil along with the warmth that radiated from my mother. I kept moving closer, and then something changed. My sister was no longer standing beside my mother. She was now a baby in my mother's arms. My mother was smiling at me and told me not to be afraid. She laid my sister down tenderly and told me to come closer. As I drew nearer I felt her love pour over me. For the first time in my life I felt joyful. For some time we faced one another, absorbing each other's love, not speaking, and then my mother told me that I had to listen to her and then leave her again. I tried to protest, but I was unable to speak. My mother began by telling me how much it hurt her that I had grown up not knowing the truth and living with the guilt of having stolen my sister's spirit and the fear that I was evil. The truth, she said, would be painful to face, but it would free me from that fear and shame.

She began by telling me that, from the beginning, she had known that there were two spirits growing in her womb. She was confused and troubled because she sensed the presence of good and evil at the same time. She had dreams of us as young women, both strong and beautiful, but in her dreams a dirty yellow cloud would form around one of us and the other would be in peril from this cloud. As the dreams became more frequent the cloud became stronger and denser and would choke one of the women and dim her from view. My mother's grandmother came to her in a dream telling her that she must not give birth to this evil one. She had to protect the other and she would know what to do when the time arrived. My mother grieved for those months we were in her womb and, as she was about to give birth, she had to set the good child free and take the evil one with her to her grave. After I was born, my mother used every bit of her strength to combat nature and keep my sister in her body. She held her legs together and refused to push the child out of the birth canal. It took a long time and the pain was horrible, but eventually she began to hemorrhage and she bled to death taking my sister with her.

It was not I who had stolen my sister's spirit. Our mother had kept her with her to protect me and to keep my sister in the spirit world. My mother told me that my sister must never be born. Her spirit was alive, but it must not be given a body until the evil in her was destroyed. She told me about the visions she had of my sister as a woman. She would have murdered me in a jealous rage, betrayed her people, destroyed many lives and brought eternal shame to the family. My mother told me I must return to the physical world. She told me that I must have children of my own and they must have children. Each time a girl child is born, it would weaken the spirit of my sister. Over time and many generations her spirit would be mended and she would lose her desire to destroy. Then, and only then, would she be allowed to enter the physical world. I didn't want to go back. I wanted to stay with my mother, but I also wanted to escape the cold evil I sensed in my sister. I knew I had to return to the world that my mother had abandoned to make the way for me. I had to have children and see them bear children while my mother would watch over my sister's spirit and, in time, see that spirit earn her way to life. My mother loved my sister and wanted to help her and to protect me and our family.

I awoke back in the forest, cold, injured and lost, but I struggled to my feet and saw one more image of my mother showing me the way home. I found the trail and stumbled into our village having been gone for three days. I knew that I would marry and bear children and they would bear children and with each new birth my sister's spirit would be diminished and eventually my mother could rest. I told my grandmother my story and she grieved over the unhappiness she had caused me. My mother had come to me because my fear that my spirit was evil was going to cause me to allow my life to end without fulfilling my destiny.

Fear is the source of all unhappiness and evil that enters our lives. Bird of Light feared her own spirit because of what she didn't know. Yet the real demon was in that which she sought, her sister. The boy in Glen's story feared the wolf, yet the real danger was in something he walked by every day without fear, the old rusty plow. We live our lives thinking we can avoid the things that will bring us harm, but in truth, we can't know the real threats. We can avoid foolish and obvious dangers. We can lead healthy lives, avoid drugs, follow the rules of society designed to protect ourselves and others, and this we should do, but whatever perils await us will find us in their own time and in most cases we won't be able to anticipate their arrival or their nature.

To lead a fearless life is the greatest good we can seek for ourselves. Conquering our fears will give us peace and freedom. This takes faith. Faith in our Creator, faith in ourselves and faith in those we love. Those who seek to control us will use our fears against us and this is the source of most of the evils in this world. To refuse to allow fear to control us is the path to a rich and productive life. Fear and faith cannot live together in the same host. Fear of poverty causes some to become greedy, exploitive workaholics. Fear of failure causes us to embrace mediocrity instead of using our talents to the fullest. Fear of those who are not like us causes death and destruction. Fear of rejection creates loneliness and despair. I wonder if Franklin Delano Roosevelt really understood the depth of what he was saying when he said "The only thing we have to fear is fear itself". Did he see that Hitler had gained his power by exploiting the fears of others? He must have seen that throughout history the great evils committed by churches and governments were achieved by creating fear and promising protection from the evils that were created in men's minds. Those who seek power know this secret. Our country was built on the principles of freedom and foremost of those is freedom from fear. I guess I'm sounding a little preachy right now, but I am concerned about our willingness to give up our individual freedoms to our government in exchange for protection from events that are easily controlled by common sense. We must never lose faith in ourselves and our creator.

We must refuse to give up our freedom to those who would exploit our fears and make us less than we can be.

I don't know what Bird of Light did with the rest of her life, but I hope that she learned that living with fear and guilt destroys the spirit. The guilt Bird of Light carried over believing that she stole her sister's spirit was really based on fear of her own spirit. The loneliness and despair she endured was due to her self-inflicted isolation. I hope she learned to love and be loved and that she raised courageous children who embraced every moment on this earth with joy. I believe that she never again doubted her goodness and rejected any force that would rob her of the joy of living a life without fear.

GLEN

Kate had been on my mind since the first time I saw her. At first I thought it was admiration for her dedication to her tribe, but I soon realized it had gone far beyond that. Watching her those past few days had been like opening a door to my future dreams. Of course Kate would want children! I was an idiot to hope for any possibility that we could share a future. I am fifty three years old, past the age where it would be reasonable to start a new family even if my injuries hadn't robbed me of that opportunity. I knew Kate was fond of me, but I doubted that she had considered me in any role other than friend, and a temporary friend at that. When this is over, we would both return to our lives. She would go back to the reservation to work for her tribe and I would go back to---what? My children have busy lives. I have a few friends, but no one special waits for me at home. With my friend Aaron and my wife both dead, I had done little to fill the gap they left. I could see that I needed to do some thinking about how I was going to spend the rest of my life. Meeting Kate had made me aware that I was missing something and that there must be more out there for me. I can always be thankful for that. Meanwhile, I vowed to enjoy every minute of her company.

I noticed old Bernie had been awfully quiet for a couple of days. Sam must have found some way to put a muzzle on him, but if he made one more crack about Kate and me, I would take off one of my legs and beat him with it. That guy is a total creep, but I must have a dark side because I was looking forward to hearing some of his memories. God must have not been watching when he let that one slip through the net.

My story about the boy didn't go over too well, but as I told the group, we are here to talk about our memories and that was one of my first. I did feel a little bad for Etienne, but that point Kate made about fear was a good one and I could see that Etienne "got it", although he doesn't seems to harbor many fears anyway. I love that kid. We all do. I didn't know what was really going on with his mom, but I hoped for both their sakes that things would turn out well. It just seemed strange to me to have her leave him here by himself even though I knew that everyone welcomed the opportunity to help.

Sam looked tired and stressed. I knew he'd feel better when Amanda returned with his granddaughter. I was looking forward to that myself. I think having Etienne here had reminded me that there are some great young people. That is easy to forget when you go to the mall or any public place and see the many variations on the human theme. The baggy pants balancing precariously midway down the butt is of special concern to me. Where did that come from? Multiple piercings? I think about all the needles that pierced my body after my accident and I wonder how anyone would want to inflict that upon themselves. Is that some sort of rite of passage? If so, we can do better. I have seen little baby girls, still in a stroller, with pierced ears. It is strange to me that if you swat your child on the butt for throwing a tantrum in a supermarket, you might get in trouble, but you can stick a needle through your baby's ear followed by a steel post and no one will say a thing. I look at some of the young boys in my neighborhood and am always surprised at how pale they are. So many don't leave their computers and go outside and play as we did. They stay in their rooms and sleep all day and play computer games all night. I call them the provimi veal people because their coloring and physique remind me of the pale, tender meat that comes from calves that are kept on special diets in tiny stalls and are not allowed to move about for fear they will develop muscle that would make the meat less tender. It's easy to forget that most of these kids will grow up to be intelligent adults in spite of how they appear now, and often we don't get to see the kids that excel in school, do public service (voluntarily) and are active in their community and churches. The hoodlums on the street are more conspicuous.

Etienne was asking Kate if she had any children. Kate replied that she had never met the right man but that she had many nieces and nephews as well as students to fill her life and, though she would like to have children of her own, she could be content with her life as it was. Hearing her say that, I had to remind myself that ours was a passing friendship and that I had to stop having thoughts beyond that. She was moving back toward the seat by me and I was smiling at her as I took her hand and gave it a tiny squeeze, like any friend would, and I decided to simply enjoy the pleasure of having her next to me.

KATE

Glen was looking at me strangely. I wondered what he was thinking. He was smiling but there was some sadness behind his smile. I felt like he was looking through me. I couldn't believe we had known each other for only a week. I wondered if I knew him as well as I thought I did. I knew for sure that I liked everything I saw in him and I loved the way I felt when I was around him. This was something new for me. I didn't know what it would be like when it came time to leave, but I was not going to worry about it then. I decided to enjoy every minute I had with him even though I believed that we would part in the end. I have to go home and I doubted that Glen would come with me. From our conversations, I knew that he has no real ties to anyone except his children and, by his own admission, they are busy and he doesn't see them very often. Yet the thought that he might take such a huge step and change his life so completely was out of the question. I had to stop thinking like that. It wasn't realistic and anyway, it was impossible to think about a traditional family of my own.

I can't have children. I had a tumor in my right ovary when I was in my twenties. It proved to be cancerous so it was removed. Later tumors developed on my left side with a high probability of cancer cells developing so the decision was made to remove that as well. It was terrible for me at the time, but since then I have realized that I might not have been able to accomplish some of the good I have done for the tribe if I had a child. I have worked hard and traveled much and that lifestyle would not have been good as a mother. I have many children in my life that I love and enjoy and I pray that my work will protect and enhance their way of life.

Until I met Glen, I never minded the prospect of growing old alone, but once I experienced what it is like to be near someone you respect and care for, I knew that it was not carved in granite by the Creator that I should live my life alone. That day when he and I went to lunch together I was walking very fast as I am prone to do. Suddenly I realized that Glenn was not beside me. I turned around to see him stopped on the sidewalk several yards behind me. He was smiling at me and shrugged his shoulders as I realized that he couldn't keep up with my fast pace. At first I was ashamed by my lack of consideration, but he was not angry or frustrated, he just waited for me to notice and was amused by the fact that I had been walking along talking a mile a minute with no one beside me. I hadn't even noticed that people were looking at me strangely as I rushed along talking to myself. There is no false pride in him. I ran back to where he was standing and we laughed and continued on, arm in arm. It is a small, but great memory and I looked forward to many more before this time is over. I don't know what the future will bring, but I will take the lesson from Bird of Light and enjoy today and live without the fear of tomorrow.

Chapter Twenty-Six

A WHOLE LOT OF DRAMA

SAM

I didn't know what to think about Kate's story. I decided I would have to think that one through and I knew Amanda would want to hear about it when she returned. I was sure she would be able to explain it to me.

We broke for happy hour and dinner and everyone was in high spirits. Serena produced a feast in honor of Etienne's homecoming. I don't know anyone else, including Amanda that can make meat loaf taste like a gift from the gods. This, accompanied by huge bowls of mashed potatoes, cream peas and pearl onions, Waldorf salad and homemade rolls made its way around the table several times. Bernie ate so much so fast that he gave himself a severe attack of hiccups. I was afraid his chair would collapse under him with each violent spasm. This continued through dessert which consisted of chocolate cake that was so rich each piece weighed slightly less than five pounds. Bernie was suffering badly and was unable to share in the dessert but asked Serena to save him a piece for later. I had a mental image of Bernie sneaking out into the kitchen late at night, buck naked as I had seen him on my boat, looking for his cake. I shook off the grotesque image and made a mental note to place the dessert in a conspicuous spot to shorten the duration of his search should my vision become reality. Again I ask, where do these thoughts come from?

I returned to my boat shortly after dinner to catch up on some sleep. I honored my earlier pledge to make the trips back and forth on foot. This seemed like a particularly good idea that night considering the meal I had just consumed. I saluted again as I passed my favorite rock and it was then that I came up with an idea that I believed at that time to be one of the most brilliant in my life. Kate's speech about overcoming our fears hit home with me and I had decided to be more aggressive in my pursuit to reclaim my spot in Amanda's heart. After all, I knew Amanda better than anyone on earth, what did I have to fear?

Amanda was to return the following evening and I decided to give her a tender and very private welcome home. I would decorate her room with fresh flowers, her favorite chocolates, soaps and scents, candles, and I would write her a poem. (Have I mentioned that I have been told I am quite the poet?) The idea was to bombard her with all of her sensual favorites in the hope that it might remind her of the ultimate sensual experience and seek me out, if you get my drift. I had most of the "ingredients" aboard my boat including a small bottle of B&B, her favorite liqueur, which I would place with a snifter on her bed stand. The plan was to run into the village before lunch and buy several bunches of fresh flowers and sneak them into her room along with the other gifts while everyone else was eating. I knew there was little chance of discovery if the group had food in front of them. Armed with this plan, I settled into my favorite chair and composed my poem.

SOUL ANGEL

Every life needs a soul angel
An angel to feeds one's soul with hope and faith
An angel who will receive the depth of your love
An angel to follow you into each different life
I feel you in my heart when I look upon you
My love is deeper with each meeting
God's plan for soul perfection is a
forever deep and lasting love
Each day I speak a prayer for you, my soul angel,

Friday morning was ugly and cold. There was a solid sheet of rain, but it didn't spoil my good mood. I put on my rain gear and made the walk to the house. Breakfast was late due to the fact that Serena had arrived soaking wet. I had forgotten that she had lent her car to Amanda and would be riding her motorcycle or I would have arranged to pick her up. She was not upset, just wet. None of the women could provide her with a change of clothes since Serena was at least two sizes larger than any of them, but Glen came up with a shirt for her and Alfie provided a pair of lounging pants and some dry socks. The effect was less than charming, but Serena was not inclined to be self-conscious as she happily went about preparing breakfast.

Breakfast dragged on and no one seemed inclined toward the story pit so there was a lot of lounging around. That was fine with me as I was anxious to get moving to execute my plan. Late in the morning I drove to the boat and collected the gifts I had set out the night before, then I drove into town for the flowers. When I returned, it was clear that sneaking into the guest cabin was not going to be a problem. It was still pouring down rain and no one wanted to set foot out of the house and leave the warm comfort of the fireplace.

Amanda's room was a mess. I realized how busy she had been over the past week dividing her time among the many emergencies and playing hostess to the group. Clothes were thrown over the chair and some were on the floor. There were some wet towels strewn about the room and her bed was not made. Ok, this was going to take longer than I thought. I hung up her clothes, grabbed the towels to take to the laundry and made the bed. Then I placed chocolates on her pillow and made an arrangement of soaps and scents on her dresser. I positioned the B&B with a snifter and took the flowers downstairs where I found large glasses to serve as vases. In all, there were five bouquets of flowers and several candles positioned throughout the room. I placed my hand-written poem on the pillow under the Ferraro Rochet chocolates and decided to sneak in later to light the candles so that by the time she retired, the room would be filled with the glow and scent of the candles and the flowers. I was quite proud of myself.

I returned to the house and spent the next couple of hours just visiting. Glen and I swapped stories about our travels during our business careers. We discovered that we had both spent a lot of time in Alaska so there were plenty of adventures to share on that subject. Bernie went to his room remarking that we should call him if there was anything interesting going on. Jenny, Alfie, Adrian, Kate and Etienne set up a card table in the den and began working on a thousand piece puzzle depicting Mount Rushmore. Adrian had very definite ideas on how this should be done and instructed everyone to find the edge pieces first and to turn all the pieces face up as they were making that search. Once the frame was built, then, and only then, could they begin working on the inside pieces. There was a great deal of laughter and chatter coming from that room and the whole scene throughout the house was warm and friendly. I was totally content and anticipating the arrival of Amanda and Samantha that evening to complete the picture.

Shortly after four pm the front door flew open and Samantha exploded into the room. I was sitting in my armchair by the fire as she jumped onto my lap. I suffered the pain inflicted by her bony elbow to my rib cage in silence as she recounted the story of how school had been let out early due to the severe rain and flooding in Snohomish County. She had called her grandmother immediately and they were able to catch an earlier ferry to the island. After a couple of minutes of incessant babbling, she finally noticed the others that had gathered around us in the room. Amanda came through the door at that moment carrying two large suitcases and behind her followed Thelma, carrying only her purse. Amanda met my astonished expression with a shrug of her shoulders and a rolling of eyes. Fortunately, Samantha was running from one person to another introducing herself, giving me a chance to cover my displeasure.

OK, I thought to myself. I can get through this. Thelma is an uninvited guest on my turf. She will have to make some effort to be civil. It is true that she can be quite charming when she wants to be and I decided that she would probably be on her best behavior, although I couldn't imagine what that would look like. The first words out of her mouth were "Hello Sam. Is it happy hour yet?" This annoyed Amanda who suggested that it might be nice for everyone to meet each other before we move onto anything else. That would have embarrassed a normal person, but Thelma just pointed out that there is no better way to get acquainted than by sharing a cocktail. I replied that if I knew she was coming I would have bought an extra case of wine. Amanda gave me “the look”. Not so good a start to a long weekend.

Just then, Serena waddled into the room in her stocking feet and baggy clothes. She had not taken the time to go home and change out of her makeshift “outfit”. Thelma looked her up and down and said “Oh goody, a pajama party”. Serena laughed and took her by the arm and ordered her to help set up the cocktail bar since she was in such a hurry. Thelma followed obediently. Did I ever mention how much I love Serena?

Samantha was totally oblivious to all this as she had noticed Etienne in his wheelchair parked in the doorway of the den. She was suddenly shy and looked to Amanda for an introduction. Etienne, on the other hand, wheeled himself forward and introduced himself. He couldn’t have been more self-assured. Samantha regained her composure and asked if he was in any pain. Before he could answer she grabbed a cushion off the couch to place under his extended leg. In doing so she inadvertently fell forward onto his lap causing the wheelchair to move backwards and her torso ended up on top of his wounded leg. Amanda reached down and pulled her off the leg and set her upright at which time Samantha burst into tears through embarrassment and at the thought that she had caused further injury. Etienne laughed and assured her that he was fine and that the doctor would be by later to fix any damage she might have done. True to her nature, Samantha went from tears to smiles in under two seconds.

Introductions were made and the adults gathered for cocktails, leaving the kids to get acquainted. Thelma explained to the group that she just had to come along to see what this séance was all about. Glances were exchanged, but no one bothered to correct her. Amanda followed me to the deck and explained that she had been visiting Alex and Tiffany the day before when Thelma arrived and invited herself along. She had tried to convince Thelma that there wouldn't be any place for her to sleep, but Thelma had heard her say that Antoinette was gone so there must be an empty room. Amanda said Samantha would occupy that room, but Alex jumped in and said that he wanted Samantha to stay on the boat with me instead of with a houseful of strangers. Thelma declared that the issue was settled and she would pack a suitcase in the morning and be ready to go at any time. The next day Samantha suggested that, since they would be catching an earlier ferry than originally planned, they could just pretend that there wasn't time to collect Thelma. Amanda was considering that plan when Thelma showed up at her door saying that she had decided to come early so she and Amanda could spend the afternoon with just the two of them. Welcome to Thelma's bag of tricks.

After half an hour and two glasses of wine, Thelma had already managed to make the rounds of the other guests and she and Bernie were engaged in a private conversation. I had never seen Bernie so animated and Thelma was hanging on his every word. I'm sure she had identified him as an easy mark to obtain information about the goings-on here. I know she was desperate to find out if Amanda and I were a couple once again. I overheard a part of their conversation where Bernie was telling her how fond he was of Amanda. I choked on my drink so violently that some of it ran out my nose. Adrian was nearby and, hearing this exchange, gave me a sympathetic look as she cleaned the front of my shirt with her napkin.

Serena got dinner on the table within a few minutes. I think she was protecting me from prolonged exposure to the team of Thelma and Bernie. Dinner went slowly with Thelma leading all conversations. I excused myself from dessert and sneaked out to the cabin to execute the rest of my plan for Amanda's room. I lit the candles and re-arranged a few items to make them more noticeable. I was feeling very pleased with myself as I re-joined the group. After dinner Amanda announced the sleeping arrangements during Thelma's visit. I felt sorry for Kate because for the next three nights she would be sharing the master suite with Thelma since Adrian had moved to the cabin to be near Etienne. I was fairly confident that Kate could handle the situation, but I felt badly that this was sprung on her without warning.

Samantha and Etienne were already sharing a secret world of their own. Etienne took her to the guest house to show her the living room, which was now relabeled as his room. He proudly displayed the big screen TV, fireplace, computer and the small kitchen which Serena had stocked with all his favorite beverages and snacks while he was in the hospital. I knew that staying with me on the boat would seem like small potatoes to her now, but she didn't seem too disappointed.

Following doctor's orders, Adrian sent Etienne off to bed early and Samantha and I retrieved her backpack and headed for the boat. The rain had stopped so Samantha was happy to make the trip on foot. She has always tried to get me to get more exercise so she was quite impressed with my resolution to walk back and forth.

Samantha was uncharacteristically quiet for the rest of the evening. She asked about Etienne's mother and I gave her the same story we gave him, but she kept at me for more details. It was clear that she believed there was more, maybe Etienne had confided some suspicions he harbored. She said she felt sorry for him and she wished she could stay here longer. Finally she fell asleep on the couch and I moved her to her cabin. I laid out her pj's and left the room. It wasn't that long ago that I would have helped her change and tucked her in, but those days were gone. Young as she is, she has developed that strangeness that accompanies womanhood. I felt the sadness of knowing that that each year would take us further apart in some ways. There would be others that would know her better than me. There would be a man in her life that she would love and respect and share her thoughts and dreams and I would be a smaller part of her world. I just hoped that when she married, her husband would be more accepting of her memories than I was of Amanda's. I hoped he would cherish her for her differences. I hoped he would be someone like Etienne.

The next morning was clear and crisp and Samantha was her perky self again as we made our way to the house. When we entered Thelma greeted us at the door with a huge grin and a hug for me. She was wearing a flower tucked behind her ear and was biting into a chocolate that I recognized as Amanda's favorite. She announced to the group that I was just the sweetest ex-brother-in-law in the world and how grateful she was to have had her room fixed up to make her feel welcome. The next thing I noticed was the piece of paper with the poem I had written for Amanda. She was waving it around and asking everyone if they knew that I was a poet. Amanda snatched the poem from her hand and pulled her aside to whisper in her ear. Thelma quieted down, but could not stop smiling. Apparently, Thelma had decided that she didn't want to bunk with a woman she didn't know so Amanda had given up her room. She told her the room was a mess and if Thelma wanted her privacy she would have to clean it up herself. Amanda had deposited Thelma's suitcase in the living room of the cabin and pointed her in the right direction, pleased with herself that she was making Thelma do the work. That morning Amanda had gone to her room to get some fresh clothes and wake Thelma only to find her up and dressed and giddy with her discovery. Obviously, Thelma knew that all those special treats had been intended for Amanda and she had little trouble figuring out my intentions.

I was too angry to be embarrassed although it wouldn't have mattered anyway. The group was ignoring her completely to deprive her of the satisfaction of exposing my zealous gesture. Only Bernie was laughing and even that stopped abruptly when Serena smacked him on the back of the head with her spatula and gave him a look that surely shriveled his nuts. There was an awkward silence for a few seconds, broken by Samantha who had gone to the cabin to wheel Etienne over for breakfast. She came charging down the hallway, pushing the chair at breakneck speed and Etienne was laughing so hard I thought he would slither onto the floor. That eased the tension, but I had made a decision. Thelma was going home. I had put up with enough of her bullshit over the years, but this time she had gone too far. With anyone else, the situation might have been funny, but there was so much malice in the way she flaunted her findings that I could see neither humor nor forgiveness. I didn't deserve this treatment and by God, I wasn't going to put up with it.

I waited until after breakfast and looked for Amanda to let her in on my decision. I felt that was only fair. She wasn't in the house so I went to the guest house to look for her. When I opened the door, I could hear screaming and shouting the likes of which I had not seen since, as a young boy, I had traded my mother's antique washboard for a mangy old Heinz 57 dog that ate her precious banty rooster. Amanda had Thelma cornered in the kitchen area and was unloading on her big-time. Neither had noticed me so I ducked behind the big screen TV to enjoy the show. Amanda was doing a fine job of letting Thelma know that her presence there was not welcomed and that her behavior over the years had been tolerated, but no more. The B word was used several times accompanied by an assortment of unflattering adjectives. She then told Thelma to collect her belongings and that she would be sent home on the afternoon ferry. After her tirade Amanda was silent for several seconds and turned around to leave. Then she turned back around to Thelma and slapped her face, very hard. For once in her life, Thelma was speechless. Then she started crying. Oh God, I thought, here it comes. Amanda will crumble. She didn't. Instead she told Thelma to pull herself together and stay put until it was time for her to leave. I slipped out through the open door and ran for the house. I didn't want Amanda to know I had witnessed the scene.

Once inside, I realized that I had a great opportunity here. I decided that when Amanda came to tell me about her decision, I would stick up for Thelma, thereby making myself the bigger person. That idea didn't turn out any better than my scheme from the night before. Amanda was still shaking with anger when she told me what had transpired, although she left out the part about the face slap. When I piped up with the bit about how Thelma is just a troubled person and no real harm had been done, I thought she was going to slap me as well. She told me to go to hell and then stormed out of the room. I should have known better. I have never been able to manipulate Amanda. She always sees through me and I can't imagine why I would have thought it would be otherwise. To make matters worse, I turned around and there was Thelma. She had decided to ignore Amanda's command that she stay in the cabin and she had heard the whole thing and was smiling. I tried to ignore the smile and focus on the handprint that was still visible on her right cheek.

About that time, Bernie came around the corner and told us that he was going to tell a past life story and everyone was waiting in the story pit. I sent Samantha to get her grandmother and told her to be sure to let her know that it was Bernie who would be doing the telling. I knew she wouldn't want to miss that one.

When Samantha returned she positioned herself on the hearth next to Etienne's wheelchair with Adrian in her usual spot on the other side. Amanda grabbed a dining room chair and sat as far from everyone as she could get. Thelma wedged herself in between Glenn and Kate and turned to each with a sweet smile. The gesture was not returned.

Bernie was feeling his oats since it was obvious that there was now a person in the room that was at least as unpopular as he. This was undoubtedly a totally new experience for him. I was a bit nervous and concerned about whether his memory would be one that was suitable for the young people's ears. I wished Samantha and Etienne had been here for the story of Seth instead.

Bernie stood in the middle of the group to tell his story. He was the picture of confidence and composure, definitely an actor on a stage. He welcomed Thelma and Samantha as if he were the official host of some grand event. The body language of the rest of the group indicated that they were experiencing some of the same nausea I was feeling. Still, I was anxious to hear what he had to say. Was anything from his past lives carried forward to explain his fractured psyche in this life? Was he ever anything more than the bitter, cynical man we saw before us? Had he ever loved and been loved. Was he ever a hero to someone? Would I believe it if he said he was?

Chapter Twenty-Seven

LUTHER AND LUCY

BERNIE

"My name was Luther and I was born in England sometime in the early 1800's, but the memory begins with me as an old man and I am looking at my thin, weathered face in the mirror as I am shaving in preparation for nothing. I am remembering my life, trying to make some sense of it and wondering if I took the right path. I had choices, but I really can't say that any particular course would have worked out better for me.

My parents were both thieves and by the time I was nine years old I was a thief in training. Prior to that time we had lived with a number of wealthy families with my parents acting as servants. They were an attractive couple and were able to fool their employers into trusting them. They would work for several weeks or months until an opportunity arrived to steal money and valuables and disappear before the employers returned and discovered their loss. Then we would live in splendor until the money was gone and it was time to find new employment. They were well connected with forgers, fences and other thieves, possibly even murderers, so for several years they had no trouble obtaining papers in fictitious names with letters of reference. My name changed along with theirs and I was always afraid that I would slip up and use the wrong name. That happened once and I was brutally beaten by my father. My mother felt bad for me and explained that the beating was necessary because if it ever happened again we could all be hung or end up in prison for the rest of our lives.

On my ninth birthday we were at a beach resort where we had been spending a few weeks enjoying the fruits of our last and most successful heist. We were just finishing a sumptuous dinner in the hotel dining room when my mother suddenly went pale. She had spotted a couple entering the room, former employers, (or should I say victims?). She alerted my father and he told us both to shut up while he plotted an escape route. Fortunately for us, the couple was seated with some other guests on the other side of the room. There was a set of double doors to the right of us which led to a patio. He was to slip out first and then after a couple of minutes my mother and I would follow when we could see that the waiters' backs were turned. This plan worked well, but the problem was that we were on the second floor balcony making it necessary to find an escape route to the ground. I was proud to announce that I could climb down the lattice that was supporting a thick wall of ivy. My father was hesitant, but it was the only viable way out and we needed to move quickly before we were spotted. I went first, then my mother, but as my father was stepping over the side the lattice gave way and he ended up falling clumsily to the ground. He had managed to grab on to clumps of ivy to break his fall. When he hit the ground my mother was laughing and I joined in, believing he would not be angry since my mother thought the situation was funny too. I was wrong. He picked me up by one arm and carried me all the way back to our cabin where he gave me another beating. This time my mother tried to interfere and he struck her several times as well.

That day marked the beginning of our decline. My father had expressed concern for some time that we were becoming too well known to continue on our current course. The incident in the dining room only proved that. That evening we left the hotel hurriedly with just what we could carry in our arms. My father had paid in advance for the first week thereby establishing his credibility, allowing him to set up an account for the rest of our stay. He always tipped the wait staff generously in cash, making us favored customers and ensuring there would be only good reports made to management and nothing to arouse suspicion. We skipped out on a sizeable lodging and restaurant bill and set out on foot so there would be no carriage driver to point the authorities in the direction we took.

We stayed off the roads and walked for many hours until we finally rested in an orchard near a small, but well-kept farmhouse. We slept on the ground behind a haystack and in the morning my father decided we would go to the house and tell the owners that our carriage had broken down a mile down the road and see if they would offer us breakfast. At least that is what he told us we were going to do. In spite of our long walk and little sleep, we still looked like a respectable family dressed as we were so the farmer and his wife believed our story and were gracious in offering us a hot breakfast after which the farmer said he and his hired hand would ride out to find the carriage and work on repairs. I guess they figured that my father, dressed as a gentleman, was not likely to be of any help and might be a hindrance.

After breakfast, I went out to the yard to play with their dog. My mother remained in the kitchen with the farmer's wife while my father was giving the farmer directions to our so- called breakdown. They took some tools with them in the farmer's wagon and assured my father that they would be able to fix the carriage and bring it back to us within a couple of hours.

The minute they were gone, my father started exploring the farm to view the possibilities. My mother was very nervous. I could tell she was wondering, as was I, what would be said when the farmer returned having discovered that here was no carriage. Neither of us knew what my father had in mind since he didn't seem to be in any hurry to make an escape. He entered the kitchen and took my mother aside telling her to take me and return to the orchard and retrieve our belongings and place them behind the barn. We were gone but a few minutes and when we returned, the farmer's wife was nowhere to be found and my father was sitting at the kitchen table. Lying on the table was a gun, some coins and a large bundle. He had changed into some of the farmer's clothes and he threw the bundle at my mother telling her to change into one of the wife's dresses and to put the clothes she was wearing in the bundle. He looked at me and started laughing, ordering my mother to put me in a dress and to put a bonnet on my head. At age nine, I was nearly as tall as the farmer's wife but had not developed a beard or any masculine characteristics that would reveal me as anything but a rather ugly girl. I think my mother and I both knew what my father had in mind and what he had already done, but we were afraid of him and afraid to be without him so we didn't question, we just obeyed. He told us to pack up any food we could find and await his return.

My father took off on foot in the direction the farmer had taken. The gun and the coins were gone as well. We just sat there in our dresses and waited for him to return. My mother was crying and I felt sick with fear. In less than an hour the farmer's wagon pulled into the yard with my father at the reins, no farmer, no hired hand. We loaded our bundles into the wagon as he filled the back with bales of hay and any baskets of produce he could find. We now had a perfect cover for whatever direction we decided to take. Not only did we look like any farm family, but we were a family with a young girl, not a young boy. My mother cried for a while, until my father struck her with the whip and told her to shut up. I knew better than to say a word. I just sat there like a good little girl. Luther became Lucy at that moment and stayed that way for the next few days as we traveled around, sleeping in our wagon, trying to figure out our next move.

We finally made our way to London and were able to trade our wagon for living space in a loft above a warehouse. We at least had shelter for the next few months. The owner offered my father a job in the warehouse, but he quickly rejected that idea.

When we had exhausted what little money we had left plus the coins we had stolen from the farmer, things really got desperate. My mother sewed deep pockets into my dress and I was trained in the ways of a petty thief. My hair had grown long enough to style as a girl and my mother took great pains to keep me clean and well groomed so I didn't look like the thousands of street urchins that haunted the city. I aroused no suspicion as I browsed through a mercantile, outdoor market or bakery discreetly filling my pockets with food and wares that could be consumed, sold, or traded by my father. I also became quite skilled as a pickpocket. I had observed these clever beings on many occasions and I practiced on my father. As a girl, I could arrange to fall down and wail loudly until some pre-selected passer-by, would stop to help me and offer comfort. It was easy to lift whatever was available posing as a damsel in distress. I would then make a quick recovery, offer my tearful thanks to the kind stranger and head off in the opposite direction of our home. These activities provided us some comforts on a day to day basis, but gave us no prospects for the future.

By my tenth birthday I was an accomplished thief, an unwitting accomplice to murder and a female impersonator, quite a resume for one so young. The bright spot of any day was to spend an hour or two in the park that was within walking distance of our warehouse home. Sometimes I would go there after an afternoon of performing my petty larcenies dressed as Lucy. Other times I would sneak out in my Luther clothes, which I hid from my parents in a bin behind the warehouse, and I would play with the other boys, but that was rare and very risky. If my father caught me, I would be beaten and he would also take his anger out on my mother. This was happening more frequently.

I knew nothing about my parents' prior lives; where they grew up, who their parents were, how they met, nothing about their pasts, and I was forbidden to ask so I didn't. I did know that my mother deeply loved my father and I could see her pain as he became more bitter and cruel.

One day I was sitting quietly in the park dressed as Lucy and wishing I knew how to read a whole book like some of the young ladies sitting about. My mother had taught me enough to survive, but my father didn't see the need for me to become proficient. I had become used to wearing dresses and, with my hair styled around my bonnet, I was not at all self-conscious, although I usually avoided conversation with other park visitors. It was late in the afternoon when an elderly gentleman sat beside me. I felt no threat from him so I allowed him to draw me into conversation. We talked for a long time. He was a retired banker and a widower. All of his family was deceased including his only daughter who had died of consumption a couple of years before. He was a very sad and kind man. I told him my mother was a widow and she supported us as a seamstress, and that I hoped to attend school someday and learn to read better and to write. We became friends that day and continued to meet on a regular basis. I can't explain why, but I totally adopted Lucy as my identity from that point on. It was easier. I had given Lucy a story and it was nice to pretend I had a life that had a beginning, a middle and a future and I had a friend for the first time in my life. Luther was a boy in my past. It was better that way.

My father was becoming more abusive to my mother, but he left me alone as I was the breadwinner. I was free to wander as I pleased as long as I showed up with the goods. I spent more and more of my time in the park with Mr. Horace Spencer. He told wonderful stories and educated me about life for those who did not steal and run. I would make up stories about the garments my mother was making for her customers and tell him about our little apartment and our make believe neighbors who were always doing crazy things. I could make him laugh anytime I wanted and that gave me so much pleasure. He told me that I reminded him of his daughter and that he hadn't laughed since she died until he met me. It made me happy to know that I could bring him joy. This feeling was new to me and I was proud of myself even though I was living a lie.

Of course I never told my parents about Mr. Spencer. My father would have forced me to make him a victim and I never wanted to hurt him or lose him as my friend. Over this same period of time, my mother was growing more distant. She was loving and kind to me as she would have been to a stray dog, but she had no strength to offer me. I began to see my mother as I had never seen her before. She was not an evil person.

She was an adventuress whose adventures had cost her too much. She hadn't judged herself as a thief and a liar. She just wanted to live as she pleased. She had been selfish and willful and was paying the price. My father was a different story. He was a bad man and I wanted my mother and me to be free of him, but I knew that would never happen.

As I drifted further into life as Lucy, my mother was succumbing to her own torturous world. She seldom ate and she slept most of the time. My father would yell at her to prepare his dinner and tend to his needs, but she would just look right through him. She didn't shrink from his blows or display any anger or grief at his treatment of her. I tried as best I could to make her life easier. I would take extra risks to steal lovely pastries that would whet her appetite and I would tell her stories meant to make her laugh. She tried to respond, but her soul had left her body. One morning I rose early and prepared a special tea I had stolen the day before, but when I went to her bed she was gone. Her body was there, but it had no life. I didn't know if she was breathing or not, I just knew that wherever she was, she wasn't coming back. My father had risen early and was gone, probably for the whole day as was usually the case. I packed up my scant Lucy belongings and left the warehouse, never to return.

I was to meet Horace Spencer later that morning at the park and I guess I knew what he would do if I told him my mother was dead. I was right. He believed I was alone in the world, which would have been better than my true circumstance. He guided me to his huge townhouse overlooking that very park. From his salon I could see the park bench where we met, which explained why he so often showed up when I was there even when we hadn't planned to meet. I was touched and humbled by his concern for me. He gave me my own room and told me I would always have a place to live. He offered to take care of my mother's burial, but I assured him that one of her wealthy customers had already seen to it. Two months later, he called in his solicitor and told him to draw up adoption papers. I was to be his daughter and the heir to his fortune.

Horace was old, but in excellent health and I knew that in time I would start developing as a young man. In spite of my fondness for him, I wondered if he would die before my deception became obvious. I decided to put those thoughts out of my mind until a later time and just give and take whatever comfort I could for the time being. I was given a generous allowance which I stashed in a box under my bed. I figured I would need that money later when I was cut off. Perhaps I could save enough to give me a start in life as a tradesman. I certainly knew how to spot and avoid people who would steal from me, so I was fairly confident I could be a success at business. Horace offered to provide a personal maid, but I assured him that wasn't necessary. That would have made my deception more difficult or impossible. He brought in a dressmaker to give me a wardrobe befitting my status and I sweat blood as she commented on my broad shoulders and muscular legs, although she never mentioned these attributes to Horace for fear of offending him. On the contrary, she commented continually about what a heartbreaker I was going to be. I remember hearing her say this and thinking that the only heart that would be broken would be Horace's. I felt terrible, but could see no way out.

Horace and I settled into a routine that did not include a lot of socialization. I was nervous about going out in public because I knew my father would be looking for me. After all, I was his source of food and drinking money. We went to the park on occasion, but I was careful to wear large bonnets that would conceal my face and I made use of some of the tricks I had seen the young ladies I met to confirm my appearance as a young girl. I pinched my cheeks to give color, I curled my hair to frame my face and I always wore a lace shawl to conceal my broad bony shoulders. All in all, I was not bad looking. I took some comfort in knowing that my father would not be looking for a well-dressed, prosperous young girl accompanied by an old gentleman. Still I was ever watchful and often declined Horace's offers to take me shopping or to other events. He believed I was just shy and was content to spend most afternoons and evenings playing gin rummy and improving my scant reading and writing skills. I was an avid student as I knew that I may have to find my own way in the world when and if the time came that my identity was exposed.

The next year went by as described and on my eleventh birthday Horace took me to the same seaside resort I had visited with my parents. I did not fear recognition by the staff, but I had to be careful at first not to let Horace know that I was familiar with the layout. We spent an enjoyable two weeks and returned home to discover that there had been a seedy character making inquiries about Horace and his daughter. I refused to leave the house for several weeks after that and spent most of my time in my room feigning illness. After a while I began to relax, believing that if the man was my father, he had not discovered the truth.

Finally, on one especially lovely day, Horace convinced me to take a walk in the park. I took the usual precautions wearing my shawl and a large bonnet. We were sitting on our usual bench when I saw my father approach and occupy the bench opposite us. It was clear that he had discovered my secret. He established eye contact, but made no overtures. I didn't want to aggravate the situation so I just sat there with my head down until Horace suggested we leave. As we walked past my father, he chose that moment to stand, and in doing so, bumped into Horace, apologizing profusely while he slipped a note into my hand as Horace was regaining his balance. That night I retired right after dinner and opened the note. It contained no greeting or threat, just a time and location to meet with the words "BE THERE".

The next evening Horace was going to his club for his weekly chess match with his oldest friend. My father must have been watching the house for some time and knew that Horace would be going out. I slipped out and ran the few blocks to the address in the note and found him waiting for me. I had brought all the money I had saved up over the past year hoping to buy his silence. It was a considerable sum, but I knew how fast my father could go through money so I was only going to offer it as a last resort. He told me to relax as he had no intention of exposing me. He praised me for my resourcefulness and let me know that he knew about the adoption and my being the sole heir. He went on and on about how our life would be when Horace died and inquired about his health in general. I asked where my mother was buried and he just laughed. It was clear that he had a plan that did not involve waiting several years for Horace to pass away and I was sure I was expected to be part of that plan.

As I listened to him, I realized that I would never be free of him. I pictured my mother lying in her bed all those weeks and months, dying of shame and despair, tied to this cold blooded murderer and I wondered if that would be my fate as well. I said nothing as he described his plan to have me leave a door unlocked. He would enter during the night and smother Horace while he slept and then disturb a few items in Horace's bedroom to make it look like a burglary. No one would suspect me and we would be wealthy beyond our wildest dreams. There seemed to be no doubt in his mind that I would go along with the plan rather than risk exposure.

I asked him when he planned to execute this plan and he said it would be that very night because Horace would be extra tired from his night at the club and would be sleeping soundly. My father had done some careful snooping around the house and was familiar with the layout so he knew where to go to find Horace. I was to unlock the parlor door that opened to the garden after everyone had retired. In the morning I would go directly to the kitchen as always. Then I would simply stay with the servants until the body was discovered. I knew the plan would work. I turned and left my father saying only "tonight then". I returned home and went immediately to my room.

When the police arrived the next morning to inspect the body, it was not Horace that they carried away, it was my father. I had waited until Horace returned home and everyone was asleep and I unlocked the parlor door as planned. Then I moved a decorative screen to the top of the staircase and hid behind it. As my father arrived at the top of the stairs, I jumped out and struck him as hard as I could with a bronze statuette. He fell backwards and rolled down the stairs. He didn't utter a sound. I raced to the bottom of the stairs and discovered he was still breathing, but unconscious. I took a cushion off the sofa in the parlor and held it over his face for a long time. He wasn't breathing when I removed it. I used the cushion to muffle the sound as I broke a small glass pane in the parlor door, then I replaced the cushion to the sofa. I stepped around my father's body and went back up the stairs. I returned the screen and the statuette to their proper places, went to my room and fell instantly asleep. I awoke in the morning to screams from the maid and rushed to the top of the stairs. Everyone assumed the burglar had tripped and fallen to his death. The servants recognized him as the man who had been making inquiries while we were on vacation. There was no further investigation.

I did not suffer over my part in my father's death, but I did come to realize that I was in many ways no better than him. The next few weeks were troubling for me as I struggled with the idea that I should tell Horace the truth. On the one hand, if I told the truth, I would hurt him deeply and destroy the pleasant life we shared and leave him to a lonely, possibly bitter existence. On the other hand, if I didn't tell, I would be forever bound to my father even in his death. I did not blame myself for my earlier thieving and lying activities. I had the excuse of youth and desperation, but now I was bound to make the right choices or forever live as a shadow of my father. My soul was at stake.

I had learned social skills and I had my savings which Horace had told me many times was mine to use as I wished so I had a small start in life should I decide to run away. So why was the decision so hard for me? I didn't want to be like my father, yet I lacked the courage to tell the truth. I couldn't bear to see the look on Horace's face when I told him, nor could I imagine leaving him a note. If I left, I had to know that he was alright. On any given night I would go to sleep with the resolve that I would tell Horace the truth in the morning, then the next day would pass with Horace treating me with love and kindness and that night I would swear that I would never hurt him with the truth. I had no one to confide in and nowhere to go for answers. The days and weeks passed with the same questions haunting me. It was near my twelfth birthday that I discovered the answer. I was struggling through one of Horace's philosophy books. The subject was ethics and I came across the word "hypocrite". I asked Horace what the word meant and he told me it was a person who professed one belief, but lived another way. I knew that was what I was doing. All my anguish over my decision was really just a front to protect me from the truth about myself. I realized that I had no intention of confessing my lie to Horace. All this suffering was just a way to camouflage my selfishness and weakness of character. It's true, I didn't want to hurt Horace, I loved him as the father I should have had, but I also knew that I didn't want to hurt myself either. I vowed I would no longer provide myself the luxury of believing that I was a young man caught in a moral dilemma. I had made my decision long ago and I would have to face my flaws. On the other hand, I also promised myself that I would become a better person. Horace was seventy eight years old and was moving slower and becoming weaker. He would likely die before my deception became obvious. I would accept his fortune and I would give myself a comfortable lifestyle, but use the bulk of the money to do good for others. I may have been a liar and a cheat, but people can change and I would have the opportunity to prove myself as a man of character, not my father's son. I made peace with myself and lived the next two years secure in the knowledge that I would redeem myself while providing Horace the love and companionship he deserved.

It was near my fourteenth birthday that Horace came down with pneumonia and passed away. He left his estate to me, but his solicitor held control of everything until my eighteenth birthday. The next four years were difficult as I attended a private girl's school and had to retain my identity as Lucy. Fortunately, I was able to live at home rather than as a boarder so I spent most nights in my room plucking hairs from my chin and upper lip and arranging my wardrobe to disguise the Luther body that was emerging. I was naturally slender, so that was a blessing, but it still required a great deal of attention to maintain Lucy.

In the meanwhile, I was getting the education geared toward a young lady, not a man who would make his way in the world, so I took advantage of Horace's extensive library to fill in the gaps. I made few friends and I had to be ever watchful to guard my secret. I was lonely, but not unhappy and I filled many hours by volunteering at the nearby orphanage and spending a large portion of my allowance on the children there, many of whom had been even less fortunate than I. I called these the Limbo years and I dreamed of the day when I could take charge of my fortune, abandon Lucy and begin my work as a man of means out to do good in the world.

I knew I would move from London and become Luther Spencer. I would have to convert any holdings to pounds so that I could open accounts in my new name. I thought perhaps I would live in Scotland or maybe France or even move to America. As the time drew nearer I realized that if I was going to start over as a new person, America would be my best choice. The cities were growing and there were many new industries emerging. Perhaps I could be a gentleman farmer. The dream took hold and on my eighteenth birthday I went to the solicitor and told him to convert all my holdings to pounds and turn them over to me. He resisted of course, wondering what a young woman alone in the world would do with all that money. He offered to set up accounts for me, but I refused his help and insisted on cash. Ten days later I left his office as Lucy carrying a huge duffle bag stuffed to the brim with pound notes. That very afternoon, I entered the bank of England dressed elegantly as a young man named Luther Spencer and deposited those funds. Meanwhile I had placed the townhouse on the market and within a few days I was sitting, dressed as Lucy once again, receiving even more funds from that sale, in cash as I had directed. That money took Luther to America and provided the seed for his new life.

I booked passage on a beautiful ship although not in first class, as I was not yet ready for that level of social participation. Hell, I wasn't even used to wearing men's clothes, let alone handling the many questions I would be asked and, God forbid, fielding the flirtations bestowed upon a wealthy young man by young ladies anxious to fulfill their romantic and economic fantasies. Having been educated in a girl's school, I was quite familiar with the affectations and schemes designed to ensnare the hearts and fortunes of unsuspecting men. I would never allow myself to be flattered into believing that any young woman would be smitten by my charms and I wanted no part of raising a family.

I arrived in New York and moved into an elegant, but moderately priced hotel suite. There I remained for the next few months as I made arrangements to shift the rest of my money from England to my adopted country and investigated the many possibilities available to a young man with ample funds. I traveled to the south and was enchanted with the beautiful cotton and tobacco plantations. I was fortunate to find one available near Atlanta. The husband had died and his widow wanted to take her children back to England to be near her family. Neither she nor her husband had adapted well to life in America and, judging by the state of neglect of their property, he had not been a good manager or businessman. I was able to purchase the property at a bargain price and began immediately to restore the house and grounds to their former glory. Making the farm a profitable enterprise would be more challenging, but I had the funds to weather the storm.

The purchase price included some twenty slaves, darkies they were called. I felt deeply for their predicament, but it was also obvious that I could not afford to hire the necessary hands to work the farm at the going rate, even if a reliable labor force was available. I had a couple of sharecroppers on the property, but their skills were even less developed than that of the former owner. I felt bound by my promise to perform good works with my inheritance, yet I could see no way to greatly improve the lot of these people in the short run. I made the decision to continue with the existing structure until I could turn the finances around at which time I would reward the good workers by sharing with them the fruits of our labors.

It took four years to learn the farming methods necessary to turn a profit. I found that I had a gift for managing the workers. Having come from such humble beginnings, I understood how they thought and I knew what it would take to motivate them to give their best. I took great pains to improve their living conditions. I had no life but work, so I had no need of an overseer. I dealt directly with all hands and was able to set up a crude system of rewards for improved performance. This worked well for most, but there were those who only responded to fear of punishment and there were some who responded not at all. I had no patience with the latter two groups. For one thing, they reminded me of my father. They were sold or otherwise displaced. All were given a chance, but the bad apples were removed when I became convinced there was no hope for them becoming contributors to my plans.

By the time I reached the age of thirty, my plantation was prospering. Cotton was my main crop, but we also grew food and enough livestock for our own consumption. Any excess was given to the workers to sell and they were allowed to divide the proceeds among themselves. I required little income from the property as I still had the bulk of my inheritance at my disposal. I was not popular with most of my neighbors due to my generosity. The benefits I provided my workers incited jealousy within the ranks of their slaves and sharecroppers causing the owners added grief at a time when the whole concept of slavery was suffering serious scrutiny from other parts of the country. Still, I held steadfast to my promise to myself and felt little concern over the growing hostility from my neighbors. I had no time for world affairs, politics, or involvement in the social life of the area. I was content with my small world and believed I was well on my way to repaying the kindness that had been shown me by Horace Spencer. I seldom thought of my father and suffered no remorse over his murder. I did sometimes visualize my mother as if she was sitting on my veranda in peace and comfort, enjoying the beauty and security that surrounded her. Over time, even those images faded.

I never felt the need for a family. There were children born to the slaves and sharecroppers and I enjoyed watching them play. It was also my rule that no child would be forced to work at anything besides minor household chores and some gardening before the age of twelve. Women were not forced to work in the cotton fields, but were given responsibility for the main house, the gardens and caring for the livestock. This division of labor was another source of irritation to my neighbors. I knew of many instances where babies were born in the fields because their mothers were forced to help with the harvest right up to their delivery time. I tried to give my workers some peace and the hope of prosperity and, all in all, my life was peaceful and fulfilling for the next few years.

My mistake was in not paying attention to what was going on around me. I had no idea how fearful the other owners were of a slave revolt and the economic issues that were fermenting between the North and South. My practices were seen as fuel to a huge fire that could destroy the lives my neighbors had built. In April of 1861 seven states, including Georgia seceded from the union and the confederacy was brought to life. We were at war with the north and, due to my treatment of my slaves, most of my neighbors viewed me as sympathetic to the enemy. To make matters worse, I refused to convert any of my wealth to confederate bonds to support the war effort of the South and I certainly had no intention of enlisting in the confederate army.

Within a few months, things started happening in my world. There were fires set in my fields. Two of my best slaves disappeared only to be found hanging from a tree two days later. They had been beaten brutally. My livestock was stolen and my gardens raided on a regular basis. By the time the Yankees invaded and Sherman was making his march to the sea, there was little left in the way of plunder. When the last shot was fired in 1865, my home and land was in ruins and I was alone. There was nothing left to keep me in the South. I allowed my property to be taken in lieu of paying the exorbitant taxes inflicted on landowners during reconstruction and I moved to New York City.

My funds, though somewhat depleted, were safe in a bank in New York and more than ample for my needs. I purchased a townhouse on Manhattan Island and there I remained living comfortably, but without embellishments.

My memory began with this old man, alone and without dreams, staring into his mirror and remembering his life. He is wondering if he fulfilled his promise to do good with Horace's money. He tried to do the right thing, but he also knew there was more for him to do. He had no friends or family. He was still moderately wealthy, but except for the occasional coins dropped in a panhandler's cup, he had contributed nothing to anyone for many years. He was bitter that his efforts in the South were squandered on a lost cause. He seldom thought about the other lives that were lost or destroyed by that foolish war, only his own. He had no desire to reach out to anyone, yet he wasn't proud of the man he had become. Had he deteriorated to mirror his former self or had he redeemed himself? Would Horace be proud of him? He wasn't sure. More than likely, his father would be laughing at him. If he gave all his money to the poor, could he purchase redemption or can that only happen through a true and unselfish desire to help others? Was he doomed from the start and would he die of shame and disappointment like his mother? He knew that he was not at the end of his life. He had years left. Would he ask these questions every time he looked in the mirror for the rest of his life? Did he even want to live? Does everyone have these thoughts as they near the end? What would Lucy do? He always liked her better than Luther. All of his promises and good intentions came from Lucy. Luther tried, but was unable to carry through. Lucy wouldn't have been beaten down by a war. She would still be fighting to make Horace proud of her.

The old man began to laugh at his withered beaten face. He finished shaving ever so carefully, put on his best suit and went out to buy a dress and bonnet."

I paused in my story for a few seconds to allow the implications of my last statement to sink in and then I continued, telling the group that I had chosen that memory because, of all my past lives, this was the only one that brought me any happiness. I pointed out that although it may not sound like a great life to most of them, compared to my other lives, it was a cakewalk.

As I looked around, I saw a certain amount of disbelief on some faces, but I assured them that everything happened exactly as I related. I went on to say that the only memory I have past that day is a vague image of a very old Lucy standing in the path of a runaway horse and carriage unable to move fast enough to save herself. She was thinking about how shocked her many friends would be when her true gender was exposed. She was hoping that the many good works she had performed since bringing Lucy back to life would overshadow the shock of her deception. She was sorry to be dying, but wasn't sad, just hoping it wouldn't be too painful. Then she was thinking of Horace and she was smiling.

THELMA

You have got to be kidding!! I mean it was a great story, but I had a hard time with the idea that he could actually have a memory of an entire life? I thought that when people claimed to remember past lives, it is just little snippets they remember, a moment in time, not a whole damn life. I don't get this at all. And then there is the question of why some have memories and others don't.

SAMANTHA

I couldn't believe that Thelma didn't know more about this. I asked why she had never asked Grandma about her memories and I volunteered to answer her questions. Many of the memories are just short images, but some are stories like this. It's like Bernie described looking in a mirror. When you see that person you once were, you know their whole story in a second because you have all the memories and experiences of their life. I guess it's like when people say your life passes before you at the moment you are dying. When you think of your favorite movie, you think of the whole thing, not one little scene. Some of my memories are very short and I really can't figure out who I was, but others are quite detailed. I don't know why this is so, it just is. I think the little memories are scary. I like to know who I am dealing with. That is the only way we can learn from what we remember.

ADRIAN

Samantha handled that very well. She wanted to point out to Thelma that if she was such a good friend to Amanda, maybe she should have had more interest in her memories instead of pretending they didn't exist. Thelma didn't seem to pick up on that, but I doubt that woman has ever questioned her own failures. I stepped in to give Thelma my own take on the subject.

"I don't know why some of us have memories and others don't, but I do believe that we are supposed to learn from these past lives and working toward bettering our souls. If we only had loose little "snippets" as you put it, there would be no opportunity to learn and advance toward whatever goal we are supposed to reach or maybe those memories are small because we failed to achieve our purpose in that life and there was no lesson learned. But one thing that I am seeing here is that we all seem to have at least some very detailed memories and I believe that is for a reason. I also know that I haven't had the memories in all my lives so if you don't have them now perhaps you will in a future life or maybe you have had them in past lives. I don't believe we are the "chosen ones". It's possible that we are the laggards and we had to be given the memories to help us progress."

AMANDA

It did my heart good to hear what Adrian and Samantha had to say. I always suspected that Thelma believed to some degree in my memories, but I also have wondered if she was a bit jealous of them. Perhaps she thought I believed I was somehow superior to her because of them. It would be so like

Thelma to think that way since if it were she that had the memories, she would take it as a sign of superiority. I don't, and neither do the others in our group. We are often troubled, sometimes entertained, hopefully enlightened by them, but never do we attribute this "gift" to our own worthiness.

I was admiring Alfie's restraint at not taunting Bernie about being a "cross dresser" when he piped up in his gayest voice and asked Bernie if the styles had changed much from the time he was the young Lucy to being the old Lucy. Everyone laughed and Bernie didn't seem offended, as it was obviously clear in his mind that becoming Lucy was a matter of survival, not a sexual aberration.

I did like both Lucy and Luther and I wondered what happened to interrupt Bernie's progress so that he ended up being what we saw before us instead of a new and improved Bernie. I would have thought there were some valuable lessons to be learned from that life. Is it possible that this Bernie is an improvement over the Bernie that existed prior to that life? God Forbid!

Etienne was studying Bernie and looked very serious. I was interested in hearing his reaction so I asked him what his thoughts were. He finally spoke up and we were all shocked by what he had to say.

ETIENNE

Bernie, I think it is obvious why your life as Lucy was more rewarding than as Luther. It is a matter of trust. When you pretended to be Lucy you loved and were loved. You invented this person that had not been tainted by your father. You allowed yourself to be free of the guilt, shame and fear that accompanied your life as Luther. When you were Luther, you tried to do the right things and be a part of the world, but you could never let anyone to get close to you because you didn't trust yourself or anyone else enough to be able to share your life. Luther could not repair the damage to his soul from the life he was forced to lead, but Lucy, his accidental creation, was free to keep her promises. In the end, you reclaimed Lucy and gained redemption. All in all, it was an admirable life.

SAM

Etienne displayed an unusual level of perception for one his age. I was impressed as were the others including Samantha, who was looking at him with something far beyond admiration. I was ready to call it a morning until Samantha turned to Bernie and asked a question that I did not want to hear. She told Bernie that she understood he was not gay and that she didn't think he had a split personality, but she wanted to know if he ever had s-e-x. I think she spelled it out, not because she was too shy to say the word, but so that the question would appear more innocent than it really was. Amanda broke in to say that the subject was inappropriate and had nothing to do with the content of the story. She was trying to appear calm, but I could see she was upset. The last thing we needed was for Thelma to report to Alex and Tiffany that we had children present at a past-life sex seminar. Samantha sensed her grandmother's discomfort, but continued on saying that although she and Etienne were virgins in this life, they both had the memories so they knew more about the subject than most kids their age. Etienne chimed in that his mother had always been very open about the subject. I was becoming more uncomfortable all the time when Thelma spoke up. She stated that it was an honest question and she didn't see anything wrong with hearing what Bernie had to say as long as he didn't go into great detail. This was a real leap for Thelma who had always proclaimed a disdain for the subject as well as the act itself.

Bernie volunteered to respond. He wanted to make it clear that he was not a sexual deviant such as being gay or a cross dresser. He told us he performed as a man, and rather well according to a variety of sources. (He just had to get that last part in). He went on to say that during his years on the plantation there were opportunities available to him of the sort that were quite common in that environment and in his later years in New York it was possible to find ladies who were willing participants without involving anything but money.

I jumped up and announced we would be taking a break before lunch and ended the conversation there. Samantha, sensing she had gone as far as she dared, asked no further questions, but she and Etienne exchanged a look that I couldn't read, one of those scary teenage moments. I needed a few minutes to regain my composure at the thought of my dear sweet granddaughter having carnal knowledge, even though it wasn't in her current body. I also realized that Samantha was pushing us. She was reaching the age when children starting challenging the authority figures in their lives. She was entering the secret world of teenagers, secret thoughts, secret dreams, secret schemes. I could see Amanda was struggling in the same way. Thelma was clearly quite proud of herself and was enjoying our discomfort. It was clear she intended to be the "cool", understanding adult in Samantha's life

All through lunch, Jenny was unusually quiet. She spent a lot of time looking at Bernie with an expression I couldn't define. I wondered if she was remembering his comment about not being a sexual deviant and including being gay in that category. She would, of course, be protective of Alfie's feelings, but he did not seem a bit flustered by the remark. I decided she was just reacting to Bernie in the same way we all did, part disgust and part confusion.

After lunch, Amanda invited Thelma to take a walk with her down on the beach. Considering their confrontation that morning, I would have thought Thelma would be reluctant to place herself in further jeopardy, but she accepted immediately. I knew Amanda would probably break down and apologize and that was OK with me as I wanted to stay on Thelma's good side. It was dangerous to be anywhere else. I knew that Amanda always has a tendency to blame herself for everything and that morning had given her enough time to turn the tables against herself. I have often wondered if people who shoulder all blame, regardless of circumstances, do so out of an exaggerated view of their own influence. It just might be a special kind of vanity. I decided not to explore this concept with Amanda.

Samantha and Etienne went to the guest house to check out each other's Facebook page. I pointed out that they might learn more just talking to one another face to face, a comment that elicited no response from either. I had known from the beginning that they would hit it off, but I didn't expect them to be twins from different mothers. The truth is, I wished Samantha could stay longer than three days. I enjoyed watching them together. There was something very familiar about the way they interacted. Before they left, Etienne secretly asked me if I was upset with him for speaking out that morning. I wasn't. I knew that he was showing support for Samantha more than being interested in Bernie's response. At least I hoped that was the case.

Chapter Twenty-Eight

ETIENNE AND SAMANTHA

ETIENNE

Bernie's story about Lucy and Luther was a real trip. I thought it was cool how Luther managed to fool everyone for so many years and I really think he did the right thing even though he lied to Horace. It wasn't his fault that his life got all messed up and he did make Horace Spencer's last years a lot better. Luther kept trying to do good things, but then he gave up for a long time. In the end he went back to being Lucy and did a lot of good for people so I think Horace would have been proud of him. Samantha agreed with me on that point, but she thought Luther should have told Horace the truth and that Horace would have understood and it would have made Luther's life a lot easier. She said that the truth was always better than a lie, but then Samantha has always lived in a very open and loving family so I thought maybe she didn't understand how things are for people who grew up in a world of secrets, although I was soon to discover that all was nor what it seemed with Samantha either.

She confessed that she felt bad about asking Bernie the question about his sex life. She could see that Sam and Amanda were upset with her and she hated doing that to them. She said that lately lots of things had been coming out of her mouth that she didn't mean to say, especially with her mother. She said she kept promising herself that she will do better, but it seemed at times to be out of her control.

When Samantha arrived that Friday afternoon and burst into the room, I felt like I had swallowed a firecracker and it had gone off in my stomach. I watched as she jumped into Sam's lap and then went around the room meeting everyone and talking a mile a minute. First of all, she is beautiful. Her hair is long and the color of butterscotch with streaks of cinnamon and her eyes are an incredible shade of blue, so much so that I wondered if she was wearing tinted contact lenses. She is slender but not tiny like my mom and she has the kind of skin that looks slightly tan year round. She looks a lot like Amanda, only prettier. But it was more than her looks that turned me to mush. She seemed familiar to me and I felt like I had known her all my life. I was glad that she didn't see me right away so I had a couple of minutes to get my head on straight.

When she did notice me sitting in my stupid wheelchair it was all I could do to move my chair toward her and try to appear cool. I think I did a pretty good job of hiding my excitement but it wasn't easy. I had been feeling pretty bad all day because I was worried about my mom. I was sure that there were things about her leaving that they weren't telling me. Adrian and Amanda looked like they were going to cry every time they looked at me and everyone was trying too hard, pretending everything was alright. Samantha took my mind off my worries and I felt like I had someone I could talk to. We spent that whole evening together while she talked and

I mostly listened until Adrian made me go to bed early like I was some little kid. Then the next morning Samantha filled me in on the battle between Amanda and Thelma. Thelma had taken Samantha aside to make sure she heard her side of the story first. Apparently Thelma had done something to embarrass Sam and Amanda was furious with her and threatened to send her home early. Samantha was worried that if Thelma left she might have to go with her, but that didn't happen. They made up, but Amanda got mad at Sam for some reason even though it was Thelma that had messed up in the first place. Samantha said it was always that way with Amanda and Sam and not to worry because they would get over it.

After lunch we went to the guest house because Samantha wanted to see my Facebook page and she was really anxious to show me hers. Of course she had lied about her age to get on Facebook, proving that she is not totally truthful all the time. I had put my page up about a year before, but I really didn't go there often and even when I did there wasn't much to see. I had posted a picture of myself from my confirmation day in the Catholic Church. Father Karl took the picture of me in my blue blazer with a white shirt and tie. I listed my hobbies as gardening, sketching, piano and violin and included that I am fluent in English and French and that I like to play soccer, although I didn't mention that I am really good at soccer because I thought that would sound like I was bragging. I also mentioned my love of Cadillacs and asked anyone who was interested in them to contact me. I guess I really am a nerd because I only had two contacts and both of them were even nerdier than me. Samantha had little to say about my Facebook page other than giving me a long sympathetic look and suggesting that we go to her page. That was when things really heated up.

The picture she had posted was obviously professionally done and though she looked beautiful, she looked like she was about twenty one years old. She was wearing a lot of makeup and her hair was done up in a style no girl her age could do herself. On top of that she was posing with her back against a tree, wearing a thin dress and not much else that I could see. She had one bare foot raised behind her and resting against the tree so her knee was extended outward and she was reaching up to a limb with her arm strategically placed in front of what would one day be her boobs. I suppose this was done to conceal the fact that she really didn't have much to show as yet. I told her that I thought the picture was sleazy and dangerous for a girl her age and she replied that at least she didn't look like someone who ran around with a book in one hand and a model car in another; an obvious slam toward me. Then she told me to quit acting like I am so much smarter than her just because I'm older.

We were getting pretty mad at one another when Sam walked in to see what we were doing. I think he was bored and maybe a little worried about what was going on with Thelma and Amanda during their walk. He looked over my shoulder at the picture of Samantha and seemed to enjoy what he was seeing. Then he realized who he was looking at and his face changed completely. His eyes kept going back and forth between Samantha and the computer and I swear he turned a little green. Samantha was smiling up at him. I suppose she was expecting to see a look of approval, but I knew that he was thinking what I was thinking. The first words out of his mouth were, "Has your grandmother seen this?". He shouted this at her and her smile disappeared immediately. He started telling her the same things I had been saying and she was not at all happy to hear them. I didn't think it was possible to see Sam so upset. Finally, Samantha jumped up and ran from the guest house crying. Sam sat in her vacated chair and asked me to turn off the computer. We didn't talk for a couple of minutes and then Sam looked at me with kind of a weak smile and said "I think we handled that well, don't you?". We both laughed, but it wasn't fun laughter.

Sam suggested that we should just let her cool down and have Amanda talk to her when she and Thelma returned. I was happy to go along with that idea and I decided then that Sam could teach me a lot about how to handle women in spite of his history with Amanda. I guess there are times when a guy just has to back off and let the women take over. It's safer that way. I hated having Samantha angry with me. Still, I couldn't back down. She was in danger of losing her way and I had to protect her. I knew I had been in this position before and I had failed. I guess Sam returned to the main house to wait for Amanda, but I really don't remember because I was already in another place. I had been there before, but this time the memory took on a new meaning.

Chapter Twenty-Nine

RAOUL AND YVETTE

I was in France and World War II was finally over. I lived in a village in the area of Alsace Lorraine but I had traveled to Paris to find Yvette. I didn't know where to look, I only knew I had to try. I hated myself for being so fearful when Yvette needed me to be strong. I had failed Yvette and I wanted another chance.

My name was Raoul and I was twenty two years old. I was five when Yvette was born. Her family lived on a small farm next to ours. Our village was small and everyone was very poor. The village had been ravaged during the war, but not destroyed like so many others. We were pretty isolated and I guess there wasn't that much to destroy in the first place. A few villagers joined the Resistance, but most of the action took place near the larger cities.

I remembered Yvette's mother, Veronique. She was kind and beautiful, loved by everyone. Yvette's father, Raymond, was not born in our village, but had come from the Pyrenees Mountains to buy some lambs. It was said that he took one look at Veronique and he never left. He was short and stout and incredibly strong. As a child and then as a young man, I had seen him perform some incredible feats of strength and we were all in awe of him. He was gracious and funny and went to work for Veronique's family as a farmhand. He worked hard and saved his money and eventually fulfilled his dream of marrying Veronique. A few months later, not enough, she gave birth to a son. This was all before I was born, but I grew up hearing rumors that Veronique had been abandoned by her lover and Raymond had eagerly stepped in to serve as her husband and father to her son.

When Veronique's parents passed away within one year of each other, Veronique and Raymond inherited the farm and the family prospered in a small way. Raymond loved and was proud of their son, but Veronique adored him. He was her life and anyone could see that she worshipped the ground he walked on. Perhaps he was all that she had left of the man whom she had loved, but who had deserted her. Her son fell off the barn roof when he was sixteen and never regained consciousness. Veronique was pregnant with Yvette at the time and she and Raymond had been overjoyed that they were finally going to share a child. Veronique sat by her son's bedside for many weeks crying and praying for his recovery. When he finally died, she became so despondent that many feared she would lose her baby. Raymond did everything he could to bring her out of her depression, but she was never the same. Yvette was born two months later and everyone hoped that the new baby would bring Veronique back to life, but it wasn't to be. When Yvette was six months old, Veronique hung herself in the same barn that took her son's life.

Raymond carried on with the farm and everyone in the village looked after him and Yvette, including my parents. From the time she was a baby, Yvette spent many days and nights at our home. I often bragged that I helped raise her since I shared so much of the responsibility for her care, but she would get annoyed with me whenever I made that claim. I thought she was like a sister to me but, as we grew older we were closer than most siblings.

On my eighteenth birthday my mother gave me a party and the whole village was invited. Everyone was asking me about my plans for the future. Most assumed that I would be leaving the village and moving to the city to attend school or develop a career. My parents were still quite young and there was little need for me on the farm. I was embarrassed to admit that I had no plans. I stayed at home for that entire summer, wondering what was wrong with me that I wasn't anxious to go out into the world. Finally, I realized that I never wanted to leave Yvette. I simply did not want to be where she was not.

Yvette was only thirteen at that time, so it was not a revelation that I could share with anyone, although I think my mother suspected. I stayed on with my family for another four years waiting for Yvette to get old enough to claim her as my bride. At first I never considered that she might reject me, but as she matured, she began to confide in me about her crushes on other boys, and over time, it became obvious that she loved me as a brother. Still, I knew that someday she would realize that we were meant to be together.

Raymond remarried when Yvette was ten years old and he and his new wife had two children of their own. The new wife had little time for Yvette and Raymond was busy with his farm and his other responsibilities. Yvette grew more and more distant and began to change. By the time she was fifteen, our village had become boring to her and she often traveled to a larger neighboring village to visit new friends. Raymond tried to control her activities, but Yvette ignored his rules and, over time, he gave up and concentrated on his second family which had grown to include four children. I saw less and less of her and, when we did get together, my role was chiefly as confidant leaving me feeling depressed and frustrated.

As Yvette drifted further away from me, she was engaging in some dangerous activities. She was smoking and drinking and had a string of boyfriends. The final straw for me was when she introduced me to her latest "suitor". He was a slimy character who had no respect for Yvette or women in general. He secretly let me know that they were having sex on a regular basis and that Yvette was very experienced and, as he put it, "knew some great tricks". I just listened and chose not to believe him, hoping he would be as temporary as the others had been. Later, I confronted Yvette and told her what he had told me. She wasn't even upset about that, but she hit the ceiling when I told her she was behaving like a whore and that her lifestyle would bring her nothing but pain. I told her she needed to stop running around with these new friends and return to the sweet girl we all knew. She cried and ranted and said she never should have trusted me. She accused me of trying to run her life just because I was older than her. We seldom spoke to one another after that. She was pleasant to me when we ran into each other, but it was clear that she felt angry and betrayed.

Finally, Raymond came by my house asking if I had seen Yvette in the past few days. She had not come home and he was concerned. I knew she had run away, probably with her slimy boyfriend. The creep had mentioned that he was going to move to Paris and it wasn't hard to imagine her begging to go with him. It also wasn't hard to imagine where she would end up.

So there I was-Raoul in Paris- searching for Yvette. I knew that I had failed her. I should have fought harder to stay in her life, but I was afraid that if I pushed harder it might drive her further away or she would turn on me and order me out of her life. I was afraid of that finality.

I don't know if Raoul ever found Yvette. I believe he did not because I have had the same memory several times and it never goes beyond the point where he is in Paris searching for her. After my fight with Samantha, I knew why she had seemed so familiar to me. The remark Samantha made about my thinking I was smart because I was older than her brought back my memory of Raoul. I wondered if Raoul and Yvette were being given a second chance through Samantha and me. I will remain in Samantha's life and I will not fail her as Raoul failed Yvette. I will not allow myself to be driven away by fear.

You may think that I am too young to understand the commitment I am making; that it is the romantic notion of a boy with his first crush on a girl, but I will remind you that I have the memories of Raoul at the age of twenty two. I can't claim to have all the wisdom of a man that age, but I do know what it is like to love and lose another.

I didn't share this story with the rest of the group, certainly not Samantha, but I was wishing my mother was there because I could have talked to her and, even if she didn't understand, she would have listened and given me some advice. I needed to confide in someone, but I didn't think it would be wise to talk to Sam or Amanda. They might think I was going to stalk their granddaughter. I decided to wait and see if Samantha was in a better mood later and if I needed help, I would go to Adrian.

SAM

Etienne stayed in the guest house while I returned to the main house to wait for Amanda. As I crossed over, I could see

Samantha heading toward the winding path to go down to the beach. I suspected she was trying to get the jump on me by finding Amanda and telling her side of the story first. It isn't that I think my granddaughter is sneaky. It's just that I have long been aware that women don't like to wait for the other shoe to drop. They want to get to the heart of the matter right away and get their point made without giving the opposition time to gather his thoughts. This keeps us men constantly on the defensive. Usually it turns out that, even if we are clearly right about what we have said or done, we are still under attack for the way we did or said it. This has the effect of lessening the guilt of the other party, at least in their own eyes. I had no idea what to expect from Amanda when she returned, but I did know for sure that she would not like the Facebook page and she would deal with it immediately. I sure as hell didn't know what to do.

AMANDA

Thelma and I had a nice talk about the events of that morning. She offered what I considered to be an adequate, if not thoroughly sincere, apology for her behavior and she promised to treat Sam with more respect. She didn't go so far as to imply that her opinion of him had been elevated, but she was willing to be more accommodating for my sake. I decided that was as good as it was going to get so I accepted her apology with the understanding that if she didn't hold up her end of the bargain, I would have to beat her up again. One thing about Thelma, she has a good sense of humor and we ended up hugging and laughing about my physical assault. Even after several hours, she still had a small welt on her cheek where I had slapped her, likely caused by my ring or possibly a fingernail. I told her the next time I would go for permanent disfigurement. I was proud of myself in that I did not accept any of the blame for the event. That was something new for me. The old Amanda would have caved in and apologized and accused myself of overreacting. To be honest, as unladylike as my behavior was, I was not the least bit sorry. Thelma had needed to be slapped for a very long time. She is one of those people that others tolerate just to stay on her good side. She rules by fear and it was time for me to call a halt to her reign of terror.

We were just heading back when I caught sight of Samantha running down the trail. I could see that she was crying. Thelma spotted her too and was running to her. I grabbed Thelma by the coattails and told her to wait where she was while I dealt with my granddaughter. She wasn't happy about it, but she obeyed. I knew it would be a matter of time until she cornered Samantha to find out what was going on, but I guess you can't change a lifetime of habit by one slap in the face.

Samantha told me about her innocent little Facebook page and that Etienne had called her a slut and her grandpa agreed with Etienne. I knew that I was not being given the whole story and Samantha knew that I knew because she kept rattling on and on about how cruel they had been to her. There is nothing in this world that would convince me that Sam would ever be cruel to Samantha, so I already had a pretty good idea of what I was going to see when I got to her page. We proceeded up the long trail to the house with Samantha saying how she hated Etienne, and Thelma following us trying to put the pieces together so that we could all benefit from her pearls of wisdom whenever she found an opening. By the time we reached the house, I was fairly perturbed with both of them.

We went to the master suite that I was sharing with Kate during Thelma's visit. Kate was not there so Samantha and

I logged on to my laptop and went to her Facebook page. I'm sure Samantha knew that I would not approve of that picture, but she probably thought she could slip it by me as a lack of judgment or an innocent mistake. She was wrong. I was once twelve (actually I have been twelve several times) and I know how a girl that age can be. It is a very sexual time in a girl's life. She is becoming a woman and many girls that age are very aware of the effect they can have over boys, or worse yet, men.

In today's world, a young girl that age may still be a virgin, but they are not exactly innocent. There is too much on TV, in magazines, at school and on the internet for them to miss the not too subtle details of sexuality. They are being told that a pretty face and a perfect body are tools to get what they want. Even girls of good character can be led in the wrong direction because our society pays attention and homage to these spoiled, self-centered little prima donnas. Parents often see their daughters as these happy young innocent treasures and they delight in treating them like little princesses. Who wouldn't want to give their child a fairy tale life, especially if their own childhood had been less than ideal? Too often though, these girls come to believe they are princesses. What does that say about their expectations versus reality?

A twelve year old girl does not have the full picture of what it means to be a woman, but they sure are in a hurry to grow up. It came as no shock to me that Samantha would indulge in unacceptable behavior at some point. I was hoping it would be later, but I was ready for it anyway. I told her that she needed to get that picture off the internet immediately and that she was too young for social media. She started to argue with me and that is when I told her that she was not fooling me a bit with her attempt at appearing unaware of what she was doing. I mentioned her question to Bernie that morning and now this picture and I told her that I was not buying into her routine. I let her know that I understood her feelings and what was happening around her world, but that I was determined to keep her safe and on the right path.

I was not surprised when she admitted that Alex and Tiffany didn't even know that she was on Facebook. It was also clear that she didn't want them to go there. I think she thought I would reprimand her, make her change the picture, but keep her secret. Wrong again. I told her I was calling Alex that evening and would direct him to the page. She became very upset and began to cry like the little girl I knew. She whined that I had always told her she could come to me with anything, but now I was betraying her. I patiently explained that she had not come to me with this for advice. She came because she knew Sam would show it to me and she was trying to beat him to the draw. I told her that, in addition to the picture being inappropriate, she was also being sneaky and manipulative with the people who love her and are responsible for her. The last thing I said to her before she ran from the room was that I understood why she was doing these things, but that I would never accept that behavior from her.

I'll admit that I was more than a little afraid of losing my relationship with Samantha. I didn't want her to turn away from me, but I also couldn't try to be her friend at that point. She needed leadership and direction and I wanted to offer Alex and Tiffany the support they would need when they were confronted with this issue. Children have such power these days. There are so many ways they can hold their parents hostage if they don't get what they want. Being a parent right now would be, for me, one of the scariest jobs in the world.

Actually, I have always been a little afraid of children. I think it might be because I was never a child myself. In this and in many other remembered lives, circumstances took that time away from me. But I do remember the thoughts and fantasies that accompany young womanhood and that made me even more afraid for Samantha. I have lived lives that took me on the short path away from my values and left me stranded or alone to travel the long road back. I knew I had to hold my ground with her and pray that she had the character to accept my judgment as an act of love.

I went to find Sam, as I knew he would be in a state of agitated confusion. He never could see anything but the angel in Samantha. It's that pedestal thing with him. I found him hiding in the den pretending to read. I felt sorry for him as he tried to make it appear that he wasn't overly concerned about Samantha's behavior and that he was accepting it as a normal part of growing up, but I could see that he was upset and clearly didn't know what to do. I relayed the key parts of my conversation with Samantha and he seemed relieved that I appeared to know how to handle the situation. He was even more relieved when I said I would be the one to take the problem to Alex and Tiffany. It was clear that he never wanted to see that picture again, let alone discuss the emerging sexuality of our granddaughter with her father. He looked so pathetic that I almost started laughing. Instead I gave him a hug that ended up being a bit more intimate than the situation called for. I wanted to crawl on his lap and stay there for an hour or two like the old days. Actually, I wanted to do more than that. I kept seeing in my mind the ill-fated candles, flowers, B&B and chocolates he had placed in my room the night before and I craved that quiet contentment we had shared for so long. If he had invited me down to his boat at that moment I would have gladly accompanied him, but there was so much going on that I'm sure it never occurred to him. That is probably for the best.

SAM

By now you must know that there are some things that I just can't deal with. I was so relieved that Amanda took the lead with Samantha. I probably would have taken some watered down approach and tried to be her friend instead of standing up to her when she needed it. Amanda has no fear. I'm sure she didn't worry that her relationship with Samantha would be damaged. She always knows what to do when it comes to children. She simply has no fear of them at all. I'm glad she couldn't see how helpless I felt. She obviously came to me for strength and for that I got something more than a hug. I'm not sure what we were doing, but it wasn't hugging. I do know that she still prefers underwire bras and she hasn't lost anything in that area. I was glad that I didn't have to stand up for the next few minutes and I found myself remembering some pretty hot moments that we have shared. I thought about inviting her down to my boat, but I knew for sure that she wouldn't be interested just then. I thought it better to wait until things settled down. I was sure I made the right decision. Meanwhile, I was wondering how Etienne was doing and if he and Samantha had made up. I decided to let Amanda handle that as well so I stayed in the den and continued to pretend to be reading. I wondered if I would ever actually read that Grisham novel.

SAMANTHA

I hated everyone that afternoon for at least two hours. I knew I would forgive my grandpa and even my grandma and I was sure that they would not be mad at me for too long. They were just being old people. But why was Etienne being so mean to me? Did he really think that just because he is two years older he can boss me around? This was none of his business- so why did I feel so bad?

I knew all along in the back of my mind that my parents would have a fit over that picture if they saw it, but several of my friends had done the same thing and it was no big deal. My friend Hope has an uncle that is a photographer and he took the pictures for free. He is a really cool guy. He doesn't have a studio because he says he likes to take pictures in natural settings, not with some phony backdrop. He has a friend that does our hair and makeup for us at his apartment and they have lots of clothes there so we can dress up however we want and then we go "on location" to take the pictures. It's like being a famous model or something. He called me a couple of times to see if I liked my picture and said that if I didn't he would take more any time I wanted. Some of the girls have several pictures, but I had a hard enough time getting away to have that one taken. I was glad grandma didn't ask me how I got the picture and I wondered why that would bother me. I guess I knew there was something funny about the whole thing. I started to feel kind of sick at the thought of grandma showing the picture to my parents and I wished I could make the whole thing go away. I remembered that grandpa told me more than once that "If something doesn't feel quite right, don't do it!". I wished I had listened.

After a couple of hours, I was feeling so sick and miserable that I couldn't stand to be alone. I wasn't ready to face my grandparents so I decided to go and see if Etienne was still mad at me. I never have been able to stand having people mad at me. I'm like my grandma that way. He was still in the guest house so I knocked on the door and heard him tell me to come in. He was sitting in his wheelchair facing the door and I had the feeling he had been in that exact position for a long time.

I could tell by his big smile that he was not mad and I felt so relieved that I started to cry. I knelt on the floor and laid my head on his bad leg and cried my eyes out. He was so sweet as he stroked my hair and told me everything would work out. I told him that grandma was going to show the picture to my parents and that I dreaded what they would think about me. I also told him about Hope's uncle and his eyes got very wide and angry. He told me that I had to tell my parents about the uncle and his friend so that they could alert Hope's parents. I didn't want to get anyone else in trouble or be a snitch, but I wanted to do the right thing and Etienne was pretty sure that the uncle was not just a nice guy. I knew that there were freaks out there that tricked girls into bad things, but I never thought it could happen to me or my friends. I still wasn't sure that Hope's uncle was a freak. He never tried anything weird with me, and none of my friends said anything bad about him. Etienne said the man was just taking advantage of the vanity of young girls and pointed out that it would be my fault if something bad happened to one of my friends. I guessed that being two years older really does make a difference. We sat and talked for the rest of the afternoon and Etienne told me how worried he was about his mother. I couldn't imagine what it must be like to not have a father or grandparents and be separated from my mother without knowing the whole story. I forgot my own worries for a while.

Etienne told me that my grandparents would help me as much as possible with my parents but that everyone would be keeping a closer watch over me in the future and that I would just have to learn to accept that. He said he hoped we would e-mail each other every day and be close friends in spite of the fact that we lived in different countries. I wanted the same thing and I thought it would be cool to have an older boyfriend in a foreign country. I was already planning how we could visit each other in the summer. Then it occurred to me that I had never seen Etienne in a standing position and I wondered if he was taller than me, not that it mattered, well it sort of did. Sometimes I don't know where these thoughts come from, but I'm glad I held my tongue and didn't ask such a stupid question at such a serious moment. That is something my grandpa would do, but it's funny when it happens to him. Grandma usually laughs when he does that, but sometimes she gets mad. That was the first time I have ever been mad at my grandpa and it was the first time he ever yelled at me. I wanted it to be the last time.

SAM

After the events of the day, that is witnessing a catfight between my beloved and her best friend on my behalf and coming to the realization that my granddaughter is less angelic than I had imagined, as well as nursing this nagging feeling that I might have passed up an opportunity to unleash my passions on Amanda, I felt I was due a reprieve for the evening. I was anxious to join the rest of the group to hear about their adventures of the afternoon and perhaps enjoy a few laughs. My instincts were reinforced when I saw Samantha pushing Etienne in his wheelchair from the guesthouse. Both were smiling so I could see they had made peace with one another. I don't know why I was so relieved about that, but my mood was immediately improved.

The group was gathered in the dining area gearing up for the cocktail hour. Amanda was nowhere to be seen and I had the suspicion that she was on the phone in her room talking to Alex and Tiffany. Samantha had come to find her earlier and they had a private conversation. Then Amanda grabbed Samantha and hugged her as if she was afraid of losing her. Samantha had returned to the guest house and Amanda related to me the details of how the picture was taken and the information Samantha had given her about Hope's uncle. Then she turned and went to her room with an angry and determined look on her face. It is so like her to dive right in and deal with the problem head on, rather than let it fester. She probably wanted to give Alex and Tiffany a couple of days to digest the information so they could deal with Samantha with cooler heads. I know she was also anxious to get word to them about Hope's uncle so they could contact her parents. There was little doubt in my mind or hers that the uncle had ulterior motives with these little girls and needed to be confronted and investigated immediately. I felt bad for Samantha because she had no idea what a mess she would be returning home to, but I was also grateful that we had stumbled across the problem in time to save her from possible damage. I have never considered myself a "macho" man, but at that point I wanted to kill that filthy, camera toting bastard. Instead I said a quick prayer of thanks and poured myself a drink almost as stiff as Bernie's.

Speaking of Bernie, he was in high spirits that evening and I was wondering if he wasn't putting his best foot forward to impress Thelma. If so, I actually felt a wee bit of sympathy for both of them. Although I can think of no more interesting match than that would be, I also shuddered at the thought of putting that much nastiness together. It would be like making "nasty soup" and it could have far-reaching effects on the environment if not handled properly. They might even form a new government agency to deal with the long term effects of such a mess. I could be arrested or fined as the perpetrator of a terrorist event. I didn't know if Thelma was impressed with Bernie's efforts, but she didn't gag when looking at him so that was probably taken as a positive response in Bernie's book. I guess he had finally given up on Serena. As kind and gentle as Serena is, she had still managed to make it very clear that she had no interest in spending more than a nanosecond with him. Good for her!

Thelma was also eavesdropping on a conversation between Alfie and Paul, who was joining us for dinner once again. I enjoyed having him around. Alfie became even more lively than usual when Paul was with us. Jenny would sit and watch the two of them joke and laugh and you could see on her face the joy she felt for her friend. The three of them kept the rest of us in stitches and I must say, Thelma was adding to the fun as well.

One thing about Thelma, she could be as much fun as she could be a pain in the ass. Get her in the right mood and you can watch and enjoy her quick wit. Get her in the wrong mood and you can be tortured by it. That night she oozed warmth and merriment. She even saved a place for me beside her (not that anyone was competing for that spot) and made a little too much of including me in her conversations. Lady Bountiful she was. I didn't care, I was just glad to have that day come to an end.

Adrian and Serena had cooked up a special surprise for our dinner. Adrian's grandmother was from one of those countries in Eastern Europe that have seven syllables and keep changing their government every few years. This brings many high caliber immigrants to this country; thrifty, hardworking, honest, and damn good cooks. I have always loved the dishes that were born in those regions. Amanda knows how to cook in that style, but hasn't done so in years, at least not for me. Adrian had volunteered to make cabbage rolls from her grandmother's recipe. Now, many cooks would have had their ego bruised to have another in their kitchen, but Serena has such a generous nature that, not only did she accept the offer graciously, but she participated in the rather lengthily process. I had heard them in the kitchen laughing and sharing culinary secrets all afternoon, but I didn't know what they were up to. The end result was a dinner consisting of cabbage rolls that were even better than Amanda's, a dish called fried noodles that was nothing more than bread dough rolled into noodles, seasoned with a savory blend of spices, steamed and browned in water and oil. Serena had also baked some caraway rye bread and we had pickled beets, pickled herring with sour cream and a dessert that was also a specialty of Adrian's grandmother consisting of a thick layer of very heavy custard on a sweet crust with cinnamon and apples made into a thin pie and cut into triangles. I couldn't understand why Adrian made eight of these pies until I tasted one. Piece after piece, I couldn't stop, even after consuming two cabbage rolls and a huge plate full of those incredible fried noodles. I bowed politely to the pickled herring, but did not indulge. As for the beets, Amanda took care of most of those. She loves beets and gets a kick out of her pink pee the next day. I'll never forget years ago, the first time she called me into the bathroom to check out her deposit. I wanted to rush her to the hospital immediately. She played along for a few minutes before telling me the origin of the offending peepee. I was not amused and I found her behavior odd because, though she is somewhat comfortable with off color jokes and often tells them herself, she is not fond of bathroom humor as a rule.

Amanda joined us as we were sitting down to dinner. She gave Samantha a big hug which was answered with a tearful smile from Samantha. She gave me a reassuring nod and whispered something in Samantha's ear that kept her smiling through her tears. My suspicions were confirmed that she had been talking to Alex and Tiffany. That night I began the dinner by asking everyone to join hands and give thanks to God for our fortunate companionship. Samantha and Etienne kept holding hands long after the prayer ended. It worked out fine because Etienne was to the right of Samantha and she is left handed and he right handed so each could eat without difficulty. It was just downright sweet watching the two of them.

After dinner everyone gravitated toward the story pit. It seemed that we all wanted to be together. Thelma spoke up and said she wanted to hear another story. She pointed out that she and Samantha had such a limited amount of time with us that we should get on with it. It was comical the way she pouted out her request. Everyone laughed, but there was an awkward silence before Adrian rose and volunteered a memory. Serena usually left after the dinner was over and cleanup was finished, but this night she asked to stay. Of course no one objected so she settled comfortably beside Amanda. I should mention here that Thelma, through cunning and subterfuge, had thoroughly acquainted herself with the situation involving Samantha. This was made obvious by a few skillfully placed comments throughout dinner (these in spite of warning looks from Amanda) designed to let Samantha see that she, Thelma, still deserved to be considered the coolest adult in Samantha's world. It was also obvious that she had shared her knowledge with Adrian and Serena and who knows who else. I suspected that Adrian might choose a memory that would provide some insights to Samantha and I was also anxious to hear her story.

Chapter Thirty

VANITY TAKES A DIVE

ADRIAN

"Throughout history beautiful women have always been celebrated for their beauty and, if they happen to have a generous nature and half a brain, well, that is fine too. Today is no different. We scoff at some of the beliefs and traditions of the past, yet in our "enlightened" age, we still honor those who, through no effort of their own, are born with the right DNA. To add to this, we now have beauty products and medical procedures that can turn a troll into a princess if enough time and money is applied. What do you suppose Paris Hilton would really look like if she hadn't been born to riches? Take a close look at her and see that she is not an example of classic beauty. She is glamorous, but so is a pine tree when loaded with decorations at Christmas time. The difference is that the pine tree is still beautiful in its natural state, but there is nothing of that natural beauty in so many of these female celebrities. That kind of beauty comes directly from God through the soul.

Our media would have us believe that doing whatever is necessary to enhance or alter what God has given us is an art form in itself and the results should be glorified with adulation and envy. One would think that mature individuals would reject this premise on the simplest grounds, yet enough people take notice of these poor misguided children, that they come to believe that they have earned the attention they are given.

We demean ourselves as a society when we value a nose job over improving a soul, or a breast enhancement instead of enlarging an intellect. The end result is a staggering amount of attention going to dim-witted little bitches and precious little to the good works of so many truly beautiful people. To add to the disgrace, we enable these poor creatures to build a life that will never be anything but destruction to themselves. I have a painful memory of myself as such a being and I can speak with full authority when I say that to worship physical beauty is to sentence oneself to a life of pain and fear. When we assume our value lies largely in our physical appearance, obviously, we must concede that when our beauty wanes we will be left with nothing. That is the pain. The fear is that at any turn we might encounter someone who is as beautiful, or even more so, and that person might have other talents or qualities that add value to their existence. Unless we develop as a whole being, vanity will lead us to doom.

My memory begins in the year 1900. I was seventeen years old and I lived with my parents in the most fashionable neighborhood in New York City. My father was an executive and large shareholder of Standard Oil. We were extremely wealthy and becoming more so every day with the advent of the automobile. I was not an only child, but you wouldn't have known that by the amount of attention I received from my family and our circle of friends. My sister was two years older than me and she was kind and loving to me in spite of the fact that I had inherited my share of beauty and hers as well. For as long as I could remember, people would praise Adele for her grace and sweet nature, but they would rave about my beauty. Adele was short and somewhat stocky, while I was taller (but not too tall) and willowy. Adele was pale and plain with thin, mousy brown hair and I had a slightly olive complexion with thick and glossy auburn hair. Her eyes were a muted greenish color while mine were brilliant blue. She was thin lipped and had tiny little teeth and a weak jaw that gave her a sweet, but rodent-like smile. I had full lips and perfect teeth and I was often told that my smile could light up a room. I used that smile often, and sometimes it was sincere.

The date was December sixth of the year 1900. The social season was in full swing and no one was enjoying it more than I. Life magazine was sponsoring a contest which began with the issue coming out on this date. Twenty ladies from the highest society in the city had been selected as the subject of this contest. These were considered to be the most beautiful ladies in the city. There had been little doubt that I would be included and, in fact, I was informed that I was among the first to be chosen. An artist had been hired to attend the brightest social events of the season and that artist would surreptitiously sketch his subjects at the various events. His sketches would be compiled on one page of the magazine and would be featured in the four weekly editions for the month of December. Of course, the fathers or husbands of each were notified to gain permission to use the sketch of their beloved in the contest. No one refused as it was considered great fun to be included in such a popular magazine.

This was not a beauty contest in that the prize would not go to the women who were selected, that would have been considered bourgeois. The object was for the readers to tear out the page and number the beauties from one to twenty with the number one being considered the most beautiful and so on down the line with the number twenty being the least. The reader would then write his or her name and address on the same page and mail or hand deliver it as their entry to the magazine office. There was no limit on the number of times any reader could enter. The contest would be open until January 14th at noon. Each entry would be recorded and the beauty with the most votes for number one would be first and so on. The contest entrant that came the closest to guessing the actual results would win the one hundred dollar prize.

At first my father was hesitant to give his permission. He felt the contest was beneath us, but several in our circle of friends had daughters or wives that were included so that, along with my own tearful pleading and tantrums, convinced him to authorize the use of my sketch. My mother was steadfast against the whole matter, but my father never paid heed to her opinion in any matter, especially when it came to my upbringing or future prospects.

I was beside myself with anticipation, knowing full well that I would be selected and celebrated as the number one beauty in the city. I was being courted by any number of the most eligible bachelors from the best families in the country. That was proof enough to me that I would take the lead. It never occurred to me that the fortune that accompanied my hand in marriage might be a contributing factor to my popularity.

My victory was of such certainty to me that I was not the slightest bit hesitant to share my beliefs with my family and friends. My sister cautioned me that the outcome might not be as glorious as I expected since any reader could enter multiple times, therefore the votes could be swayed in favor of anyone who launched a campaign to be selected first. She told me this to protect me from disappointment, but it had the unanticipated effect of striking fear in my heart. I knew personally all but three of the entries and some I knew to be at least as desirous as I to be selected as number one. But would any of them be so vile as to stack the deck? I answered my own question with a resounding yes, mainly because I knew myself capable of such deceit. My sister read my expression as I thought this through and she immediately tried to retract her statement when she saw that I was already in the initial stages of planning my strategy. She begged me to ignore her comment, but it was too late. My mind was spinning.

I should tell you that this was not my first venture into the world of intrigue and manipulation. It was a lifestyle with me. I had inherited my beauty from my mother's side of the family, but my drive and thirst for recognition came from my father. My dear sister had inherited my father's physique but my mother's kindness and intellect. It would not be long before I would envy her inheritance over my own, impossible though that thought would have seemed to me at the time.

I had never aspired to be anything more than the pampered, self-centered child that I was. Why would I? I would never want for anything and there was no reason for me to toil over books or charitable works to set myself apart. I was born with everything I could ever want. All I had to do was make the most of my gifts, and I was diligent toward this end. There was not a fabric so rich that I couldn't afford to have it made into a dozen of the most stylish dresses designed to fit my perfect form. I had the best maid in the city to care for my every need and arrange my glorious hair in the most flattering styles. I used the best creams to enhance and protect my flawless complexion and I had my own personal scent made in Paris and delivered to me on a regular schedule. Our chef designed delicious but sensible meals especially for me to ensure that my waistline remained so tiny that I had to special order my corsets. I had the finest undergarments that enhanced my bosom to appear slightly, but tastefully, provocative. My petticoats were handmade with the ruffles at the hem in colors to match my dresses. This was my own innovation and one that was soon copied by some of my friends. All this was due me by my provident birth and I was a careful student of any innovations that could provide further benefits. My father had given me a large allowance starting on my sixteenth birthday so that I could make my own purchases without going through my mother, who was more inclined toward teaching me values of a less superficial nature. What I couldn't afford to purchase with my allowance was given to me as gifts from my father. I had but to ask or demand.

None of the other girls my age had the freedom and privileges that I enjoyed and I loved showing off my many treasures and seeing the awe and jealousy on their faces. I knew that I was lacking in compassion for those less fortunate than myself, but I didn't care. I didn't have to be compassionate because I would never need compassion. Besides, I questioned the sincerity of those more generous than me, believing their charitable and kind actions were performed to impress others which, in my opinion, was just as vain as spending a large portion of a day primping in front of a mirror.

My conversations were limited to the latest fashions, recollections of the fanciest parties and the ever enticing bits of gossip that floated about and found their way to my ears or originated with me. I made certain that my own behavior would invite no criticism or embarrassment, (my father's only condition for his generosity toward me) and I never failed to spread the word about the indiscretions of another, always with just the right tone of concern for the victim. I was safe from being accused of reading any of the trashy novels that abounded at that time since I never read any books at all. I spoke enough French to appear stylish, but on my three trips to Paris we had always taken an interpreter. Besides, money speaks the same in any language. I knew nothing of politics and avowed publicly that all politicians were scoundrels and not worthy of my time unless they could be of service to my father in increasing our fortune. I cared not for the issues of the day, especially women's rights. I was clever enough to know that, with those rights would come expectations and responsibility and I could see no reason to make that trade since I already had everything I could possibly want. Adele was active in a number of organizations and had a special interest in child labor laws. I thought that I might get involved in that cause when I was old, but right then I didn't have time to spend on activities that weren't fun or didn't center around me. I went to church every Sunday with my mother and Adele, but I was more interested in what everyone was wearing than in what was being said in the pulpit. Do you think that I considered myself a sinner for my lack of caring about others and my lack of fervor in the pew? I did not. I believed I was living the life that God had given me and if he had wanted me to live otherwise he wouldn't have elevated me to the position I occupied.

I did have one little concern that was a source of guilt to me. I never wanted to have children and I knew that when I married I would use whatever means available to avoid becoming pregnant and I would conceal this from my husband. I justified my deception with the thought that I would not be a good mother and that I would save a child from a lonely life. I also promised myself that I would make up for my unwillingness to provide a child by being the best wife imaginable. After all, any man would be proud to have me as his wife and, if I took great pains to provide him whatever comforts I could, that should be enough. My father was another story. He had failed in producing a son so he was counting on me or Adele to give him a grandson. Since Adele was not in great demand as a prospective wife, this responsibility would likely fall on my shoulders. It pained me to think how unfair it was to expect me to take on such a demanding role. Every time my father brought the subject up, I would simply smile sweetly and try to look joyful at the prospect. I have to admit, this brought me some guilt, but not enough to make me change my mind.

So now you have a picture of the person I was on December 6th 1900. I sent my maid to the newsstand to pick up a copy of Life magazine. There it was, a full page describing the contest rules with the artist's sketch of each of the twenty beauties. I looked for the sketch of myself and flew into a rage. Seventeen of the women had individual sketches, but mine was thrown into the same sketch with two of the other entrants. I recognized them and I even knew when the sketch must have been made. The three of us were standing together in our ball gowns talking and I remember we were gossiping about one of our friends whose father had fallen on hard times. Life as she knew it was coming to an end and we were counting the many deprivations she was suffering. This girl had never been close to me since she was a rival beauty in my eyes and she continually insisted on talking about current events that were of no interest to me. I was somewhat relieved that I wouldn't have to evade her conversations in the future since she would no longer be on the favored guest lists.

The artist captured the fact that the three of us were engaged in a secretive conversation, and his sketch of me was less than flattering. Granted, he did a good job of capturing my best features, but my expression was a bit haughty and hinted of contempt. I was furious to have my sketch lumped with two others and on top of that to have been portrayed in such a manner. The family had gathered to view the page and Adele tried very hard to comfort me, saying that I didn't need to have a spot of my own to stand out as the most beautiful. My father said he would call the magazine and ask to have the artist do another sketch of me, but I knew that even he did not have that kind of influence. My mother spoke up quietly and said that the artist had captured perfectly an expression that she often saw on my face. I assumed her remark was born of jealousy even though I knew she wasn't given to low thoughts. I had little in common with my mother so her opinion mattered little to me. It didn't occur to me until much later that I had never heard my mother say anything cruel before about anyone and how disappointed she must have been in me.

I was sure that if all of our social contacts participated in the contest, I would be the winner so I went right to work to make sure everyone knew I was a contestant and I asked my father to do the same. I had to be subtle or I would expose the depths of my vanity, but at every ball, every afternoon tea, every outing of any kind and to every visitor at our home, I alluded to the contest making comments about how frivolous the whole thing was, but how fun and entertaining. I was disappointed to hear so many of them say that they had no time for such silliness. My suitors all avowed that they would certainly post at least one entry and I would, of course, be their first choice. I fully trusted their sincerity, but I needed more than their promises. It had never really occurred to me to question whether I had any true friends, but suddenly I realized that if my acquaintances were anything like me, I couldn't count on them at all. By the end of the first week, I was frantic. I had become obsessed with being publically recognized for my beauty and I searched my brain for a way to make that obsession a reality.

My father had always claimed that his fortune was a result of his staunch belief in taking control of any situation, not depending on others to further his goals. I decided that I would follow his lead. I took my entire allowance for that month and had my maid hire young boys off the street to buy up every issue they could put their hands on for the next three weeks. She gave the boys money to purchase the magazine, tear out the entry page and deliver that page to her untouched. (For the sake of discretion I didn't want my maid to be seen carrying a pile of magazines into our home.). For each page I would pay an additional fifty cents. This was no small amount in those days especially since most of those boys probably stole the magazines in the first place, leaving themselves with a sixty cent profit per magazine for very little work.

I then had my maid place numbers on each of the sketches with me in first place and bring them to me as she completed them. I dug out all my dance cards which I saved throughout the social season and began to forge the entries from the signatures on the cards. Getting the addresses was no problem as my mother kept a very thorough address file for sending out invitations to our parties and other social purposes. I made several entries from each person and was careful to alter my handwriting as I moved from one to another. I considered myself quite clever in this regard and could see no way any suspicion would be aroused. I instructed my maid to walk all over town and post the entries at different mail drops, again to deter suspicion. I lost count of how many false entries I provided. But I laughed to myself, because at sixty cents each plus posting fees, I had spent more than the winner would receive as a prize.

That effort was the closest thing to actual work that I had ever done and I was certain that through my labor, I had earned a victory and I went on with my glorious life for another month. I told no one but my maid about my adventure and I threatened her with loss of her position if she told anyone else. This would insure her silence since, in my mind at least, there was no better position in the city than serving as my maid. In the end, it wasn't her disloyalty that brought me down, it was my own failure to see the obvious.

The votes were to be tallied and the results announced after January 14th. Even the New York Times was set to announce the results on the society page, which was the only page that mattered as far as I was concerned. In spite of the fanciful nature of the contest there was, just as I had expected, quite a buzz throughout the city as the day drew near. The holidays were over and the social season was drawing to a close so, as we would say today, there were some slow news days.

Well, the results were published all right and yes I was selected as the number one beauty in the city, but there were seventy one entries that had selected exactly the same beauties from one to twenty – seventy one first place winners. My maid had numbered all the entries the same from one to twenty instead of creating different combinations. I was first on every entry, which was what I wanted, but the other beauties occupied exactly their same spot, two through twenty, in every entry. Even I could see it would be a mathematical impossibility for seventy-one people to choose the exact same progression. It was a disaster. It was clear to everyone that the contest had been manipulated, but at least it wasn't clear in the beginning as to who had been the mastermind. The Times did a tongue in cheek article in the editorial section stating that New Yorkers may never agree on their politics or anything else, but they obviously have a very clear view of what constitutes beauty. They also ran the artist's sketch of me with my "disagreeable" face, identifying me and adding the caption "APPARENTLY NEW YORKERS BELIEVE THAT BEAUTY TRULY IS ONLY SKIN DEEP".

That was bad enough, but at least I could feign innocence and let on that it must have been the work of an overzealous admirer. What happened next sealed my doom and made me the laughing stock of the city and placed my father in a very embarrassing position. When Life magazine contacted each of the winning entrants, all but twelve denied that they had even entered the contest and, of those that did enter, none of them had made the selections as listed in the article containing the results. Clearly I or someone in my family had masterminded this plot. No one believed it was my father, because as he severely pointed out, if he had been responsible it would not have been done so stupidly.

The magazine re-tabulated the results, throwing out the phony ballots and I was not the winner. I placed twelfth indicating that there were few legitimate votes for me. Life magazine never implicated me in any way, but the truth was out there. This frivolous little contest became a major scandal in our society for several months and it even spread to other cities. I was the butt of many jokes from that time on and my humiliation was almost unbearable. My father, who had only asked that I never cause him embarrassment, withdrew all my privileges and most of his affections. There were times that I could see he felt sorry for me and once he even told me that he felt partly responsible for my lack of character and intelligence, but overall my relationship with him was permanently damaged and he turned me over to my mother to clean up the mess he had made of me. My sister stood by me and even shouldered some of the blame for her suggestion that others might manipulate the contest which had set me on my disastrous course. Because of her sweet nature and her reputation for kindness, no one persecuted or snubbed me in her presence. They knew it would cause her pain. The same was true of my mother, who never chided me for what I had done. Her only comment was that I would finally be free of my vanity and could become the person I was meant to be.

I remained on everyone's guest list due to my family's influence, but for the next two years I seldom left the house and then only in the company of my mother and sister. I fired my maid for being so stupid, still unable to accept responsibility for my own actions, but my mother hired her back and gave her to my sister. The maid was ecstatic to be free of me and told me as much on the day I fired her. The truth is, I was no smarter than the maid because I don't remember even looking at the ballots as I was forging the entries and I doubt that I would have been smart enough to see the outcome anyway. At one point I even wondered if the maid had set me up on purpose.

During those two years, I learned a great deal about myself and what it means to be a human being. Oh, I was still seriously flawed, but I did gain some insights and I did learn to appreciate kindness and compassion for the wonderful traits they are and I began to feel the stirrings of a human heart. At Christmas time the year after the disaster, I spent many hours trying to decide what gifts I could give to my family that would show them how much I cared for them. This was a breakthrough. In years past, my Christmas shopping had consisted of sending my maid to pick out gifts. That year I even bought a gift for the maid I had fired as well as my current maid. However, I wasn't fully healed as I found myself taking way too much pride in how considerate I was being. A couple of times I caught myself thinking that not only was I beautiful, I was also thoughtful and generous. I guess one cannot erase a lifetime of ignorance and conceit in one year.

At the end of the second year, my mother suggested that I go to Philadelphia and spend some time with my mother's sister, Aunt Olivia. She was a widow and was anxious to have some company. I loved the idea as I was still quite uncomfortable in New York and still suffering jokes and insults although fewer in number. Aunt Olivia was warm and kind like my mother and, although news of my antic had spread to Philadelphia, knowledge of the details was not as widespread or exaggerated and I would be able to present myself in a better light and possibly make some real friends. Finally, I remember thinking that of the two of us, Adele was the lucky one. My memory of that life ends with my arrival in Philadelphia and being embraced by my Aunt. I could feel her warmth, love and concern for me in that embrace and that moment makes this memory one of my favorites.

This memory came to me the first time when I was about fifteen years old. You maybe can't tell it now, but I was quite a looker when I was young. Fortunately, I had parents that focused on my character rather than my physical attributes. In spite of that, by the time I was fourteen, I was beginning to become a bit preoccupied with my appearance. My parents were prosperous enough to buy me nice clothes and I was spending a lot of time admiring myself in the mirror and I was developing an attitude (a modern term for being spoiled and arrogant). My mother kept at me, but I was more concerned with the attentions boys were paying me than her chidings. I was in danger of becoming my former self. The memory came at the same time as my best friend abandoned me. Her name was Inga and we had been friends since the first grade. I noticed that she was spending more time with other friends and I wasn't being invited to go on picnics, bike rides and to the movies. Inga and I had been like sisters so I decided to go to her house and confront her with my hurt and anger and ask her why she was excluding me. She just looked at me for a long time and then told me that she didn't even know me. She said I wasn't the same girl I used to be and that she didn't like the new girl that I had become. She told me I was boring because all I ever talked about was clothes and boys. She went on to say that her parents really didn't want her to spend so much time with me. Then she told me to go home. I was crushed and went home and cried for hours. My mother tried to comfort me, but I just knew she didn't understand. I was convinced that no one in the history of the world had ever felt the pain I was experiencing. I moped around for days, ignoring my parents and refusing to go anywhere. My father threatened to give me a damned good spanking if I didn't show them more respect. I had never had a spanking before so I didn't take him too seriously.

Then came the memory! I didn't have to be hit with a brick to understand the message. My life changed back immediately. I had been raised with good values, so all I had to do was return to the world that loved and cherished me. Inga died three years ago, but throughout our lives, we remained the closest of friends and I thanked her often for setting me straight. She became a school teacher and brought her love and wisdom to many young girls through the years. At her funeral, there were dozens of grown women ranging from twenty to seventy years of age that credited her with saving them from drastic mistakes through her love, wisdom and candor. Many said they hated her at the time, but they never forgot her words. There is no substitute for the kind of love that protects us from our worst selves.

I told my husband this story shortly after we married. He looked at me very seriously and said, "I don't get it, you're just not that good looking". That was his kind of humor and I loved him for it."

SAMANTHA

I tried so hard not to cry, but when she started talking about her parents and how they loved her and how mean she had been to them, I couldn't help it. Then I looked at my grandma and remembered the harsh things she had said to me that morning and I realized how hard that must have been for her and how much she must love me. I knew from the beginning that I was wrong to deceive my parents and I had sensed that there was something wrong with the way we were getting the pictures. I was embarrassed and ashamed, but in a way I felt relieved too. By the time dinner was over I was feeling better and I decided to call my parents to let them know how sorry I was. They had already met with Hope's parents and told them about the uncle. My mom said Hope threw a fit and swore she would never speak to me again. This upset me, but my mom said I couldn't hang out with Hope anyway until she changed her attitude. I wasn't looking forward to going back to school on the next Tuesday, but I was glad the worst was over. Thelma took me aside and told me I could always come to her with problems if I didn't want to go to my parents or grandparents. I didn't understand why she thought I would rather talk to her. I still don't, except that she always tries to be more important to me than my grandma. She must be really lonely.

AMANDA

I have never been more proud of Samantha than I was that night and I could see that Sam shared my feelings. He just kept hugging her. He also came to me and told me I was amazing and thanked me for taking the "bull by the horns". He was almost tearful as he described how helpless he felt when he saw that picture. Poor Sam. I have often thought it was fortunate that we never had a daughter. She would have turned him inside out and I would have been forever forced to play the villain. The evening ended on a positive note and when Sam and Samantha left to return to the boat, Samantha took his hand and I expected to see a puddle of water around him from his melting heart. I wished I were going with them.

During that evening, Etienne and Samantha made Sam promise to take them on a cruise the next day. The weather was predicted to be sunny and warmer than usual so the idea was appealing to everyone. It was decided that we could all go along and depart right after breakfast. Serena said she would pack sandwiches and we could make a day of it. Bernie was the only one who declined saying that he had already seen the boat and he didn't enjoy all the rocking. He said it had made him sick and he didn't want to experience that again. Apparently he felt the fifth of bourbon he had drank that night had nothing to do with his discomfort. No one encouraged him to change his mind including Serena, who would have the rest of the day off leaving right after breakfast and not returning until Monday morning.

Bernie was obviously disappointed that he wouldn't have her to himself for the day, but he didn't change his mind about going. Jenny suggested that he settle in with a couple of good movies and she and Alfie left the room giggling. Glen was concealing a grin as well, so I knew there was a story behind that remark. Bernie's expression grew even nastier than usual as he poured himself and Thelma another drink.

Chapter Thirty-One

THE LOVE BOAT

SAM

The next morning was beautiful as predicted. Everyone was set to go at exactly 9AM. They chose to walk as a group to the boat. Serena followed in the Escalade with enough food and drink to supply a cruise to Hawaii. Spirits were high, but no one was more excited than Etienne. He had been cooped up for several days and was ready for some fresh air and adventure. Paul and Jenny easily lifted his chair with him in it and set it on the back deck. Paul had been elevated beyond guest status and it was assumed that he would be part of any of our social events.

There was plenty of room for everyone aboard my boat and they could choose between a seat on the deck or the comforts of the main salon. Samantha decided to show off a bit by acting as crew. She gave a "stewardess" speech including hand gesture about safety precautions and pointed out the location of life jackets as well as describing the procedure for lowering the dinghy in case of emergency. She handled the lines during our departure and instructed Jenny to haul in the fenders after we left the dock, pointing out that failure to do so would make us look like a bunch of amateurs. I hadn't realized how much she had learned during our many cruises over the years.

Amanda went to the galley to stow the food and prepare the traditional peppermint schnapps and hot chocolate. There was still a bit of a chill in the air although the sun shone brilliantly so the drink was accepted with enthusiasm. Not a big surprise-all food and drink is met with enthusiasm from this group. I have made it my rule to never consume alcohol while driving the boat so Amanda brought me coffee on the fly bridge and stayed with me, silently enjoying the moment and many memories of past cruises. There was still a bit of mist in the air and I could see her perfectly coiffed hair succumb to the unruly curls that so annoyed her. Humidity has never been her friend, but today she seemed unconcerned with her appearance and totally at ease with everything and everyone.

Thelma decided to act as tour director. She had found a book about the San Juan Islands in the salon and placed herself at center stage to identify and give some of the history of each island and point of interest. I have to admit she did a good job and everyone seemed to enjoy her commentary. Glen and Kate stayed in the salon for most of the morning.

My boat is equipped with dual stations, one on the top deck and one in the salon. About an hour into the cruise I had Samantha take the helm on the top deck so I could visit the head. The cabbage rolls from the night before were working their magic on me and I suspected my visit would not be a short one so I asked Amanda to go to the lower station in the salon as a safeguard in case Samantha ran into trouble. There had been a storm earlier that week and there was quite a bit of debris floating offshore that could destroy my propellers.

Amanda was an expert at spotting deadheads and Samantha was easily distracted so I didn't want to take any chances. I found out later that when she entered the salon Glen and Kate were not there, but she could hear familiar sounds coming from the forward cabin, Samantha's room. She stayed as quiet as possible to not disturb or embarrass them but when they emerged a few minutes later, they realized that there had been a witness to their escapade. It was awkward for a moment or two, but then Kate and Glen started laughing (or giggling as Amanda put it) and Amanda just shook her head and asked if they wanted to share a cigarette. When I emerged from the head, I could tell that something had transpired, but once again, I was totally in the dark.

The day was otherwise uneventful except for the beautiful weather, awesome scenery and Serena's fantastic picnic. By the time we returned to the dock it was after five PM. Amanda had already cleaned up so we could just tie up and walk back to the house. Glen and Kate lagged behind the group partly because Glen couldn't walk as fast as the rest of us and partly to have a few more minutes alone. I wondered what would become of their relationship when all this was over.

As usual, Samantha took charge of pushing Etienne's wheelchair and they were yards ahead of the rest of us. The trail was well traveled and hard packed so it was not difficult. About halfway there she decided to let us catch up and darned if she didn't sit on my favorite rock to rest. The memory of my one-sided sexual interlude caused me to flush with embarrassment as I walked beside Amanda. I wanted to get Samantha off that rock. I felt like a dirty old man. By the time we caught up with them, Samantha had already stood up and was pushing Etienne's chair again. Amanda noticed my red face and thought I had overexerted myself and suggested that I sit on the rock and rest. I started to laugh, which she attributed to a macho reaction to her suggestion that I was in a weakened state. This annoyed her and she gave me a look of exasperation and proceeded to jog the rest of the way to the house. I stepped up my pace, but remained behind watching her backside jiggle ever so slightly as she moved along the trail. Alfie and Paul were beside me by that time and smiled knowingly at each other as they followed my gaze. I was still laughing and the more I laughed the faster she jogged.

About this time I heard a commotion behind us. It was Glen and Kate. They were both on the ground and Kate was on her hands and knees with her back to us performing some kind of act on the lower part of his body. He was sitting and leaning back on his hands with his pants pulled down and a big smile on his face. I couldn't believe what I was seeing!! I thought we were all going sex crazy until I realized that one of Glenn's legs had come loose and Kate was trying to help him get it back on. He had warned us that this might happen and was not the least bit embarrassed. Kate was flustered at first, but soon was laughing and rolling on the ground along with Glen. He waved us on and they arrived at the house just a few minutes after we did. They were acting like a couple of teenagers. Kate had lost all of her reserve and Glen looked like he had slipped into a time machine and traveled twenty years to the past.

I spotted Bernie in the den passed out on the leather couch with an empty drink glass on the floor beside him. He was drooling profusely onto a couch pillow and I made a silent note to destroy that pillow at the first opportunity. I closed the door to prolong our freedom for as long as possible. Everyone went their separate ways and it was clear that there had been enough camaraderie for that day. I made one sneak trip into the den to retrieve the Grisham novel that I still hadn't read.

Bernie was still sleeping and drooling. I left him there and slipped out quietly.

I went to the kitchen and made myself a huge sandwich and headed back to the boat for a quiet evening. Samantha had asked to stay at the house with Amanda for the night. They are used to sleeping in the same bed since Amanda's condo only has one bedroom. It really was a non-issue anyway because as I was leaving, I caught a glimpse of Kate sneaking into Glen's room so I was reasonably certain that there would be an empty bed in the master suite from then on.

When I got back to the boat, I grabbed a Coke, my sandwich and my book and settled into my bed for a leisurely read. I awoke the next morning with a half-eaten sandwich and a warm coke on my bed table and the book, open to page four, lying under my right arm. I assure you that I hold John Grisham in high esteem as an author, but you couldn't prove it by the progress I had made with his book. I was ravenously hungry so I ate the rest of my sandwich in spite of the warnings I had heard all my life about eating anything with mayonnaise that hadn't been refrigerated. I don't believe these warnings are valid anymore. The mayonnaise we buy now is so loaded with preservatives and chemicals that you could put it into a time capsule and safely consume it twenty years later. Having lived alone for so long, I have often pushed the rules of food safety well beyond their limits with no ill effects. I once read in a trade journal that the biggest cause of salmonella in the United States is not chicken or fish or mayonnaise, it's cantaloupe from Mexico. I know that our farmers and food processors are subject to all kinds of rules and restrictions, yet so much of the fresh produce we buy comes from countries that have no such oversight. I don't understand this as I don't understand so much of what our government does. I guess it is the Texan in me that rebels against being told how to live.

One time in Seattle, I rode my bicycle without a helmet just because I wanted to see if I could get away with it. Gutsy, huh? If you think I'm bad, Amanda is worse. She once drove all the way across the Evergreen Bridge in the HOV lane as the only person in the car. Halfway across the bridge they have a sign with a number you can call if you want to snitch on drivers misusing the HOV lane. She memorized the number and when she got across the bridge and close to home, she called the number and taunted them about what she had done and made fun of them for trying to turn everyone into snitches against their neighbors. She loves to do stuff like that.

When I arrived at the house, still hungry and ready for breakfast, I opened the door and peeked into the den to see if Bernie had survived the night. He was still there and he had removed all of his clothes and partially covered himself with a small throw blanket. The blanket was added to my list of that which must be destroyed. He was barely awake and mumbled something about dinner. He apparently thought it was still the same day as when he went to sleep. Then he started to get up stating that he had to "pee like a racehorse". I set him straight about the time and ordered him to put on his clothes before emerging from the den. His hair was in a rooster tale and he had bags over and under his eyes big enough to block out the sun. Altogether, he was the most repulsive sight I had ever beheld and I felt pity for all who would have to look at him before putting something in their stomach.

Sometime around noon Bernie casually mentioned that my father had called while we were on the cruise. I told him my father had died two years ago and he didn't bat an eye. He just shrugged his shoulders and walked off. I finally figured out that in his drunken haze he must have isolated the word "father" and that it was probably Father Karl that had called. I knew it would do no good to ask if there was a message so

I placed a call to Father Karl immediately. His housekeeper answered the phone and informed me that the priest was out, but she would have him call me when he returned. I debated whether to tell Etienne about the call and decided to wait until I heard what he had to say. I hung out by the phone all afternoon as I wanted to be the one to answer when his call came through. Finally around five o'clock, he called back. The news was neither good nor bad. Antoinette had not been charged with the murder, but was told that she could not leave Scotland. In fact, the police had confiscated her passport. Father Karl went on to say that Andrew had been brutally beaten with a heavy object and his skull had been fractured in numerous places. They also suspected that he had still been alive when buried although he was most likely unconscious. Evidence pointed to suffocation as the possible cause of death, although I have no idea how they could discern that after so many years. They were doing forensic studies to see if any more evidence could be found. Apparently, Antoinette was still a prime suspect. Nothing he told me gave me any hope that Antoinette would be returning soon, if ever.

I discussed this news with Amanda and Adrian and we decided not to mention it to Etienne. We couldn't have told him the truth and none of us felt like lying to him. I felt sick inside. Amanda began to cry and Adrian threatened her with bodily harm if she let on that anything was wrong. Samantha's visit was helping to keep his mind off his mother and she was determined to keep him happy as long as possible.

Jenny volunteered to share a memory after dinner. I was glad to see her perk up as she had seemed a little distracted for the past couple of days. I was beginning to worry that she was getting bored, especially with all the time Alfie was spending with Paul. Of course she was always included, but I know what it is like to feel like a third wheel. It occurred to me that, although she was a lively part of all our activities, she really hadn't formed a noticeable bond with any of the other women. She did seem to seek out Serena from time to time, but Serena was so busy with her duties that there really wasn't much opportunity for intimate conversation between them. I made still another mental note to pay more attention to her and encourage Amanda to do the same.

Making that mental note reminded me to take care of that compromised sofa pillow and blanket. (I can only hold one mental note at a time.) I went to the study, collected the offensive items and threw them over the balcony onto the rocks below knowing that the incoming tide would deal with them appropriately. When I re-entered the den from the balcony, there was Bernie. He had seen it all. His glasses were lying on the end table by the sofa and he picked them up, shrugged his bony shoulders and left the room. I felt terrible. As repugnant as he was, I still felt sorry for him in much the same way I felt bad for a skunk or rodent lying dead in the road. I am not a cruel man and had no desire to add fuel to Bernie's jaded view of the world. I knew there was nothing I could say to mask the reason for my behavior. It was just one of those things that had to be left alone and allow some time to pass.

Thelma was in such a hurry to hear Jenny's story that she actually helped Serena clean up after dinner and enlisted Samantha to do the same. Serena had once again asked if she could stay. I told her it was not necessary to ask. She had the friendship and trust of everyone here and her constant devotion to making our stay as pleasant as possible earned her whatever privilege she wanted.

I was glad for the distraction of a good story to keep my mind off my conversation with Father Karl and my unfortunate collision with Bernie. Everyone settled into their usual spots except that Kate and Glenn sat down early, very close together in the middle of their couch to prevent Thelma from sitting between them as before. Thelma took notice and grabbed a chair from the dining room and set it down noisily by Bernie. Kate gave me a triumphant smile. I liked that woman more every day. Jenny sat on the floor in the middle of the group to tell her story.

Chapter Thirty-Two

CELESTE'S JOURNEY

JENNY

"I chose this memory because it surfaced most recently. If I had ever suspected that my memories were nothing more than dreams or hallucinations, this one would have convinced me otherwise. First of all, let me say that prior to this memory which surfaced about a year ago, I had no interest or education in the history of this part of the world. It was because of this memory that I did some research to try to determine the time and place this life occurred. It was easy to figure out where to start looking and I found a great deal of information as well as some conflicting theories about the circumstances surrounding this life. It may be that I could fill in some knowledge gaps for archeologists and historians if I found some that would move away from hard science long enough to listen to my story, but I realize that this would serve no purpose since they could not prove anything that they could publish and they would subject themselves to ridicule from their peers if they tried to present my story as support for their theories.

You may have heard of the Bering Land Bridge. This is a narrow strip of land that was exposed for a period sometime between 11,000 and 25,000 years ago connecting northern Asia with Alaska. Scientists differ on the length of time this land bridge was exposed, but for my purposes, I don't care. It was a long time ago and that's all I need to know. Most agree that there was a migration of people from Asia and possibly other parts of the world over this bridge into Alaska. Whether these migrants were the first Americans or there were already Native American tribes living in North America is up for debate. I can only tell my story.

I have named this person Celeste because in that life I believed that all was guided by the stars and the moon. I was one of these migrants. We were a band of about fifty. I guess you would call us a tribe. I was young, probably about twelve or thirteen since I had just started my menstrual cycle. I think we were a migrant tribe in our homeland and I know my mother carried me on her back for the first few years. We were traveling across a huge plain in search of this land bridge which would take us to a gentler environment. Our leader had made the trip as a very young man with his father and he spoke of a land where the temperatures were more moderate and food was plentiful.

In our homeland, we struggled constantly to find enough roots, berries and game to feed and clothe ourselves. Every minute of every day was spent on mere survival and often there was not enough of anything to sustain our numbers. Death, through starvation, disease or exposure to the elements, was part of our everyday lives. Most babies died within weeks of their birth and the old and sick had no defenses against the harsh environment. We gathered roots and berries in the warmer months and ate sparingly even during these times to preserve enough food to get us through the long winters.

We hunted for meat and hides for our clothing. Everyone had their duties to contribute to the survival of all. The children that did survive were taught to help with food gathering and preservation, making clothing from hides, and the strongest were trained as hunters. Our elders were treasured and cared for as the teachers for they had survived many seasons and we depended on their knowledge to teach us needed skills and keep us in touch with our ancestors who could help protect us from the spirits that sought to destroy us.

I was disappointed to be a girl. I wanted to be a hunter, but instead I was doomed to the tasks given to women. We dried meat, worked and sewed the hides, and gathered food from whatever vegetation we could find. My brother was allowed to hunt and enjoy the glory bestowed on the hunters after a successful kill. The older hunters traveled ahead of our band to seek out the larger prey while the younger ones and the old men traveled with the women and children to protect us and hunt small prey such as rabbits and birds. My brother was allowed to go on the big hunts at a very young age since he had proven himself as able as any of the men, including my father. He was very proud of his skills and made my life miserable by turning me into his personal slave when he was in camp. He knew how I envied him and he boasted to me and teased me incessantly. Our family was well respected because we were so strong and healthy. We never suffered from the various ailments that plagued others. We did more than our share of the work and provided most of the meat. I worked with the hides, turning them into warm clothing that withstood the elements and hard use. My cloaks were the warmest and the softest and my blankets were lighter to carry, but every bit as warm as any others. The boots I made from the thickest hides did not leak and I knew how to use the toughest part of the hide to protect our feet from protruding rocks and chards of ice. I took pleasure and pride in this work, but not as much as making a big kill would have afforded me.

There was still another problem that plagued me every moment of every day. We moved so slowly. I wanted to run or at least walk faster. I knew the journey would be long, but I believed if we could just move faster we would all have a better chance of survival. I could easily carry the load of two people with energy to spare and I was constantly frustrated at having to move at a snail's pace to accommodate the others. My mother chided me about my restlessness and often sent me to walk with the elders as a way to teach me patience.

There was another like me in the group. He was the best of the small game hunters, so much so that he was prevented from accompanying the large game hunters. Rabbits and birds were our most dependable source of meat and the rabbit hides were an absolute necessity. It was decided that his skill at finding and killing this small game was of more value than he could provide on the big hunts. Rabbits, beavers and other rodents were nearly always available, but months could go by without spotting a caribou herd. At first he was proud of his contribution, but as he grew older, he craved the adventure of the big hunt. He took younger boys under his wing to teach them his skills so that he would be free to accompany the big hunters, but none of his students was anywhere near his equal.

We had played together since we were babies and, as we grew older we shared our dreams and frustrations. Forced to stay behind while others hunted, he was well aware of the contribution the women made. He knew that without our skills and hard work, no one would survive. Making the big kill was only a small part of survival. Harvesting and preserving the meat and organs and turning the large hides into shelter were the real work. He understood my anger at my brother for all his bravado and he respected my skills. A couple of times I stole away with him to hunt small game and he taught me to use a spear and saw that I had more strength than most of the young boys he had taught. He was also a great navigator. He had studied the stars with his grandfather and he spent as much time as possible with our leader to understand the path we were taking across the tundra, over the land bridge and into the area of plenty in the new land.

I must have been at least twelve or thirteen and we were in the process of turning our childhood friendship into a lifelong love. We were away from the group lying between two of my hide blankets looking up at the stars. It was early spring so it was still cold, but there were large patches of bare ground and the nights were warm enough to venture away from the small fires.

We were young and strong and we sought adventure and love. We talked about the new land and what we would face when we arrived. I had secretly been thinking how wonderful it would be to run ahead to this land and prepare the way for our group. He had the same thoughts. We had no doubt about our ability to reach our destination and begin to harvest the bounty that awaited us so that when our families arrived, we would have already prepared a place for them to live in comfort and cease their wandering. We had never spoken of this before, but once the dream was shared, it became an obsession. The time was right because we would have the warmer months to travel and would still have time to begin our preparations once we arrived. At the speed our tribe was traveling, they might arrive during winter, which could be dangerous or they might have to make a winter camp along the way and delay the rest of the journey until the following spring. Either way, this added a huge element of danger and created a certainty that some or all may not survive.

Food was easier to find for the tribe during these spring and summer months so we would not be so greatly missed. We made the decision to leave within a few days. Of course, we could not tell anyone of our plan because it would not be allowed. I was to gather what we would need for the trip and hide it away from the camp so we could pick it up as we left. He would gather even more information from our leader so that we would have a definite course to travel and we would recognize the destination when we arrived.

Once we made the decision to change our lives and the lives of our tribe, it never occurred to either of us to change our minds. For the next few days, I gathered everything I could without being discovered and I made each of us a new pair of boots that would survive the trip. I worked day and night to prepare us. When the night came for our departure we did not suffer at leaving our families for we knew we would see them soon and they would be proud of us for our achievements. We believed that we could travel light because food would be plentiful along the way and we both had the skills needed to provide fresh meat. We had a good supply of spears and we were confident we could avoid any predators by using the skills we had learned from our elders. I was finally going to be able to run and run and run.

The first few days were filled with joy. We ran, then slowed to a fast walk, then ran some more. We ate on the run and slept deeply in each other's arms. We believed our ancestors were watching over us and we were fearless. We stopped one evening earlier than usual and performed our own marriage ceremony so that we would be bound to each other for eternity. We had shared the same bed and explored each other's bodies, but we had not consummated our bond until that night. From that point on, we stole a few minutes each day to share our bodies and absorb the love and energy each of us brought to the union.

We had to travel for several weeks just to cross the tundra of our homeland before reaching the land bridge that would take us to our new home. We were convinced that the further we traveled, the easier it would be to find food. This did not prove to be true. The closer we got to the sea, the sparser the vegetation and fewer the small animals to be found. Our progress was slowed as we had to spend more time each day to hunt and gather. Still, we were not discouraged. I was glad that I was experiencing none of the bleeding and pain that I had endured for several days each month before we left. We remained in good health and spirits. We were not sure how far we had traveled or how far we had to go because we were not able to measure our progress. At the time we left, our leader had told the tribe it would take six to eight full moons to reach our destination. We believed that at our rate we would arrive in three full moons.

We also knew that when we reached the new land, we would have to turn away from the North Star and travel south to find a shore on the great sea. Our leader had said that the tribe would need large spears to protect our members from bears. Toward this we planned to spend part of our evenings making spears. We could find an abundance of stone to make our arrowheads and I had made many leather strings to attach the arrowheads to the spear. We didn't bring any wood with us to make the spears because they would be hard to carry but we brought tools to make the spears as we got closer to our destination. We were disappointed to find that there were very few trees to be found and those that we did find were not strong enough to provide us with the wood for spears. This worried my husband, but I had bigger things to worry about. True, I wasn't bothered by the monthly pain and bleeding, but

I finally realized that I was carrying a child. I kept the news to myself because I felt guilty about bringing on an additional burden at this time. I was torn between joy and shame. I just kept praying that we would arrive before I gave birth or became too heavy to maintain our pace.

We did see some very large animals from time to time that seemed to be on the same path as ours. We were not equipped to hunt them but we were reassured that the hunters in our tribe would be able to provide food as they made their trip, especially since vegetation was so scarce.

Most of the time we were able to put our concerns aside and just keep moving, but there were times when we would fall silent and our fears would overtake us. I was tiring more easily, but I would not slow down. I wanted our child to be born in the new land where he would have the best possible chance of survival. I never questioned whether we were on the right course, so confident I was of my husband's ability to guide us. We had close calls a couple of times from some large cats that we knew to be dangerous to man. We saw them in a distance, and we stood very still until they passed out of sight. It was as if everything on that journey was driven on the same course and would allow no distractions to reaching their destination. Further proof of this came when we discovered a huge animal that had been killed and partially eaten. It was fresh and there was plenty of meat left. We feasted that night and took the next two days to cut and dry more meat that we could carry with us. We weren't able to use our normal methods because that would have taken several days, but we were able to speed up the process by cutting very small strips so it would dry more quickly. We carried enough dried meat with us to last for a month if we were careful and by that time we should be close to where we would settle. I was also able to clean enough hide to make a small shelter when we arrived. It was heavy, but we determined that we might need it, so we carried it between us open to the sun to dry it out. I can still smell the stench as it dried. Normally, we would hang the hides on a tree far away from our camp to avoid the smell and the insects.

The final weeks of our journey were the hardest. We were tired and had been deprived of the vegetation that made up so much of our usual diet. We were also running out of water. There was not much snowfall on the land bridge or on the tundra on either side, therefore we were having difficulty finding snow to melt for water. It had rained a couple of times, but we could not carry much water with us and maintain our strength. We were often hungry and thirsty, but we kept walking, and if either of us doubted our chances of survival, we never shared our doubts, although I had the added strain of keeping my secret and trying to find enough food to feed myself and the child growing inside of me.

After many weeks, I began to suspect that we were lost. I would wake in the middle of the night to find my husband gazing at the stars perhaps hoping for some sign to guide him. He became quiet and withdrawn and I was determined that he would not sense my suspicions. Each day became more difficult until one morning he announced with a conviction that I knew to be false that it was time for us to turn south. I followed without question and praised him for his skills. This decision gave use a short-term boost of spirits in that we could allow ourselves to believe that our journey would soon be over. I felt stronger and happier than I had in weeks and decided that it was safe to share my secret with my husband without adding to his burdens. He was proud and happy and he walked taller and seemed more certain of himself than ever before. We walked very quickly for the next few days, stopping only to sleep for a few hours at a time. This was not difficult since there was no night. The sun would rise and set at nearly the same time. This was confusing to us since our leader had not told us that the new land would have eternal light. We decided that this was a good thing as it would give our tribe more hours in the day to hunt and gather food. Still, I worried that we were entering a strange place where none of the knowledge of our elders would be useful to us.

Finally, we were seeing more vegetation and wildlife giving us hope that we were nearing our destination, but how would we know it when we got there? My husband was confident that our ancestors would give us a sign. After a few more days of drifting, we came upon a huge expanse of open space without a sign of vegetation. We ventured a short distance before we realized that we were no longer on land. There was nothing but ice and water below us. We knew we had to change course and go around the water. We skirted the edge for several days until we were in an area where trees were plentiful and there were wildflowers, grass and much more wildlife. I was finding it more difficult to walk and I was secretly hoping that we would be given the sign that we had reached our destination. We kept watching and praying, but none came.

By this time we were also noticing that the daylight hours were diminishing and there were a couple of hours of darkness. We couldn't tell how long we had been traveling because we couldn't study the moon in the way we had learned, but we knew that winter was on its way. Finally one morning I was especially tired and feeling irritated that my husband would not slow his pace. He was running several yards ahead of me when I heard him shriek. I ran to catch up with him but I couldn't see him, I could only hear his cries. I ran in circles looking for him and finally came to the edge of a deep crevice. He was lying at the bottom screaming with pain. I knew there was no way to reach him and for the first time I realized that we were going to die. I fell to the ground and covered my ears to block out his screams. Finally he was quiet. I didn't know if he was dead or just asleep. Even if he awoke again I knew there was no way to rescue him and so I prayed that he was dead to save him any more agony. People who had injuries did not survive in our world and I wanted to spare him the slow death he would face.

Our weapons, tools and much of our protective clothing were lying at the bottom of the crevice with my husband. In many ways, he was more fortunate than I because I knew I couldn't survive either. I was carrying our scant supply of food and water and our child. I decided that I would not leave my husband. I would stay where I was and die beside him. We would be a family in the next world.

I never heard another sound from my husband and I wished that I could find a way to make my own death come quicker. I threw my food into the crevice so I would not be tempted to eat and prolong my misery. It had grown dark so I laid down and prayed for sleep. When I awoke, it was light and I was surrounded by the first human beings I had seen since we left our tribe. They looked like us, but different and they spoke in an unfamiliar way. I wasn't frightened because I was sure I was going to die anyway and they might make it happen more quickly and with less pain. In my homeland, it wasn't unusual for outsiders to be killed to protect the tribe. There were five of them and I suspected they were a hunting party. Lying next to me on the ground was my husband and all of our possessions. I couldn't imagine how they had gotten him out, but I could clearly see that he was dead. He was lying on a bed of some sort with poles on either side. They lifted me onto one just like it and then two of them took hold of the poles at our head and our feet and carried us off. I didn't try to talk or communicate in any way. I just allowed myself to be carried.

I was thinking about my child and that I had to at least try to find a way to bring him to life. I came to believe that I was not meant to die nor was my child. I was sad to have lost my husband, but I had hope for my child and that I might see my family again. My time had not yet come and I would fight to live. I would be reunited with my husband and my God soon enough.

I don't have a memory of this life past that point, but in many ways I learned more from this life than any other. It takes place thousands of years ago, before man became "civilized", yet the emotions and other facets of what is often called "the human condition" were already present. Hate, fear, jealousy, greed, lust, and all the other bad stuff was there too right along with love, loyalty, courage and all the good stuff. We just didn't have a name for everything in those days. When God created man, he gave us all the good stuff, when man betrayed God we gave ourselves all the bad stuff. The struggle throughout the history of man has been to survive but I believe that, from the beginning we have also struggled against our darker nature to reunite ourselves with our creator-however we may view him or whatever we call him.

When I run into the danger of fooling myself into believing that our struggles are new and expanding in our complicated world and that it is somehow harder to keep in touch with God today, I remember Celeste. We may have more choices and distractions and we may consider ourselves more evolved, but our basic natures are the same. I don't know if Celeste and her child lived or died, but I believe she fell into kind hands and had some sort of life. I guess with a memory this far in the past, it makes me an "old Soul", though maybe not. It's possible that we can go thousands of years without being reborn. I have memories of five lives including Celeste and the rest are all in recent times.

There are those who believe that when we die we go to a place where we are loved and taught to learn from our lives and then, when we are ready, we return. This does not insure that we will be better or wiser than in our former life. We are still stuck in a mortal body with a limited brain and we suffer the ills that befall all of mankind. Our quest is to improve as we move along, but we still have free will and a wide range of emotions that can cause us to be sidetracked or damaged.

One other thing and it's important! I have shared a past life with someone in this room. I am not going to explain this now because I want to see if that person comes to the same realization. In addition, I have often wondered if Alfie was my husband in my Celeste life. We were drawn to each other instantly and I have always felt like I have known him all my life. I have read accounts by others that they have encountered the same people in different lives in different relationships. Glen alluded to this when he spoke of that couple that had been reunited after their lives had been cut short the first time around. I'm not trying to be mysterious about that other person and our other life. I think it will be interesting to see if that person recognizes me."

SAM

Well, that was an interesting development. There was silence around the room for a moment as everyone pondered over what she was saying. I was anxious to know who in the room had shared a life with her. Etienne was the first to speak and he supported her premise, saying that he believed that we might get a second chance to set things straight. He spoke so earnestly that I wondered what that sweet boy could have done in any life that would need to be corrected. Judging by the respectful silence following his statement, I guessed that the others were thinking the same thing. Thelma ended the silence by shouting "Wow! This is good stuff". For some reason everyone started laughing at her outburst and she pretended that that was the result she had intended. Thelma is not one to turn down attention of any sort.

Kate spoke up next and asked Jenny if she was that person. Since she is Native American and the belief is that many of the North American tribes had arrived here through that same route, she thought she may have played a role in Celeste's life. Jenny responded that she wished that were the case, but no.

Once again, Thelma spoke up and asked if we could have another story and she looked directly at Amanda. Amanda replied by staring right back at her and asking why she was suddenly so interested in hearing from her when she had never bothered to ask before. Thelma didn't have an answer, but Samantha jumped up and begged Amanda to talk. Amanda hesitated, but decided to go ahead with the warning that although the life she was remembering was not a happy one, it has had a profound influence over her other lives, including this one. She looked at me when she spoke and I knew I was going to find out the story behind her comment made so many years before about losing children. I didn't know for sure if she was doing this out of kindness to satisfy my curiosity or as a rebuke to me for not pursuing the subject sooner. I chose to believe it was because she had finally decided to trust me.

As Amanda rose to tell her story, I noticed there was something different about her. Her hair was all frizzy from the boat cruise, but it was more than that. It took me a minute to figure it out but I finally realized that she had changed clothes since we returned and she was wearing one of my old shirts. She used to wear my clothes all the time, even though she had ten times the wardrobe that I did. It never annoyed me. I kind of liked it. I realized that I hadn't seen that shirt in years and she must have taken it when we split up. I wondered why she would bring it and wear it on this trip. Was there some message in this or did she just forget where the shirt had come from? Was I just looking for some sign that things were changing for the better? Probably.

Chapter Thirty-Three

FROM DUST TO DUST

AMANDA

"My name was Lorretta and I lived in a tiny cabin in Oklahoma with my husband, Chad and my three daughters. The year was 1937 and it was my birthday. I was 37 years old. My father had settled the 160 acres he was given by the government when he moved there with my mother. He had prospered over his lifetime to where, at the time of his death, he was able to leave Chad and me a farm that was debt free and could produce a reasonably sound living.

We had two work horses and several head of cattle that could feed off the land and be sold to meet out modest needs. I had a huge vegetable garden, twenty or so chickens, a couple of milk cows, some pigs, and we owned a plow and all the tools needed to support our farming activities. Chad often did carpentry work for other farmers and the income from this gave us a few extra dollars for some luxuries like linens and featherbeds. I had the prettiest set of china in the county. Our two older girls were well dressed and had dolls that were purchased from a mail order catalog. We enjoyed our neighbors and were active in our church. At least this had been our life until a year or two years before that day.

Things had changed drastically. Even at the beginning of the draught we saw some of our neighbors fall on hard times. Many were severely in debt to the bank and when crops began to fail they were forced to sell off their livestock to make their loan payments and all they could do was pray for a better harvest the next year. It didn't happen. The draught continued and worsened. The winds began to strip the land of topsoil. At first we survived because we didn't owe the banks and were so well established. As the situation worsened, more people abandoned their land as their wells went dry causing even more crop failures. The winds continued and more soil was lost. Eventually there were no crops at all and even the native grass had disappeared leaving our cattle with nothing to eat. We had to sell them for whatever price we could get or watch them starve to death. We kept only the animals we needed to feed our family and at first I was able to keep a small garden alive.

One day Chad was working on the well, trying to get more water for the garden and I was washing our clothes on the front porch using only a couple of gallons for a week's worth of laundry. The wind was blowing so much dust that the clothes looked dirtier than when I started. I was trying to hide my tears of frustration from Chad. He felt that he had failed me and betrayed the trust my father had placed in him by giving us the farm. I saw him walking toward me, but to my horror, there was a huge wall of dust behind him moving toward us. It was so thick that it appeared black and I couldn't see where the wall ended. The sky had disappeared and it became very dark as if night had settled in within a matter of seconds.

We had had dust storms before, but nothing like this, and it was just the first of many to come, each worse than the one before. My two girls were in the house and I was about to give birth to the third. We rushed inside and lit our lamps to wait out the storm. It raged for hours and when it was over, there were piles of dust everywhere and on everything, including us. My girls were coughing violently and I felt as if I were going to pass out from lack of air. Chad and I held our girls and prayed long into the night. The next morning was clear and we began to believe that the worst was over. Chad went to the pasture to check on the two remaining cows and bring us some milk. When he hadn't returned after two hours I was worried and went to find him. One of the cows had made it to the barn and was lying on her side struggling for breath. The other was dead in the pasture, her mouth caked with dust. She had suffocated. When Chad opened her up, her lungs were full of dust. The other cow never recovered and we had to butcher her for meat instead of keeping her for milk.

We spent the next few days working feverishly to seal our home with oilcloth should we face another storm. Every crack we could find and all windows and doors were sealed. The front door provided the only light and the only access to our home and we kept more cloths nearby to seal that as necessary.

Our preparations paid off as the storms kept coming and we kept praying. We still had a workhorse that could pull a plow and we continued to plant small crops, most of which failed. How we guarded that horse and our few remaining chickens! When we could see a storm approaching we would bring all the animals, including the horse, into the house to keep them safe. We never considered giving up and moving on like most of our neighbors. We just prayed and believed. We never lost our faith in God.

On that day, the morning of my thirty seventh birthday in 1937, Chad had insisted that I stay in bed and spend the morning reading and poring over the catalog looking for items we would buy when things got back to normal. Our youngest daughter was just nine months old and Chad and my two older girls had fed and changed her, played with her, and then put her down for a nap. She loved her naps and was the sweetest baby ever born. They went out to the barn to finish working on my birthday present. Chad was building me a new table with four matching chairs. He had been working on it for weeks and the girls were helping him apply the lacquer and put on the finishing touches. It was supposed to be a surprise, but the girls had been dropping too many hints in their excitement. It was a beautiful morning and I was convinced that this was the turning point in what had been years of torture and disappointment. They had been gone about an hour when I got up, still dressed in my nightgown, to get a glass of water. The front door was open and as I passed by I saw the biggest dust storm ever coming our way. It looked like a mountain moving across the prairie. I knew they wouldn't be able to see it coming from where they were in the barn and I had to get to them. I wet a blanket and placed it over the baby's crib as I always did during storms, because no matter how carefully we sealed the house, the dust found its way in. I closed the front door and ran to the barn, calling out to them as I ran. They couldn't hear me as my throat was already clogged with dust and the cloud descended when I was halfway to the barn. I couldn't see more than a foot in front of me and I was blinded by the dust in my eyes. I screamed noiselessly and cried, but I couldn't find my way. I covered my nose and mouth with the hem of my gown and kept moving feeling in front of me with my free hand. For several minutes I touched nothing but air, but finally I felt a wall and I followed along the wall looking for a door or window. I thought I was at the barn, but I had turned around and I found myself back at the house. I tripped over the step leading to the porch and fell. I kept crawling until finally I found the porch floor and made my way to the front door, which had blown open. I crawled inside and felt my way to the cradle and my baby. It seemed to take forever. As my eyes cleared a little, I tried to pull the blanket off the cradle, but it wouldn't move at first. It was so heavy. I got to my feet and pulled with all my strength and finally it gave way. It was coated with several inches of dust and underneath, where the blanket was wet, the dust had formed a thick mud coating. I reached into the cradle and pulled the baby to my breast, but I knew instantly what had happened. The dust and mud had pushed the blanket down into the cradle and suffocated my baby.

I screamed at the top of my lungs, but no sound came out. I was overcome with shame and I wanted to run and hide so that I didn't have to see Chad's face when he realized what I had done to our child. I couldn't move from that spot. I didn't try to shut the door and seal it. I wanted the dust to kill me. I laid there coughing and crying. Then as suddenly as it came, it ended. It was quiet and so dark in the house. Still holding the baby, I managed to clear away enough dust to light a lamp so that Chad and the girls could find their way back to the house, but they never came. I sat rocking my poor dead baby for hours. I didn't go to the barn to look for them. As long as I could pretend they were safe in the barn, I didn't have to face what I knew in my heart had happened.

The next morning our neighbor came to check on us and he found me still sitting with my dead child in my arms. He asked about Chad and the girls, but I couldn't answer him. My voice had disappeared along with my will to live. He didn't try to take my child from me, he just went outside and I could see him walking toward the barn. He was in there a long time and when he returned his dusty face was streaked with tears. He told me that the barn just couldn't provide enough shelter. He had found Chad and the girls huddled under a horse blanket. He said they appeared to be asleep at first, they looked so peaceful. I tried to believe him, but I knew how hard I had struggled for breath and it didn't seem possible that they died peacefully. I envied Chad for not having to see his babies all dead. I was mad at him, mad at myself and mad at God. I could see no end to my anger and grief.

The neighbor tried to get me into the wagon and go home with him where his wife could tend to me, but I wouldn't budge. He left to bring his wife to me, hoping that she would be able to help. I didn't want help. As soon as he left I carried my baby and Chad's gun out to the barn. The neighbor had left my family as he had found them with Chad spreading his arms over the girls trying in vain to give them a little more protection. I didn't look at their faces. I tried to remember them as they had been the prior morning, full of anticipation at giving me my birthday surprise. I laid down beside Chad with the baby on my chest and prayed for forgiveness. That is all I remember, but I know I took my own life.

I warned you that this was not a happy memory. The first time it came to me, I was about twenty years old and it sent me into a tailspin for weeks. I have never been able to forget that feeling of despair nor have I ever fully let go of the shame I felt for leaving my baby unprotected. Those feelings followed me into this life, challenging my faith. Bad things happen to good people and we don't know why, but it is our job to build our faith to be strong enough to accept it and believe that God has a reason for everything. I still struggle with the fear that everything I love will be stripped from me. When Alex was sick I used that fear to fuel my resolve that nothing would happen to him. Poor Sam, he couldn't have realized the full extent of the turmoil in my head and heart. I didn't dare let down for a minute and open the door to the possibility that Alex wouldn't survive. I know I gave Sam little or no comfort. I had to save my strength to fight my own despair.

In this life I have often struggled with my faith in God. I have never been jealous of those who seem to live untroubled lives, but I wonder at times what purpose God could have in mind that would explain the suffering of innocent people. Most of the time I accept the fact that we will never know or understand His plan and that our time on this earth is just a moment in eternity, making our suffering here of little consequence in the long run. I believe that Chad and my daughters are safe and happy in heaven or perhaps enjoying new and happier lives. There are times when I see a child that reminds me of one of my daughters and I wonder if she has returned and will be allowed to live out her new life. I try so hard to remember what happened to my soul after I took my own life. Did I see my family again? Was I judged for my despair? I do know that there is a plan, a purpose for each life we are given, and that we must use our gifts to discover that purpose while accepting that God's plan may be different from our own.

Sometimes it is hard to translate the many small details of our lives into the whole picture but we serve God and those we love by living each moment aware that every tiny act leads to another, every thought gives birth to others, and every joy and sorrow has its place. It is our job to see that we remember at all times that our thoughts and deeds in these bodies we are given can either strengthen or weaken our souls and the souls of those around us. Joy and goodness are contagious but so are fear, anger and despair. I fail so often to live as I believe and I would like to say that I do the best I can but in reality, I don't believe any of us ever do the best we can. We are always capable of doing better and we all know it. Maybe that knowledge is God's way of keeping us on our toes. He doesn't demand perfection from us and we have no right to demand our view of a perfect world from Him."

SAMANTHA

I have always wondered why grandma sometimes laughs at things that upset other people. She has a way of finding humor at the weirdest times. Some people love her for this because it helps them get over a sad moment. I think it's called perspective. Other people think she is just insensitive. My mom gets upset with her because grandma makes little jokes about things that happen that aren't really funny unless you look at it as she. She often does the "good news, bad news" thing like when you burn the dinner and grandma says the bad news is that you burnt the dinner, but the good news is that you get to order pizza. (Grandma loves pizza and can eat six large slices at a meal.) Another time my mom got a dent in her brand new car and she was really upset. Grandma said that at least she could stop worrying about getting the first dent and just relax and enjoy the car. My mom looked at her like she was some kind of nut and went to her bedroom until grandma left. I guess when you have memories like grandma's you don't sweat the small stuff. I don't know what problems I will face in my life, but I hope to be very brave and strong and I hope I have grandma's sense of humor. Even though she can annoy some people, a lot of other people really like the way she sees things.

When grandma said that each tiny act leads to another and each thought gives birth to others, it reminded me of my situation with my picture on Facebook. I knew what I was doing was not right but I did it anyway because my friends were doing it. Then I tried to conceal it from my parents, which is the same as telling a lie. Then I tried to pretend like I didn't know it was wrong and got angry with my grandpa and Etienne. One wrong act leads to another and I can see how easily people mess up their lives. Grandma knows this and made me face up to what I was doing and then she helped me fix it. I know that when I get back home my friends are going to be mad at me, but that's OK.

Everyone was really quiet after grandma told her story and grandpa got up and went into the den for a few minutes. I think he is sorry he didn't listen to her before. It's not his fault. Most people have trouble believing our stories. It's hard enough to find someone to share your life with and it's even harder if you are asking them to share all of your lives. Hey, that's kind of funny!! I think I'm starting to think like grandma.

SAM

What can I say? My failure was out there for all to see. I know that Amanda believes everything she was saying about how we are to live our lives. I also know that she fails from time to time, but she does keep trying and for the most part she is successful, which is more than many of us can say. All this time I had been trying to win her back, partly to make up for my own failures and help her in her struggles, but I was missing the point. I need her as much as she needs me and it isn't just because she makes me happy or because she is my "dream girl". She is part of my purpose in life and I think I am part of hers and together we can perform the little deeds and think the thoughts that move our souls forward and take others with us. I'm not saying that we are anything special in this world. We are simply meant to live together as beautifully as possible and that is what God intends for any married couple.

Years ago I read somewhere that some prominent man (I can't remember who it was) was talking about the divorce rate in this country. He said that maybe we were going about it all wrong. He said that maybe a couple should have to spend twenty or thirty years together and then, if they did a good job they would be granted the honor of getting married. In other words, they would have to work every day to earn that reward. This goes against our Christian principles and I realize that we can't have people living together and procreating without some sort of legal and social order, but the idea of marriage as an honor and privilege has not been given enough attention. We talk about the bonds of marriage but what about the honor we bring to each other? We say love, honor in the marriage vows, but in that context they are verbs. If we view them as nouns as well, we can see them not solely as a duty, but also as a gift. I had that gift and I want it back.

THELMA

Amanda told me when we were in our teens about her former lives. She didn't go into detail because I wasn't interested. I still wasn't sure if I believed that the memories were real rather than just vivid dreams, but I had to ask myself if it really matters. If Amanda believes she was Lorretta then the effect is the same whether it is true or not. In that case, I wished I had been a better friend to her. I was wondering if I had always been a little jealous of her. It's not that she is better looking than I am because she isn't (at least not in my opinion). What has always confounded me is that she has managed to be happy with so little. I have been a successful business woman and a careful steward of my money. Amanda treats money like it has a disease and wants to get rid of it as fast as possible. The end result is that I own a lovely home and grounds, have traveled extensively and am able to afford anything I want within reason. I am financially secure and have been for many years, whereas Amanda has never known that kind of freedom. Even the condo she owns, which she calls cozy but I call small, is a gift from Sam. She has a minimally comfortable income which leaves not much for additional pleasures such as traveling with me, yet she won't allow anyone to pay her way. She doesn't mind missing out on the adventures that most people find attractive and she takes great pleasure in shopping in thrift stores. I doubt that woman has seen the inside of a Nordstrom's store in twenty years yet she enjoys dressing well. In fact, finding the bargains is the part she enjoys most over actually wearing them. She has managed to be successful in some of her endeavors, but she has never really tried to take anything to the next level and make some real money. I didn't know if I could be happy living in her shoes, (many of which are second hand) and I think that has always bothered me.

I could see that our relationship was changing, just like it did when she first met Sam. Prior to that we had spent most of our free time together and shared many experiences. All that changed when she married Sam. I guess that is natural, but it didn't make it any easier. Then when Alex was born there was even less time for me. I was married for a few years, but that didn't work out well since my husband was jealous of my success. It could have been otherwise. He was a decently talented architect, but he wouldn't listen to me on business matters and ended up working for a second rate firm at a third rate salary. We never could find much in common. Fortunately for him, he later managed to start his own firm and got a few good commissions that brought him some success in his field. I'm happy for him, but he could have saved himself a lot of grief if he had just listened to me in the first place.

Sam, I recognized as a lost cause from the beginning. He had been in sales all his life and he made a fairly good living most of the time but where do you go from there? He and Amanda always seemed to have such a good time but they lived pretty much paycheck to paycheck. Neither of them seemed to mind very much and I guess I am a little in awe of people who can be happy with so little. They are both risk takers and they seem to thrive on doing things the hard way and they never demand what is due them. I think Amanda is a lot like her dad in that respect and Sam is just a good natured schmuck. She could have done a lot better and I thought she might show better judgment after they divorced, but it looked to me like they were going to get back together. At least Sam has a lot of money this time, as long as he doesn't give it all away. I can easily see him as one of those lottery winners that end up penniless ten years later because he gave handouts to every loser that approached him with a tale of woe. I have to give him credit though. This project may be expensive, but it certainly is fun and interesting, and it sure got Amanda and Samantha's attention. I decided I would show up here again but I would have to do some fence mending with Amanda before that would be possible.

I got a real kick out of old Bernie. He sure knew how to get under Sam's skin. If Sam had a set of balls he would have sent the guy packing the first week and avoided this whole mess with him dying. People like Bernie just have a way of making sure others don't get too complacent. They tend to bring out the worst in people. I'm glad I'm not like that.

GLEN

Amanda's story really touched everyone. I had read some of the accounts of the dust bowl so I wasn't surprised about the severity of the conditions, but hearing that story firsthand was pretty hard to take. Sam left the room and, for the second time in just a few days, I could see that he was gaining a full awareness of why his rejection of Amanda's memories had cost him so much. I felt sorry for the guy, but I suspected things would work out for them in the long run. I think this is one of the reasons I never shared my memories with Peggy when she was alive. Maybe I didn't have enough confidence that she would take them seriously and would disappoint me. Obviously, I don't have that problem with Kate. As a matter of fact, I don't have any problem with Kate. I am in love, or should I say we are in love. I have no intention of losing what I have found. I know she is dedicated to helping her tribe and an idea was already starting to take shape in my mind.

BERNIE

Wow. I could see why Amanda is such a hardass. I decided I could be a little nicer to her if for no other reason than to give poor old Sam a break. He was taking that story pretty hard and I was sure that Amanda would grind it into his groin about how he failed her. Old Adrian was standing up and I figured she was getting ready to impart some of her wisdom to the group. I wanted to get out of there before she got on her soapbox. I had better things to do than listen to that old crone. Sam had returned from his little pity party in the den and he was looking at her like she was the Dali Lama. Why do people think that just because someone is old, they are wise? I know a lot of really stupid old people.

ADRIAN

"It's hard to imagine anything more terrible than what Lorretta went through. Thankfully, although we remember the pain, we don't experience it fully in this life as we did in the past life. If that were the case, none of us could survive. It's hard to describe how we can have the memories of that life without being devastated by events like this. We are separate yet the same. It's as if there is some kind of filter that lets us know the pain without absorbing it. We are more than just observers, but we don't totally participate. That's about as good an explanation as I can give. Nevertheless, it affects how we live in our later lives and it is up to us to make sure the effects are positive. Amanda faced despair in that life and it consumed her. In this life she has learned to overcome her fears."

SAM

Everyone seemed to agree with Adrian's description of how the emotions pass into future lives. I guess it is like remembering the pain of a past physical injury. We remember the pain without experiencing it. Amanda spoke up and said that it is like the pain of childbirth. If a woman felt the actual pain every time she remembered the birth, few women would have a second child. The memory of the joy is much stronger than that of the pain. Bernie interjected that he couldn't remember much joy but he certainly remembered the pain.

Etienne replied that that was his choice and it didn't appear to be serving him well.

I was wondering if any of the characters in their past lives had memories of former lives. Did Lorretta have the memories? Amanda said she didn't think so. Alfie spoke up to give us his take on that subject.

ALFIE

"I have a memory of myself as a woman who had memories of prior lives. Her name was Rachael and she lived somewhere in what is now the Middle East. I can't say when she lived, but it was a long time ago. Rachael had several children and was married to a prosperous man. She was a beautiful and somewhat outrageous woman for her times. She may well have been one of the first women's libbers. She had many servants so she was not restricted by daily chores. She spent most of her time shopping in the marketplace and visiting with her many friends. Rachael often spoke to her husband about a past life when she was a slave. She worked in a stone quarry preparing food, such as it was, for the other slaves. She was ugly and uneducated and abused in every way imaginable until one day when she fought back. One of the overseers, who was also a slave, had made her life even more miserable by tormenting her about her ugliness and calling her lazy and worthless. One day, the woman was bent over the well getting water and the overseer was hurling his usual verbal abuse at her and decided to take it one step further by urinating on her back. He was laughing and others laughed too, not wanting to offend or anger him. She grabbed a clay pot and hurled it at him striking him in the forehead. Blood was gushing from his wound but his rage was greater than his pain. He thrust her head into the well and held it underwater until she drowned. Rachael remembered this woman's thoughts as she was dying. The woman was relieved to be freed from the bondage of her miserable life.

Rachael carried this memory with her and it was that which made her fearless in her next life. She was intelligent so she never went too far beyond the bounds of convention, but she tested the limits every day of her life and taught others to do the same. Because of her beauty and the joy she took in every aspect of her life, her husband adored and protected her. She lived a long and happy life and raised her children to be brave and successful. When she was on her deathbed, her husband sat with her for days on end and told her that when she passed he would kill himself immediately so they could be together. She was the bravest of all my memories. Living a fearless life does not always turn out so well, but no matter what the outcome, it is better than living in fear. I have learned that the uncertainty we find in life is to be enjoyed rather than dreaded."

JENNY

Alfie meant every word of what he was saying. Bernie views him as a prissy little queer, but Alfie has more strength than anyone I have ever met. He is a champion in my book. I could see by the way Paul was looking at him at that moment that he felt the same way. I had a feeling that life for Alfie was about to change dramatically.

Of course that meant my own life would change as well. That's OK. I'll never lose him completely and this experience was teaching me to be a little braver in how I live. I am going to have to reach out more to others. I'm not shy. I can do that.

It's just that with Alfie constantly at my side, I haven't felt the need to include too many others. I knew then that I want a bigger life. Before, I wanted to keep other people on the sidelines because I didn't want the pain that relationships can bring. I wanted to stay in my happy little world. Now, after meeting these wonderful people and hearing their stories, I can see that I have been missing too much of what makes us grow. I know how to be happy within myself, but I am not really part of the whole and I think I won't grow unless I join the world and stop protecting myself.

God wants us to be part of a community. That is different than just having a few friends. A community has a life of its own and through that community we learn to live and love fully. We can learn from others so that we don't have to make every discovery and suffer every mistake by ourselves. It's kind of like creating a shortcut to a good and full life. Alfie has been my refuge for too long. He deserves a life of his own and I am ready to explore and share my world with others.

ETIENNE

I couldn't stop thinking about my mom. I knew they weren't telling me the whole truth about why she had to leave, but I also knew that it was her decision to keep me in the dark. I wondered if she was sick and in a hospital somewhere all alone. I was a little angry with her for not being honest with me and not trusting me to be strong enough to help her. When Alfie was describing Rachael as strong and beautiful, I was picturing my mother. She is strong and very beautiful, but I have always known that she was hiding something. I had started to suspect that it had something to do with my father. She wouldn't have lied to me all these years if she wasn't trying to protect me. My father must not have been a good man if she left him and the fact that she told me he had died before I was born means that she didn't want him in my life, and I trust her enough to believe that she probably made the right decision. Since she learned that he really has been dead all these years, I wondered why she wouldn't tell me more about what happened between them. She obviously had nothing to fear from him if that was what was worrying her.

I decided to go to Sam and demand the truth and if he wouldn't tell me, I would go to Adrian or Amanda. I knew they were all in on the story and I was determined to get the truth out of someone. Samantha had stayed an extra day because there was still flooding where she lives and the school buses couldn't run so the schools were closed. She and Thelma were to leave the next afternoon and I decided to wait to confront Sam until after they left.

Samantha was very sad to be leaving, partly because of what she was going to be facing when she got home but also because she didn't want to leave me. I felt the same way but I knew that we will be in constant touch with one another and I was and am sure we won't drift apart—ever.

SERENA

When all this first started I was a little skeptical about the past life theory but I thought it would be interesting, and I have always had a little bit of a crush on Sam so I was glad to be included. By this time I was wondering if it was such a good idea. I had always loved living on this island and being part of the island culture, but how could it ever be the same for me? After meeting these people, hearing their amazing stories and the way they view their lives, past and present, I was afraid that everyone else would be boring. What would happen when Sam and his group leave? It had been less than two weeks since they arrived and already I felt like I knew them better than any of the people I grew up with. I didn't want to lose them, with the exception of Bernie. I couldn't wait to be rid of him but I didn't mean for it to come about in the way it did. I was afraid everyone would leave before I found out what happened to Antoinette and the thought of never seeing Etienne again was painful. I believed that everyone would keep in touch with one another and Sam would keep me in the loop, but I was still sad at the thought of not seeing them every day; laughing, eating, crying, eating, sharing secrets, eating, happy hours, eating. This job for me truly was and is a labor of love. I don't know what to think about Bernie's death except that I know that there isn't a person here that would have harmed him no matter how obnoxious he was. I think he drank himself to death and I hope that if he comes back in another life it will be somewhere on the East coast or another continent, perhaps Paris or New York City-he might fit in there.

Anyway, after hearing Amanda's story about Lorretta I was exhausted and I decided it was time to go home. Paul was getting ready to go too. He offered to walk me to my car. He asked if we could talk for a minute or two, so we got into my car and turned on the heater. He had changed so much since meeting Alfie. I had always liked Paul and at one point I had even thought he was interested in me because he was so thoughtful and attentive whenever we ran into each other. I had no idea that he was gay so that took me by surprise. Since meeting Alfie, it was like he exploded into this funny, outgoing, thoroughly charming person. If that is what love does for you, I wanted it. Paul told me that he would be leaving with Alfie and wanted to know if I wanted to take over the kite shop. He said he would just hand it over to me, with all the inventory, for nothing. I wasn't too surprised that he was leaving, but giving the business away for free seemed strange. He explained that the business wasn't profitable enough to afford a living plus paying him so he wanted me to have it if I wanted it. He suggested that I could cut down on my inventory of kites to make room for some of my baked goods and he was certain that the store would make more money that way. The rent on the store is month to month and very cheap and he was sure I could make a better living than he had. He assured me that money was not an issue with him and that he had been more successful with his video games than he had let on. I had never thought of myself as a business woman so I was taken aback by his offer and was amazed to discover that my mind was already working on ways to increase revenues. I was actually thinking in terms of revenues; a word I had never used before! I had always thought in terms of an hourly wage-and a low one at that. Sam was paying me much more than I had ever earned before and I was saving as much as I could for when I would return to my usual level of earnings.

Sitting in that car with Paul, I discovered that I needed more challenges than I had given myself. Me, Serena, a business owner! I wanted to jump out of my car and start working immediately but I didn't want to appear too excited in case Paul changed his mind. I told Paul that if he still felt the same way by the time he left with Alfie, I would be happy to take over his business. He assured me that he would not change his mind and he leaned over and kissed me on the cheek and told me I was beautiful. Then he got out of my car and I was left alone staring into space dreaming of my new life.

I realized then that I could have had this adventure at any time. Spending time with these people had made me see that though I had lived well, I had lived fearfully and without passion. Now, that old Serena was gone. I drove home and stayed up all night, too excited to sleep. I was no longer afraid about how I would feel when everyone left. I would be sorry to see them go and would miss them, but I had a life and it was going to be bigger than I had ever imagined. My little shop would be a success and would grow into something I could be proud of. I had visions-no doubts, no fears. My new friends would stay in touch with me because they love me. I wouldn't have to hear about them through Sam. I would take short vacations and visit my friends wherever they live. I would see Etienne as he grew into a man and I suspected Samantha would be with him in the years to come. Glen and I would exchange letters and business tips and Amanda would be coming to the island with Sam. I would make sure that I had a place in all their lives. Serena would not be invisible.

SAM

I was pretty tired and decided to go back to the boat and get some sleep. Samantha stayed at the house with Amanda again and Amanda had given her permission to spend a couple of hours with Etienne since it would be her last night with us for a while. She gave her a twelve o'clock curfew. Trusting Etienne was not an issue with her as it wouldn't have been with me.

Thelma had settled into my usual chair with a full bottle of wine and asked Amanda to sit with her for a while. I could see that Amanda was not in the mood for any "drunk talk" with Thelma so she begged off saying she was exhausted. Thelma was clearly offended and, as Amanda left the room, she loudly proclaimed that she would check in on Samantha and Etienne from time to time, implying that Amanda was being negligent. Amanda gave her a cold "whatever" and went to bed. Thelma was looking around for someone else to inflict herself upon as I went out the door. I said goodnight to her and got a grunt as a response. That was more than I was usually given.

Chapter Thirty-Four

CHANGES

SAM

The next morning brought another glorious fall day. These days are cherished on the island because of the gloomy wet weather that would soon set in and last for five or six months. I arrived at the house before 6 AM and brought my Grisham book with me. It was my intent to spend a couple of hours in the den reading and enjoying the sunrise. Serena's car was already in the driveway, but I didn't think much of it since she often came early if she was preparing a special meal. I figured I was in for something really good and I was hungry, so the day was looking even better than before.

I could smell coffee as I headed to the kitchen. There was Serena, all smiles and looking fantastic. She was wearing a black skirt and sweater and her hair, which is her best feature, was arranged in a very flattering up style. She was wearing makeup! Not much, a little lipstick and some eye stuff, but I had never noticed how pretty her eyes are. She looked really nice. I was careful not to rave too much about her appearance for fear of making it sound like I thought she was a troll before. That is the kind of mistake I usually make. Amanda would be proud of my restraint. I know I mentioned before that Serena was no great beauty and I have to stand by that, but that day she looked "kind'a cute" for want of a better expression and she was moving about in a distinctly feminine manner. There was a sort of mysterious air to her that was new to me. She has always been a cheerful person, but now she seemed playful and confident. As I poured my coffee and scrounged around for a bagel or something to tide me over until breakfast, I swear she was flirting with me. It was nothing that obvious, just the way she moved and looked at me out of the corner of her eye. I didn't know how to act and she seemed amused by my discomfort. I got out of the kitchen as fast as I could.

I went to the den intent on some serious reading of Mr. Grisham. I had made little progress so I decided to start over at the beginning rather than try to remember what had happened thus far. By the time I reached page ten I realized I just had too much going on in my own life to be able to concentrate on anything else. I decided to take a walk.

I started out along the road in the opposite direction of the village. I had gone about half a mile when I noticed Adrian sitting on a rock, looking out over the water, deep in thought. I was reluctant to disturb her, yet afraid it would be rude to just pass by. I stood there for a moment trying to decide what to do. Finally, she turned around and saw me and, judging by her smile, I felt welcomed to join her. She told me that she was an early riser and didn't want to disturb anyone in the house so she often took early morning walks. I sat beside her and we were silent for a couple of minutes when she said that she had wanted to talk to me about something for a few days. I was afraid she was going to say that it was time for her to leave, but that was not the case.

She asked if she could invite her granddaughter, April to join the group. I knew that she suspected all along that April had the memories and that some of the short stories she wrote were really about her past lives. April was the one who had encouraged Adrian to come in the first place. Since her arrival, Adrian had spoken with April on the phone a couple of times and apparently April had finally come clean and admitted that Adrian's suspicions were right on. I told her that I had no problem with the idea and we had room for April with Antoinette gone, but that I felt we should run it by the rest of the group, although I knew there would be no objection. That seemed fair to her and we agreed that we would bring the subject up at breakfast.

Adrian's eightieth birthday was in four days so I thought it would be a great thing to get April here for that celebration. Serena had already made plans for a special dinner and everyone was trying to decide what to give her as a gift. What do you give a healthy and beautiful eighty year old woman who was already blessed by every gift God could bestow? I made a mental note to insist on inviting April myself so that I could enlist her help with a gift idea.

We walked slowly back to the house as Adrian told me what to expect with April. She has many friends but has had only one real romantic involvement in her twenty eight years and that had ended several months before when the love of her life chose another. Adrian had never liked him in the first place. Apparently he was very controlling and made a habit of making little jokes at April's expense and was jealous of her modest success as a writer. He was a real estate salesman who claimed his specialty was commercial properties. In fact, he had only sold one property in the past four years and that was his father's which he managed to sell at a ridiculously low price. Still, the sale generated a commission large enough to support him until recently. The money had run out and April couldn't afford to "loan" him any more so he decided it was time for him to move on. April's replacement was another agent who was on a fast track in the business and was willing to partner with the jerk. His explanation to April was that he needed someone who lived in the real world, not her fantasy world, and the new woman wasn't afraid to invest in his future. He claimed they had several deals in the making and he would be repaying his loans from her in a short while. Adrian said that April seemed pretty indifferent about the whole matter, but it was hard to be sure since she was so good at masking her true feelings. Adrian was convinced the timing was right for April to take this step and it was clear that she was excited at the prospect of her joining the group. We agreed to call her right after breakfast unless there was opposition from the others.

Breakfast was a feast consisting of pork chops and eggs, fried potatoes and hot biscuits with Serena's homemade blackberry jam. We stuffed ourselves as usual and then lingered over coffee since we were too full to move. As expected, no one had any objection to Adrian's request except Thelma who pointed out that there would not be room for her when she visited again. She was serious, but no one responded so she pouted for a while. Finally, Amanda spoke up and told her that she didn't have a vote in the matter and that we hadn't planned to have visitors in the first place. Thelma gave her a "yeah, right" and gave Paul, whom Serena had invited for breakfast, a dirty look. Amanda ignored her. We all did.

We made the call to April and she seemed happy to be invited. I asked Adrian to let me talk to her alone for a minute on the pretense of laying out the rules, as if we had any. April agreed to arrive in time for the birthday party and said she would take care of getting a gift. This day kept getting better! When I returned to the dining room, I was informed that Samantha was going to share a memory before she and Thelma had to leave. I had heard some of her memories before and was surprised when she came up with a new one. Samantha stood with her hand on Etienne's wheelchair as she told her story.

Chapter Thirty-Five

THE INCREDIBLE SHRINKING JANE

Her name was Jane and it was her sixteenth birthday. She woke up screaming. She was lying on her back in bed and she had rested her hands on her tummy when she felt two large, hard lumps, one on each side. She panicked as she thought she had broken some bones or had tumors. Her aunt Leona came rushing into the room when she heard her screams. Jane threw back the covers and showed her aunt the lumps. She was dumbfounded when Leona started laughing. Finally Leona explained that those weren't lumps and there were no broken bones, Jane was just feeling her pelvic bones for the first time. You see, Jane had been an extremely fat child since birth and she had finally lost enough weight to allow her to feel those bones.

Leona was Jane's father's sister. Jane had come to live with her over a year before that after her mother died. Jane's father didn't feel he could take proper care of a young girl, especially one as troubled and unpleasant as Jane. He was not a bad man but he had been through hell with Jane's mother's depression and ill temper for years before her death, and as Jane was exactly like her mother, it seemed her father would have the same problems with her. Leona had always been close to her brother. She was a widow and very lonely and offered to take Jane into her home and give her the care she needed. Jane's father was relieved to have Leona's help.

When Jane's father met her mother, Irene was the spoiled, but charming and lovely daughter of one of the richest men in the county. His wife had died shortly after Irene was born so she was raised by her father's housekeeper who dealt with Irene's temper tantrums by giving her anything she wanted. By the time she was married Irene had become a cheerful and fun young woman as long as she got her way, but as soon as they were married, Jane's father realized that he had married a spoiled, bratty child who didn't know how to run a household and didn't want to learn. He made a good living and was able to afford a housekeeper, but he was not wealthy like Irene's father. Irene's lifestyle changed and she did not like it one bit. She cried and screamed and pouted, but she couldn't get her way. She was miserable and was determined to make everyone else miserable too. That turned out to be the only thing that she did well.

In her misery, she turned to food. She lived on pastries and chocolates and was capable of eating a whole chicken at one meal. The housekeeper kept her supplied with goodies just to shut her up. After a couple of years, she had gained so much weight that she didn't even realize she was pregnant until three months before Jane was born.

Jane was born fat and every time she opened her mouth her mother gave her food to keep her quiet. By the time Jane was three years old she was so fat she could hardly walk. When Jane was five, her Aunt Leona's husband died and Leona moved back to be near her brother. The first time she saw Jane she couldn't believe her eyes and she begged her brother to do something about Jane's weight while he could still control her, or she would become as hideous as Irene. Jane heard Leona talking to her father and told her mother what Leona had said about her. Irene banned Leona from the house from that time on.

When Irene died suddenly of a heart attack, Jane was fourteen years old and a miserable child. She weighed over two hundred fifty pounds and was still gaining. Jane's father dropped her at Leona's house and left immediately so he didn't have to listen to her screams. Leona sat Jane down and told her that she was not going to allow Jane to become like her mother. Jane was to lose the weight and she was going to become a respectful young lady. She gave her chores to do and spent several hours each day tutoring her in her studies. Jane had never attended a real school because she was so fat and her mother said the other children would be cruel to her. Leona told Jane that the tutor Jane's father had hired had not done a very good job, but that she could see that Jane had a good mind and she would be expected to use it.

Jane was miserable, but there was no one to listen to her complaints. Leona controlled everything in her life; what she ate, what she read, when she went to bed, when she got up and Leona made her take walks with her for an hour each day. At first the walks were very hard and painful, but little by little they got easier and Jane didn't mind them so much. They helped take her mind off her constant hunger. Leona was a good cook, but she gave Jane only one serving of everything and there was only fruit for dessert. There were no pastries, pies, cakes or chocolate. Jane begged for even one treat per week but Leona said that sugar was addictive and even one treat would make it harder for Jane the rest of the week.

Within a couple of months, Jane had settled down and stopped screaming and throwing tantrums. It was no use, they never worked anyway. She felt abandoned by those who were supposed to love her. She cried herself to sleep, hungry and miserable and she could see no end to her tortures. She didn't hate Leona, but there were times when she would fantasize that Leona had died and she would be returned to her father's house where she would be allowed to do and eat whatever she wanted. That fantasy was destroyed when her father came to visit and brought his new wife. The woman was pleasant and Jane liked her well enough but she knew that now there wasn't any place for her in her father's house.

She had lived only for food for her entire life so it never occurred to her that there could be other things that would make her happy. She had never had a friend, never dreamed of romance, never imagined a normal life with interests beyond what was in the kitchen. Leona taught her how to sew and make her own clothes. Jane was shrinking rapidly and everything she had brought with her was falling off her body. Even the new dresses she made were soon too big for her as she continued to lose weight. It took a long time for Jane to realize that this was a good thing. She had lived all her life as an obese person with no idea that she could be anything else. By the time she had been with Leona for a full year, she had lost over one hundred pounds and, though still plump, she was not so fat as to draw attention from others. She and Leona started going to church together and taking trips into town. Jane still cried at night but it was more from habit than anything else.

As her sixteenth birthday neared, Leona asked Jane to be thinking about what she wanted for her birthday. Jane told her she just wanted a huge gooey chocolate cake and tons of ice cream. Leona took her by the hand and led her to her bedroom and sat her down in front of her mirror. She told Jane to really look at what she saw. For the first time Jane realized that she was an attractive young girl. Leona said that she should be asking for something outrageous for her birthday, not a stupid cake. She told Jane that food was no longer the center of her life. She should have other things to look forward to. Leona promised her the chocolate cake because she deserved a reward, but she wanted Jane to want more. When Leona left the room Jane stared at her reflection in the mirror for a long time and she began to cry. She understood what Leona was saying and she understood then that Leona loved her as no one else ever had, but she still couldn't grasp what she was supposed to want. She still couldn't see herself as much more than an eating machine. She was doing well in her studies, but to what end? She had no dreams or goals. Even the fact that she had lost all the weight was not her doing, it was Leona's. What was she supposed to want? Even if she knew what she wanted to do with her life, how would she get there? She had never done anything on her own. She laid down and cried herself to sleep.

Later that evening Leona brought her dinner on a tray. Also on the tray was a stack of books, all by the same author, Jane Austen. Leona told her to read the books and it would help her understand what a woman could be. For the next few days Jane barely left her room. The other Jane, Jane Austen, became the first friend she had ever had. She loved Elizabeth, laughed at Emma, pictured Mr. Darcy in her mind and, for the first time wondered if a man would ever love her. Jane Austen taught her more about herself in one week than she had learned in all of her life. She wanted to be a woman of character, like Elizabeth. She wanted to be in control of herself. She wanted to bring people into her life and share her thoughts. She still didn't have a dream, but for the first time she craved adventure and companionship instead of chocolate. She began to believe that there were things she could do on her own.

Three days before her birthday she went down to breakfast as a changed person. Her hair was combed and curled and she had on the new dress she had made the month before. She sat up straight and ate slowly, pushing her plate away with a few bites left. She thanked Leona for teaching her to sew, but asked if she could be involved in choosing the fabric from then on. After breakfast, she asked if she could be excused to take her walk alone for once as she had some thinking to do. Leona was excited and happy to grant both her requests. Before Jane left for her walk she told Leona that she wanted two things for her birthday. First, she wanted her father to come for the dinner. She hadn't seen him in several months and she realized that she missed him and she was excited to have him see her as she looked. Perhaps he would love her. Second, she wanted Leona and her to spend the day in town, just walking around and looking in the shop windows and watching people. She told Leona that she still wanted chocolate cake, but it was because that's what people did on their birthdays.

The morning of her birthday she felt the lumps and was certain she was dying just when she had finally decided to live her life. When Leona laughed and explained what the lumps were, Jane realized how little she knew about her own body, let alone the world around her. She still wasn't convinced that she would ever have what others have in their lives. That type of knowledge doesn't come in one week, even when you have Jane Austen as your teacher. But instead of feeling lost and alone as she would have felt a month earlier, she felt excited, and looked forward to all the discoveries awaiting her. The only fear she had was of her own weakness, but she knew she was changing and she would grow to be a strong and courageous woman.

That is the last I ever heard from Jane but I believe that she lived a good life. I think of her whenever I see a person who is grossly overweight and I wonder if they think the way Jane did. There was a very large girl at my school last year and I tried to make friends with her, but she wanted nothing to do with me. I asked her one day if she had ever read any of Jane Austen's books, but she just gave me a blank stare and moved on. Some of the kids made fun of her and were cruel to her so maybe she was just afraid I was trying to trick her or something. She isn't at school this year so I don't know what happened to her. I can't even remember her name and that makes me feel bad.

SERENA

Samantha is such a sweetheart. That girl at school probably took one look at her beautiful little face and perfect little body and decided that they would have nothing in common and that Samantha couldn't possibly imagine how she felt. I can identify with Jane to a certain extent, because I have never been pretty and slender and I had no mother. What made the difference for me is my wonderful father. He never would have allowed me to indulge myself in self-pity or any serious bad habits. He is such a happy person that no one around him can fail to thank God for the gifts we are each given. Even so, I didn't really see the possibilities in my life until that night when Paul offered me his little shop. I had accepted everything as it was and though I was happy, I wasn't opening any new doors. I guess I was ready to listen and look in the mirror. I'm also going to re-read my Jane Austen books.

JENNY

What an adorable story. I hadn't had a chance to spend much time with Samantha, but I hoped she would come back soon. I vowed to make every effort to pry her away from Etienne for a few minutes and get to know her better. One thing is for sure. Her world is not small and never will be. She is an adventuress and I hope she will stay close to her parents and to Sam and Amanda so they can watch over her until she is able to take care of herself. I picked up on what was going on with the Facebook page. That is exactly the type of thing that can ruin a young girl, especially one as trusting as Samantha seems to be. Etienne, on the other hand, is every bit as sweet and kind as Samantha, but there is an awareness in him of how evil the world can be. I guess you can be innocent without being naïve. I have a feeling he too will be looking after Samantha. Alfie and I have been watching out for one another for a long time, but that is going to lessen now as Paul has entered the picture. I'm very happy for both of them and, as I mentioned before, it's probably good to force me out in the world a little more. I was looking forward to meeting April. She is closer to my age and it sounded like we might have a lot in common.

AMANDA

I am so proud of our little granddaughter. There is so much I can teach her and so much I can learn from her. She is such a brave young girl. People always told me I was brave when I was young, but that is not true. Much of what I did in those years was because I didn't have any other choice, or at least I didn't perceive other choices. I hope Samantha will let me and Sam help her to see her possibilities and make the right choices. I was so grateful to Etienne for spotting the danger she had placed herself in and for having the courage to stand up to her in the face of her anger. Not many young men would have done that.

Samantha wanted Etienne to tell a story next. They had shared some of their memories and there was one in particular that she wanted him to share with the group. We were all anxious to hear from him but none of us wanted to push him too hard because of his injuries and what was happening with his mother. However, he seemed perfectly at ease as he wheeled himself to the middle of the room. He and Samantha exchanged secret smiles as he began his story.

Chapter Thirty-Six

THE NATURE OF EVIL

ETIENNE

"My name was Harold and I was evil from the day I was born. There was no reason for my bad behavior other than my evil nature. I wasn't beaten or abused and my life was no harder than that of anyone else in my family or my village. This life took place in what must have been medieval times and we lived in Scotland. My father was a blacksmith and my two brothers and I helped him in his shop while my sister kept house with our mother. Everyone in my family was happy and healthy except me. I was only happy when I was causing trouble and bringing pain to others and there were few in my village that had not experienced some sort of cruelty from me. I made fun of the old and sick. I terrorized young children and tortured animals enjoying their pain and the power I had over them. My father had tried all sorts of punishment and rewards to get me to change my ways and my mother prayed for me constantly as she was convinced I was possessed by a demon.

When I was sixteen years old, I stole a horse from our neighbors and slit its throat. This was a huge crime as our neighbor depended upon this horse to feed his family. The horse pulled his delivery cart with which he supplied our village and surrounding villages with sausages and cheese and milk. His son, William, was my age and we were bitter enemies because of the many lies I had told about him and I had often beaten him up and stolen food and coins from him. This had been going on since we were very young, but the final straw came when I told lies about his younger sister. She was very pretty and I tried to kiss her one day and she slapped me. Enraged, I went around the village telling everyone that I had seen her naked. I said that she lured me into the woods and took all her clothes off and tried to get me to lie with her. Usually, as children, we settled our differences without involving our parents but this time William had gone to his father and told him what I was saying. The father questioned his daughter and she denied everything but was humiliated at the thought that some people might believe my story even though everyone knew I was a liar. Her father came to my father and I was beaten severely and told that if I did even one more bad thing, I would be turned away from my home.

Like most bad people, I blamed my trouble on someone else rather than admit that I had brought it on myself. Again, like most bad people, I believed that I was smarter than everyone else and governed by a different set of rules. The plan to destroy their horse fit well with my desire to get back at all of them at the same time. I wanted to bring disaster to their entire family.

The village was small and remote, so when the horse came up missing and was found with its throat slashed, there was little doubt in people's minds as to who was responsible. No one else had any motive and there were few travelers that found their way to our village. I didn't care because I had been clever and knew that there was no way they could prove it was I who was responsible. On the other hand, I wanted that family to know who had brought them to ruin. What fun was there in causing pain if the victims didn't know the source? I denied everything but made no effort to pretend that I felt badly for the family.

For two days everyone avoided me including my own family and I was confident that I had made my point and that no one would mess with me again. My mother cried every time she looked at me and my father and brothers didn't speak to me at all, but none of that disturbed me. On the third night, my father asked me to help him deliver some horseshoes to a neighbor outside of town and, even though I knew he could handle the job by himself, I went willingly as the silence in our house was boring me. We walked silently to the top of the hill and the last thing I remember was seeing my father's muscular arm with a hammer clenched in his fist flying toward my face. I assume that my father decided to put an end to my evil life and spare others the pain I would inevitably bring them. I have no doubt that I was capable of murdering a human and any number of horrible deeds and I believe my father killed me out of love for me and his family.

I don't know why God allows such evil to exist. Maybe it is to remind us to be vigilant regarding our souls. It is his way of demonstrating that without faith and belief in his goodness, we are all capable of incredible evil. Most of us are born good and, with care and love, we develop into good people even though we are flawed. There are those, however, that are born with none of the qualities that make us children of God. Harold was one of those and I believe that I have learned more from that life than any other. I have no compassion for Harold because he didn't fight for his soul. He chose pride, greed, lust and hatred instead of love and goodness. He forced his father to murder his own son and created havoc in his village which distracted others from their pursuit of goodness. I hope that by his example others were able to see the destructive power of an untamed soul."

SAM

I don't have to tell you that there were some perplexed people in that room after hearing this story. We all sat silently for several moments, unable to believe that there could be a connection between this young man we had all grown to love and the demon that was Harold. Glen was the first to speak.

"It is difficult to define morality without reference to that which is immoral. To say that we should not kill our neighbor or steal from him is easy enough to understand, but it doesn't address all the problems that are created beyond the loss of that one life or the torment to the victim's family. There are obvious consequences such as the hatred and mistrust that arises in others from witnessing the evil in one such as Harold. Facing the grief or the paralyzing fear that follows evil deeds stifles our ability to love and live our lives fully. These things drain us of energy that could be directed toward nourishing our souls and the world we live in. As an example, look at the time and resources we spend protecting ourselves from vandals, thieves, murderers and rapists. We install locks on our doors and front gates. We buy expensive alarm systems and teach our children how to lock the world out. We buy protection from identity theft and shredders to thwart the efforts of those who want what we have. We pay attorneys to make sure we are protected from frivolous lawsuits that could bring us financial ruin. We spend hours each week locking and unlocking our homes and cars. Businesses spend thousands of dollars each year on background checks and drug testing of employees. If we totaled up the time and money that ninety five percent of us spend protecting ourselves from the five percent that would do us harm, the results are staggering. But even worse is the effect it has on us individually and as a society. We are forced to use our time, energy and money to protect our families instead of enriching their souls and lives. We have to teach our children to fear the unknown instead of exploring it. Evil is more than just the deed itself, it robs us of our innocence and incubates hatred and more evil. It is this knowledge that makes Etienne the person he is and will keep him vigilant. There will always be evil doers and we do have to protect ourselves, but the greatest challenge is to learn to keep the evil from spreading by not allowing ourselves to become brittle with hate and fear. Love and protect as best we can, and then live our lives in such a way that we enjoy each day and bring happiness to others. Fear feeds hatred and hatred feeds on itself."

As Glenn was speaking I was reminded of the many times I had enhanced the effects of a wrong done to me by my own reactions and I could see others nodding in agreement and probably thinking the same thoughts as I was. At the same time, I can't imagine anything more challenging than this assignment. Then again, all I had to do is think of Bernie to see that Glen was right. Bernie may not have been an evil person, but he certainly was an example of someone who robs the world of joy through his fear and bitterness. However, as I looked at him I was surprised to see that Bernie appeared pensive as if he was giving some credence to what Glen was saying. Of course, the second he saw me watching him, his expression changed to reflect his usual sour disposition.

Etienne did not seem uncomfortable or worried about the effect his story would have on the others. He smiled at Glen and accepted hugs from Adrian and Samantha. It was clear that in his mind Harold was dead and he was alive, well, and living a better life thanks to the lessons learned from having viewed life from the dark side.

It was time for Samantha and Thelma to leave in order to catch the ferry home. I volunteered to drive them to the dock, but Amanda insisted on taking them herself. There was a tearful goodbye to Etienne from Samantha and Thelma gave an unsolicited promise to the group that she would try to come back for another visit. No one reinforced her promise but, as usual, Thelma didn't seem to notice the lack of enthusiasm. Amanda gave me her "Don't worry, I'll handle this." look as she ushered Thelma out the door. Samantha gave me a hug that was both tender and painful to my left shoulder and whispered to me to take care of Etienne because she loved him and to please keep her informed if there was any news about Antoinette.

I was beginning to wonder about the long term effects of this project. We had brought so many new people into our lives and they are people that we will never want to lose. I couldn't imagine leaving them behind and never seeing them again or knowing what happened in their futures and losing the benefit of their knowledge. Admittedly, I could live without ever seeing Bernie again, but that has become a moot issue. It was impossible for me to imagine that Etienne and Samantha would drift apart and we were already a part of the drama surrounding Antoinette and I knew we would be there to see it through with her no matter what. Jenny, Alfie, Glen and Kate (I was already thinking of them as a couple), and Adrian as well as the new and improved Serena, all had brought a richness to our lives that we would never want to give up. I could visualize Amanda and me making many trips together to visit our new friends and, of course, we would be spending some time in Toronto with Samantha visiting Etienne.

After Samantha and Thelma left, the house was a lot calmer and everyone seemed anxious to get down to the business of whatever our business was. April was scheduled to arrive in three days in time for Adrian's birthday party and Serena was busy making plans for the event and performing even more miracles with her physical appearance. She was emerging more each day as a young woman who has discovered her worth not only as a kind and generous being, she always had those qualities, but as a person to inspire and lead others. She was more than just a generous heart. She was becoming a leader, someone worth watching, someone we can learn from instead of simply admiring the gentle goodness she seemed to be born with. She was actively expanding her world. She disappeared for hours at a time, making trips to Port Townsend to buy special items for the birthday dinner and mysterious bundles for herself. She announced that the event would be semi-formal so we were all told to dig out our "glad rags". She was having the time of her life, yet still managed to provide us with fabulous meals. Amanda enlisted my help in taking over more of the household chores to give Serena a little more freedom. Jenny took over laundry duties and Alfie and Paul placed themselves in charge of party decorations. Bernie was in charge of aggravation as usual.

We continued with our memory sessions and Alfie provided us with a couple of winners. He described a former life in which he was a female acrobat in a circus. Apparently this woman had the ability to fold herself into a small package and then explode her body to its natural form in one swift movement. A catastrophe occurred when one of the clowns fell on her when she was in her folded state, crushing bones and joints which prevented her from regaining her former shape. She had to be "detangled" forcibly and was never able to sit or stand on her own again and she lived in constant pain. Just listening to this tale caused us to wince and damaged the atmosphere in the room so he quickly followed with this story to lighten things up. We could tell Alfie loved this memory as he launched into his narrative.

Chapter Thirty-Seven

LEONARDO'S GIFT

ALFIE

"His name was Arthuro. He was born in Florence Italy in 1483. Even as a child he believed he was destined to be a great artist, and the fact that he reached his twenties at the height of the Italian Renaissance only served to confirm this belief. His contemporaries were DaVinci, Rafael and Michelangelo along with a great many others whose genius was overshadowed by the brilliance of these three men. Arthuro, however, never wavered in his faith and desire to find his rightful place in the hearts and purses of the Italian nobility. He studied with the best teachers and on several occasions he, along with several other students, spent a few hours with the great Leonardo.

By the year 1509, as he celebrated his twenty-sixth birthday, Arthuro was making little in terms of a living and his family was tired of supporting his dreams. For the first time, he had to support himself. Arthuro was not a stupid man. He knew the time had come when he had to sit down and give himself an honest appraisal of his prospects. He forced himself to accept the fact that he had some severe limitations. The only money he had ever made was as a portrait artist and even with his skill in that area, commissions had been few and far between and not from the wealthiest families. His dream of creating beautiful landscapes and seascapes had not materialized. He simply didn't have the sense of depth, color and proportion necessary to produce great works. He also didn't possess the knowledge of the human body that Michelangelo and DaVinci had and he didn't have the ambition to engage in the intricate studies necessary to gain that expertise. In short, he realized that although art was his calling, he was too lazy to compete with the greats. He was a personal friend of Raphael and was privy to the rigorous devotion Raphael brought to his work and he knew well the pleasures and leisurely activities forfeited by DaVinci and Michelangelo to perfect their works. He realized that, although he was intelligent in a crafty way, he lacked the basic intellectual curiosity exhibited by these great men. He finally concluded that he would have to develop his limited talent for portrait art and find a way to win the huge commissions paid by the wealthy families.

He had seen an unfinished portrait by DaVinci of the wife of one Francesco Del Diocondo. Though unfinished, it was creating quite a stir in the art community. The woman's name was Lisa and though she was no great beauty by traditional standards, Leonardo had captured some essence or quality that brought the woman to life. Arthuro studied the painting and realized that it was truly a work of art but he couldn't quite distinguish what it was that set it apart. He needed to learn that secret if he was ever to become rich and famous as a portrait artist.

It took several months, but he finally succeeded in getting a private audience with DaVinci. He decided to be honest with the great man and tell him of his motives from the start. He knew DaVinci would not be threatened by him as a competitor since DaVinci's skills ran far beyond that of a portrait artist and he was in great demand for any number of projects with huge commissions. That was a good decision on Arturo's part. DaVinci was impressed with his honesty and certainly not threatened in any way by his talent. Besides, Arturo took great pains to feed DaVinci's massive ego. DaVinci set aside an entire day to tutor this "wannabe" in the secrets of portrait art as a business, as well as an art form.

Arthuro went on and on about the mysterious qualities of the subject, Lisa. He quoted all the rhetoric and speculation he had heard from the artist community about this enigmatic woman. After several minutes DaVinci threw up his hands and started cursing. This was not the reaction Arthuro expected, so he quit talking and opened his ears trying to memorize every word spoken by the great master.

DaVinci began by saying that the reason the portrait was not finished, even though he had started it almost six years earlier was because he was totally bored by the subject. He went on to say that it was true the Lisa Gheradini Giocondo was no great beauty by any standard, but it was also true that she was neither mysterious, nor enigmatic and certainly no model of perfect womanhood as had been suggested by many. In fact, she was vain, arrogant and totally witless. He had begrudged her every minute that he was forced to spend in her presence and, had he not spent the commission advanced at the time of the contract, he would have abandoned the project long ago. As it was, a completed work was long overdue and Francesco had recently demanded a finished portrait or a return of all the money he had paid. Leonardo was glad that he was presently in a position financially that allowed him to repay the sum, which meant that he now owned the painting and could do with it as he pleased. Had it not created such a stir among his students and art collectors, he would have destroyed it at the time he took ownership, but instead he decided to keep it, possibly finish it at a later date and give it to one of his students.

DaVinci went on to say "What people see in that portrait is what Lisa Giocondo wants them to see. She believes she is enigmatic, mysterious and wise and that those traits make her beautiful in a way that cannot be duplicated by nature. Lisa believes she is the personification of womanhood and a model for the Madonna so I gave that to her. I didn't change her features to make them more pleasing. I just transformed them to give her the appearance she wanted. The knowing smile, the direct steadfast gaze with no hint of coyness, the complete absence of anxiety or any form of discomfort, the erect yet relaxed pose, the way the light features her face against the darker background, all of this gives an image of how Lisa wants to be seen, not as she truly is. Study this portrait carefully and you will see what I am telling you. You must interview your subjects and learn how they see themselves so that you can give them what they want rather than an exact reproduction of how they appear. You will learn to see them as they imagine themselves in their finest hour. You will erase the flaws in their character that show themselves in subtle ways on their faces and transform their features into their idea of a perfect model. You will paint what they want to see. Arthuro, you are talented enough to learn these secrets and lazy enough to be content with the art you will produce. You will finish the portraits on time and go on to the next and you will achieve some level of wealth. I envy you your freedom from the forces that drive me. You can do the work you set out to do, yet live a full life without being a prisoner of your art. I admire you for your self-assessment and your courage in facing the truth about your talent."

Arthuro was pleased with what Leonardo told him and flattered that he believed Arthuro could master the intricacies he described. Again, Leonardo surprised Arthuro by volunteering to accompany him to Arthuro's studio to examine the two portraits he was working on and demonstrate his methods. Arthuro knew his subjects well enough to give him an idea of how they saw themselves and would like to be seen. In a few short hours, Leonardo shared enough of his secrets to enable Arthuro to develop techniques that would set his work apart. Arthuro was ecstatic and eager to put these newly acquired techniques to work. For the first time in a long time, he knew what he wanted to do and he believed fully in himself once again. After all, if Leonardo DaVinci said he had the talent, who was he to disagree?

Within a month he completed the two portraits utilizing his newly found skills. His clients were well pleased with the results and paid the rest of the meager commissions they had agreed upon. More importantly, one of them was so impressed with his work that they introduced Arthuro to a wealthy merchant who wanted to commission a portrait of his eldest son who had distinguished himself as a soldier. The family had acquired their wealth through trade rather than family lineage and they hoped to capitalize on their son's military success to enhance their social standing. Arthuro was able to demand a huge sum for this portrait and his career was launched as he employed Leonardo's methods and produced exactly the portrait that the father wanted to see. After all, the father was writing the check, not the son. From this commission, he received more, each at a higher rate until Arthuro found himself debt free, living quite comfortably and being recognized as one of the most prominent portrait artists in Italy.

His wealth grew to the point where he could afford to become bored and begin to look for more challenges. Over the years, that same merchant's son had visited Arthuro regularly and they had become friends. The son was not a happy man. His family doted on him, and his military career ended well, bringing the family the elevated status they sought, but the son was miserable. He was living a lie. Finally, he confided in Arthuro that he saw himself as a woman and he wanted to live as a woman. It wasn't so much that the son feared bringing shame to his family, rather he was afraid of losing their financial support if their war hero son was exposed as a dandy. His military pension was not sufficient to keep him in the style to which he was accustomed and he had no interest in the family business. He begged Arthuro to paint him as he desired to be seen. He dressed himself in an elegant gown, applied a wig and made himself up as a woman, a femme fatale. This gave Arthuro exactly the challenge he had been seeking.

Arthuro applied all of his practiced skills to this task and the end result was impressive indeed. The son was thrilled and convinced Arthuro to produce more portraits of him in various poses and gowns. All In all, Arthuro produced seven paintings of the mysterious "woman". These he hung in his studio so the young man could visit them at any time. As fate would have it, some of Arthuro's other patrons fell in love with the portraits of the anonymous woman and, sharing the proceeds with the son, Arthuro sold all but one of the paintings for very large sums. Purchasers of these paintings claimed to be smitten by the beauty and grace of the subject "lady" and many a man proclaimed her as his "ideal". Arturo's refusal to divulge her identity only added to the mystery. The son enjoyed visiting the homes of these wealthy collectors with his parents and seeing his portrait hung in their halls. It was a pleasant joke for the frustrated young man.

Arthuro would never have revealed the true identity of his subject, but the son spilled the beans by showing up at an annual masquerade ball dressed and made up as he was in one of the paintings. It seems his vanity got the best of him and he wanted to receive the adulation that he deserved. Needless to say, the paintings became a scandal and a joke, and there were some very embarrassed art collectors. Arthuro was publicly shamed by the revelation. He made one last visit to Leonardo to apologize for his misuse of Leonardo's gift. Leonardo was not offended. He seemed more amused than anything else. He told Arthuro that he often injected some subtle surprises into his works to see if anyone would notice. However, Leonardo told Arthuro that his offence was unlikely to be forgiven and that his career as a serious artist was over for the time being and it would be good for him to live in obscurity for a few years and enjoy whatever wealth he had acquired. Arthuro took his ill-gotten fortune and moved to a secluded village by the sea. He continued to paint, but never offered his works for sale. Instead he painted portraits of every man woman and child in his village as well as commemorating weddings, births, and baptisms. All of these, he donated to his neighbors as well as secret donations of money to those in need. He lived a long life and no longer sought fame and fortune. He was content with the good wishes of his neighbors and being part of a community.

The soldier/son enjoyed the notoriety created by his stunt and the many male admirers that surfaced due to "outing" himself. Though rejected and shunned by his family, he found happiness with one of these admirers who purchased the formerly valuable paintings from the embarrassed art collectors at a mere fraction of their original cost. The son was eventually murdered by the jealous wife of one of his suitors."

SAM

We all enjoyed this story and Alfie delivered it in a flamboyant style that made it even more fun. To be honest, I never have been able to see what all the fuss was about regarding the Mona Lisa. She always did look a little dull to me. I was relieved to learn that I wasn't a total idiot for not experiencing some kind of artistic orgasm in her presence. Amanda was impressed that Arthuro overcame his desire for recognition and was able to find contentment by bringing joy to others and becoming part of a community.

Etienne had been unusually quiet since Samantha left, but he seemed to perk up after Alfie's story. He asked to be excused until dinner and went to the guest house. Actually, he spent more and more time alone for the next few days. He would sit in on our sessions and he was pleasant during meals, but he retreated to his quarters at all other times. Adrian and Amanda kept a close eye on him but both stated that he didn't seem depressed. He did have some catching up to do with his studies and he was spending a lot of time with his notebook, but never shared its contents with anyone. I was staying pretty close to the phone hoping for word from Father Karl or Antoinette. I wanted so badly to be able to go to Etienne with news that his mother would be returning. I hated lying to him, but the alternative was to come clean with the whole story and I didn't feel I had the right to go against Antoinette's wishes, even though I wasn't sure she was doing the right thing by keeping him in the dark. I knew he suspected there was more than he was being told and I wondered if he was imagining something worse than the truth, although I couldn't think what could be worse than the truth. Adrian confided to Amanda and me that she was praying that Antoinette was innocent of the crime and I had to admit that the same thoughts had occurred to me. Amanda refused to allow any doubts about Antoinette's innocence and was a little short with Adrian for suspecting otherwise. I was glad I had kept those thoughts to myself.

Chapter Thirty-Eight

ADRIAN HAS HER DAY

SAM

That Friday was the fifteenth day of our time together and it was Adrian's birthday. We had made no attempt to conceal the fact that there was going to be a party nor that April would be arriving that afternoon. Keeping such a secret in this crowd would have been an exercise in futility. Besides, Adrian was enjoying all the attention. She was turning eighty and stated openly that she deserved any accolades she was given. Amanda found Adrian's attitude refreshing as opposed to the fake humility usually demonstrated by honored guests. I had to agree that it is more rewarding to spend time and money on one who openly appreciates the effort than on one who feigns embarrassment or pretends that they were undeserving.

The weather that morning was about as unpleasant as it could get with no promise of improvement later in the day. It was drizzling rain and the wind was gusting to about forty mile per hour, but there was no cause for concern as we hadn't been foolish enough to rely on good weather for any of our activities.

I planned to meet April's ferry at four o'clock and take a few minutes to get acquainted before exposing her to the group. Adrian suggested that April and I stop off for a latte before returning to the house so that we could get comfortable with one another. I thought this was good plan because it would give me a chance to compensate April for the money she had spent on Adrian's birthday gift as well as discover what the gift was. Amanda, Jenny, and Kate were going to take Adrian to the Sandcastle for an early happy hour to give Alfie, Paul, Glen and Etienne a chance to put up the decorations. Serena would set up the bar and appetizers and complete the dinner preparations. Bernie was put in charge of nothing, but surprisingly, he volunteered to make sure that the alcove in the master bedroom was cleaned and had fresh linens for April since Amanda had returned to her room in the guest cottage. Kate said she would take care of that duty, but Bernie insisted that he could make up a bed as well as any woman and would attend to any other details as well. I could tell Kate was upset at the idea of having Bernie enter the living space she and April would share, but there was no real reason to object without making an issue so she backed down. Serena showed Bernie to the linen closet and he eagerly set about his task. I gave Kate a sympathetic smile and she gave me a dirty look. Glen chuckled to himself, but Kate heard him and I caught her giving him the finger, which made him laugh out loud.

At three o'clock I left to meet the ferry, knowing that I would be early, but I wanted to stop off at my boat and change into my only suit. It is a charcoal grey that Amanda had picked out for me years before to wear to Alex and Tiffany's wedding. I would wear it with the burgundy tie and the pale gray dress shirt she had selected to go with it. This would only be the fourth time I had worn the suit and I hoped that I had not outgrown the waistline. Bernie complained that he had not brought anything dressy as he hadn't been informed that there would be formal events. I told him I would lend him a nice sweater and tie that he could wear with any pair of slacks and he would be just fine. I was surprised again as he seemed relieved. I guessed maybe he really was trying to be more civil and I vowed once again to give him the benefit of the doubt.

The suit fit fine except the waist on the trousers were a little more snug than I remembered, but I rationalized that that would just keep me from overeating. Looking at myself in the full length mirror on the back of my cabin door, I decided that I looked presentable if not handsome. I grabbed the sweater and tie for Bernie and arrived at the dock just as the ferry was landing.

Adrian had given me a brief description of April so I was looking for a woman in her late twenties, (which meant nothing to me since women between the ages of twenty one and forty one all look to be pretty much the same to me) with reddish brown curly hair and bright green eyes. I guessed this meant I would have to get close enough to each brown haired woman to see the color of her eyes, a situation that could cause me to be looked upon with suspicion. It was a Friday so there were many more passengers than other days and I saw three women that could fit the description. I ruled out the first woman because, although she sported a mass of reddish brown hair, she was accompanied by a dog, a black and white border collie that was straining at the leash, determined to befriend anyone that would establish eye contact. The next woman was kind enough to drop her umbrella giving me a chance to pick it up and return it to her as I cleverly searched her face for the appropriate eye color-they were brown. Having disqualified the first two candidates, I confidently approached the third reddish brown haired lady, not bothering to check eye color and proceeded to introduce myself to her as I tried to relieve her of her suitcase. I mistook her resistance for self-reliance and soon found myself the object of her scorn. It occurred to me belatedly to ask her if she was April. She gave a forceful negative response and eyed me suspiciously as I apologized. I heard laughter behind me and turned to look into the bright green eyes of the young woman with the border collie.

"You must be Sam" she offered. I was flustered and embarrassed but I managed to respond and then compounded my embarrassment by asking her if she was April. "Of course she's April, you idiot", I told myself. My next question was even more stupid. "Are you Adrian's granddaughter?" She responded with "Adrian who?" which really threw me for a loop. Still the wordsmith, I said "I didn't recognize you with your dog". More laughter from her as she handed me the leash and said "It's not my dog, it's my grandma's. This is her birthday present! Her name is Camille. Grandma has always loved border collies. They always had at least two of them on the ranch and I know she has missed not having a dog so I thought this would be the perfect gift for her."

I recalled that Adrian said she lives in a condo in downtown Portland so I had no clue as to how she would react to getting a dog of this size. Most condo dwellers, if they had pets at all, chose dogs that are slightly bigger than a rat with little personalities to match their size. This was a border collie, bred to herd cattle and sheep, requiring space to run and jump and demanding a great deal of attention from their masters. It took a minute or two to sink in that this was the gift April had selected to be our gift to Adrian for her birthday. Adrian or Amanda or both were going to kill me for sure. I started to confess my misgivings to April when she told me not to worry. She had another surprise for Adrian that would make me feel better and she asked for my patience until that time when all would be explained. I decided to relax, since there was nothing I could do about the situation anyway. Besides, I love dogs and they love me. Amanda has often said I am a dog whisperer and this animal was beautiful. I knelt down to pet her and she stuck her tongue in my ear so far I thought it was going to come out the other side. I fell in love on the spot and decided that if the gift ended in disaster for Adrian, I would be only too happy to take the dog off her hands. In all the years I lived in Texas, we always had at least two dogs on the farm and Australian shepherds and border collies were our favorites.

I took the leash and we walked up the dock, dog and dog's best friend, with April following behind struggling with her large suitcase. When we arrived at the Escalade I realized my oversight and began to fumble again with my apologies as I finally grabbed her bag. April laughed again and I wondered if it was my fate to be a constant source of amusement to her.

I decided to forego the latte and head directly home as I didn't know if this dog was well trained enough to take to a public place. I loaded April's suitcase in the back and opened the passenger door for April at which time Camille made a mad dash for the front passenger seat and would not be coaxed or coerced to get in the back seat. She sat on her hind end and stared straight through the windshield ignoring all our distractions as if she were the copilot on a 747. April finally gave up and climbed into the back seat and we drove to the house.

On the way April gave me the history of Camille. She is two years old and belonged to a friend of hers who worked for a software firm and was transferred to India. Camille had been her friend's cherished pet since she was eight weeks old, but the transfer offer came with a huge promotion and a salary too good to refuse. April assured me Camille was a perfect lady, well trained, well cared for and would bring no harm nor foul to my home. She did require regular exercise but April vowed that between her and Adrian, Camille's needs would be met. Actually, I was already visualizing Camille and myself romping on the beach or running through the fields by Patrick's home. I didn't know for sure how Patrick would feel about having a dog as a tenant, the subject had never come up, but if Camille was as well trained as April claimed, I couldn't see a problem.

I wondered if Amanda would see it my way. She was a bit overwhelmed at the time with the responsibilities she had assumed with the group. Would Camille put her over the edge? Amanda liked animals, especially dogs, but had never wanted to be tied down as so many dog owners are. She grew up primarily on farms and pets were pets, not family members. They were cared for, fed, played with and loved, but they did not go on airplanes for family vacations and they did not sleep in the same beds as their owners. Amanda would often point out that, left to their own devices, dogs sniffed at and rolled in things that were dead or had been previously consumed. Knowing this, why would anyone want to sleep with them? She also enjoys her freedom too much to have to run home every five or six hours to let a dog out to pee or poop. She has often pointed out that so many people claim to love their dogs so much, but ignore the fact that the animals are left alone for eight to ten hours a day and often don't get enough fresh air and exercise and she thinks that is cruel and selfish. I have to agree with her. I guessed that there wouldn't be a problem with Camille where Amanda was concerned as long as she was not put in the position of being her caretaker. Besides, it wouldn't be a permanent arrangement and it's not like we were all going places all the time. There were plenty of people around to give Camille the attention she needed. I further reasoned that it was really my decision, not Amanda's and I would just be firm. OH YEAH!

When we arrived at the house, the women had already left for their happy hour and the men were busy putting up decorations. Alfie and Serena had decided on a New Orleans theme; with feather masks, jazzy music and lights, lights and more lights. Alfie and Jenny had made some fake street lamps to be placed throughout the main rooms and on the deck. To these were hooked clusters of clear round light bulbs that were draped with some sort of fabric to give a soft glowing effect. There were brightly colored paper flower arrangements, feathers, iridescent beads and streamers hung everywhere. Serena had rented white pillars to create a restaurant effect sort of like the Commander's Palace in New Orleans (although I have been to the Commander's Palace and believe me, our rendition looked a lot fresher and cleaner than the real place). The dining table was converted into a huge buffet and the living room furniture had been moved to accommodate several smaller tables seating either two or four with white linens and candles to complete the fine dining motif. Glen was in charge of the music and we were treated to the best jazz that could be found in the island music shop. He had a much better knowledge of Patrick's surround sound than I, and it sounded like we had a real live jazz band.

Paul was there, helping Alfie with the finishing touches and both were splendid looking in their tuxedos. (I couldn't believe I knew two people who owned a tuxedo, let alone would bring one to the casual capital of the world.) Bernie accepted my sweater and tie, but emerged a few minutes later in a bright red dress shirt with a dazzling black velvet sport coat on loan from Alfie. We made quite a fuss over him and he glowed in the spotlight. I was sure our problems with him were behind us. Etienne returned from the guest house wearing a black sport coat with a black shirt and a shimmering silver tie of a fabric that I didn't know existed. He looked suave and elegant even in his wheelchair and I could tell that Alfie was wondering what he would have to offer Etienne to get him to sell that tie. Glen wore a navy blue blazer, white shirt and black slacks, but no tie. It didn't matter because Glen is pure class and anything he puts on looks like a million. How does a guy with fake legs carry that off? I'll tell you. He's just the real thing to start with.

Serena wore a simple full length black dress with a slit up the side, her version of the not-so-little black dress, but she looked great. The cut was perfect for her as it accentuated the right parts and camouflaged the rest. Her hair was fixed in that up style that was so flattering. She wore some big drop earrings with yellow stones and black suede shoes with ankle straps. (All men love ankle straps-don't know why-it's just a fact.) Most importantly, she wore a stunning smile and it was clear she was having a great time.

I directed April to her room in the master suite praying that Bernie had done as he promised. It was perfect! Better than perfect, he had even placed a fresh flower arrangement on her bed table and there was a little tray with a tiny glass and that small bottle of B&B that I had previously placed in Amanda's room beside the flowers which I recognized as those purchased for Amanda. Nice touch Bernie! April was delighted with the accommodations and I left her to freshen up and change into her evening clothes-or glad rags, as Serena would say.

By six o'clock everything was ready and we were just waiting for the girls to return. Bernie suggested that we go ahead and open the bar and that seemed like a good idea in spite of its source. Camille was resting comfortably by the fire in the guest house until her unveiling later that evening.

She is very obedient as long as she is given her way. I had no qualms about leaving her there alone and Etienne promised to check on her from time to time. I decided that I would not tell Amanda about Camille until the unveiling.

By six thirty we were beginning to wonder if the girls would be returning soon or if their happy hour had become a little too happy. It was then that I remembered that I was supposed to pick them up at six. We had agreed that they shouldn't drink and drive and since no one of them had volunteered to be the designated driver, it was decided that Serena would drop them off and I would pick them up. Serena was busy in the kitchen and had lost track of time and I had just plain forgotten my promise. I forced Glen to go with me to act as a buffer in case they were mad at me for being late. He volunteered to say that we had deliberately delayed the pickup time in order to complete the preparations. My oversight covered, we made the short drive to the Sandcastle in record time only to find out that the ladies had just ordered another round of drinks and our departure would be delayed by a few more minutes. No problem. It was Adrian's day and she was having a ball. They had all dressed for the evening before leaving the house and I can assure you, the Sandcastle hadn't seen a group like this in a long time, if ever.

Kate was amazing looking in this sort of Native American formal dress which I can't begin to describe. Her hair was parted in the middle and drawn back into kind of a fancy bun with feathers around it. She looked like someone out of an international fashion magazine. Jenny was wearing a very short lacy off white dress with (I assumed) a brown lining that matched the color of her skin, bare legs that gleamed, and stiletto heels. Adrian wore a dress that was the brightest red I have ever seen and it looked perfect for her. Eighty years old and she was still the lady in red--accent on" lady". She wore silver sandals and her feet looked like those of a young girl. Her toenails were polished to match her dress and she was wearing some very expensive silver jewelry-lots of it. Still, I couldn't take my eyes off her feet! They were so perfect and delicate. I knew that Amanda must have been jealous as hell about that because she had always complained about her ugly feet and she was right to do so. Amanda's feet were not large at all, but she had little short toes that did not look good in sandals or flip flops. She has always been very self-conscious about her feet and does not like being seen barefoot. That is the one thing I could never tease her about.

So, where was Amanda? She was nowhere in sight so I assumed she must be in the ladies room but when she didn't return within five minutes I became concerned so I picked up her drink and finished it off. Jenny said she had seen her head toward the head, but that was some time ago so I asked her to go check on her for me. As she rose to her full glorious height, I realized that she was more than a little tipsy. It might not have been so obvious on a shorter woman, but Jenny resembled a skyscraper during an earthquake. Upon closer inspection I realized that Adrian wasn't in much better shape. Turning to Kate I saw a happy, but sober woman. I asked her if she would mind checking on Amanda and Jenny as she seemed to be the only one that wasn't three sheets to the wind. She laughed and crossed her arms in front of her Indian style and said in a low voice "Indian woman can't take much fire water". Glen had not said a word since we arrived. He was just staring at Kate the whole time looking like a lovelorn sixteen year old. Kate grabbed his face between her hands, planted a big kiss on his lips and headed for the ladies room. She emerged one minute later and went straight to the bar, returning to the ladies room with two cups of coffee. I ordered a third for Adrian and we settled into our chairs for what turned out to be a half hour wait.

When they finally emerged they looked like three respectable ladies, but Amanda's hair, which she wore in a loose up-style was looser than usual and tilted to the left. Jenny was perfect as always and a lot more stable. Adrian finally remembered to ask if April had arrived and was suddenly in a great hurry to get home. I checked with the bartender to see if we owed any money and he presented me with a bill that resembled the annual budget of all of Island County. Drink prices at the Sandcastle are not that high so I knew I was being hustled, but I paid the bill as presented (no breakdown of charges was provided), and left a very small tip. I am not cheap, but I hate being ripped off.

It was after seven o'clock when we arrived back at the house. I apologized to Serena for all the extra effort it took to keep the food fresh, but she brushed it off as no problem stating that it was Adrian's party, not hers. Paul, Alfie and Etienne had been playing poker and Bernie was content to stay near the bar. April and Serena had spent the time getting to know one another and all was well as the birthday celebration got underway.

The decorations were a huge hit and Amanda was enchanted with the whole arrangement. She was still a little drunk and seemed to have forgotten that we were no longer married as she commandeered one of the intimate tables for two for us. I graciously complied with her wishes while trying to remember if I had left my room on the boat in a condition that would be appealing to an overnight guest. More drinks were served and Serena put out a fabulous buffet that included turtle soup, jambalaya, catfish, and a host of other New Orleans favorites. Everything was perfect. April stood and toasted her grandmother and shared a few memories of "grammy" from her childhood. Anyone could see that the two of them had a great relationship.

It was time to give Adrian our gift. April said that first she had an announcement to make that would shed some light on the reasoning behind the choice of gift. It seems that she had not devoted her efforts only to short stories. In fact she had been working for three years on a novel which she finished a few months prior. One of the major publishing houses had agreed to pick up her novel and had given her a large advance as part of the contract. Everyone applauded and Adrian had tears in her eyes, so proud she was of her granddaughter. April said that she had always had a secret dream to live in the country on her own small farm. She announced that she had used the advance money to purchase such a farm just a few miles outside of Portland and that she was hoping her grandmother would move there with her and enjoy the country life once again. April went on to say that she wanted some chickens, a couple of horses, perhaps a cow or two, a garden and lots of flowers. She asked Adrian if that would appeal to her.

Adrian jumped up and hugged April stating that if she lived in such a place she would make sure that she lived to be at least one hundred. When things settled down April explained that with that lifestyle in mind, she had chosen Adrian's birthday gift. At that point I left and returned with Camille on the leash. Adrian ran to her and, throwing modesty by the wayside, sat on the floor in a most unladylike fashion to hug her new pet. Camille was all over her licking her face and trembling with doggie delight. Our gift could not have been a bigger hit.

As Adrian returned to her chair, I turned for a sideways glance at Amanda in time to see her picking up a chocolate truffle and admiring it before biting it in half. Camille must have seen the other half because she leaped across the room in one flowing movement only to land at Amanda's feet sniffing the remaining tidbit. Everyone knows that dogs can't have chocolate and Amanda was laughingly explaining this to Camille, but Camille was having none of that. She had been trained not to jump on people, but it was obvious that she had to control every muscle in her body to restrain herself. Her legs were moving a mile a minute in very short gestures and she was trembling all over. She finally became so excited that she lost control and peed all over Amanda's shoes. This was not good!

Amanda jumped up and looked so shocked and helpless that no one dared laugh, although everyone wanted to. In the excitement, she dropped the truffle and this long tongue came out of nowhere and scooped it up and swallowed it in one gulp. Then Camille lay down in a submissive position to demonstrate her shame. Amanda stared at her for a moment or two and then burst out laughing, which gave the rest of us permission to do the same. I was so proud of Amanda because I know what a weak stomach she has. She left the room and I followed to see if I could be of any help. She entered one of the bathrooms, turned on the shower and stuck her feet-shoes and all- under the spray. She drizzled her feet and shoes with shampoo and let the shower do the work. Then she removed her shoes, dried her feet and returned to the room barefoot, as if nothing had happened. I couldn't believe she was actually exposing her feet in public! I guessed it must have been the booze and I wondered if she would lose any other inhibitions that night. While we were gone, Glen cleaned up any pee that had escaped her shoes. When Amanda sat down, Camille ran to her and placed her head in her lap, looking up at her with one of those pitiful expressions that smart dogs are so good at. It was clear that Amanda was smitten and Camille would be part of the group. Everyone took turns getting acquainted with April and playing with Camille, who seemed to have an inexhaustible supply of energy as well as a huge appetite for anything containing sugar. Adrian fell right into her role as mistress of the dog and finally forbade anyone to give Camille anything more to eat.

We partied until three AM and it would have lasted longer had I not pointed out that if we didn't call a halt to the festivities, there would be no one sober or awake enough to tend to our wounds and fix breakfast. The threat of missing a meal was enough to sober everyone up. Serena stretched out on the couched and announced that breakfast would be served no earlier than eleven AM –no exceptions.

I decided to spend the night on the couch in the den even though I had discarded the sofa pillow and afghan after Bernie's naked night. Everyone else dispersed and the quiet was deafening. It must have been about five in the morning when I awoke to find Amanda sprawled on top of me, fast asleep. I don't know how long she had been there but she was out like a light so I just went back to sleep. When I awoke at nine, she was gone and I wasn't sure if it had really happened, but I was certain that if I had dreamed it there would have been a lot more action. My dreams have always been more exciting than my reality.

Chapter Thirty-Nine

ALL ABOUT APRIL

SAM

The next day was spent cleaning up the mess from the night before--the house and its occupants. Breakfast was served at eleven, but before Serena could cook, she had to deal with leftover food and dishes from the night before. April was the first one up and she had started the process, but with Serena asleep on the couch, she had to be as quiet as possible. I awoke around nine, but stayed in the den pretending to sleep and revisiting my "dream" of Amanda's visit. Finally I heard Adrian come over to help and Etienne brought Camille with him. He had her on a leash and she was pulling him along in his wheelchair. He thought that was pretty clever of her, but I suspected that Camille just wanted to be where the food and all the people were and she had to drag Etienne with her to get there.

The rest of the group drifted in and breakfast was a pretty quiet event by the usual standards. Serena was still dressed in her basic black evening dress, but the total effect was less effective than the night before. I was still in my rumpled shirt and suit pants and I felt and looked like a beat up door-to-door salesman. Amanda was nowhere to be seen and no one felt brave enough to wake her. I was surprised to see Paul emerge from the master suite where he had spent the night in Kate's bed, which apparently had been permanently abandoned. I felt bad for not making sure that he didn't drive home the night before and was relieved that April had the presence of mind to offer to share the master suite. I guess she felt pretty safe with him. After breakfast there was a feverish rush to take down decorations and put the house back in order. I think everyone wanted to get the work done so they could crash. I sent Serena home after breakfast and told her to take the rest of the day off, leaving us on our own to graze for dinner. I didn't think anyone would mind and I was right. About six o'clock Glen and Kate made a mercy run to the Sandcastle and returned with huge bags of hamburgers and french fries, providing the ever popular hangover grease. They even brought a burger for Camille since neither April nor I had thought to buy dog food. Camille didn't seem to mind. She had eaten a huge bowl of oatmeal with cream and sugar for breakfast and the hamburger disappeared, bun, pickles, lettuce and all into her smiling jaws, followed by a tour of the room begging for fries. I wondered if we would have a case of doggie diarrhea, but it didn't happen.

Amanda came down about two in the afternoon, but was back in her room by five. I ate her hamburger for her thinking that was the least I could do. I wanted to ask her if she had made that visit to the den that morning, but thought better of it. Bernie was no different than usual. He was used to being hung-over. Everyone was in bed by eight except Etienne who was occupied with his computer, probably e-mailing Samantha. I returned to my boat, showered and shaved and went to bed with no pretense of spending any time recalling the events of the past two days or even trying to read my Grisham novel. I did take a minute to worry over April. No one in the group had been themselves that day and I wondered if she was disappointed with our lack of energy, or maybe she thought we were just a bunch of drunks. To be honest, I didn't remember if she had spent any real time with anyone that day except Adrian, and even she was not quite herself. Oh well, as Miss Scarlett would say, "Tomorrow is another day". In case you are wondering, I have seen GONE WITH THE WIND two or three times with Amanda and Samantha and those two are always quoting Scarlett O'Hara. So, as I drifted off to sleep I vowed that I would "think about that tomorrow".

That Sunday was the third day in a row that the weather had been rainy and blustery. This was also our third Sunday on the island and none of us had mentioned or expressed any desire to attend a church service. I had often attended services at the little non-denominational church in the village and I planned to go that day and invite anyone else who wanted to attend. There is a Catholic Church on the island but it is over by the hospital which was a twenty minute drive. I decided I should ask Etienne if he wanted me to take him there, but I hoped he would opt for the village church. Amanda was raised Catholic although she seemed quite at home in any church. Still, I thought she might volunteer to make the drive if Etienne wanted to go.

I arrived at the house early, but everyone was already up and about and Serena was scurrying around the kitchen trying to get breakfast on the table. As quiet as everyone was the day before, they were making up for it that morning. They were in high spirits and talking about the birthday party as if it had happened the night before. Apparently, Saturday was just a lost day, kind of like in that movie, "Lost Weekend" starring Ray Milland. Amanda had fully recovered and she and April were engaged in a battle over who the dog loved the most. Amanda was claiming that in view of the fact that Camille had chosen her to pee on, that marked her as the favorite. April countered that it wasn't Amanda that Camille was excited about, it was the truffle. They were on opposite sides of the dining room and both were calling Camille to see which one she would come to. Amanda won, but April caught her in the act of giving Camille the piece of bacon she had hidden behind her back and she called foul on the contest. Adrian intervened stating that Camille was her dog and she would forever be the favorite. Camille seconded that notion by jumping on her lap and licking her eyelids.

I brought up the subject of church and, to my surprise everyone except Bernie opted to attend. Etienne said the village church would do just fine so we all prepared to attend the eleven o'clock service. I figured our presence would just about double the size of the congregation and that the pastor and members of the church would be anxious to get a look at our strange little group.

The church looks like the one in LITTLE HOUSE ON THE PRAIRIE and Pastor Kurt is a very real person with a huge heart. There were the usual scripture readings and the sermon was about the call to thank God by serving others. The best part was the singing. Everyone had a hymnal and a man named Earl served as sort of a music director. He would announce the hymns, give the page numbers and which verses would be performed and then lead the group in song, accompanied by his wife on the oldest functioning organ I have ever seen. I pictured in my mind what it must sound like to someone on the outside walking by, and again, visions of LITTLE HOUSE ON THE PRAIRIE. Looking around, I could see that our group knew their way around a bible and hymnal and it struck me that, with the exception of old

Bernie, every one of them was deeply spiritual. Amanda had backed away from Catholicism due to their stand on women as church leaders and the focus on church dogma rather than emphasizing the bible, but she insisted that had nothing to do with her faith in God or Jesus Christ. She often maintained that if Christ came back on earth today, he would not favor any of the organized religions. He would just teach as he had before and each person would be judged by how they carried out their lives according to his teachings, not by what church they belonged to. I tend to agree with her. Born a southerner, I was introduced to the bible at a very early age and my faith was fed as I grew up by the goodness and love of my neighbors and family. Over the past few years I have become acutely aware that my life in the secular world has overshadowed my spiritual training and I have been trying to work my way back to my roots. Not an easy task.

We didn't linger after church in order to avoid the many questions the locals were undoubtedly dying to ask us. Ours is a private endeavor and not one easily explained even if we wanted to do so. We returned to the house and the next couple of hours were spent visiting with one another and getting to know April. She had brought each of us a copy of a collection of her short stories; stories that Adrian had always believed were actually memories of her past lives. April explained that some of the stories were, in fact, her memories. Others were an expanded version of small glimpses of past lives, ones where she did not get to see the whole life, rather just a moment in time. She said she enjoyed taking those tiny glimpses and building a scenario around them. She joked that she didn't like to waste a memory, no matter how small. She confessed that she felt like she was cheating as a writer by simply recording her larger memories and that by creating a story from a mere glimpse of a character, she was redeeming herself. She went on to say that her novel would be published in the early spring of next year and that it was totally her own creation, not based on a memory.

I asked her if she would like to share a memory at that time and she said she would rather wait a day or two until she got to know everyone better. That was fine with me as Amanda had hinted earlier that she had another life she wanted to tell us about. She had looked pretty excited about this one so I thought it must be a doozy. I will never again pass up an opportunity to learn about her through her memories now that I better understand the impact they have on this life.

While the others were visiting with April, I took a few minutes to thumb through one of her short stories. I was amazed, confused, agitated, and aroused by what I was reading. It was loaded with torrid sex scenes. As I read on, the prevailing theme was carnal desire, sex, passion and that mixture of love and lust that Amanda refers to as lovst. The writing was excellent if measured by my anatomical response. This girl had really lived! Realizing that this was likely one of April's past lives, I became more uncomfortable with each passage and even more so when I looked up and saw Adrian watching me with an amused expression. I tried to cover my embarrassment by waving the book in the air and giving it the thumbs up, but I was sure that she could tell which story I was reading and that I was having a hard time reconciling the words in those pages with my vision of what Adrian's granddaughter should be.

I decided I would have to confiscate Etienne's copy immediately. It was sitting innocently on his lap as he listened to April talk about her farm and the bull she was purchasing for breeding purposes. Adrian followed my glance and took the hint. She reached over and removed the book as if she was going to put it somewhere for safe keeping. Etienne barely noticed the gesture, but April noticed and gave her grandmother a nod of approval.

Lunch consisted of Serena's famous clam chowder (September is one of the months ending in "R" so the clams are fresh and safe to each as long as there is no red tide warning.) Her chowder is the best in the world and she guards her two secret ingredients with her life. I happen to know what they are and I will share that information with you: a bit of horseradish and a dollop of cream cheese. Don't tell anyone. Amanda topped off the chowder by making a huge pile of her homemade white cheddar crackers. Fresh fruit for dessert and we were set for the afternoon session led by Amanda.

Everyone found a comfortable chair except April who sat on the floor by the coffee table. She had the rest of Amanda's crackers on a plate in front of her alongside a large glass of sauvignon blanc. She beamed at the group stating that life doesn't get any better than this. Jenny tried to steal a cracker and April slapped her hand. This began a wrestling match between the two of them ending in the spilling of April's wine. They were apologetic, but laughing so hard that I doubted their sincerity. Serena was enjoying the spectacle and added to the fun by grabbing April's jacket from the back of a chair and using it to wipe up the wine. April gave false protest but it was clear that she could take as good as she gave. I was glad to see Jenny and April enjoying each other's company and the change in Serena continued to amaze me. Amanda was laughing as she rose to get April another glass of wine and as she set it down she grabbed April by the ear and told her to behave herself. Once again, I felt envious of how women relate to each other and how they can make fun of each other without presenting challenges. If I ever had a past life, I hope I was a woman. I'll definitely keep that thought to myself.

Chapter Forty

LILY

AMANDA

"This is a happier story than Lorretta's, and I hope you enjoy hearing about Lily as much as I enjoyed being her. This is my all-time favorite memory because it contains a little bit of everything: love, luck, strife, victory, adventure and, unlike my dust bowl disaster, it ends well.

Lily grew up in a seaside town on the east coast. She was the daughter of Milo and Chloe Hanson. Milo owned three fishing boats and had made a good living for many years. He was handsome, strong and dedicated to Chloe and Lily. Their home was filled with fun and laughter.

Chloe was one of those women, a rarity in those days, who could take anything in stride and laugh at whatever joy or challenge life threw at her. She was educated, but not really intellectual, delicate and ladylike but not frail, and she loved Milo and everything about him. Milo would come home from a fishing trip and tell her all the bawdy stories and jokes he shared with the other fisherman and she would laugh until she cried. Every so often she couldn't resist the urge to share a particularly good story with her lady friends only to be reminded that not every lady was as open minded as she. Still everyone loved her and she had no shortage of friends.

Milo was the undisputed king of the village. He had a big heart, a ready laugh and the strength of a giant. Milo and Chloe were generous to others with their time and their money and Lily was raised to be kind and loving, but most of all to be her special self. She was delicate looking like her mother with the blond hair and pale blue eyes that reflected her Nordic ancestry. Chloe was every bit the Christian lady, but her spiritual side made room for some "other worldly" beliefs which she shared with Lily. Milo, on the other hand, believed that God put us on this earth to do the best we can and enjoy our lives. He didn't worry about heaven or hell, he just lived, loved and laughed and shared whatever good fortune he earned with others. In that respect, Sam often reminds me of Milo.

Jeremy came into her life when Lily was nineteen. Many of the villagers had wondered if she would ever fall in love, as most of her friends were married and had started a family by the time they were that age. Lily had never cared. There were many young men who had pursued her and she had turned them into friends, but never anything more. Chloe was partially responsible for this since she had always taught Lily that when the right man came along, there would be an unmistakable sign. Chloe believed firmly in signs and she passed the belief on to Lily that if she waited for a sign she would find her soul mate just as she had found in Milo. Chloe had told Lily many times about the day she met Milo and Lily was convinced that the same "magic" was waiting for her. The joy and love that Chloe and Milo shared served as proof of this belief.

The story went like this. Chloe was seventeen when she traveled to New York City with her father. He had agreed to take her along as she had never been outside of her village. One day she was sitting alone in the dining room of their hotel enjoying her breakfast when Milo walked into the room. She couldn't take her eyes off him, but of course, there was no way for her to meet him. Her father had left her there to finish her breakfast while he went down the street to the tobacco shop to buy his yearly supply of cigars. He was to return shortly and then they were going to take a walk after which her father had scheduled a business meeting.

Chloe continued to nibble away at her breakfast while stealing glances at the handsome stranger. Her heart was pounding and she was adjusting her chair so that she could get a better view of Milo without being obvious. A waiter carrying a tray loaded with food tripped over her chair leg and the tray he was carrying swayed ominously over Chloe. Apparently, Milo had his eye on Chloe as well because as the waiter tripped, Milo shot out of his chair, leaping toward them. He swept the tray out of the waiter's flailing arms and secured it with his own. Only one fried egg had been sent flying and that landed squarely on top of Chloe's bonnet. Milo deftly handed the tray off to the grateful waiter, picked the egg off her bonnet with his bare hand and placed it on top of a toast point on Chloe's plate with such grace that he appeared to be offering her a gift. Chloe laughed and clapped her hands causing others in the room to join the applause. Her father entered the room in time to view this spectacle and hurried over to express his gratitude to Milo. He invited Milo to join them for coffee and, by the time the three of them went their separate ways two hours later, Chloe and Milo were in love. By the time the dinner they all shared that evening was over, Chloe was trying to think of a way to explain to her mother that she was going to marry a man that was a perfect stranger to them.

Milo told them that he was in town to purchase a newer and larger fishing boat to replace the old and decrepit one he was using at the time. He let them know that he had a small but profitable fishing business and he had saved every penny toward the purchase of the new boat and that he planned to save enough to buy two or three more. He would eventually manage his own fleet and this would give him and his wife, should he marry, a very comfortable living. Chloe's father told her that he had no doubt that Milo would accomplish his goals, convincing Chloe's mother would be a challenge. For the remaining four days of their trip Chloe and Milo spent every waking moment together, often unchaperoned as Chloe's father went about his business. He obviously trusted Milo, and Chloe pointed out that they were anonymous in a large city so she could see no harm in relaxing some of the rules of propriety.

The day they left to return home there were no tearful goodbyes between Chloe and Milo. Milo would come the following week for a visit. As they waited on the station platform to board the train, Chloe spotted a bird's nest in the rafters and, just then, a small egg fell from the nest and landed on her bonnet. Milo rescued the little blue egg from her bonnet and returned it to its nest. If Milo's daring rescue of the serving tray had not been enough, this second egg on her bonnet served as a sign to Chloe that they were meant to be together. Six months later Chloe and Milo were married and Chloe moved with Milo to their village.

Chloe had told Lily this story many times and Lily fully accepted that the eggs on the bonnet were too much of a coincidence to be anything else but a sign. Lily's sign was a long time coming, but finally just a few weeks before her twentieth birthday, fate stepped in and brought Chloe the love of her life.

Jeremy had moved to their village looking for work. He intended to work very hard and save his money so that he could travel west and explore his dream of becoming a fur trader, a prospector, a rancher or whatever other possibility presented itself. He found work with Milo and quickly proved himself to be an able fisherman as well as a great foreman. Within a few months Milo placed him in charge of the fleet, which freed Milo to spend more of his time managing his assets and assuming the role of mayor of his town. Jeremy had a talent for getting the most out of their workers and he found many ways to cut costs and make the business more profitable. Milo admired him very much, but he said that he always knew Jeremy would follow his dream to go west and he would lose him.

Lily and Chloe never went down to the docks because Milo had always insisted that they would be a distraction. Besides, the docks were dirty and smelly and could be dangerous. Lily had often heard her father singing the praises of Jeremy, but she had never met him until the Christmas of the second year he had worked for her father. Chloe suggested that Milo invite Jeremy for Christmas dinner as a reward for his fine work and because he had no family. When Jeremy arrived, Lily answered the door to find a tall handsome stranger wearing a decent, but outdated suit and carrying beautifully wrapped gifts. She knew instantly that this was the Jeremy her father was so fond of and she regretted that she had not taken the time to meet him before.

The dinner went well and Jeremy seemed to be at ease and enjoying himself. After dinner they all retired to the parlor for hot cider and to exchange their gifts. Lily's father presented Jeremy with a beautiful wooden box containing a pistol which appeared to be very expensive. Jeremy was deeply touched as Milo explained he would need this when he went west. Jeremy gave Chloe a beautiful lace table cloth and Chloe told him how amazed she was that a man could exhibit such good taste. Milo pretended to be offended by her comment.

Lily had spent most of the day admiring Jeremy's bright blue eyes and fine physique as well as enjoying the sound of his voice. Finally, Jeremy presented her with a small black box trimmed with gold ribbon and decorated with a tiny bird's nest. When she opened the box she nearly fainted. Inside was a hollow egg that had been beautifully painted in bright colors. It was the most beautiful and delicate thing she had ever seen and.......it was an egg! She stared at it in awe and then looked over at Chloe who was dumbstruck. The irony was not lost on either of them, and yes this was a sign, her mother's eyes told Lily. Lily could not speak for several seconds and when she did, her voice was ragged. Jeremy told her that he had purchased the egg in Charleston, South Carolina from a Russian fisherman. He had bought it originally for his mother, but she had passed away before he could give it to her. He hoped she liked it. Lily jumped from her chair and ran to him and gave him a big hug which embarrassed him and amused Milo. Everyone in that room knew the significance of that egg except Jeremy.

They were married the following spring and lived with Milo and Chloe so that they could save money for their westward trip. Chloe's belief in "the sign" was so strong that she never questioned the fact that Lily would be leaving them to follow her husband as much as it hurt her to think about losing Lily. She often told Lily that, no matter what happened, a man must have a dream and Lily must have been fated to be a part of Jeremy's dream.

One year after their marriage, Jeremy and Lily set out for the great frontier with Milo and Chloe's blessing, Jeremy's savings, and enough money from Milo to buy the horses, wagon and provisions they would need to make the trip. Jeremy was embarrassed by Milo's generosity, but Milo argued that Jeremy would need to use his savings to get them established in whatever trade he decided to pursue.

Leaving her parents was agony for Lily, but she was strengthened by the knowledge of the love her parents shared so neither of them would be lonely. She was so much in love with Jeremy that she didn't worry about her own happiness or well-being. Fate had brought them together and she knew they would share their lives forever.

They took themselves and their belongings by train to Saint Louis where they purchased a wagon and horses and provisions for their trip. They joined a wagon train headed for California, but like many of their fellow travelers, they were uncertain as to their final destination. They might break off on their own and travel to Wyoming or Montana or wherever they were called.

There were forty wagons in the train and Lily and Jeremy soon made friends and formed a makeshift and temporary social circle. Lily thrived on the adventure of traveling across lands that few had seen, and she became known for her excellent outdoor cooking skills. Many evenings she would pool their provisions with their neighbors and Lily would create a splendid dinner for ten or twenty travelers. She was never happier than when she was cooking over an open fire and she invented some new techniques that allowed her to make dishes and breads that had never before been seen on the trail. One fellow traveler introduced her to the use of the Dutch oven and Lily took it from there. Jeremy made himself useful to the wagon master in many ways, including acting as a scout and hunting for fresh meat. Lily and Jeremy proved many times over that they were cut out for the life of pioneers.

From time to time along the trail, they would be joined for a few days by one or more of the mountain men who originally blazed the trail they were following. Jeremy made it his business to get to know these men and it took little convincing to get them to share their tales with Jeremy and Lily. The further west they traveled, the more adventurous these tales became until several weeks into their journey, Jeremy and Lily decided that California would not be their destination. There were too many opportunities in the less developed areas such as Wyoming and Montana. They wanted to be on the cutting edge of the frontier and California was quickly becoming too populated and civilized for their tastes. There were rumors of gold and silver deposits in Montana and the fur trades in the Montana and Wyoming territories were thriving and provided ample opportunities for someone who was young, strong and well provisioned. Land was there for the taking and the climate wasn't that different than it had been in New England so they weren't afraid of the winters.

This was their thinking when, in the early spring, they and five other wagon families split from the train and took a northerly route led by a mountain man named Isaac. Isaac had been born and raised in Philadelphia but left the city to answer the call of the frontier. He wasn't any older than thirty, but he looked forty. Unlike so many of his counterparts, he had retained some elements of refinery from his upbringing and he had a gift for storytelling. All mountain men embellished their stories, but Isaac was, by far, the most convincing. He assured Jeremy that they could travel to Wyoming, trap for furs through the summer months, sell the furs in the fall and proceed to Montana the following spring, laden with money to explore the possibilities in that territory. Gold or furs, it didn't matter, there was plenty of each in Montana. If nothing else worked out, they could always travel on to Oregon.

The plan had appealed to some of their fellow travelers as well, which meant that as they traveled and settled temporarily in Wyoming, Lily had the company of other women while Jeremy and their husbands went into the mountains to do their trapping. They were mostly looking for beaver pelts which were much in demand in Europe for the making of gentlemen's hats. The pelts would be sold to the American Fur Company at the "rendezvous" held at the mouth of the Green River in the fall. The young boys and older men would remain in camp through the summer with the wagons, children, and women and it would be their job to build a large camp house to be shared by everyone during the coming winter months. The women would spend the summer growing vegetables and foraging for food.

By the end of summer the camp house had been built and stocked with food. The men remaining in camp had hunted and found plenty of meat to get the group of seventeen people through the winter. One of the men was sent to Laramie to purchase more flour, sugar, coffee and a few other necessities. He returned with all of the supplies plus enough fabric to make a new dress for every woman and girl child in the group. Lily placed herself in charge of cooking all the dinners. Another woman was in charge of breakfast and still another handled lunch. Lily was also an excellent seamstress and she looked forward to spending the long evenings in the winter designing and stitching the new dresses.

Just before they moved into the camp house, Jeremy and the other trappers passed through on their way to the rendezvous where they would sell their pelts. Jeremy looked rugged and strong and more mature, making him even more attractive to Lily. They had been very successful with their trapping under the direction of Isaac and everyone was assured a full purse when they returned. It was agreed that each trapper would give Isaac one-fourth of his proceeds in return for his guidance.

Lily and Jeremy spent two blissful weeks after their long separation and spoke of the hours they would spend that winter planning their trip to Montana in the spring. They were like two children on Christmas Eve. The trip so far had been pleasurable and had cost them less than anticipated due to Lily's thrifty habits and the pooling of provisions with the other travelers. They were well bankrolled and the proceeds from the fur sales would bring even greater rewards. There was no reason to question whether they had made the right decision in moving west.

While the men were away selling their furs, those left in camp were to move into the camp house and provide as much shelter as possible for the animals and wagons. The men continued to hunt and dry meat and everyone worked feverishly to make sure all was prepared when the trappers returned. Lily had planned a homecoming celebration with music, dancing, sweets and even some whiskey for the men.

It was a three day ride to the rendezvous and the men planned to stay only five days, bringing them back in less than two weeks. The rendezvous was an annual event where all the trappers gathered to sell their pelts to the trading companies. It had developed into a huge encampment complete with tents that served as hotels, restaurants, saloons and brothels. It lasted much longer than five days, but Isaac warned them that the temptations of liquor, wild women and gambling had left many a trapper penniless as he departed, so it was better to get in, get business done, and get out. Besides, food and lodging was prohibitively expensive. Isaac had learned that, in many cases the only people who made money at these events were the provisioners, the professional gamblers, and the whores. He promised he would take care to see that the men in his charge were not taken advantage of and would return with all their money.

They did return, but only after eighteen days. Lily had begun to worry, but everyone assured her and themselves that it probably just took longer to sell the furs, or that the journey was longer than anticipated. It was late afternoon and Lily woke from a nap in the wagon where she had gone for some privacy and quiet. She had spent most of the night before nursing one of the women who was sick with a fever. She could hear shouts and wailing and cursing from her neighbors. She stumbled from the wagon and spotted a very solemn Isaac and some of the other men immediately, but no Jeremy and there were two other men missing. She didn't want to ask where Jeremy was. She just wanted to go back into the wagon, go to sleep and wake up with everything as it was before. One of the women was crying and screaming and Lily noticed that her husband was one of the three missing men. The husband of the sick woman was the other, and the third was Jeremy. Isaac approached Lily and she turned and ran to get away from him. She didn't want to hear what he had to say.

Isaac said the men had arrived at the encampment in record time, taking only two and a half days. They had set up camp on the perimeter to save money by sleeping in their own tents and cooking their own food. The next day Isaac went about the task of negotiating a good price for their pelts. It took all of that day and most of the next to sort the pelts and line up with the buyers. He wanted to hold back some of the pelts to see if he could get a better price on the third or fourth day, but that plan didn't work out. Jeremy and two other men had decided to take a hike to the river after dark and get a much needed bath. On the way back they were attacked by a pack of wolves. Two men were found the next morning. One was dead and the other was still alive, but he was too far gone to help. He died later that night. There was no sign of Jeremy. Isaac said he left immediately to search for Jeremy and the others stayed to bury their two companions before joining Isaac in the search. After a few days they returned to the encampment, completed their business and started the somber trip back to their families.

Listening to this story, Lily wept and was gripped by grief and fear. She was alone, far from her parents, and her soul-mate was gone from her. Suddenly, the tears stopped and the fear was gone. She refused to believe that Jeremy had not survived. Perhaps the wolves had injured him, but she had heard tales of Indians finding injured white men and nursing them back to health with their secret herbs and chants. Perhaps that is why they couldn't find him. He was being cared for in some secret cave. Or perhaps he just lost his way while running from the wolves and he would find his way home. Lily believed that if Jeremy was dead, she would have been sent a sign and she had received nothing. She and Jeremy were meant to live out their lives together just like Chloe and Milo, otherwise why would there have been signs to bring them together in the first place? Lily could not and would not accept Jeremy's death without a sign. She would remain where she was and await his return.

The winter passed with everyone staying in the camp house with the exception of one of the women whose husband died. She was taken to Laramie to catch a stage and begin the long journey home. The other woman, the one Lily was nursing, died of fever and grief leaving two children behind with no parents and no one to claim them. The girl, Abby, was six years old and her brother, Adam, was nine. Lily took charge of the children along with most of the cooking and sewing. She was busy from morning to night and, in her few free moments, she prayed for Jeremy and his safe return.

Isaac had stayed through the winter to help out since the group was short three of the most capable men and he had no particular place to go anyway. He had been successful in obtaining a good price for the pelts, especially after the disaster with the wolves. He said that even the most hardened trader could not help but be generous in his offer in view of the tragedy that had occurred and the families that were left behind. He distributed the money and many believed he took less than his share from the three widows.

When spring came, the group was ready to move on. Isaac had agreed to escort them as far as Bozeman, Montana and then he would return for another year of trapping. Lily refused to leave. She believed Jeremy would return and he would find her waiting. The two children, Abby and Adam, were to remain with her as no one else volunteered to take on the responsibility. That was fine with Lily. She had grown to love them and Isaac felt it would be good for her and the children if they stayed together. He promised to return early in the summer and check on her. He didn't like leaving her there all alone, but she wouldn't budge so he had no choice. Before he left he helped her plough the garden plot and he made the thirty mile trip to LaGrange for seeds and other provisions. He also brought back some chickens and a mangy dog he had found along the way. At least Lily had plenty of supplies to sustain her and the children. One of the travelers left behind a cow so they had fresh milk and Lily had learned how to make cheese and butter. She was confident that Jeremy would be returning any day.

When Isaac returned in mid–June, he found her and the children in excellent health and spirits and the garden was beginning to flourish. Lily had also staked out what she claimed as her property in case Jeremy wanted to stay put when he returned. Isaac was surprised to see that there were two other families that had settled nearby. They had built small cabins and were already planting gardens. Lily now had neighbors and that made Isaac feel much better. He told her that she was positioned in one of the best spots in the state as far as he could see. She had a river that ran through her claim, plenty of trees and the soil appeared to be responding well. He guessed a person could make a life for themselves there if they wanted to work hard enough.

Lily and the children did quite well on their own that summer. Their nearest neighbor was less than a mile away and Lily had made friends with the woman who volunteered her husband to build a pen and a coop for the chickens, a swing for the children and they traded meat for some of Lily's eggs and milk. The garden provided everything else they needed. Lily worked on the camp house to make it more comfortable and snug and she spent a couple of hours each day schooling Abby and Adam.

Slowly over those summer months Lily had begun to accept the thought that Jeremy might not be returning. She stayed so busy that she didn't have time to mourn and she had the children to love and care for. She looked forward to Isaac's return in the fall. She sensed that Isaac was in love with her and little by little she began to think about him in different terms. She knew she would never love another man as she loved Jeremy, but Isaac was good and kind and he had often remarked that it was time for him to settle down. He had hinted many times that he had saved up a healthy sum of money to start a farm.

Lily never considered returning to her home in New England. She had written her parents a few times, but had not told them that Jeremy was missing. She knew they would insist that she come home but, as much as she loved and missed them, she knew that there was no life for her there. Besides, she had the children now and they were happy and didn't need to be uprooted and taken to a strange place. In addition, she held on to that small hope that Jeremy would return.

These were the thoughts in Lily's head the day that Jeremy returned. She was working in her garden when she looked up to see two riders approaching on horseback. She recognized Isaac immediately but the other man was a stranger. As they drew nearer, Lily began to feel agitated and a little frightened. When they came within a few yards of her, Lily recognized the other rider and fainted. She awoke seconds later and looked into the eyes of the man she loved so dearly. Actually she looked into only one of his eyes, the other was covered with a patch. He was also missing an ear and had deep scars over half of his face. His left hand was gone and Isaac had to help him get up from the ground as he didn't have the full use of one leg.

Jeremy stood leaning on a cane as Isaac helped Lily to her feet. Lily threw herself at Jeremy, nearly knocking him over and wrapped her arms around his thin body. Jeremy was weeping and couldn't speak. Isaac helped him into the house while Lily just stood outside for a few moments, not knowing what to do. It had never occurred to her that Jeremy would return in such a state. She felt sick about what he must have gone through and that she hadn't been there to help him. Finally she went inside and sat at the table with Isaac to listen to Jeremy's story.

The wolves had come out of nowhere and all three men were attacked at the same time. Jeremy had managed to get his knife out and was fighting two of the wolves off at once. He could hear the screams of the other men. The wolves were in such a frenzy, they didn't seem to notice the wounds he was inflicting on them. After just a couple of minutes, which seemed like hours, two mountain men came upon the scene and began shooting. They killed three of the wolves and the rest ran off leaving one man dead and the other two barely alive.

News of the attack reached Isaac in the encampment and he went out alone to do what he could. He found Jeremy in a horrible state but he believed that with care, Jeremy would live, although he would lose his hand and probably his leg. The one eye was destroyed and there was damage to the other eye so it was possible that he might be blind as well. The doctor in the encampment did what he could for Jeremy, but told Isaac he would have to get him to his home which was twenty miles away in order to give him the care that would save his life. Jeremy was fully conscious and begged Isaac not to let the others know that he was alive. He did not want to return to Lily as a blind man missing an arm and leg, let alone the disfigurement of losing an ear and an eye along with the deep scars to his face. Isaac begged him to let him tell Lily, but Jeremy was adamant and Isaac understood his fear of being a repulsive burden to the woman he loved. Isaac took Jeremy to the doctor's house and explained his own absence to the others by saying that he had been out searching for Jeremy. He went along with the charade of searching for Jeremy because he didn't believe he could trust the others to keep Jeremy's secret.

Isaac lived out that winter watching Lily bravely waiting for Jeremy's return. He led the other settlers into Montana and then returned to the doctor's house to see about Jeremy before returning to Lily. He was happy to see that Jeremy had not lost his leg, although he would never have the full use of it, and that the one eye was healing so it appeared he would not be totally blind. The scars were every bit as bad as he had imagined, but that didn't seem to bother Jeremy. Isaac and Jeremy talked long into the night and it was decided that if Jeremy still had his eyesight in the fall when Isaac returned, he would go back to Lily. Jeremy refused to consider returning as a blind man.

Not surprisingly, Lily's relief and joy at Jeremy's return soon turned to confusion and then to anger which was directed mostly toward Isaac. He had witnessed her misery and said nothing. He had no right to make that agreement with Jeremy, who could be forgiven because of what he was going through.

The reunion of Lily and Jeremy was not what she had dreamed. Jeremy held back his true feelings because he didn't want to put an unfair burden on Lily. She reassured him time and time again that everything would be as it was before, but he could not get over his fear that she would stay with him out of pity. Lily was young and beautiful and full of life and he was a scarred, half man who would not be able to do all the work that needed to be done. There would be no adventure in their lives. They would stay where they were not by choice but because he wasn't fit for anything else.

Lily worried that he would not want to keep the children with them. She worried that he would become bitter and brittle and they would not share the laughter that had been such a big part of their life together. All of these concerns caused them to be uneasy around each other and they both felt like they were pretending to be married. Isaac stayed on for a couple of weeks to help with preparations for winter and over that time Lily's anger with him subsided, partly because she realized that Isaac had paid the doctor out of his own money. Jeremy thought the payment had come from his share of the fur sales, but Lily knew that Isaac had paid that money to her. She didn't tell Jeremy and Isaac refused her offer to return the money stating that he was quite well off and the doctor had enjoyed Jeremy's company and this had been reflected in his bill. Lily was deeply touched and felt ashamed that she had been so hard on him.

Adam and Abby had been very fond of Jeremy before and that attachment grew over those first couple of weeks, especially for Adam. He questioned Jeremy about the wolf attack and Abby wanted to know if their father had suffered. Jeremy told him that their father had fought bravely and that he had not uttered a sound as he passed away. He told them that their father was buried in a beautiful spot on a mountain top and that someday he would take them to see his grave. This seemed to help them get over their grief and Adam bound himself to Jeremy in a way that was touching to watch. He never left his side.

One day Jeremy was outside trying to repair the fence around the chicken coop. He was having a difficult time keeping his balance and working with one hand. Adam stepped in and gave him exactly the help he needed without making Jeremy feel useless. They worked perfectly as a team. Lily was sitting on the porch watching them when she started laughing. Jeremy looked at her and she yelled out "It looks like you found yourself an arm and a leg." Jeremy looked at Adam, who was so proud and happy to be able to help and smiled for the first time since his return. From that moment on everything began to fall into place. Jeremy became Jeremy and Lily was herself again and their love for each other was stronger than ever. The four of them became a family and over the years they were blessed with three boys of their own. Jeremy had always been a good business man and together with Isaac, built a mercantile to provide the basic necessities and a few niceties to the new settlers and the mountain men that came through in the spring and fall. Lily made jams and jellies to sell and she perfected and sold blends of spices and herbs that could turn a drab stew into a masterpiece. The story of Jeremy's wolf attack spread and many stopped and shopped to get a look at the "wolf man". Jeremy often joked that he was making a good living by just being ugly.

Isaac built a cabin on the outskirts of their property and eventually took a wife who made his life a living hell. He spent most of his time in the mercantile or helping Lily with her gardening. After five miserable years of marriage, his wife ran off with another mountain man and Isaac returned to a life of unwedded bliss. He was still alive when Lily died.

Milo and Chloe paid a visit a few years after Jeremy's return and, though initially shocked at the extent of Jeremy's wounds, they left knowing that their daughter was happy and well cared for.

Abby went to live with Milo and Chloe when she was twelve years old and eventually married a young doctor, but only after there were sufficient signs to prove he was the one for her.

Jeremy died at the age of forty six and Lily lived on for another twenty years with her sons and Isaac living nearby. She had fourteen grandchildren and each of them was taught to wait for the sign before marrying. She was loved and cherished to the end.

This was a happy life, full of joy and love. The memory of this life started when I was four years old and came to me in bits and pieces over the years. My last memory of Lily happened about ten years ago. She was ill and lying in bed. Isaac was at her side holding her hand and she was looking past him at Jeremy standing as he had been on that first day. He was young and strong and he was holding something out in his hand and offering it to her. It was a beautiful egg, glowing from the inside with light in many colors. Chloe and Milo were on each side of him. Lily's heart soared before it stopped."

GLEN

I could tell Amanda really enjoyed Lily. Lily reminded me of Peggy, my wife, in many ways. There was no end to her devotion to me and her children. At first I thought she was just grateful to be in a decent relationship after the hard times she had with her first husband. She once told me that for a long time after he left she would wake each day expecting him to walk in the door and she felt horrible because she didn't want him to return. She said she even fantasized at times that she would get word that he had died. Then she would feel so guilty that she would talk herself into wishing he would come back. Years after we got married she still carried a sense of dread that he would show up and demand to see his children. We never did find out what happened to him.

Peggy gave her all to those she loved and I could easily picture her holding on as Lily did. Peggy never seemed to notice that I was handicapped in any way. When I took my legs off at night it was no different to her than when I removed my shirt. If I woke up in the middle of the night and had to go to the bathroom I would scoot along on my hands rather than going through the trouble to assemble my legs and it was as if it was the most natural thing in the world to her. She did everything she could to make life easier for me, but never made it obvious. There was not an ounce of pity, only love and support. Some women just have the ability to absorb that which would be abhorrent to others and, by doing so, they soak up any bitterness, self-pity and anger into their "love sponge", and squeeze them out, leaving only the good stuff. I was so fortunate to find her and now, with Kate, I think I have hit the jackpot again, if she will have me.

I know what I want to do now. It's something I have thought about since the cruise. My career as a corporate executive is over and I am getting tired of all the travel to speaking engagements. Air travel has become a nightmare, even though I have enough frequent flyer miles to be upgraded to first class on most flights. That helps, but there is still the struggle of getting to, from and through airports, airport security, delayed flights, missed connections, bad or no food service, and fellow passengers, some of whom do not seem to have a clue about personal hygiene. I love garlic as much as the next guy, but it is the height of rudeness to consume a whole loaf of garlic bread and then expect the person next to you on that four hour flight to want to engage in a conversation. Even in first class, you can't put enough distance between your nose and that infested mouth. Then there are the nut cases that talk incessantly whether you are listening or not, and mothers who let their toddlers hang over the back of their seat drooling onto your lap table or your laptop.

When I was younger I used to find it interesting to talk to the person next to me. I found that people will often open up to a stranger more than their own friends or family and I enjoyed listening to their dreams and problems. I guess the world hasn't changed that much, but I have. I am sorry to report that I now find that only about one in three conversations is interesting and enjoyable. This makes me sad.

At times I worry that my advancing age has brought with it an indifference to the persistent angst infecting the public at large. So many people seem to be desperately searching for a lot more than they have materially and emotionally. It's like they believe they have been cheated out of a life they were promised. I find few people that are content with the life they have chosen. They want a better job, a better home, more money, a perfect spouse, and children that are a reflection of themselves as they wish they were. I have been a motivational speaker for many years and have always tried to make clear the difference between contentment and complacency. Contentment does not mean that we no longer have goals. Quite the opposite, it means that we have positioned ourselves to enjoy our lives while we achieve our goals. This makes it easier to be better people, better parents, better employees or employers, better neighbors and better citizens without the constant strife I see written on the faces of so many.

I am also a magnet for every zealot that books a flight on any airline. I don't want to hear their views on global warming, paper versus plastic, the tyranny of having to look at a Christmas tree in an airport, evil corporations, political scandals, proper pet care, the glass ceiling for women, any subject dealing with low self-esteem or depression, gay rights (no matter which side is being taken), ADD, ADHD or any human condition that has existed since the beginning of time that is now considered a "disease" curable by all the experimental drugs that are being developed and sold at astronomical prices. I especially do not want to hear about one more child being put on Ritalin because he or she has trouble sitting still in a classroom.

It isn't the subject matter that bothers me so much, it is the total lack of perspective in many people that I find terrifying. One can't simply have an opinion, or God forbid, a sense of humor about an issue. We have to "subscribe" to a belief and accept the conclusions of the self-appointed experts. If your opinion differs from one of these, you have not "evolved" and their followers look upon you with a mixture of pity and contempt. The old debates about capital punishment and nature versus nurture that used to bore me are looking more attractive all the time.

You may have guessed that I am ready to drop out of the mainstream as it appears to me today. Living on an Indian reservation in the northwest sounds pretty good to me now. My plan is to open a small gourmet coffee shop and country store. I think I would be good at running a business like that. It would still keep me in touch with people, but I could pretend to be busy if the conversations turned to any of the above subjects. Besides, rural communities are concerned more with local issues that I still find interesting. I have plenty of money to start a business like this and to cover the losses that will likely be ongoing. I'm not trying to get rich. I just want to do something simple and enjoyable. I haven't spoken to Kate about this yet, but I hope she will be pleased and willing to continue our relationship. I want that more than anything.

I told Sam that I would like to tell a story that night after dinner. He laughed and asked if this was another animal attack story like that of "wolf boy". He said we had heard enough about wolves. No one took that memory seriously for some reason, but it is one hundred percent true. Even Kate just smiles and shakes her head whenever it is mentioned. I assured Sam that this next memory would knock his socks off. He looked down at my legs and said "as long as it's just my socks". That struck me as a pretty good joke, much better than he usually comes up with. Actually, Sam is funniest when he is just being himself. He gets really flustered at times and says the strangest things. It's what makes him so lovable, at least that's what Amanda says. I like Sam a lot and I hope we will become friends and see more of each other in the future. It would be fun for the four of us to get together, assuming things work out for me and Kate.

I have no doubt that Sam and Amanda are heading toward reconciliation, but they need to keep Thelma out of their lives. Amanda does seem to realize now what a negative impact Thelma has on their relationship, but it's more than that. I wonder if Thelma likes Amanda at all. She seems to want to usurp Amanda's place in Samantha's life. What that means

I don't know but the day they left I went out on the deck and Thelma was there with Samantha and Etienne and asked me to take a picture of the three of them. No big deal until Thelma started orchestrating the picture. She stood behind Etienne's wheelchair with her arms draped around him and she told Samantha to kneel beside Etienne and look up at her smiling. It would have been a great picture if it was spontaneous and real, or an ad for an insurance company, but it was totally contrived and I felt sad for Thelma. Samantha didn't seem to notice, but Etienne looked as uncomfortable as I felt. She had me take three shots to be sure I got it right, whatever that meant. I wonder if Thelma's entire life exists only in her mind and has no connection to the outside world.

SAM

I could see a lot of Lily in Amanda. She has a mystical side to her that could cause her to look for "signs" whether she will admit it or not. Amanda talks to God a lot--often out loud and in public places, so I think she would consider Him the source of any signs she might be given. In spite of the fact that we are divorced, I don't think Amanda ever really gave up on me. One time she told me that she was ashamed that she didn't fight harder for our marriage. I took that as a sign.

Everyone liked the story and it was nice to see a happy ending. Personally, I really liked Chloe as much as Lily and I would have liked to know Milo, although I'm not sure I could let a daughter of mine run off to the frontier with some guy just because he gave her a pretty egg, let alone help finance the expedition. I mentioned that to Amanda and she said it was just further proof that it was fortunate that we never had a daughter. Maybe so, but having a granddaughter like Samantha is almost the same thing.

Glen volunteered a memory after dinner that night. He said his story would "knock my socks off". I looked down at his legs and made the statement that I hoped it would just be my socks. He laughed and was not at all offended. I think Glen thinks I am quite clever with jokes. Amanda says I don't need to tell jokes because I am funny enough as I am. I don't know why that doesn't offend me. Perhaps it's because she doesn't say it to offend me and anyhow, I like to make her laugh any way I can.

Dinner that night was a real adventure. Serena got a good buy on some king crab and she covered the table with layers of newspaper and we all sat around the table cracking the shells and pulling the meat out of the legs. Some of the legs were two inches in diameter so there would be about eight to ten ounces of solid crab in each leg. She served some hot, with garlic butter, and some cold with Amanda's homemade cocktail sauce. We had several loaves of crusty bread and a massive relish tray with vegetables, pickles, olives, marinated artichokes, pickled beets, salami and cheese. It was a huge success with no leftovers (as usual). I ate five crab legs and I counted four in front of Amanda, but I'm not sure that she didn't push one or two of her discarded shells in front of Adrian so it might have been more. Cleanup was easy. Serena just scooped the shells and newspaper into a huge trash bag and set it outside the front door with instructions for me to bury the shells on the beach and burn the newspaper in the fire pit the next day. King crab is a wonderful thing, but like any seafood, there is no good to come of leaving anything sitting in the house after it has been consumed.

Dessert consisted of those tiny cups of sherbet with little wooden spoons which we took with us to the story pit. There were assorted flavors and everyone agreed it was perfect after eating such huge amounts of crab, everyone except Bernie who complained that we didn't have any "real" ice cream. (Actually we did have several cartons in the freezer in the garage, but Serena didn't let him in on that little secret for no other reason than to be mean. That is about as mean as Serena gets.)

April chose her usual spot on the floor by the coffee table. She had three containers of sherbet and was watching over them to make sure Jenny didn't steal one. Amanda threatened to send them to their rooms if there was any roughhousing like the night before. While they were joking with one another, Etienne reached over and stole one of April's containers. April threatened to wheel him off the deck to the beach below if he didn't give it back. He responded by prying the entire lump of sherbet out with the little wooden spoon and shoving the whole thing in his mouth. We felt bad for him as we witnessed his worst ever brain freeze. April embraced him, and pretended to comfort him as she managed to steal his sherbet cup, but ended up dropping it on the floor. As Etienne struggled to retrieve his cup, Camille loped across the room, grabbed the cup in her mouth and ran to the entry hall where she gulped down the whole thing, cardboard and all. I found myself marveling at the pleasure April had brought to the group. Energy takes many forms in humans, and hers was the best kind.

Glen announced he was going to share a memory and everyone booed him except April who hadn't been present for the wolf boy story. Nevertheless, everyone settled in to listen except Camille who prowled the room with her nose to the floor searching for another wayward dessert. She finally gave up the search and plopped down in front of Adrian with the look of one who has been cheated. Camille is aptly named as she is quite the drama queen.

Chapter Forty-One

THE NEAR OCCASION OF SIN

GLEN

"This memory came to me for the first time shortly before my marriage to Peggy and it visited me frequently over the next few years. It illustrates the constant struggles we all face in reconciling our beliefs with our reality. Is it good enough to adhere as closely as possible to our beliefs while still managing to accomplish our goals, fulfill our responsibilities, and maintain a right relationship with God, or must we take a rigid stance when it comes to what we believe about right and wrong no matter what the cost? As the CEO of a large company, I routinely faced this dilemma as I was presented with choices which were mutually exclusive in terms of what my faith told me versus what was best for the company, its shareholders and employees. In all cases, someone would get helped and someone would get hurt and neither path seemed totally right. These decisions weighed heavily on my mind but, as one of my contemporaries explained, "That's why we get paid the big bucks".

My memory of Father Paul served me well in those years, not necessarily giving me answers as to the right course, but rather helping me to avoid the frustrations that can cause us to question our core values or take us to a position where we cannot make a decision.

Father Paul grew up in a staunchly Catholic family with four brothers; Matthew, Mark, Luke and John. It was pretty clear that his devout mother had hopes that one or more of her sons would have a calling to the priesthood. Paul was the third son, and from the beginning, he exhibited the kind of faith that would surely lead him down that path. His mother and the parish priest nurtured that faith so that, by the time he graduated from Saint Alphonse High School, he was prepared to enter the seminary.

He was a gifted student and a perfect example of what a priest should be. His goal was to live his life helping the members of his flock to live their faith fully and to pass their beliefs on to their children. He did not aspire to rise within the church hierarchy as his mother hoped he would. Instead, he exemplified kindness and humility.

After his ordination he was sent to a parish in a small town in Illinois to begin his work. He was loved and respected by everyone and took a special interest in the young people. He started many youth programs that were funded by donations from parishioners as well as local businessmen, and were open to all boys and girls, not just Catholics. The boys had their sports and community service programs and the girls were offered activities that included music, arts and crafts and fundraising for charities. Of course there were also catechism classes that were encouraged, but not required for participation in other activities. As each program grew, so did the donations and tithes to the church. After just five years the diocese took note of his accomplishments and decided to move him to rescue a prosperous parish in Chicago, whose membership and donations were shrinking.

Father Paul hated to leave, but he obeyed without question. Life in the city church was different than he was used to, but he found that many of his programs translated very well to his new parish. Again, he gained the love and trust of his community and, though the youths of that community were more sophisticated and troublesome to deal with, it soon became obvious that he was making progress: and nowhere was this more evident than in the collection box. The city parents were busy and less connected to their children than those in the small town and gratefully offered the dollars necessary to support his programs and their church in exchange for the guidance and leadership Father Paul provided their children. In short, Father Paul was credited with being a prime mover in the betterment of the community as a whole as well as the church. He worked day and night and had intimate knowledge and understanding of most of the families inside and outside of his congregation. He was happy and fulfilled and thanked God for giving him the gifts he needed to serve his church.

His success as a spiritual leader, mentor, and moral compass was not limited to the youth of the community. He was sought after, in and out of the confessional, for help and guidance by those experiencing grief, hardship or a crisis of faith. He turned no one away and judged no one. He provided comfort and tried his best to help people reconcile their problems and tribulations with the teachings of Christ. He prayed for wisdom and guidance and taught others to do the same. There were times when he was unable to reach a troubled soul and he wept over his failures, but his faith never faltered. He never questioned his calling to be a priest and never viewed the sacrifices he made as anything but trivial compared to the rewards he was given and the joy he experienced in serving God.

Father Paul had been a handsome child and young man and, as he reached the age of thirty, maturity brought with it characteristics that were very attractive to women. He was well built due to his participation in the sports programs he created, and he possessed the self-assuredness that accompanied his strong beliefs and were amplified by his successes.

Since he had no experience with women other than his devout mother, he knew nothing of the passions that inhabited the souls of the ladies in his parish. He had only seen the pious and obedient side of their natures. They were mothers and caregivers and though he was aware of that "other kind of woman", he seldom had occasion to mix with them. To top it off, he was unusually sympathetic to the plight of women as they were viewed by society and the church at that time. He quietly objected to their being treated as chattels of their fathers and husbands and he believed that they were intelligent and had more to contribute to the world than they were allowed to give.

There was one woman in particular of whom he was especially fond. Her name was Polly Sinclair and she was recently widowed. Father Paul had been a friend to her husband who met his death in an explosion in one of the mills he was inspecting. He had spent several hours praying with Polly, but she was having a difficult time accepting her husband's death.

One Sunday afternoon Polly came to the rectory in tears. She had not been able to sleep for many nights and she confessed that she felt angry with God for taking her husband and leaving her poor and lonely, without hope. She was afraid she was losing her faith and would never get it back. Father

Paul did his best to reassure her that everyone faced that struggle at some point in their lives and that she needed to pray for strength. Polly was not consoled. She wept and collapsed at his feet. He helped her onto the sofa and stroked her hair, speaking softly to her, not about God or her faith, but about how beautiful and good she was and how God would not have gifted her with all that beauty and goodness if he didn't intend for some man to worship her throughout her life. She looked up at him with tears in her bright green eyes and, for the first time in his life, Father Paul was lost in the sweet, complex, confusing, delicious, intoxicating spell of a woman.

Like any boy, Paul had experienced the normal sexual urges including the "midnight visits" that result in soiled sheets or the embarrassing outward signs of arousal. He understood that this was normal, but that he was bound by his beliefs to fight these urges and avoid any circumstance that would allow them to surface. Placing himself in situations that could incite these urges or failure to eliminate temptation was a sin in the same way that deliberate sexual activity would be. He prayed for help in avoiding this, "the near occasion of sin". He had devised many exercises that would help him defeat the betrayal from his body. If he awoke in the middle of the night in a state of arousal, he would get up and pray or find some physical work he could do until the urges passed. This was relatively easy for him since he had no history of contact with any female other than his devout mother, so there were no images to erase. They were just biological functions brought on by the devil and he could erase them entirely because there was no real person that would ignite temptation. Over time, these occurrences were less frequent and Father Paul was not overly concerned-until that afternoon with Polly

That Sunday Father Paul consoled Polly less as her priest and more as a man to a woman. Holding her lightly and appropriately as she wept, he absorbed her beauty, gentleness and her passion and, for the first time in his life, the arousal came from a source outside of himself. In the course of holding and comforting her he experienced a full erection and the ensuing explosion that accompanies such a profound physical reaction. He was humiliated and ashamed and he began to weep openly and bitterly. Polly was not aware of his predicament and attributed his tears to a deep empathy for her sorrow.

Father Paul was unable to move for fear of exposing his weakness so he simply sat and held her until she was all cried out. Finally she was able to compose herself and she apologized for her weakness, but assured him that, through his kindness and understanding, her faith and hope was restored and she departed a much happier woman. After she left a devastated Father Paul ran to his room, removed his soiled clothing and bathed himself over and over again, weeping and praying the entire time. He spent the rest of the day and evening on his knees, praying for forgiveness and strength. That night, after hours of tossing and turning, he finally fell into a deep sleep only to be awakened by another erection even stronger than the earlier one. He feared that his contact with Polly, innocent as it was, had unleashed a demon in him

Polly, on the other hand, was so touched by his compassion that she shared with her female friends her belief that Father Paul was a true saint who could erase all bitterness from one's heart and restore one's faith. He was besieged with girls and women of all ages wanting to share their innermost fears and passions and receive his tender ministries. There was a constant stream of sad and troubled females in and out of the rectory to the point that he was having difficulty finding time to perform his other duties, but that was the least of Father Paul's problems.

In the days that followed Polly's visit, Father Paul finally convinced himself that his experience with her had been an isolated incident brought on by his overconfidence that he had his carnal inclinations in check. He believed that God was giving him a warning that he was letting his guard down and was as vulnerable as anyone else to the sins of the flesh. Perhaps the incident with Polly had been a sin, he wasn't sure, but at the very least, God had given him a lesson in humility.

He dreaded conducting mass the following Sunday for fear that seeing Polly sitting in her usual pew would bring on another attack and he would lose his concentration on the service and humiliate himself and disappoint God. For once he was grateful for the flowing vestments he would be wearing, but he felt terrible for that thought, as the vestments had meaning that was much greater than simply hiding his shame.

Sunday morning arrived with rain and gloom that matched his mood. He arose an hour early, intent on spending that extra time in fervent prayer. By the time he entered the church, he was confident that the worst was behind him. Imagine his joy when the mass went off without a hitch and he was able to stand at the entrance after mass and greet his parishioners, including Polly, without incident. He returned to the rectory and fell on knees, thanking God for deliverance. His mood improved and by midafternoon he was feeling more like himself.

Around three o'clock his doorbell rang and he opened it to discover a very distraught young woman. He recognized her as Sarah, the wife of one of the wealthier members of the congregation. She tearfully pleaded for a few moments of his time and he directed her to his study. Just as the Sunday before when Polly made her visit, his housekeeper was gone to spend the day with her family. He found himself wishing that she were present to add the insulation he might need to protect him from his weakness, but he quickly dismissed that thought, confident that God would be his protector.

Sarah fumbled with her handkerchief as she began her story. Within minutes that handkerchief was soaked with her tears and Father Paul was weeping right along with her. Sarah told him that she had been aware for some time that her husband was routinely unfaithful to her, and with more than one woman. Father Paul told her to pray for her husband and promised that he would do the same. He spoke of God's grace and forgiveness and offered her the comfort that through their prayers, her husband would find his way back to her and they would share eternity in heaven. To his surprise, Sarah broke down further and told him that it was not fear for her husband's soul that brought her such grief; it was fear for her own. She did not want to have more than the two children she already had and had been denying him his rights as a husband for two years, forcing him into the arms of other women, thereby making his transgressions her sins rather than her husband's. Her guilt was increased by the fact that she was interfering with God's plan by refusing to have more children. She was ashamed that she did not seem to have the same motherly instincts as other women. She dearly loved her children, but was content to allow them to be raised by a governess. She didn't feel that she was a good enough person to raise the children she had, let alone the others God might send her. She went on to say that she didn't understand her children and lived in constant fear that she would not provide them the guidance they needed. It was easier to leave that to the governess who seemed confident in her ability to teach the children good Catholic values. In short, she believed herself to be a failure as a wife, a mother and a Catholic and, through her failures she was forcing her husband toward his own condemnation in the eyes of God.

Father Paul was overcome with compassion for this woman and prayed for the wisdom to help her. As she wept, she leaned over and buried her face in Father Paul's shoulder. It wasn't long before he realized that he was no longer praying for her, rather he was pleading once again for himself. The specter of his sinful nature had, once again, raised its ugly head. From his experience with Polly, he knew he had to separate himself physically from Sarah before he experienced another explosion, but she was clinging to him and he didn't know how to pry himself away without hurting her feelings. His solution was to lift her from the sofa and tell her that they must both drop to their knees and pray for answers. She complied, but her tears continued to the point that she couldn't support herself kneeling and she ended up sitting on the floor. Father Paul continued to kneel and pray and it soon became obvious that he would have to remain in that position or his own weakness would be exposed. He hated his body for betraying him.

After the explosion, he felt calmer and he was able to focus once again on Sarah's plight. Somehow the right words came to him as he explained to her that perhaps her problem was not that she was weak or evil, perhaps she was just young. He went on to observe that since her husband was a lot older than she and extremely successful, he often treated her as a child and thereby contributed to her feelings of inadequacy. She admitted that he didn't seem to have any respect for her opinions and often told her that he would do all the thinking and it was her job to play with the "other" children. Father Paul told Sarah that her failure was in not believing in herself and not having the faith to ask God for help in raising her children. He explained that if she could reach the point where she believed in herself and God, working together, her fears of having more children would likely disappear and she could be a true wife to her husband. He also said that if, at that point, her husband sought pleasure elsewhere, she was not to take responsibility for his actions. He asked her if it was possible to learn to take God as her partner and grow into motherhood. She stopped crying and put her head on her arms remaining silent and immobile for several minutes. When she lifted her head, she was beaming and it was as if she had changed in those few minutes from a child to a woman. She rested for a short time and then thanked Father Paul and went home to become the mistress of her house and a mother to her children, leaving Father Paul to wrestle with his own demons. As he watched her leave he felt and immense love for her, just as he had for Polly.

Over the next weeks, He occupied himself with his normal duties, prayers and fasting, and the visits from a parade of distraught women. Father Paul tried desperately to rid himself of the disease that was attacking his soul. Still, he did not despair, he just prayed for answers. The impulses occurred spontaneously and out of his control, so he prayed for mercy and to be freed from his torment. He worried that one day he would lose himself totally and act on his urges. The women who visited him were vulnerable and in need of comfort. It was not hard to imagine that they would respond to his advances and, if that happened, he would be lost and take them with him. Over time he stopped praying for relief, but rather prayed that his affliction would not get worse. Every Sunday he would stand in his pulpit delivering his sermon and looking out on the growing number of women with whom he had experienced an explosion. At the same time he could see that these women were happier and seemed to be uplifted and relieved of their miseries through his counseling. He believed that God often works in strange ways, but he could not believe that it was his "affliction" that may have helped him to find the wisdom to help them perform miracles in their lives. He couldn't imagine how all this would end.

He had another problem. Week after week he heard the confessions of his parishioners yet he had not made a confession of his own since before the first incident with Polly. The priest in the neighboring parish or the bishop would normally be available to him but he had not garnered the courage or the clarity of mind to approach either of them. On top of that, he was giving and receiving communion when he may not have been in a state of grace which was in itself a sin. He knew that his erections were not his fault and he did everything in his power to dismiss them and nothing to encourage them, but allowing himself to be alone with these distressed women, knowing the effect it had on him-that was a different matter. Those meetings, for him, were placing himself in the near occasion of sin-which was a sin. On the other hand, it was his duty to counsel the troubled, and God seemed to be giving him the wisdom to help them so how could he turn them away? Did the good that he was performing justify putting his soul in danger in God's eyes or would God want him to strictly adhere to what he had been taught regarding temptation? Was he lacking in humility by believing that God had placed him in that place at that time for the purpose of healing these souls? Was this a test and if so, what was being tested?

As time passed and Father Paul continued to struggle with his dilemma, more women were showing up at his door and in some cases he was confused as to what they were seeking from him. His kindness and understanding, coupled with his good looks, began to attract females of all sorts, many of whom were not even Catholic. In some cases he suspected that he was not sought for his spiritual guidance at all. Often the women were just lonely and some even seemed to be flirting with him. In his naiveté, Father Paul did not know how to deal with this type of woman and he was so uncomfortable that he would say a few kind words and then make an excuse to get rid of them. It was a huge relief to him that he did not experience with them the arousal that occurred with the faithful ladies seeking God's help. He decided that his reactions must be guided by something other than pure lust and he became even more confused.

Finally he concluded that he could no longer face this problem on his own and that he had to overcome his pride and shame and seek guidance from his bishop. Until that time, his only contact with the bishop had been quite formal and consisted mostly of receiving praise for his fine work and discussing budget issues. The bishop had often heard Father Paul's confession in the past, but there had been little to confess and certainly nothing more than the usual sins that accompany being human. By this time Father Paul had suffered so greatly with his secret that he was actually looking forward to his confession, no matter what it might bring.

They met in the bishop's private quarters. There was no need for the anonymity of the confessional since he had made the request that the bishop hear his confession. He saw the arch of the bishop's eyebrows when he told him it had been over three months since his last confession. He knew that this would be a warning that something pretty serious was about to be revealed. The bishop never took his eyes off Father Paul's face as he struggled to explain his problem, ask for forgiveness and seek help in how to deal with the future. He knew his confession was awkward and sounded somewhat childish, but Father Paul kept talking until he had spilled out every event, every fear, all his guilt and confusion, then he fell silent waiting for the bishop to speak.

The bishop rose and began pacing the room and finally came to a halt staring out of his window with his back to Father Paul. Several minutes went by without a sound between them. Father Paul waited silently for the bishop's words of wisdom. He knew the bishop would be inspired by God with the answers to his problem. If the bishop told him he would be sent to an assignment where he would not have contact with women, he would accept his fate. On the other hand, there was always the possibility that the bishops prayers, coupled with his own, would give him the added strength necessary to overcome his sinful nature. He felt an immense relief. After a few minutes he noticed that the bishop was hunched over leaning with his hands on the windowsill. His shoulders were shaking and he seemed unable to stand up straight. Father Paul assumed he was weeping for him and he felt his shame even more deeply for disappointing this great man of God.

He walked over to the bishop, placing his hand on his shoulder to let him know that he could accept whatever God told the bishop to do. The bishop turned his head slightly and Father Paul could see the tears running down his cheek, but the bishop was not weeping, he was laughing. Father Paul didn't know what else to do so he laughed with him. This caused the bishop to laugh harder but Father Paul stopped laughing. Soon the bishop was able to regain his composure and he apologized to Father Paul stating that he was painfully aware of the anguish Father Paul was suffering and he didn't mean to make light of his anxiety, but he also couldn't ignore the spectacle of Father Paul's boyish innocence, so rare in a man his age. He put his arm around Father Paul.

"My son," he said, "I can only explain this in the following way. Our souls are not perfect and, though we try our best to cleanse them and make them holy, they still reside in our imperfect and unpredictable bodies. Our souls look toward

God, but our hearts and minds are bombarded by the whims and wiles of earthly things. I believe that what you experience is an almost supernatural level of compassion for these ladies. Your earthly mind cannot grasp the depth of your feelings so it interprets it as passion and it sends that signal to your body. I do not see sin in what you are experiencing so long as you continue to pray and you do not act on these urges. Let me ask you this. When you are in this state of arousal, do you have fantasies about having sexual relations the women involved?"

Father Paul responded immediately, "Of course not, but I fear that someday I will be swept with carnal desire and I will not be able to control myself and that, by continuing to counsel these ladies, I am putting my soul and theirs in jeopardy and would not that be as great a sin as the act itself"?

"Ahh, but this is the difference", the bishop replied. "You are not experiencing carnal desire for these women, but rather a sort of rapture at being witness to their innate goodness and your being in a position to help them maintain their relationship with God. Remember, the word compassion has two parts and one of those parts is "passion". I don't believe you would ever violate God's trust. I believe your body misreads the intensity of your respect for their souls and your desire to nurture their faith and sends an inappropriate response. You are uniquely gifted with empathy and love and it would be wrong to turn your back on these gifts. I apologize for my earlier reaction to your confession. Perhaps I was taken aback by your sincerity and innocence and my own flawed brain didn't know how to react. We all have to fight to overcome our imperfect humanness in order to protect our souls. Continue to pray for strength and thank God for placing his trust in you. I will pray for you as well. If God sees your continued contact with the ladies entrusted to your care as sinful, he will respond to our prayers in his own way. Go in Peace."

My memory takes me no further than this. I only remember that Father Paul left with a sense of joy and relief. He accepted the words of the bishop and believed that God would give his soul the strength to conquer his wayward body and the guidance to counsel with wisdom and love.

As for me, I struggle with the many forces that attack my soul every day, but through my memory of Father Paul, I have learned to accept the fact that my mind and body are imperfect and it is only through faith that I can find the strength to live as God wants me to live. When I fail, and I often do, I have to believe in God's grace, love and understanding. I believe that it is God's understanding of our human frailties that allows him to forgive us over and over again and that as long as we keep fighting our weaknesses, he will continue to bless us and that even when we fail, he continues to love us."

Etienne said that the story of Father Paul made him miss Father Karl and I could see that he was struggling with being separated from his mother. Adrian put her arm around his shoulders and April spoke up, perhaps trying to get his mind off his troubles.

Chapter Forty-Two

A GLORIOUS FUTURE

APRIL

"We have all heard the expression, "The spirit is willing, but the flesh is weak", but I don't think most people fully comprehend the struggle between the soul and the body. We know that our minds and bodies are under constant attack. Our bodies crave sugar, alcohol, drugs, sex, cigarettes, or any number of stimulants that can diminish the quality and length of our lives. Our fragile egos can wreak havoc upon our ability to form healthy relationships. We are subject to destructive emotions such as fear, anger, hatred, jealousy, greed and pride, and our brains tell us that we are suffering and deteriorating, but we are often too weak to overcome the enemies we create in our minds. Some find the battle too hard and they give in. Most of us continue to fight but I don't think we always know what we are fighting for.

We want to be better people so we will be loved. We want to do good things so we will go to heaven. We want to develop self-discipline so we can look better or make more money. We want to create a legacy so we will be remembered. We want to make the lives of our children easier than our own. We want to achieve so we will be admired. We want to create a world of comfort and security so we can be happy and once we are happy everything else will fall into place and we can afford to be kind, generous, trusting and wise. None of these goals reflect the true nature of our quest and, somewhere in the back of our minds, we know it. Perhaps that is what we call "the human condition".

I have written several of my memories in the book I gave each of you so I don't intend to repeat them now, but there is one memory that you won't find in those pages. I tried several times to make it into a story, but failed because it has no beginning and no end. I will try to describe the essence of what I experienced. Perhaps some of you have had a similar experience but have found it too hard to relate within the limitations of our language.

My memory began as one of my lives ended. You will not find this life story in my book because there is nothing about that life that I wanted to share. It was not a happy or productive life. I died alone and friendless and I deserved that fate. I had not fought the weaknesses in my mind or body. I had allowed my soul to lie fallow during that life. When I died I had to face the reality of the life I had wasted.

Upon my death I was greeted by many souls I had known before. Some were from that most recent life, but many were from lives prior to that. I was aware that I had been in this place before so I was not surprised when I was embraced by these souls with love and understanding, but there was not the joy in this reunion that I remembered from other reunions. My mothers and fathers from many lives were there and they treated me with tenderness, but I knew that I could not go with them and bask in their love. I had to go a different direction and relearn that which I had already learned in other lives. I felt sad, but not abandoned.

I was led away by a beautiful soul who told me that I would be forced to spend some time at rest and during that time I would be called upon to review my failures in that life and answer to myself for the weaknesses that I had allowed to damage my soul. I was not to be punished, but I would not be allowed to move forward until I identified and repaired that damage. If I worked hard and listened to my teachers, I would be successful; if not, I would not be allowed to return to life and continue to work toward building my soul to its full potential.

I was isolated, but never alone. My guide was with me whenever I reached out to her for knowledge. She offered no comfort when I wept because I couldn't weep and learn at the same time. Yet, I was allowed to weep because it was part of my resting period. As I was shown the weaknesses that I nurtured during that worthless life, I was filled with shame, but my guide never allowed me to transform that shame into self-hatred or despair because those were the flaws that caused my failure in the first place. My job was to replace that shame with a commitment to abolish my weaknesses and repair the damage to my soul in a way that would make it even stronger than before. By doing so, that infertile life would become valuable as a source of learning and would not have been wasted.

Does this sound complicated? Well, it's not. It's just hard. There is no concept of time in that place so it is impossible to say how long I spent resting and learning. Finally, I was free to move on and be reunited with other souls. My time in isolation made that reunion even sweeter to me, and my success in emerging from that painful process brought joy to those around me. I guess you can compare it to someone coming out of drug rehab after years of abuse. In much the same way there were more challenges to come. I had to go through a strengthening and growing process before I could be released to another life and take on another imperfect body. This process was difficult, but not unpleasant because everyone was sharing the journey. We were all there for the same reason. Some were further along than others and they would help us along the way. Every soul was there to build strength in themselves and others. There was no judgment, envy or jealousy, only dedication and love. We all knew that we couldn't stay forever. The fact that we were where we were meant that we had to go back and use the knowledge and strength we were gaining to make better lives for ourselves and others and to work hard to improve the world we would rejoin. There were other souls that had completed their transformation and they went on to a place of peace and glory. There were also souls that would never grow and they would languish forever in a hopeless vacuum that they created for themselves.

This is what I remember, but I can't relate to you the full sense of what I experienced. Nowhere on earth does that sense of communion prevail. There is great beauty in that place, but it is not physical beauty, it is all feeling. My guide was beautiful; not as a woman is beautiful, but as a soul is beautiful. I remember her as a woman because that is how my mind remembers her, but in truth, she doesn't have a gender. She is gentleness, love, light and wisdom. This is the only way I can describe her. I wonder if any of you have a memory such as this. If not, I can only wish this for you because once you have been there, you will never doubt the goodness and grace of God and his great plan for us."

JENNY

"I don't have a complete memory of a "between life" as April does, but I did have a glimpse into that world and it fits her description perfectly. I was a young white girl, part of a large, happy farm family. My parents were the kind of people that were born to raise children. I mentioned this life before and I told you that I went back in this life to the farm, and many of the members of my prior family, including my mother, were still alive and living on that farm. In that life I had been named Pearl and I was the youngest of seven children. I was loved and protected by my parents and all my brothers and sisters. When I was just nine years old, I died from a fall out of a tree I was climbing. It was then that I had my visit into the "between life". It was very short, but I remember being embraced by my grandmother, who had died the year before. I wanted to stay with her in that beautiful place, but instead I was sent almost immediately into another life. Grandma told me that my soul was strong and I was ready to continue my journey, but that she would see me again. I was then sent to the life I am living now. I believe that the love and warmth I received from my family in that life is what sustained me through the early years of this life. I had the memory of what a family could and should be so I didn't blame myself for the emotional vacuum that was my childhood.

When I returned to the farm to visit my former family, I wasn't going to try to make them believe that I was their departed daughter. I pretended that I was doing research on interior designs for country living. They were open and charming and allowed me to tour their home and gardens. During the tour I inadvertently asked about a garden shed that used to be in a certain spot but was no longer there. The shed had been removed twenty years before my visit. The woman that was my mother kept questioning me as to how I knew the shed had been there and I couldn't give her a coherent answer. When we came to the tree I had fallen out of, I stopped and the memory of my family looking down on my broken body overcame me and I began to cry. My mother embraced me and cried with me, calling me her precious Pearl. She knew who I was. It remains in my memory as the happiest day of my life. We didn't tell the rest of the family but when my mother made me stay on for a week, no one questioned her decision. We spent every minute of that week together and when I was leaving we decided that we would not meet again until that time when our souls would be rejoined. That was seven years ago and I have not had contact with them since, but I do subscribe to the small weekly newspaper in that area and I recently learned that my mother had passed to join my grandmother. I was not sad because I know where she went and I remember the joy and peace that she found in that place."

AMANDA

All the while April and Jenny were talking, I kept looking over at Sam. He was leaning forward in his chair, so intent on what they were saying that the house could have slid down the embankment and he wouldn't have noticed. He had brought us all together to find some answers for me and Samantha and what we heard that day brought answers along with many more questions. No one in that room seemed to doubt what had been told to us, including Bernie. For me, that day marked Sam's mission as a success. I could see it on the faces of everyone, most importantly Sam's. When he looked at me his eyes were saying "Are you seeing what I'm seeing?"

Sam and I have never been especially religious people. Sam was raised Methodist and I Catholic, but in our adult lives we have never really attached ourselves to either religion. Yet, our training has followed us and we have both tried to live by the values we were taught as children-sometimes more successfully than others. Sam's faith is very simple and direct. He has always been able to accept God's grace and love without question. I have had to struggle to believe that God forgives and loves us unconditionally. Sam is well versed in the bible and the teachings of Christ, while I was educated more in church dogma. His faith was built on trust, mine on fear. Sam has a personal relationship with God. I studied the rules but was never fully sure I was in the club. Sam feels shame for his sins, but believes that he is forgiven and goes on to live better. I have wallowed in guilt and hoped that by spiritually flailing myself, I could earn God's love. I have had the advantage of my past life experiences, yet Sam is the one who has the real understanding. Samantha, thankfully, is more like Sam.

I have learned so much in these past few weeks that I know my life will never be the same. I still don't know how all this works. I don't know if everyone has multiple lives or if some souls get it right the first time and the rest of us have to be put in multiple bodies before we get where we are supposed to go. I have even wondered if all bodies have souls. Did Ted Bundy have a soul? All I know for sure, and I learned it here, is that there is a God that wants us to succeed and he will patiently train a willing soul. To believe otherwise leaves us tromping through the universe alone and hopeless. Some people call faith a crutch. It is!! What's wrong with that? If you try to walk on one leg you need a crutch, and living without faith is like walking on one leg.

I was exhausted and I wanted to be alone to think about all I had learned that day, so I went to my room. Before I left, I went over to Sam and gave him a big kiss on the lips right in front of everyone. Afterward, I felt uneasy because I was afraid it would appear that I was giving alms to a beggar. I didn't mean it that way at all. I just wanted to show him how grateful I was for his love and caring for Samantha and me. He had fearlessly put himself "out there" to help us and demonstrate his faith in us.

SAM

What a night that was! April and Jenny's experiences with the "in between" really blew me away. Apparently it had a huge effect on Amanda too because I saw her looking at me like she did in the old days. Then she got up and gave me a big juicy kiss and went to her room. Being the creep I am, my first thought was that she might want me to follow her, but I quickly realized that she was excited about our session and wanted to be alone to sort things out. I have to admit that I was feeling pretty proud of myself. We were really beginning to make some exciting discoveries and, for the first time, I was certain that this experiment was a success. Amanda appeared happier and more excited than I had ever seen her. I believed then, and I still do, that Amanda was making peace with her memories.

Chapter Forty-Three

ANTOINETTE AND JOHN

SAM

I didn't sleep well that night. Etienne cornered me before he went to bed and was asking questions about his mother. I knew that he suspected there was more to the story than he was being told. I put him off by saying that I was hoping to hear from her soon. Adrian rescued me by telling Etienne it was time for bed. He obeyed, but I could tell that he would not give up. I kept going back and forth in my head as to whether I should tell Etienne the truth about his mother's absence. On the one hand, I felt a little resentful that I was put in the position of having to lie, but I also didn't want to see him worry. Of course he was worrying anyway, but I couldn't imagine anything he might be thinking that was worse than the truth. Amanda was no help as her concerns were the same as mine. Adrian was staunchly against telling him that his mother was a suspect in his father's murder but she left the final decision to me.

By morning I had decided to call Father Karl and ask for his advice. He knew Etienne and Antoinette better than anyone and I decided to follow his lead no matter what. I arrived at the house around six thirty and was just about to make the call when the phone rang. It was Antoinette. I was overcome with relief but at the same time I couldn't help but notice how weak she sounded. She was obviously ill or seriously distressed. I offered to go get Etienne so she could talk to him but she wanted to talk to me first.

The news was good. She was not going to be charged with murder. The authorities still did not have any idea who did Andrew in, but they had reached the conclusion that a woman as small as Antoinette and pregnant as well, could not have inflicted the type of wounds they found on Andrew nor could she have moved and buried him. There really wasn't anything concrete that could implicate her. There were plenty of other people that had reason to want him dead, mainly the fathers of several young girls in the area, but no one stood out as a suspect so they were closing the case for the time being. Antoinette was free to leave the country and she wanted to return to our group rather than go back to Toronto. That was fine with me. None of us were ready to lose Etienne so soon and it would be too difficult for him to travel with his bad leg.

I sensed that there was more to come so I just shut up and waited for her to speak. She started to cry and the next thing I knew I was talking to John, Andrew's brother. He explained that Antoinette was not well. The whole mess had taken a huge toll on her and she had suffered a small stroke. Fortunately, there was little or no permanent damage, but she was very weak and would need some care and, although she definitely was not up to traveling at that time, she refused to stay in Scotland to recuperate. He would be traveling with her and wondered if there was a chance that he could stay on for a few days to help care for her. I couldn't refuse and I decided not to worry about accommodations at the house. I knew that we could rearrange things and that everyone would want to help. I was so relieved I would have agreed to anything at that point.

Antoinette came back on the line and asked to speak with Etienne. I had already signaled Serena to go get him and she was pushing him through the door at that very moment. He nearly fell out of his chair as he reached for the phone. Apparently Serena had made enough noise in the guest house to wake everyone because Amanda and Adrian came running in at that point and Etienne had to ask us to be quiet so he could hear his mother. Their conversation was short and when he hung up there was such an eruption of joy that everyone in the house came running. Etienne was openly crying and clinging to Adrian. Everyone, including Bernie, was laughing and crying at the same time. Well, Bernie wasn't crying, but at least he appeared happy for Etienne.

I didn't know how much information Antoinette had shared with Etienne so I didn't mention her illness and it was obvious that Etienne still didn't know the reason she had been detained, but if he had questions I could tell him to ask his mother when she arrived. I took Amanda aside and filled her in on the details. Antoinette and John were scheduled to arrive in Seattle late that evening. John said they would spend the night in the city so Antoinette could rest and they would catch a ferry the next day. That gave us the better part of two days to figure out where we were going to put everyone. I said it made sense to put John in the guest house with Etienne and Antoinette, but where would Amanda sleep? It was an innocent question! Amanda nixed that idea because she didn't want Antoinette climbing stairs. She said Etienne and Antoinette would share the master suite and John would stay on the boat with me. April would take over Etienne's spot in the guest house and Amanda and Adrian would keep the two bedrooms over there. That left what to do with Kate. With a shy smile, she assured us it was no problem. Glen was grinning in the same way I would have been had my plan been adopted. Amanda's plan made sense, damn it.

The rest of the day was spent moving Etienne into the master suite, April into the guest house and preparing the tiny cabin on my boat for John. Adrian hinted that Bernie might offer his room to John and move onto the boat with me, but thankfully, Bernie adamantly refused and I made a mental note to find some appropriate way to torment Adrian for making the suggestion. What had I done to deserve such treachery?

When I left for the boat that evening, all was ready for Antoinette's return and Etienne was e-mailing Samantha with the good news. Etienne told me that Samantha had a pretty rough week. Her friends were mad at her for outing the photographer and getting them all in trouble with their parents. Everyone, including Samantha, was grounded and being heavily supervised. He said she was taking it pretty well but was in a hurry to get back here to meet Antoinette. Amanda had spoken with Alex and I guess they were pretty happy with the way we handled things from this end so I figured it wouldn't be hard to convince them to let her come for another visit. Apparently, Thelma had given a good report on the goings on here, probably in the hope that she would be accompanying Samantha on her next visit. That was not going to happen.

The next day seemed endless as we waited for the four o'clock ferry. Naturally, Etienne wanted to go with me to the dock to meet Antoinette and John and he and insisted that we get there in plenty of time in case the ferry was early. By three o'clock he was fidgeting nervously so we left early and went to the village to get her some flowers. When the ferry arrived he was shaking so hard his chair was rattling.

Antoinette and John were among the first to get off. John had her arm and I could see that she was struggling to appear calm. The scene of their reunion was so touching that I had to turn away. John did the same and we averted our "man tears" by making our own introductions.

John is a very large man, probably six foot six inches and sturdily built. I was having trouble picturing him crawling into the little cabin that was to be his home for the next few days. It would be like putting a bear in a foxhole. I reconciled myself to giving up my cabin to him and taking the smaller one. He took me aside and thanked me for letting him stay. His concern for Antoinette was obvious and he let me know that there were other matters that had to be discussed and settled before he could return to Scotland.

Antoinette appeared exhausted and looked as if she had lost several pounds off her already tiny frame. I knew that Serena would take one look at her and start planning how she was going to fatten her up. She was preparing a welcome home dinner, although I had warned her that Antoinette was not well and might want to go directly to bed. I pushed Etienne's chair back to the Escalade and John took Antoinette's arm again. She was struggling, but trying her best to hide her weakness from Etienne. I returned to the dock to collect their luggage and we wasted no time in getting back to the house. Everyone was in the front entry to greet us. Antoinette used what must have been her last bit of strength to give a jaunty wave as we came up the walk. Amanda took one look at her and started with the tears, but quickly pulled herself together and directed John to the master suite where he deposited Antoinette on the edge of the bed. Amanda ordered everyone, including Etienne, out of the room so that Antoinette could freshen up and rest before dinner. I thought this was rather pushy of her, but when I saw the grateful look on Antoinette's face, I realized that, as usual, women had the best instincts. Etienne didn't seem to mind either, he was just happy to have her back. Besides, he seemed anxious to get to know his uncle. John told me that he and Antoinette had decided to tell him everything about the reason for the trip and also about Antoinette's stroke. John was obviously a take charge kind of guy, but there was a gentleness about him that put me at ease. He asked where he and Etienne could talk in private and I showed them to the den and left them alone. When they emerged an hour later, Etienne looked like he had matured by five years. He smiled at me, gave Amanda and Adrian each a big hug, and wheeled himself to the master suite. He didn't knock first, just opened the door and went in to his mother.

John agreed that it was "a fine time for a wee bit of scotch" as I presented my bottle of McClendon's Twelve Year Old. It is a long way down to a chair for a man of his size, so the least I could do was to offer him my usual chair, the largest and most comfortable in the room.

To call him handsome would be an understatement. If you apply that word as well as virile, distinguished, confident, strong, forthright, and polished you still might not get a complete picture of what he brings to a room. These qualities were not overlooked by the women I can assure you. Amanda, April, Serena, Adrian, even Kate could not take their eyes of him, but Jenny took the prize. She didn't sit down like the others. She stood straight up, sort of frozen in place as if her high heeled boots were full of cement. Glen and I exchanged glances and I'm sure he was wondering, as was I, if any of them would notice if we dropped off the face of the earth. If Andrew looked and carried himself anything like John, I could see why Antoinette would have been swept away and her lack of judgment could be explained. What a sight those two must have been as they traveled the world.

Serena delayed dinner by an hour and finally Etienne and Antoinette emerged. Antoinette looked a little better, but it was obvious it would be a short evening for her. Etienne just looked happy and relieved. Dinner was halibut cooked in parchment with a sauce that I can only describe as "soft". There was fresh asparagus, glazed carrots, rice pilaf and pea salad. This meal was unusually heavy on vegetables and I suspected that Serena was trying to get Antoinette healthy in one sitting. Her efforts were rewarded as Antoinette packed away a pretty good meal. John said she ate more at that dinner than he had seen her eat in all of the past few weeks. He made more than one trip to the buffet himself and declared Serena a world class chef. She beamed all the way through the cleanup and before she left made it a point to ask John what he would like to see for breakfast. His reply was "absolutely anything as long as it is prepared by you, Serena". The funny thing is that at no point did he seem ingenuous.

Etienne and Antoinette retired almost immediately after dinner and I suggested to John that we could go down to the boat if he was tired. He wanted to stay for a while and get to know everyone better. He also wanted to hear more about our "project" and seemed genuinely interested. Antoinette had filled him in and he wasn't in the least bit skeptical about the whole idea. He said that if Etienne had memories of past lives, he wanted to gain as much understanding as he could because he intended to be more of an uncle to Etienne from this time on. Bernie grunted and asked if he wanted to be more than a brother-in-law to Antoinette as well. The implication was obvious, but John didn't flinch. He looked directly at Bernie and said that he intended to be whatever they needed, as family should be. Bernie said no more but left shortly thereafter for his room.

By midnight I was getting pretty tired but John was still going strong. He and Jenny were engaged in a conversation about the restoration of the many castles in Scotland and John was describing their family home. I finally suggested that we retire and John apologized for keeping me up so late.

Although John had seemed very enthusiastic about staying on the boat when I mentioned it to him, I worried that he might find the accommodations less than comfortable and very cramped. After all, John came from a very wealthy family and who knew what luxuries he was used to. My fears went away when we stepped foot in the salon. He seemed totally at home and quite pleased. I showed him to my room and told him that is where he would be staying but he insisted on seeing the other cabin. In the end, he would not hear of me giving up my space and insisted that he would do very well in the smaller quarters. There was no arguing with him so I gave in on the condition that I didn't have to watch him ooze his body into that tiny space.

The next morning it was still dark when I was awakened by a horrific howl followed by a huge splash. I jumped to the rear deck just in time to see John's head emerge from the watery depths of the marina. He was sporting a huge grin and, from what I could see, nothing else except a pair of boxer shorts which led me to believe that his dip in the chilly waters had been deliberate. He took another dive, re-emerged and effortlessly pulled his huge frame onto the swim step. I handed him a towel and he made all sorts of pleasurable sounds as he dried himself off. As we entered the salon, the teakettle was whistling and I guessed that this was all some sort of morning ritual that he performed in Scotland. I apologized for not warning him that the waters here seldom rose above fifty degrees, but he said they were no colder than what he was used to at home. He asked if I minded if he used my shower as the one in the guest cabin was too small. Of course, I had no problem with that and was pleasantly surprised that he washed his huge body in less than two minutes, leaving me enough hot water to shower as well. Most people don't realize that the hot water tanks on boats are a lot smaller than those in homes.

I shaved, showered, dressed and returned to the salon where John had prepared our morning tea. I glanced longingly at my coffee pot, but decided I could forego that luxury until we reached the house. John asked if we could talk for a while as he had some things to tell me. It was only six-thirty and still dark so that seemed a good time for a discussion. I was not at all prepared for what I was going to hear.

JOHN

"My wife, Meaghan, fell in love with Antoinette the minute Andrew brought her home. Meaghan was shy and sensitive, a quiet beauty. She was the love of my life from the time we were children. More than anything we wanted to have children, but after many years of trying and praying, we had to accept the fact that this was not going to happen for us. When Antoinette announced that she was pregnant Meaghan was ecstatic. There would finally be a child in the family and she looked forward to being an auntie. We were both well aware of Andrew's shortcomings but, like Antoinette, we hoped that fatherhood would bring him to some level of maturity. At first he seemed to be doing better with regard to the business and he didn't appear to be as restless as he had been before, but it wasn't long before the old Andrew resurfaced. Meaghan was worried about Antoinette because she seemed depressed and was spending less and less time with us and Andrew was leaving her alone most of the time. I was clear that things were not going well in their household.

One day Meaghan walked over to the guest house to check on Antoinette. She could hear Andrew yelling at her and behaving in a threatening manner. He told her that she was repulsive and that she should have gotten rid of the baby. Antoinette was crying and Andrew stormed out of the house. Meaghan hid and decided to return to our home rather than embarrass Antoinette, but she told me about the incident and we both decided to keep a closer watch over her. Shortly after that, Cloris, our maid whose family had worked for our family for many years, confided in Meaghan that Andrew had made some unwelcome advances toward her and that she was afraid of him. At the same time, we had been hearing rumors about Andrew carousing and womanizing in the town. This wasn't anything new for Andrew. It had been going on for years before he left home and returned with Antoinette, but now he was a married man and soon to be a father so something had to be done. I went to our father with the stories and the worries concerning Cloris. He was furious and confronted Andrew, threatening to cut him off without a cent if he didn't change his ways. Andrew knew it would do no good to lie to father so he put on a show of being the repentant son and promised to be a model husband and father from then on. Our father wanted to believe him and so he did.

About a week later Cloris did not show up for work. Meaghan was worried about her so she went to her home and was told that Cloris would not see her. Meaghan was terribly upset and couldn't imagine what she had done to cause the girl to be angry with her. That same day Andrew disappeared along with a great deal of money from the business account. It was several days before we discovered the missing funds, and Andrew had often disappeared for two or three days at a time so we didn't realize right away that his absence might be permanent. A week or so later, Meaghan and I went again to see Cloris. We were told by her father that she no longer lived there. Her father had been our gardener for years and he was deeply devoted to our family. He had always been a strong and jovial man, but he looked old and tired as he told Meaghan and me that Andrew had brutally beaten and raped his daughter in retribution for her telling Meaghan about his advances. Cloris had tried to withhold the truth from her father, but finally broke down and told him whole story. Her father did not want to hurt our family, but something had to be done about Andrew so he and his son tracked him down and beat him. In the course of the beating, the son had lost control and killed Andrew. The father took us to the place where they had buried him. He also gave us the bag Andrew had been carrying and in it was the money he had taken. It was clear that Andrew was going to abandon his family if he hadn't been killed first. I can't begin to tell you how it felt to mourn my own brother yet, at the same time, want to protect his murderers, but that is what we did. Meaghan and I never told anyone what had happened, not even Antoinette. Nine months later Cloris bore Andrew's child, a son, and we have been watching over him and caring for his mother ever since. The money Andrew stole was given to her and she has been living in Edinburgh for the past thirteen years. Cloris knew nothing of Andrew's fate, but since the news broke of the discovery of his body, I knew that it was quite likely that she would put two and two together and guess at the truth. I went to visit her before Antoinette returned and told her the whole story and that Antoinette was a suspect in the murder and that if she was not cleared I would have to come forward with the truth to the authorities. Cloris agreed, but I could see the torment she was experiencing at the possibility that her father and brother might be charged.

When Antoinette arrived in Scotland, I confessed all to her as well. I told her that I would go to the police with the truth immediately if she wanted me to and she would be totally cleared of all suspicion. She wouldn't hear of it. She was terribly distressed at facing possible charges, but she pointed out that there was a good chance she would be cleared and she didn't want to cause any more problems for Cloris or her family. She also pointed out that Cloris's son, Robert, was Etienne's half-brother and she wouldn't expose him to the shame created by his father. In short, Andrew had caused enough pain and she didn't want it to go any further. We left it that, if she was charged with Andrew's murder, we would make our decision at that time. Antoinette asked me to ask Cloris if she could visit her and meet her son. Cloris had been very fond of Antoinette when she lived there with Andrew and she was grateful to Antoinette for what she was about to endure so she agreed to the visit.

I was not present at that meeting. I dropped Antoinette off and promised to return in one hour. When I returned to pick her up I witnessed a warm embrace between the two of them and Antoinette burst into tears the minute she got into the car. From that moment on, she was adamant that we do everything in our power to shield Cloris and her family from the heartbreak and publicity exposure would bring them.

Antoinette endured some very harsh interrogations over the following week and, worse yet, waiting for days to hear the findings of the investigators. She didn't sleep and rarely ate for the entire time. Finally, she collapsed and was rushed to the hospital where it was discovered that she had had a stroke. Several days later we got word that she was not going to be charged and was no longer a suspect. Antoinette stayed in the hospital for two more days and was released with the provision that she take complete bed rest for at least two weeks and then return to the hospital for more tests or possible rehabilitation. She was exceedingly tired, but didn't exhibit any ill effects other than a slight slur in her speech and even that disappeared within a few days. That is when she called you and insisted that I bring her here. She did not want to spend another minute in Scotland and I can't say that I blame her. You can see why I wanted to accompany her and make sure she took care of herself and that is why I am telling you about what she has been through. She must rest and she must be in a place where she feels secure for herself and Etienne. She spoke so highly of all of you and she trusts you completely or she wouldn't have left her son in your care. I even thought perhaps there was something going on between the two of you that could make her future a little brighter, but I was possibly mistaken about that.

I told the whole story to Etienne yesterday so there are no secrets between him and his mother. That alone should take some of the pressure off her especially in view of the maturity Etienne is showing regarding the whole mess. His only request is that he will get to meet his brother. That is natural and I believe the courage Antoinette exhibited in this matter earns her the right to expect cooperation from Cloris.

There are other decisions to be made concerning the family businesses. When I die Etienne would have been the only heir, but now that the truth is out about Robert, Antoinette is insisting that he be recognized and included in the estate. Etienne feels the same way, but who knows if either of them would want to take over the running of the businesses. It is a huge and lonely job and I wouldn't wish it on anyone.

When my Meaghan died three years ago, I realized how isolated I had been. Since then, my work has filled my days, but not my heart. I am only fifty years old and I am living like an ancient old hermit. I miss Meaghan desperately, but I want to go on and live a life that includes love and laughter. Meaghan and I never regretted our decision to keep Andrew's death a secret. I believe to this day that we did the right thing, but I didn't realize until recently what a burden it was. We lived in constant fear that the truth and our part in it would be discovered and this caused us to shut ourselves off from the life we could have had. I guess we believed that if we kept ourselves "small", we would be less likely to be exposed. We hoped that by keeping to ourselves we did not invite speculation about Andrew and people would forget about him.

I don't know what the future will bring for Antoinette and Etienne. That will be their decision, but I hope that by my coming here and getting to know you, I can enlist your help in watching over them in the short term and that you will contact me if there is any way I can help them. My parents are very old and provide little comfort to me so Etienne and Antoinette are my only family and I want them to be happy. Maybe I can help make up for some of the misery my brother caused. Antoinette is not angry at me for withholding the truth from her all these years, but that doesn't mean she doesn't have a right to be. I would like to stay on for a week to put my mind at ease and then I'll be out of your way. I have to admit, the company you are keeping here makes the idea of staying on a few days more inviting than I could have anticipated."

SAM

Listening to John's story, I was reminded of Alfie's memory of Isabelle's shooting of Mary's father, Etienne's memory of being murdered by his own father, and Bernie's memory of

Luther murdering of his own father. I guess if one has had many lives, it would be these that would stand out and I couldn't help but wonder how many lives throughout history have been ended in the name of love and how many people have lived their lives in fear of discovery. I don't know what would have happened to these people if they were subjected to our legal system for their crimes. Perhaps they would have been shown mercy, but I believe that, with only God as their judge, they have a better chance of being dealt with mercifully. Don't get me wrong, I am a law and order type of guy, but it is hard to imagine a reason why any of these people should be made to suffer more than they had.

Evil people are hard to overcome because they don't play by the rules. They will bring a gun to a knife fight. They hate the goodness in others and despise anything that places restrictions on their power. They view virtue as weakness and love as submission. They defy all rules of civilized human behavior and defile anything that appears wholesome or pure. Perhaps God shows a special kind of grace for those who come face to face with true evil. Maybe he doesn't ask us to turn the other cheek when we encounter evil because these people cannot be influenced through love. It's not my place to decide, but I believe that even God can lose his temper with bad people.

When John and I arrived at the house it was brimming with activity and cheer. Serena was making eggs benedict and I noticed that all the women had taken special care with their appearance, especially Jenny. Antoinette looked rested and happy and Etienne was constantly at her side looking watchful but not worried. I noticed that John made a special point of sitting next to Jenny at breakfast and I caught April making a face at her across the table. Jenny laughed and threw a strawberry at her and I thought they might get into another food fight. Alfie was smiling at Jenny and was unusually quiet as he watched her renew her conversation with John from the night before. John seemed completely at ease and divided most of his attention between Jenny and Etienne. Antoinette asked Amanda if Samantha would be returning any time soon and Etienne, who was talking to John at the time, jerked his head around to Amanda so fast that everyone noticed and started laughing. He didn't seem to care. He just kept his eyes on Amanda who promised to arrange another visit as soon as possible.

Adrian explained to John that Samantha was our granddaughter and John became very serious as he told us how lucky we are to have so many friends and family. He didn't seem a bit embarrassed to show how lonely he was. Jenny looked like she wanted to cradle his head between her perky breasts. While I was wondering where I came up with "perky breasts", I happened to glance at Amanda and she was looking at me with a loving smile. She gave me a slight nod which I took to mean that she was having some pleasant memories of us as a family, but then I worried that she might guess what I had been thinking about. I had to look away. In the past she had shown some talent at reading my mind and I couldn't take any chances. When I looked back at her a few seconds later, she looked a little sad or disappointed. I had screwed up what could have been an intimate moment.

Breakfast over, John asked Etienne if he would like to go for a walk with him. Etienne agreed and added that he would show John the spot where he had his accident. Antoinette said that was a morbid idea, but John wanted to see the spot and have Etienne recreate the story of Jenny's daring rescue. Jenny groaned, but seemed pleased at the same time. Amanda ordered Antoinette to take a nap and the rest of us were on our own for an hour or two.

I noticed that Jenny walked over to Bernie and was speaking to him in a low voice. This, in itself, should have alerted me that something strange was going to happen because no one ever deliberately invited contact with Bernie, but I really didn't give it much thought. I was just happy to have been relieved of the burden of keeping secrets and pleased that everything had turned out so well for Etienne and Antoinette. Bernie responded to Jenny with a look of suspicion, but Jenny kept talking to him in a very earnest manner. Shortly, they put on their coats and left the house, evidently to take a walk. As they passed through the front door, Bernie turned around and looked at me with an expression that spoke of confusion and possibly fear. I guessed old Bernie had never been approached by a woman for a private meeting except maybe on a street corner in a seedy part of town.

I went to the den for some quiet time and was just settling in to start my book, once again on page one, when April burst into the room followed by Camille whose tail was wagging furiously as if she was part of some great adventure. Camille jumped up on my lap and managed to spill my coffee in the process. I am convinced that dogs have no sense of size. Camille thinks she is still a little puppy who can cuddle up on a lap. She kept turning around trying to find room to lie down, but ended up with her tail covering my face and her head hanging over the side of the chair. I didn't want to hurt her feelings, but the coffee had spilled between my legs and was burning some tender parts. April called her and she jumped off my lap spilling what was left of my coffee. April ran and grabbed a towel out of the bathroom and started cleaning up the mess talking all the while she was working. She finally got around to telling me that I had a phone call. I was a little irritated because whoever was on the line had been waiting for about five minutes.

Chapter Forty-Four

RESCUE AND REWARD

SAM

I had heard the phone ring, but someone had grabbed it after the first ring and I figured it was Paul calling for Alfie. It wasn't. It was Thelma calling for me. That was almost as strange as Jenny taking a walk with Bernie. Thelma was very upset and sounded like she was crying, another first. I told her Amanda was taking a nap, but she said she didn't want Amanda. She needed to talk to me.

She needed money and lots of it. That was weird because Thelma had always made it clear that she was well set financially due to her brilliant management of all funds during her marriage and since. As it turns out, she became a little overconfident in her abilities and had set up a margin account with her broker and she was on the wrong side of the stock market and was getting margin calls. She needed fifty thousand dollars immediately. She explained that she was good for it. She just didn't have enough liquid assets at the time. She promised it would be a very short term loan.

She sounded so humble and the dark side of my nature wanted to prolong her agony for a while even though I knew that I was going to help her. I was picturing her sitting at her desk with her head in her hands desperately searching for a solution without having to call me and, somewhere in the process of inventing that image, I saw Thelma in a different light than before. She really had nothing in her life of any real value except her relationship with Amanda and Samantha. I couldn't remember the last time she had mentioned a friend, let alone a romantic interest. I guess at that moment I stopped thinking of her as the mean, nasty, overbearing, self-centered person I had known all these years and for the first time saw her as a lonely, disconnected human being. There was never any doubt in my mind that I would help her, but viewing her in this new way made me want to help her, and do it as kindly and discreetly as possible.

I could have had the money wired to her account but, believe it or not, I wanted to go there and try to offer her some comfort at the same time. I kept asking myself if I was secretly wanting to see her squirm, but I really didn't want that. I told her I would take the first ferry the next day and to meet me at the terminal and we would go directly to my bank. I also mentioned that it wasn't necessary to tell Amanda or anyone else about our arrangement. The relief in her voice made me uncomfortable. I realized that Thelma had never faced this type of adversity before, making it doubly troublesome for her. I wasn't worried about being repaid the money as I knew that she had plenty of assets that could be converted to cash given some time and I was sure that Thelma would not want to be indebted to me for one minute longer than necessary.

I made an excuse to the group and left the next day as planned. I decided that I would drop in on Alex and Tiffany after meeting with Thelma to see if I could bring Samantha back with me for the weekend. I knew she wanted to meet Antoinette and she was dying for a chance to be with Etienne again. I supposed that Amanda and I would be taking a back seat as long as he was around.

Thelma met me at the terminal and within two hours we had her all straightened out with her broker. She was pleasant, but subdued and I could see that she was struggling with some thoughts. When she dropped me off at Alex's house she turned to me and tearfully told me that I was the only person she could think of that could help her and that she had never doubted for a second that I would be willing. That was the closest thing to a compliment that I had ever gotten from Thelma and, although I wondered why she had been so confident, I was pleased to hear her say it. She thanked me once again. I barely got out of the car before she sped away.

By this time it was late afternoon and Samantha was just getting home from school. Alex was still at work so I asked Tiffany if Samantha could return to the island with me. She called Alex and he agreed. Samantha had been having a pretty rough time since her return home. Her friends were all in trouble over the Facebook incident and some of them were being pretty mean about it. Alex and Tiffany thought that a couple of days away would be good for her. We had already missed the last ferry so I called Lake Union Air to see if we could get a flight. I had to pay for the pilot's hotel room on the island since it would be dark before he could fly back. Samantha was ecstatic about getting to go plus the adventure of flying in the small plane. She is fearless. I arranged for Paul to pick us up at the harbor so we could surprise everyone.

Happy hour was well underway when we arrived at the house so everyone was in the living room. Samantha, with her usual style, burst into the house ahead of me and by the time I caught up she was already hugging Etienne and Amanda at the same time. It was just plain sweet watching Etienne introduce Samantha to his mother and, to the surprise of everyone, Samantha greeted her and carried on a short dialogue with her in French. I can tell you this; Antoinette was smitten with her instantly. Etienne knew nothing of Samantha's attempt to learn French, but looked on proudly at her as she conversed, somewhat awkwardly, with his mother. Amanda kept looking at me and smiling and I assumed that she was happy with me for bringing Samantha.

Dinner consisted of spaghetti Bolognese with Italian sausage, fettucini alfredo with chicken and artichokes (lots of pasta to fatten Antoinette), garlic bread and Caesar salad. Serena had somehow anticipated our celebratory mood and had provided us with a good Chianti, a Volpollacella and a Sauvignon Blanc. There was plenty of cannoli and sorbet for dessert. We had one of the best evenings since our arrival.

Jenny seated herself beside Bernie and I noticed that he seemed totally sober and was smiling quietly at everything that was going on. I remembered the walk they had taken the day before and I made a mental note to pry information from Jenny about their conversation. At any rate, it was nice to see Bernie so pleasant and happy and he did seem to have finally made a friend. After my dealings with Thelma and now this change in Bernie, I was beginning to wonder if maybe world peace was an achievable goal after all.

After dinner Samantha announced that she had a memory she wanted to share. By this time, we were so used to having Paul around that there was no question about him being allowed to stay and Samantha specifically requested that Antoinette remain. John simply assumed he would be included as he sat down beside Jenny and she seemed to glow more than usual. Samantha said that her story was one that would forever win her a place in all of our hearts as one of the coolest people in the history of the world- Bill Gates being the coolest. We all laughed, but it was plain that she meant what she said.

SAMANTHA

My name was Martha Swenson and I lived in Reno Nevada in 1873. My husband, Johnny, was a very hard working man but he was also a very large man. I guess I mean fat. I would buy his work pants and within a month, even the more expensive ones would split and rip around the pockets and around the waist. Because of this we had to buy the cheapest pants we could find and the material was scratchy and irritated his skin. There was a tailor in town named Jacob Davis who made pants out of a comfortable and supposedly durable material that he purchased from a company in San Francisco, but these also ripped out on poor Johnny and they were too expensive to replace every month so we had to go back to the scratchy cheap ones.

One day I was sitting on the front porch trying to mend a pair of Johnny's shredded work pants when I happened to glance over at the cover that was stretched over our wagon. This canvas fabric was no stronger than that used by Jacob, yet it didn't tear even with all the hard use. That gave me an idea and I went to Jacob and asked him to make Johnny a pair of work pants out of his special material, but instead of just sewing the pockets and the waist, I suggested that he try using rivets to hold the fabric at stress points like he did on the wagon covers. I told him that if he could make the pants stronger, people like us could afford to buy them because they would last longer. He liked the idea and a week later he delivered to me the world's first pair of blue jeans. (Well, that first pair wasn't blue but I dyed them dark blue so they wouldn't show the dirt.) Johnny was so happy. They were soft and comfortable and we could see that they weren't going to tear no matter what he did. I ordered another pair right away and, as we spread the word our neighbors started ordering them too.

Jacob decided to patent the idea, but he didn't have the sixty eight dollars he needed for the patent fee so he wrote to his fabric provider in San Francisco, a man by the name of Levy Strauss and asked him if he would like to be his partner. Levy paid half the fee and he and Jacob began the blue jean industry and were partners from then on. Johnny and I never got a dime from my idea, but Jacob did keep us supplied with work jeans for the rest of Johnny's life. Johnny died ten years later and Jacob delivered a brand new pair of jeans for him to be buried in stating that those jeans would take him through eternity. I kept every pair of jeans that Johnny had ever owned and made a quilt out of them with Jacob adding rivets to hold it together. I'll bet that quilt still is being used somewhere.

I told you I had made a huge contribution to the world and I'll bet that none of you, in any of your lives, have done anything to make a bigger impact.

ANTOINETTE

Nothing this girl could say would surprise me. When she finished her story she smiled smugly, took a deep diva-like bow, and sat down next to me. Everyone was laughing and thanking her for her contribution. Adrian said that she would contact the quilting society to see if her jean quilt was registered anywhere. I guess in America quilting is considered an art form. What a great idea. I think I would like to learn more about this. Etienne kept looking from Samantha to me.

I think he was trying to see if I liked her as much as he did. I like her very much and I think that is a good thing because I believe she will be a big part of our lives.

That was a very happy evening for me. Etienne was recovering from his accident and the doctors didn't believe there would be any lasting effects other than some scarring on his leg. John was thoroughly enjoying his stay and I remember thinking how much he deserved some happiness after all he had gone through. He did seem a little bothered by all the attention Jenny was paying to Bernie, but it never occurred to me that he would be jealous of such an unattractive and unpleasant man.

I couldn't stop thinking how fortunate Etienne and I were to have found Sam and Amanda. I believe that only God could have brought us to this place with these wonderful people at the exact time our world was falling apart. How else would Etienne have found that website and decided to contact Sam? At the same time, I was not looking forward to taking Etienne home to Toronto where we had so little in terms of friends and family. I realize now that, in trying to protect Etienne from the truth about his father and erase the memory of my poor judgment, my lies had caused me to withdraw from the world, I suppose out of shame and fear of making more mistakes. I am not a cowardly person by nature and I didn't want to live in hiding anymore. I had spoken with Father Karl and told him the whole story. He just listened and then asked me what I was going to do next. I honestly didn't know. Adele, my sister, is happy and comfortable living in Toronto, but I realized that I moved there to feel safe and hide my shame and I don't want feel the need to do that anymore. Certainly, Etienne and I can afford to live anywhere we choose. There is nothing for me in France. I have no family left there. Scotland is out of the question for me and Etienne has plenty of time to decide if he wants to live there and run the family business in the future. John is healthy and strong and can make the necessary decisions for a long time to come. I decided that night that I would ask Etienne what he wanted to do and we could make our plans together. I told myself to relax and enjoy the evening and the days to come. I had put off being happy for too long. I didn't want to end up a sad, pathetic drama queen.

SAM

It was great to see Samantha back to her old self again, especially in view of the rough time she had been having at home. She and Etienne picked up right where they left off and it was clear that Etienne was enjoying having Samantha, Antoinette and his uncle John together. It struck me how lonely he must have been, growing up without a father, siblings, or grandparents. I don't think he and Antoinette did much socializing either, yet he has excellent social skills and seems to enjoy the company of people of all ages. Even with all the attention he was getting from others, he still made time for Adrian. Most kids don't have that kind of sensitivity and loyalty.

It was still early and I had no volunteers for another story. It seems everyone but me had made plans. John and Jenny announced that they were going to go down on the beach and build a fire. John was challenging Jenny to take a swim. She was protesting, but I had the feeling she would not let him outdo her. Kate and Glen asked if they could join them. I could see a slight hesitation coming from John, but he responded enthusiastically. Bernie spoke up saying that it was too cold to go to the beach so he wouldn't be joining them. No one tried to change his mind, but Jenny did give him a nice smile and told him he was the only sane one. He seemed happy with that and retired to his room. Alfie and Paul were going to the kite shop to do an inventory so that Serena would be able to set up her books when she took over. This told me that they might be planning on leaving soon. The thought left me a little depressed as I had sensed for a day or two that we had reached sort of a pinnacle and that we would start to wind down. I hadn't given much thought to how we would decide when we were finished with our project. I had purposely left it open ended, but as I saw the end drawing nearer, I didn't know what I would do with myself after all this. Clearly, most of the group was taking their lives in new directions and I began to feel a little sorry for myself.

Serena, April and Adrian were going to the Sandcastle again and they invited Antoinette, but she was tired and Amanda had ordered her to bed. Etienne and Samantha were locked in conversation by the fireplace and I knew that would go on for hours. As everyone departed, I noticed that Amanda was nowhere to be found. I wandered over to the guest cottage, but she wasn't there either so I guessed she must have decided to go to the beach with the others.

Since I had not been invited to join in any of their plans I decided to go to the den and enjoy some quiet time and read my book starting at page one. After an hour, I convinced myself that I did not want to be there when they returned. I wanted to show them that I had any number of interesting activities to pursue so I left the house and walked to my boat. About halfway down the dock I noticed a pair of women's shoes paced neatly in the center. I couldn't imagine how they got there and they were placed so precisely, it didn't look like they hadn't fallen out of a suitcase. As I pondered this mystery I noticed an article of clothing further up the dock. It was a woman's blouse and it was laid out perfectly. I recognized it immediately as the one Amanda was wearing that night so I knew those were probably her shoes as well. I picked up those items and continued up the dock to only to find a pair of jeans and, further on, a black lacy bra. By this time I was beside myself. I gathered the clothing and tried to run, but I kept dropping items and retrieving them. I was cursing myself for spending that hour in the den when all that time Amanda must have been on the boat waiting for me and wearing---- perhaps only black lace panties that would match the bra I found. By now she could be angry or asleep.

By the time I stepped onto my boat and into the salon, I was convinced that I had blown the opportunity I had awaited for so long. She wasn't in the salon and I wanted to rush into my cabin, but I couldn't make myself go there. It has always been that way with me. I freeze when I get overly emotional. It's not that I am trying to be cool. I just stop functioning as a normal person and I take up some mundane task as if nothing is going on. In this case, I started to make a pot of coffee, but I left that half-finished and made myself a drink. Then I opened the refrigerator as if I was going to make myself a snack, knowing full well that there was nothing in there except ice and a few condiments. Then I closed the refrigerator and took my drink into the bathroom and sat on the toilet with the seat closed. I just sat there watching my ice melt for about ten minutes. Then I panicked, thinking that Amanda might have gotten disgusted and left the boat so I charged the door and flung it open just in time to have it smack Amanda, who was coming to look for me, in the face. She fell backwards and I was trying to get to her but the door was blocking the narrow hallway and I couldn't get myself calmed down enough to methodically close the door before passing through the hall. I was yelling my apology, but she wasn't responding. Finally I managed to get around the door and found her lying on the floor in my bathrobe. It had flown open exposing her lower half encased in the black lace panties that I had imagined. She tried to get up, but couldn't and it took me a second or two to realize that she was laughing too hard to be able to pull herself off the floor. I was so relieved that I forgot to be nervous so I joined her on the floor and that is where we spent the next half hour. The hour after that was spent on the bed and the salon got its share of the action as well.

I hate to disappoint you, but I guess I am too old fashioned to give a detailed description of our lovemaking as you would find in of one of those romance novels, but although I have never been one to kiss and tell, I will say that we were doing a hell of a lot more than kissing. The years of our separation melted away and the passion we had always found with one another returned along with strong evidence that I had not lost my staying power. To me, Amanda was that same angel that I had spotted so many years ago on Tom Carlson's boat and, like that day with the stolen martini, her behavior that night was not exactly angelic. At some point I began to worry about John returning to the boat and walking in on this scene. Amanda assured me that this would not happen and I realized then why I had not been included in any of the plans the group made for that evening.

We talked and laughed for hours. It was better than before. Somewhere in those years apart we had come to recognize and appreciate the essence of each other and the love that we shared. I told her I wanted to make an honest woman of her again and she turned me down. By this time I was over my nervousness so her refusal didn't bother me a bit. I asked if I could propose again the following week and she said yes, but only once per week and I could not ask on a Sunday. I know this sounds crazy, but I was totally satisfied with that response. It was exactly the answer I got the first time around so many years ago.

I finally fell asleep and when I woke up two hours later, she was gone. I was disappointed, but not upset as I finished making the pot of coffee I had started the night before. Then I retrieved and dumped my melted drink from the bathroom where I had left it and prepared to take a shower. It was then I noticed that her clothes were still lying on the chair where I had dropped them and my robe was nowhere to be found. Her shoes were missing too. I threw on a pair of sweats and went out to look for her. There she was, sitting on the end of the dock, dressed only in my robe. It was pretty cold, but she didn't seem to notice and I didn't care. Her hair was all frizzy and her makeup must have found its way to another location, but she looked like a goddess to me.

I searched her face for signs of regret and found none. I asked her why she was sitting outside in the cold and she replied that she was waiting for breakfast and that it would be nice to eat our first meal as a couple reunited, alone. I pointed out that I had nothing in my refrigerator, and she said she knew that and she had called and ordered breakfast delivered from the Sandcastle and was waiting outside to guide the waiter to the right boat. I said I was surprised to learn that they delivered and she replied that they don't but she had told the waiter I would give him a fifty dollar tip if he brought us breakfast. He told her it would be there in no time at all. I had to break the news to her that I only had twenty dollars in cash, but she didn't see a problem. She said I could give him a credit card and we could go in and sign for it later. I had never known Amanda to be so flippant with money, but it pleased me because that meant that she viewed that day to be as special as I did.

The waiter came and Amanda explained our situation and he left with my credit card that had a twenty five thousand dollar credit limit, but I couldn't take time to worry about that. Over breakfast I asked her why the sudden change of heart. She just looked at me and said, "Thelma called me and told me what you did. I know she is a pain in the ass and you would have been justified if you told her to jump in the lake, but you didn't do that. On top of lending her all that money, you weren't going to let me or anyone else know what you did. You helped and protected a woman that had no right to expect anything from you. On top of that, I believe you did it for her, not because she is my friend. That means that you are an amazing person, even more so than I ever knew. I have behaved very foolishly. First, I wanted you to understand and accept something that even I don't fully understand. Then I blamed you for not realizing how important a force the memories are in my life when I never tried to explain this to you. Then, when I did begin to accept how unfair I had been, I let my pride get in the way and we wasted more years. I know you still love me, but I can't imagine why, just like I can't imagine why you helped Thelma. I finally came to the conclusion that you have a great soul. I think you don't have the memories because you already are what you are intended to be while I am still struggling. Most of the people here are further along than I am and I have felt from the beginning like a C student who has been placed in an advanced class. I have been given a crash course in humility and, though it has been difficult, I feel honored to be honored in this way. I would love to marry you again because I never stopped loving you, but I want to give you some time to absorb all that we have seen and heard and make sure that you want me for real and not just out of habit. That is only fair. Now eat your breakfast, you paid enough for it."

I was happy to keep my mouth full of food after Amanda's speech so I couldn't say anything stupid. As she spoke I kept thinking about how she was giving me too much credit and I was wondering why she always has to overthink everything. It's very simple really. From the beginning Amanda had expectations of me that I didn't meet. Whether her expectations were fair or not and whether I didn't try hard enough to discover what she needed is the issue. She did a poor job of letting me know how important it was for me to appreciate the scope of how her memories affected her because she assumed I would sense her need and know how to respond. I didn't spend one moment thinking about helping her, in part because I didn't realize how she struggled, and in part because I was afraid I wouldn't know how to help her. We failed each other and we let our failures destroy our marriage. It's that simple.

Amanda viewed herself as damaged goods and she spent many years trying to hide the damage from me. I just bounced from day to day, believing that if I loved her enough, we wouldn't have to deal with anything that I couldn't or wouldn't understand. We may have failed each other, but we did not abuse one another. There never was an ounce of cruelty between us and there never has been any desire to hurt each other. From my point of view, there is nothing to forgive and nothing to make up for on either side. All we have to do from now on is to make darn good and sure that we take care of one another. I never have had expectations of Amanda beyond that of being my partner and the love of my life. If that makes me a simpleton, then so be it. Her world was more complex and she had every right to expect me to share her burdens as well as her joys but she did not have the right to expect me to understand what she needed without telling me. We both blew it and wasted a lot of years, but I hoped that she would realize that we just need to get on with our lives.

I set the dirty dishes out on the dock thinking that we would get showered and dressed and return to the house. We did return, but not until four o'clock that afternoon. I'll let you decide what detained us. When we entered the house, everyone was there and behaved as if nothing unusual had happened. I think they were trying to spare us any embarrassment. I did catch Glen's eye and he gave me a "man to man" nod and I couldn't help smiling. As for Amanda, she went to her room to change clothes and fix her hair and makeup. Life on the wild side is a lot harder for a woman.

Antoinette sat by me and, leaning her head against my shoulder, said "Oh Sam, you look so happy. I might someday fall in love again so I can have what you give Amanda." I looked down at her and, for the first time, I saw no sadness. She was already looking stronger and healthier and I didn't doubt for a minute that she would find love. I even had someone in mind for her if she wasn't going back to Toronto. Samantha followed Amanda to her room, probably to pry information out of her. When she returned to the house she was smiling and happy and asked if Amanda and I were going to live on the boat or in the condo. I told her to mind her own business and she laughed and said it was her business because she loves us both. Then she ran off to ogle Etienne some more.

Chapter Forty-Five

SAM IN DEMAND

SAM

Dinner was delicious, but then everything seemed delicious that evening. I only had two things on my mind. The first was where Amanda would be sleeping that night and the second was to try to get with Jenny and find out what was going on with her and Bernie. This was the third night in a row that he had little or nothing to drink and he was a perfect gentleman at dinner. He even smiled at Amanda, and not with the nasty sneer that he seemed to reserve for her.

My opportunity came right after dinner when Jenny went out on the deck by herself. I followed her and came right to the point, asking her what in the hell was going on with Bernie. She informed me that I would find out the next day. She said that she and Bernie had planned a little show for us and that I was to find out what kind of miracle I had pulled off by bringing us all together. I told her I was already overcome with miracles so why not give me a preview so that I wouldn't overburden my heart. She laughed her Jenny laugh, but then became serious and said she needed my advice. I told her I hate giving advice, but that I am a good listener.

It had to do with John. That didn't surprise me as I had noticed how much time they spent together, but why not? They are both wonderful, larger than life, fun loving people. I had assumed that there might be something going on between them since he was always finding ways to be alone with her and she seemed more than willing.

She told me that John had asked her to go to Scotland with him. She could have a wonderful career opportunity in restoring the many castles and country estates, but he also made it clear that he had deep feelings for her and hoped that over time their relationship would evolve into something permanent. Jenny confessed that she might already be in love with him but that she had never had a relationship with any man before. I stupidly thought that she meant she was gay so I asked her if John knew that she was a lesbian. She looked down at me and stated firmly, "I mean, I have never been with anyone". I said "Are you telling me that you are a virgin at your age?" With brilliant responses like that, you can see why she sought me out for advice.

Jenny laughed, but not in her usual free style. She explained that, after growing up in a house where her father was always going after her mother and having to witness his disgusting behavior day after day, she had no romantic notions about sex. She liked kissing because her father never kissed her mother, but any time things heated up beyond that point, she lost interest. She had gone to several counselors and they had given her any number of possible approaches, including one "professional" who volunteered his own body to try to awaken her libido. She thanked him for his offer, but declined his services. Finally, she spoke with an older woman who told her that if she met the right man, everything would fall into place. She accepted that as truth and waited for someone to come along. She believed that John might be that person, but what if she was wrong? She admitted that she felt strange new urges when she was around him, but what if she found it impossible to forget the ugly memories from her parents? What if she froze up at the crucial moment? What if she was frigid?

Now how was I supposed to respond to that? I became nervous and you know by now what happens when I am nervous. I grabbed the broom that was sitting in the corner and began to feverishly sweep the deck. Jenny looked at me like I was nuts and started to go indoors. I knew she was hurt so I blurted out the first thing that came to my mind. "How will you know unless you try? You know how it's done, so just do it and see if you like it. I'm pretty sure John wants to." She stopped abruptly and just stood there for a minute with her back to me. Then she gave a hearty, Jenny laugh and turned around to face me with tears in her beautiful eyes. "Well Sam, I guess it really is that simple isn't it?"

I told her that men are basically simple people who are capable of a great deal of understanding and tenderness when it comes to the women they love, but you have to spell out exactly what you need from them. You can't make them guess. They'll blow it every time. Jenny said she would give careful thought to my advice. I felt like I had failed miserably so I went inside and left her alone with her problem. When I looked back at her through the glass door, she was sweeping the deck slowly and mindlessly. I decided to make things easy for her in case she took my advice, so I went to John and told him that *I* would be staying at the house that night and not to expect me on the boat. I knew Amanda would be sharing her room with Samantha so I reconciled myself to another night on the couch in the den.

Amanda and Antoinette were deep in conversation and everyone else, including John who had joined Jenny on the deck, seemed to be busy, so I headed for the den. I hadn't even sat down when Bernie entered the room.

"You still trying to read that book?" He apparently found my efforts amusing because he was smiling when he said it. I set the book back on the desk and asked him what I could do for him. He asked if Jenny had told me that they had something they wanted to tell the group the next day. I told him she had and that I was looking forward to hearing what they had to say. I asked if he would give me a sneak preview, but he said that would spoil the fun. I thought it strange to hear Bernie using the word "fun". He sat down in the desk chair and started fiddling with the mouse for Patrick's computer. I wanted to find out what had put him in such a good mood for the past few days, but I didn't want to break the spell. I guessed that if he knew people thought he was being civil, it might scare him and he would go back to his old self. We sat in silence for a couple of minutes and finally he spoke. "Sam, do you think these lives we are given are "do overs" or are they punishments? I mean, are we given second, third or fourth chances until we get it right or does it just go on forever, one miserable experience after another, until we just fade away?"

I kind of lost my patience. "Who am I, the Dali Lama? I don't even have the memories and here you are asking me to solve the mystery of the ages. I don't want to be rude, but I don't have the answers to these tough questions. I don't even understand the questions so how can I have an opinion? I do think it's pretty obvious that each life has an effect on the next and it can either be positive or negative. You, somewhere along the line, must have had a whopper of a bad time, because you have allowed it to destroy any happiness you might have drawn from this life. That would scare the hell out of me because it could mean you aren't going to get another chance. Maybe you should quit complaining about having to come back time and time again and just be grateful for the chance to get it right. I don't know what you think you deserve that you are not getting, but if I have learned anything from this experience, it is that we should all hope and pray that we don't get what we deserve because we are all seriously flawed. What we deserve may not be to our liking."

Bernie cocked his head to one side and replied, "See, I knew you would have an opinion. Thanks for being so patient with me". Then he left the room.

I got up and shut the French doors as an indication that I wanted to be left alone, but then I opened them again in case Amanda wanted to pay a visit. She was still in deep conversation with Antoinette, but she did come in a few minutes later to say goodnight. She asked if the fact that I was sleeping in the den had anything to do with Jenny and John leaving together a few minutes before. I said that it could and she broke into a terrible rendition of the theme from "THE LOVE BOAT". Did I mention that Amanda is a terrible singer? We sat together for a while and it seemed like those years we were apart never happened. I decided not to make any moves on her since I might be needed to give some more wise counsel. I seemed to be in such great demand.

Chapter Forty-Six

EXIT BERNIE

SAM

I was asleep within twenty minutes after Amanda left the den that night and I slept like a baby. The next morning I awoke to the aroma of cinnamon rolls and bacon. Serena was busy in the kitchen as I went in search of coffee. She was singing one of my favorite Cat Stevens songs, "Morning Has Broken" and I was remembering how much I enjoyed his music before he became a Muslim and decided to hate America. I also noted how sweet her voice sounded as opposed to the screeching sounds I heard coming out of Amanda's mouth when she sang the night before.

Serena was dressed in jeans which she had rolled up mid-calf and she was wearing her hair in a ponytail. She looked like a teenager. It was the first time I noticed how much weight she had lost over the past few weeks. I could tell she liked the way she looked as she glided from stove to refrigerator to sink. She motioned to the coffee maker and handed me my favorite mug. I thought about how much I would miss her when this is over. Not just her cooking, although she certainly has performed wonderfully, but I would miss the peace and joy she brings to a room. She is always the first one to smile or laugh and the last one to complain or criticize.

As if she read my mind she turned to me and said, "I'm so excited about taking over the kite shop, but at the same time I can hardly stand to think of everyone leaving. I am so glad you hired me because this experience has changed my life. You just have to organize a reunion in a year or two. There are still so many stories to be told and everyone here has so many plans, I simply have to know how things turn out. Don't you agree?" Of course I agreed and I promised to keep in touch with everyone with a reunion in mind, but I reminded her that life has a way of taking over and that what we have experienced is a unique place in time that might be difficult to duplicate. With that, we both were silent and lost in our own thoughts until the others started drifting in.

Breakfast was a long drawn out affair that morning, confirming my suspicion that people were starting to think about leaving and that they were hanging on to every moment of our remaining time together. There was a lot of laughter and discussion of future plans, another indication they were getting ready to move on. Amanda smiled at me warmly and I hoped that she was trying to tell me that she was ready to move on with me.

Bernie did not come out of his room for breakfast, but that was not terribly unusual since he often slept in. Serena grabbed the last cinnamon roll off the platter and wrapped it up for him. John looked disappointed, but Jenny told him to quit pouting. They seemed very comfortable with one another. I didn't know if Jenny had returned to the house the night before or stayed on the boat with John and I was trying to think of a tactful way of getting the details. After an hour or so Jenny suggested that I go and wake Bernie since they had planned to address the group together that morning. I went to his door and knocked loudly and called his name several times, but there was no response. I knew from experience that Bernie was a sound sleeper and I also knew that he slept in the nude so I really did not want to enter that room. Finally, I opened the door a crack and I could see him lying on the bed fully clothed except for his shoes. Grateful for small favors, I went over to coax him awake. Now, I have seen very few dead people in my life, but it is not hard to recognize death when you come across it. Bernie appeared waxen and I had the sense that there was no soul in that room other than my own.

I just stood there looking at him for some time and when I finally turned around, there was Jenny looking as confused as I felt. She didn't even notice when I left the room. When I returned to the dining area, everyone was laughing and talking and living their lives. Amanda was the first to notice me and I didn't have to say a word, she read the expression on my face. One by one the others realized something had happened. When Jenny re-entered the room the look on her face said it all. It got very quiet except for the noise Samantha and Etienne were making in the living room arguing playfully about something. Antoinette told them to go to the guest house and continue their discussion. Samantha appeared a little annoyed, but she obeyed. Etienne looked at his mother and it was clear that he knew something was amiss, but he said nothing and left with Samantha. I guess Etienne knows how to recognize a crisis when he sees it.

Glen was the first to speak telling me that I should call the police immediately and that everyone should stay out of Bernie's room. Paul volunteered to make the call since he knew the sheriff personally. Everyone was pretty quiet until Adrian suggested that we say a prayer for Bernie. We all lowered our heads and she led the prayer. "Dear God, we ask you to have mercy on poor Bernie's soul. I never liked him and I won't pretend that I saw any value in him as a human being, but I trust that you are better than me and are able to see the good in all of us and forgive us our weaknesses. Bernie gave us all the chance to examine our hearts and try to love the unlovable as Christ taught us to do. Perhaps that was his purpose in life. I'm certain that, no matter how we each viewed Bernie, we are all sincere in asking that you bring peace and joy to his soul. Amen." I thought the prayer was from the heart and everyone else seemed comfortable with her words except Jenny, who had a strange look on her face. I couldn't read her expression, but I could tell that she was struggling with thoughts of her own.

The sheriff and a deputy arrived within minutes followed by the coroner two hours later. Antoinette and Amanda went to the guest house to explain things to Samantha and Etienne, but the rest of us just sat around occasionally making small talk while the sheriff and the coroner performed their duties. At one point I saw Glen look at the lone cinnamon roll setting on the kitchen counter and watched as his eyes drifted to John. I caught a glimpse of a smile on his face before he lowered his head. Serena caught Glen's action too because I saw her glare at him and throw the cinnamon roll into the trash. Maybe it was a form of hysteria, but that scene caused me to start laughing. I tried to camouflage my laughter by pretending I was coughing, but the look Kate threw at me told me that I wasn't fooling anyone. Still, I could feel the laughter swelling in me and I ran to the den in panic. In the past I had often seen Amanda react in this way to stress. She was afraid to go to funerals for fear of this very thing. I had rescued her from several such situations, but it was a first for me.

Finally the sheriff asked to use the den to interview each of us individually, including Samantha and Etienne. It had not occurred to me that there might be a suspicion of foul play. Paul spoke with the sheriff and reassured us that it was just a formality. In his initial inspection, the coroner had found none of the usual signs that signify heart attack or other common causes of death so he would be performing an autopsy and thought it would be prudent to interview us to see if we knew anything that might shed some light on his health and habits.

Those interviews only served to demonstrate how little we knew about Bernie. The coroner asked me about the scars on Bernie's hands and I did my best to explain them without going into the reasons why he tortured himself. I didn't believe that telling the coroner that he abused himself in order to blot out the horrible memories of past lives would be useful in determining cause of death and it would only create undue speculation about the reasons for our gathering. I did tell him that Bernie was a big drinker but that, to my knowledge, he had been very moderate in that regard for the preceding days. None of us knew what to tell him about living friends or relatives. The only scrap of information I could give him was Bernie's bank information because I had made direct deposits into his account during his stay with us. The coroner looked at me strangely as I explained that Bernie was being paid as a participant in a research study I was conducting. I assured him that we were not testing drugs or any mind altering substance.

We were each asked where we were the night before and if any of us had heard or seen anything unusual. Samantha's eyes were as big as saucers after her interview and she whispered to me that the sheriff must think one of us murdered Bernie. I assured her that was not the case and that the questions were routine, but I wasn't totally certain myself.

Jenny remained silent during the whole episode. She appeared confused as much as upset. She sat by John, who seemed to be the only one to understand her sorrow. He held her hand and tried to show his support in any way he could. Alfie and Serena busied themselves making and serving coffee. Glen suggested we open the bar and have a drink in Bernie's honor but no one seconded that motion. He was embarrassed, but Kate took his hand and gave him a sympathetic smile. April announced that she was going to write the story of Lucy and Luther and send it to her publisher as a remembrance of Bernie in his better days. Jenny perked up immediately and volunteered to help her with that project. They sat at the dining room table discussing how they would structure the story and Jenny looked almost happy. Antoinette and Amanda were busy planning a small memorial service for Bernie and I heard Amanda volunteer me to pay for all funeral expenses. Paul said there was a small cemetery here on the island. He volunteered to get information about purchasing a plot and he would talk to the funeral home about a casket. In the end, there was no plot available so Bernie's remains were to be taken to Seattle for cremation and I was to be presented with the urn containing his ashes as well as the bill. Amanda apparently thought that was amusing because she whispered that she thought the corner shelf in the main salon on my boat would be an ideal spot for the urn. Did I mention how annoying she can be?

By the time the coroner and the sheriff left with the body it was midafternoon and we were all pretty much settled down and in need of a diversion. Serena volunteered to pack up Bernie's few belongings, although we had no idea what to do with them and Amanda said she would clean the room and the bed. This left an empty room which could have served to give John more comfortable quarters than the tiny berth on my boat, but when I offered it to him, he looked at me as if I were trying to throw him into a pit of snakes. Everyone laughed at his reaction, including Jenny. A few minutes later I spotted Glen sneaking into Bernie's room and exiting a couple of minutes later with a shoe box. I didn't want to know what was in that box, but Jenny saw what he was doing and gave him gave him a warm smile as he emerged. I assumed that whatever was in that box was something Bernie would not want Serena to see. I guess maybe we all would hope that someone would hide our secrets for us when we can't do it ourselves. Glen is a real gentleman in my book.

Dinner that night was a quiet, but not somber affair. Bernie was the topic of conversation and everyone had a story to tell about their experience with him over the past few weeks. Although the stories weren't flattering, they weren't told in a malicious way either. Instead, Bernie became sort of a mascot for all the things we would like to say or do at times, but are too afraid to be seen as he was. We were laughing at ourselves for positions Bernie forced on us. Adrian recalled the day she took off on Bernie so harshly and confessed that she only pretended to be sorry for her behavior. In reality she really wanted to strangle him. There was a long pause after her confession and then John suggested that she keep that thought to herself in view of the current circumstances. That opened the floodgate and we all exploded into laughter, releasing the tension that we had held in all day. Samantha told us we were a bunch of creeps and she was ashamed of us. Etienne told her to lighten up and pointed out that she had told him many times that she thought Bernie was a ghoul. She pouted for a few minutes and then told her own Bernie story about how he had told her that Amanda was just trying to recapture her faded youth through Samantha and that Samantha shouldn't try to be like her grandmother because there wasn't another man on the face of the earth that would cater to her like Sam caters to Amanda. Samantha admitted that she might have liked to injure him, but not kill him. Kate said that she never could figure out why Bernie had taken such a dislike to Amanda. Jenny spoke up and told us that she thought Amanda was the kind of woman that Bernie feared because of her strength. Bernie had told Jenny that his grandmother hovered over him all while he was growing up, and never let him make a decision on his own and would criticize him every time he chose a friend or wanted to try something new. He mistook Amanda's strength for bossiness and Sam's love for her as submission. I spoke up and said there is nothing wrong with submission as long as you get what you want. Glen said an "amen" to that comment and Kate slugged him in the shoulder. Samantha picked up on Glen's innuendo and said "Yeouwww". That response prompted me to tell the story about the night Bernie stayed on the boat. When I got to the part about finding him naked on my couch, everyone put their forks down as if waiting for the nausea to pass. From that point on anything anyone said was met with the question "What would Bernie say about that?" and someone would try to imitate him. There were some very clever impressions. It sounds disrespectful, I know, but it wasn't intended that way. At least we found a way to enjoy the memory of Bernie as he really was rather than trying to make him into something he wasn't. It was sort of a tribute. Almost.

Amanda finally asked the question I had wanted to ask all day. She asked Jenny what she and Bernie were going to reveal to us that morning. Jenny said that she was too tired at that point but she would tell us all about it the next day. Finally, everyone got up and helped clean up the dinner mess so I could send Serena home for some rest. The day had been hard on all of us.

Chapter Forty-Seven

SAM

John walked to the boat with me and I told him that Jenny had confided in me about his invitation for her to go to Scotland with him. He stopped and sat down on my special rock and confessed that he was hopelessly in love with her. Things happen fast with this group. I took that opportunity to ask him if she had spent the previous night on the boat with him and he admitted that she had but said that was all he was going to tell me. By the involuntary smile on his face I surmised that Jenny's fears about her sexuality had been unwarranted and I left it at that. John added that Jenny had decided to go with him and they planned to leave in a few days. Alfie was going to take care of shipping Jenny's personal belongings to Scotland and putting her household furnishings in storage for her.

"Sam, I can't believe that I am going to be given this chance to be with this incredible woman. I do worry about Antoinette and Etienne and I hope I can count on you to keep us posted on how they are doing. Antoinette deserves some happiness too and I think that, with all she has been through these past few weeks, it will take her a while to find her footing. Will you and Amanda look after them?" I promised I would do as much as I could and we both knew that, through Samantha and Etienne, I would be kept informed of their decisions.

I found myself wishing that John didn't live so far away. I really enjoyed his company and I hated to lose Jenny. Then I remembered a little invention called the airplane and I thought about the fun Amanda and I could have visiting Scotland. I have to admit, it's fun being rich and able to go anywhere you want, especially when you have someone you love to share your life. Later on the boat, John and I sipped some of my best scotch and swapped a few lies before going to bed. It was a nice way to end a not so nice day.

The next morning found John splashing away in the cold water again. He and Jenny are so much alike in their appreciation of life. As we walked back to the house I asked John if he had any idea what Jenny was going to tell us about Bernie. He said he did, but that I wouldn't believe it unless I heard it from her. He said "You just can't make this shit up!!". I prepared myself for a ride.

Halfway to the house we saw Camille running toward us dragging her leash behind her. She was prancing along in that proud way that dogs do when they have outsmarted their masters. When she spotted us she ran even faster and all I could see was this fifty pound dog coming straight at me. I knew she was going to jump on me, but I didn't have time to brace myself for the impact. I landed on my ass with Camille sticking her tongue into my ear again. I tried to get her off me, but she was all love and no obey. Finally John ordered her to sit and she instantly did as he commanded. He helped me up and took the leash and she walked at his side like a perfectly trained show dog. I was amazed and more than a little jealous. I had never been able to train a dog. I always found it more fun to play with them than to teach them. I paid a price that morning because it had rained during the night and, between the ground and the mud that Camille carried with her, I was a mess from head to toe. I told John to go on to the house while I returned to the boat for some clean clothes and to wash the dog spit out of my ear.

By the time I arrived at the house I figured that breakfast would already be over, but that was not the case. Instead, I walked into a scene of total chaos. There was no Serena. No coffee was made. Nothing was on the stove or in the oven. Nothing anywhere. I thought Amanda must have overslept or she would have taken over and made breakfast, but she was nowhere to be seen either. Adrian was gone, and so was Antoinette, Jenny, Kate, and Samantha. All I found was a bunch of highly incompetent males standing in the kitchen looking totally lost and forlorn. I knew by then we were on our own and help was not on the way. My guess was that the women had risen early and decided to have a girl's breakfast at the Sandcastle. Amanda would know that I am perfectly capable of cooking breakfast for this crowd, but I thought it strange that there was no note or anything to indicate that we should start the day without them. Alfie threw out the idea that there had been a multiple abduction, but we all knew that was not possible given the nature of the potential abductees.

I set John to the task of making coffee which proved to be too much for him so Glen had to jump in. After all, isn't he the one planning to open a coffee shop? I ransacked the refrigerator and took out eggs, sausage, red and green peppers, mushrooms, onions and a huge hunk of cheddar and prepared to make my world famous one pan breakfast. Alfie was put in charge of chopping vegetables and Etienne cracked two dozen eggs into a bowl and whisked them together like he had seen on one of those cooking programs. I crumbled and cooked the sausage and then added the veggies and mushrooms, sautéing them in the sausage grease. Then we put the whole mess in a huge baking dish, poured the eggs on top, added about a pound of shredded cheese and placed the dish in the oven at 350. While that was baking, I started toasting English muffins but the guys kept stealing them as fast as I could toast them so, by the time my dish came out of the oven, we were all out of muffins. It was too late to bake biscuits so I took out a whole box of oyster crackers and fried them in butter with chopped jalapenos and another pound of cheese melted on top of that and we had "cheesy pull-aparts" to go with our breakfast. They were fantastic and Alfie is the one that gave them that name. Everyone agreed that my invention was better than anything they had eaten in the finest restaurants. This was a real man's meal. Camille got what little was left of the egg dish and she licked it so clean that I hardly had to scrub it at all. She was not happy that she was left out of the cheesy pull-aparts, so I made her a small batch of her own, leaving out the jalapenos.

Glen kept the coffee going and we added whiskey to make it cowboy coffee. After about five pots we were a pretty rowdy group. Glen and John proposed that since we had done such a great job on breakfast, we should make dinner too. We decided on chili and cornbread. I found a prime rib roast in the freezer and we defrosted it in the microwave enough so that we could cut it into small pieces. We browned the meat with some garlic and some more jalapenos and began the process of rummaging through the pantry to find the remaining ingredients. I have always been known to make the best chili around, but I backed off that day and let them have their fun. I figured I could fix it up later if it didn't taste right. John was especially excited about our project as he had only had canned chili in Scotland and was anxious to try the real thing. The chili was bubbling in a huge pot where it would remain for the duration of the day. The beans were cooking separately in deference to the Texan in me. We Texans do not put beans in our chili. You can eat beans or rice, or rice and beans on the side, but they don't go in the chili pot. This was the only point that was not negotiable with me.

The girls finally came home shortly after noon. We told them what a good breakfast we had and that we were taking over the kitchen for the entire day. Amanda looked into the pot at what we were passing off as chili, but didn't say a word other than to praise us for taking charge. It was as I had guessed. They had all decided to go to the Sandcastle for breakfast and yes, they did leave a note. It was then that Etienne discovered the slobbery, tooth marked piece of paper lying in the living room. Camille strikes again. She must have chewed the note just before she made her escape from the house. Adrian admitted that she put the leash on her to take her for a walk, but abandoned that idea when the girls decided to make their break. I guess Camille thought she should get a break too and she must have made her escape in the confusion of getting everyone out the door and into Serena's car.

Finally, we settled in the living room to hear what Jenny had to say. She sat in Bernie's usual chair which she had placed in the center of the room.

JENNY

"Sam, I know you remember that day I invited Bernie to take a walk and I know you have been dying to ask me about it ever since. We walked about halfway to your boat and I told Bernie to sit on that big rock because I had something to tell him. He didn't argue with me. I guess he was surprised to have someone actually seek him out for a conversation.

You might also remember that some time ago I mentioned that I had shared a past life with someone in the group. Well, that someone was Bernie. When he first started to tell the story of Lucy and Luther, I didn't realize that we shared that life. It was only when he got to the part where he met Horace Spencer in the park that I recognized the truth. You see, I was Horace Spencer. Everything happened exactly as Bernie told it. As Horace, I didn't realize that Lucy was really a boy for a long time. I thought that I had adopted a young girl who had lost her parents and would be left penniless to face the world alone. I had become very fond of Lucy through our many visits in the park and I was lonely after the death of my wife and daughter. When Lucy told me her mother had died, I wanted to rescue her from a dreadful fate and rescue myself from my loneliness. Those years were happy for me and I was glad to be able to provide a future for Lucy even after my death. Bernie was right. Luther made a nice looking girl dressed as he was. She was no great beauty, but with the inheritance I could provide her, I had little doubt that she would make a good match and lead a happy life. I can only imagine the efforts poor Luther had to make to maintain his Lucy body.

That day in the park when Lucy's father bumped into me, I saw him pass her the note. I had sensed before that day that there was something Lucy wasn't telling me about her circumstances, but she was young and helpless and if she had a secret that she didn't want to share, I would let her keep it rather than cause her pain or embarrassment. When I saw the note being passed, I realized that she might be in some danger or was placing herself in harm's way and I decided to keep a close eye on her. I followed her that night instead of going to my bridge game. I couldn't hear their entire conversation, but I thought I heard him call her Luther and I could sense the evil in that man. I could also see that she was frightened and upset and I suspected that one or both of us was in imminent danger. I didn't know who the man was at first, but as I watched them in the dim lamplight, I could see a strong resemblance and realized that Lucy was escaping more than just poverty. She was escaping her father. As she left him, I heard her say "tonight then" so I knew I wouldn't have to wait long for answers.

I waited until the time I usually got home from my game and then I went directly to my room and sat on the bed listening and praying. Later, I heard Lucy moving around and I heard scraping sounds as if something heavy was being moved. I opened my door a crack hoping that any sound I made would be muffled by her activity. I laid on the floor, watching and waiting for something to happen. I didn't hear the man come up the stairs, but I saw Lucy spring out from behind the screen she had moved to conceal herself and strike him with something heavy. I heard him fall and I couldn't see what else happened, but one thing I knew for sure; Lucy was not a girl. I remembered her father calling her Luther and it all fell into place. The way she moved and the force with which she struck the intruder could only have been the work of a male. She went downstairs and I crept to the top of the stairs in time to see her holding a cushion over his face. When she removed the cushion, I had no doubt that he was dead.

I can't tell you why I didn't make my presence known at that moment. I just wanted time to think so I went back to my room and sat on the bed for a long time trying to absorb all that I had seen. Little by little it came to me that what she had done was to protect me. I knew that when the body was found in the morning, it would appear that a burglar had entered and fallen. I could tell the police that a suspicious character had been around asking questions and my servants would identify the victim as that same man. No one would suspect a frail old man or a young helpless girl and there would be no apparent motive. I had to believe that, whatever her reasons for killing the man, she had to have thought that it was the only way to protect me. This was an evil person who intended to harm me and possibly Lucy, so there was no reason to step forward, just as there was no reason to tell Lucy that I knew the truth about her. I didn't want our lives to change and I certainly didn't want her life ruined. I decided to let the body be discovered in the morning and within a few days, everything would return to normal. I loved Lucy like a daughter and I had already lost one daughter so it wasn't difficult for me to go on as before. After that night I never thought of her as Luther again.

All of this, I told Bernie and at first he didn't believe me. I was able to convince him by describing several details about our lives that only Horace could have known. I was able to tell him the names of all the servants and I described in detail the room Lucy had occupied in my home. Finally he accepted the truth and he began to cry. I told him that, as Horace, I had loved him deeply and that even after I discovered his Luther identity, my devotion to him did not dwindle. I thanked him for the happiness he had brought Horace and I told him that Horace would have been proud of the way he lived out his life as Luther, even though things didn't turn out quite as Luther wanted them to. I told him that Luther was not like his father and that, with all that had happened to him in his youth, he had still managed to bring some goodness to the world and that few people could survive such a horrible childhood without becoming evil. I told him he had lived a good life.

Bernie sat there for a long time and when he looked up at me, I knew he was seeing Horace. I didn't move or say anything. I couldn't read his expression but as we looked at each other it was as if his face changed into that of Lucy's. I knelt down and he placed his head on my shoulder and I felt him melt into his former self. It was like a reunion. I didn't see that nasty person that was Bernie, and I knew he was experiencing the love he felt for Horace. When we rose and walked back toward the house he took my hand as a little boy would hold his father's. When we arrived at the house, he went directly to his room and as he closed his door, he smiled at me. He looked wonderful."

SAM

Aside from the fact that it was impossible for me to picture Jenny as Horace Spencer, I never doubted her story and I had witnessed myself the bond that had developed between her and Bernie in those last couple of days of his life. He seemed happy and, for the first time since his arrival, I felt that he believed he truly had a place in the group and maybe even in this world that he had previously viewed as such a dark place. It occurred to me that Bernie felt "redeemed" by the information Jenny had given him.

I think we have all wondered from time to time about how our lives might have been different if we had known what we didn't know. I'm not talking about the wisdom that we acquire as we get older. I'm talking about facts that we didn't perceive or that were hidden from us at the time. What if that shy boy in high school had known that the pretty cheerleader, who was the object of his dreams, actually thought he was really hot but was afraid to let him know? Would he have altered his perception of himself and become a more confident young man? Would that have allowed him to take more chances and bring him the life he secretly craved? What if the young woman who married the dark, serious man knew that he had spent his childhood watching his father beat up on his mother?

Instead of believing she was marrying a deep intellectual, she might have sensed that his quiet charm was a mask for his violent nature and chose another. What if the young executive had known that his boss hated his guts and felt threatened by his talent? He might have been more vigilant and not allowed himself to be trapped by the lies his boss told about him. I'm sure there are times when not knowing the truth has saved us from disaster as well. Perhaps a professor secretly believes that a certain young man who is struggling to be a journalist has no talent whatsoever yet doesn't voice that opinion but rather lets him believe he will be the next Walter Cronkite. Would the young man have still become a success as a world renowned journalist if he had been aware of the professor's true feelings, or would he have given up?

Bernie found out that Horace understood and approved of his life as Lucy and Luther and that was all it took to change his view of himself and the world. I guess we could feel bad that it took him so long to learn the truth, but he did learn and that brought him some happiness. I was beginning to suspect something about his death, but I didn't share my suspicion with anyone because it was kind of "out there". I wondered if hanging out with all these mystical people was turning me into Shirley McClaine.

Chapter Forty-Eight

THE FINAL DAYS

SAM

It has now been over a week since Bernie's death and what a roller coaster ride it has been. The coroner has declared that Bernie died of natural causes. The final word was heart failure, but there had been no heart attack. His heart just stopped beating. I guess ultimately, that is true of everyone who dies, but in this case the coroner was unable to isolate any specific cause. He had sent blood and tissue samples to a lab in Seattle looking for signs of poison or drugs, but the results were negative. Apparently Bernie just laid down and died, which exactly fit the scenario I had worked out in my mind. Jenny and I had a conversation along those lines and she agreed with me. It wasn't that Bernie wanted to die. It was that he wanted to get on with another life and get rid of the mess he had made in this life. Bernie had told us that he didn't believe his next life would be any better than this one, but I think, and Jenny agrees, that he changed his mind.

Bernie had told Jenny about a life after that of Luther's where he was falsely accused and convicted as a pedophile and spent three years in prison before being murdered by another inmate. During those years he was severely beaten many times and abused daily in the manner that pedophiles are often punished in prison. Prior to his Luther life he had another short life in which he starved to death as a child. There were other stories, none of them good, but Bernie claimed that his experience with our group and the reunion with Horace had given him hope that he could have a better life next time around. Jenny believes that he decided to step up the process by leaving this life prematurely. She also believes that his death was not an act of suicide. She thinks he just asked to be relieved of his Bernie body and mind, and his belief was strong enough to take him out of this world. Jenny had seen much the same thing with her mother's death and she has always believed that her mother was given another life that was better than her last. Jenny said she was happy to have served Bernie, both as Horace and in her current life.

The group is in the process of disbanding. I am sad and happy and that seems to reflect everyone's feelings. We are all anxious to get on with our lives, and every life has taken a huge turn, including mine. Each of them has rejected my offer to buy their plane tickets home and each has forbidden me to add any more money to their personal accounts as originally promised. That makes me feel good, not so much because it saves me money, but because it tells me that they believe they have benefitted by the experience.

I can't begin to tell you how happy I am with the outcome of these past few weeks. I won't take credit for all of this because I have come to believe that I was directed and guided by a higher power to be an instrument in what I and others consider to be a miracle. How else would I have thought of this project in the first place? Who directed each member of this particular group to my website? How else could Bernie and Jenny have been brought together? I don't understand the full picture of how our meeting will affect the future lives of many or all of us, but I do believe there will be significant results and I am honored to have served a small role.

As for me, my goals have been achieved. I get a "do over" and I don't have to wait until my next life for it to happen. Amanda and I will be sharing our lives, only better than before. She has agreed to marry me again and we are going to have that ceremony performed here on the island before we return to Seattle. Our love for one another has never been stronger and we now have something else to make our union complete-total trust and acceptance. There will be no more secrets, no denials, no barriers.

KATE

Glen and I are leaving tomorrow to begin our new life together. When Glen told me about his plan to open a coffee shop, I had serious reservations regarding the viability of such a plan, but I was reassured when he told me that he had the financial means to cover his losses indefinitely and still be financially secure. Not that I cared so much about the money, our life will be very simple and we won't need much to support us. I just wanted to make sure he understood what he was getting himself into. With that subject covered, I am free to experience all the joy our life together will bring. I never dreamed I could be so happy and feel so excited about the future. I will be able to serve my tribe, and love and be loved. I am confident that Glen is ready for a quieter life and we can always take little vacations to visit all our new friends. I wonder if Sam realizes what a miracle he has pulled off for all of us. However, I think he had help. I can't even remember what directed me to his website, but I knew instantly that I had to come.

I am no longer worried about losing communion with my ancestors. It's all there in my heart and my soul. I think it's there for everyone if they take the time and make the effort to bring it to the surface. The "it" I refer to is the common thread that has run through every human being since the beginning of our life here on earth. That thread is love. We are all created through our Creator's love, and our souls' are directed to love and nourish each other and our earth. It is our duty to protect our souls from getting sidetracked by the evil, ignorance and fear that our frail human minds create. Anyone can do this. We who have the memories in this life may not have them in the next so it is crucial that we build our souls to make them strong enough to carry us through the next challenge. I guess it is sort of like "carb loading" before a marathon. I have never felt stronger, less fearful, and more in love with God, our world, our people and Glen.

GLEN

I can't add a thing to what Kate has said except that I am a hell of a lot better business man than she is giving me credit for, and I plan to build a bustling business. My guess is that within a year, I will know everyone on the reservation and I plan to introduce the entrepreneurial spirit to others who want to create a satisfying and productive life for themselves and their families. I have never felt more energetic and happy. I didn't realize before I came here how isolated and lonely I had become. Like Kate, I can't remember what took me to that website, but I thank God for the nudge. Kate is right.

Everything we think and do should be about love. That is a tall order in today's world, but that's what we are directed to do and it is not for us to judge or understand why we, God's greatest creation, so often fail. We just have to try to be part of the solution, not part of the problem. I intend to give my best effort to whatever challenges God sends me.

If you get to North Idaho, take I-95 south out of Coeur D'Alene for thirty miles and stop and enjoy a great cup of coffee and some Indian fry bread or huckleberry pie.

ALFIE

Paul and I are leaving tomorrow as well. We are going to my home to deal with Jenny's belongings and to load up my "stuff" and take it to San Francisco. Paul is going to create some fun and non-violent video games and I am going to build my design business. The thought of being so far from Jenny makes me want to cry, but the happiness I am seeking lies with Paul and I suspect hers lies in Scotland. I am thankful that we live in an age when we can communicate daily and visit in person often. I told Jenny that if things don't work out with her and John, she will always have a place with us. Paul feels the same way. Who would have thought that after all these years of being the center of each other's lives, we would come to a remote island and each find a new center?

I will miss everyone, especially Sam. He is such a good and generous man and his devotion to Amanda has touched all of our hearts in a world where such loyalty and unselfish love seem to be disappearing. Adrian will have April's farm whipped into shape in no time and I can foresee many happy years still ahead for that amazing woman. I told April that I have never in this life ridden a horse, so she should have a couple of sweet, gentle ones available when we two tenderfoots come for a visit. Who knows? Paul and I may decide to drive all the way to North Idaho for a cup of coffee and some of Glen's humor. There is also talk of a two year reunion and we are game for that, although I can't imagine anything that would compare with the past few weeks. Still, I do have some more great stories to tell and I'll bet the others do too. It's strange to say this, but if we do have a reunion, I will miss Bernie. Somehow we seem to have learned more from him than anyone else. It's scary how low we can sink if we let our guard down and reject the opportunity to give and receive the gifts of love, understanding and forgiveness.

APRIL

Well, I wasn't with the group for very long, but what a trip it was. We left on the early ferry yesterday morning and everyone came down to the dock to see us off. Grandma Adrian cried and I realized that I had never seen her do that before, not even when grandpa died. I am so happy that I was able to buy my farm. It's been a dream of mine for a long time and it is giving grandma a new lease on life, not that the old one had expired. That spooky old lady will never suffer from boredom or be unhappy.

I didn't meet the man of my dreams like Kate and Jenny did (Actually I did meet the man of my dreams, but he picked Jenny instead.), but I did meet myself again. Before this trip I was beginning to wonder just who I was. I was too cowardly to come here myself so I talked grandma into coming to test the waters for me. I am ashamed of myself and I can never let myself get that lonely or fearful again.

I had such a great time with Jenny. The first time I get another lump sum of cash, I'm going to Scotland to visit her and to stare at John. Better still, grandma is loaded, so maybe I can get her to spring for the trip. She thinks the world of Jenny, so I wouldn't be able to go without her anyway. If I can convince her to go to some island to join a bunch of spooky strangers for a few weeks, I should be able to make her believe the trip is her idea. It will just take a little creativity and I have plenty of that. In any case, I am so happy that she is coming to live with me on the farm. She has always been my rock. I still have so much I can learn from her and I know she will be happy there. When we were on the ferry yesterday she asked if she could raise a couple of pigs and have a horse of her own. She's like a little kid on her way to Disneyland. I love her so much.

Everyone was talking about a reunion in a couple of years. I have a few ideas on that. My farmhouse is large with two extra bedrooms and there is a bunkhouse that could easily be divided into three rooms. I'll bet we could get old Sam off his boat for a couple of weeks if I gave him some horses to ride. After all, he is from Texas. Besides, he's going to want to see Camille again. When we boarded the ferry, everyone was there to see us off. Amanda was all hugs, kisses and crescent roll eyes. There were tears all around, but Sam really broke down when Camille jumped up and stuck her tongue in his ear. We all laughed and it took some of the edge off the moment.

For me, this experience was not as profound as it seemed to be for the rest, but I have Grandma to fill in the blanks. She is a great teacher, even when she doesn't say a thing. Her hardest moment was saying goodbye to Etienne, but he just winked at her and said, "I have a plan, see you soon". With that, we turned and left, Camille in the lead.

SAMANTHA

Grandpa called my dad the morning after Bernie died and told him what happened. Dad was on the next ferry to come and get me. I think he was pretty upset that this happened while I was here. Grandma and grandpa were worried that he would be mad at them, but I knew my dad. He wouldn't blame them.

He got here at noon and joined us for lunch. I was really excited about introducing him to Etienne. I wanted them to like each other and that made me a little nervous. I introduced him to everyone else first so that he would be able to spend the most time with Etienne. Antoinette was over at the guest house so that came later.

Etienne stepped forward and shook my dad's hand and called him "sir". I could see that that impressed dad, but what came next really blew me away. Etienne just came right out and suggested that dad spend the night instead of returning that afternoon. He told my dad that he hoped to be part of my life for a long time and he wanted dad to have a chance to get to know him and his mother. He didn't look embarrassed or nervous at all. In fact, my dad looked more nervous than Etienne. I thought that was pretty cool. Dad said we were expected home that evening, but he would think about staying. About then, Antoinette came in and I introduced her. Dad could hardly speak. My mom is really pretty, but Antoinette is so beautiful that I finally understood what people mean when they say something took their breath away. It sure worked that way on my dad! He looked really silly and when he looked at grandpa it was like they were reading each other's minds. I know my dad is nuts about my mom, but I guess men will always get all goofy around a beautiful woman, even when they are in love with someone else. I thought it was funny and I was pretty sure we would be spending the night. Then grandma begged him to stay and he said yes.

Lunch was awesome. At breakfast Serena said that since that was my last day, I could chose whatever I wanted for lunch. I chose macaroni and cheese so that was the main dish and it was better than any I had ever had. She said she used four kinds of cheese. I had two helpings and Etienne had three. We also had a spinach salad with those little oranges in it and she made a huge basket full of these little breadsticks that had some herbs all over them. My dad laughed at how many she had made, but just shook his head and smiled when he saw John and Glen fighting over the last one. He said he had never seen such big eaters, but I pointed out that he had eaten at least six of them himself. Grandpa said it was lucky the group was leaving soon or we would all have to go directly to a fat farm. Grandma threw an olive at him and told him to speak for himself. She was smiling when she said it, but I noticed she pushed her plate away with a lot of food still on it. Glen reached over and stole the half of breadstick still on her plate and popped it in his mouth. My dad thought that was pretty funny and I could tell he was really enjoying himself.

The rest of the day was really great. My dad spent a lot of time talking to Etienne and Antoinette and I could tell he liked them both. I felt so grown up introducing him to all those old people and he said he was glad I had been allowed to visit because he could see that they were some really fine people. He spent time with everyone. Alfie had him in stitches and he said Jenny was an angel. I had never heard him say anything like that before and I remember thinking that everyone there talked different than they did in the real world. He really liked Glen and they talked for a long time about business and even exchanged e-mail addresses. Dad told Glen to let him know when he gets his coffee shop open and he would drive to Idaho for a visit. Knowing dad, I'm sure he will keep that promise.

Before dinner, while everyone was enjoying "happy hour", dad had a long conversation with Adrian. They were sitting off by themselves, but I overheard enough of their conversation to know that they were talking about the memories. (I am really good at eavesdropping. I learned it from grandma.) Actually, dad was listening and Adrian was talking. He looked real serious. I hoped Adrian could convince him that they were real because I don't think he ever believed grandma and me. Anyhow, when they quit talking dad went over to grandma and gave her a great big hug. Grandma got tears in her eyes and that gave me tears too.

I felt kind of bad because if Bernie hadn't died my dad would not have come to get me and I was glad he was there. That doesn't mean I was glad Bernie died, but I didn't feel that sad either. Life sure can be confusing.

At dinner grandpa said he had an announcement to make. I pretty much knew what he was going to say, but I could see he was excited, so I kept my mouth shut. Grandma looked a little embarrassed and I was thinking that she looked kind of young. Anyhow, Grandpa tapped on his glass like they do in the movies and everyone got real quiet. Then he said that grandma had consented to become Mrs. Sam Merrick again and they would be married there on the island before they returned to Seattle. Everyone cheered and toasted with their glasses and my dad had tears in his eyes. I guess no matter how old you are you still want your parents to love each other. It makes you feel like love lasts forever and whether you are a kid or a grownup that is a good feeling. Grandma asked my dad if he and mom would come back for the wedding, and me too of course. He said he wouldn't miss it for the world. He said it wasn't everyone that gets to be present at their parents' wedding.

Everyone stayed up late and we had a great time that night. Jenny put on some music and my dad danced with Adrian a bunch of times. She did most of the leading but he followed really well and after a few dances he got pretty brave and was twirling her around. I had never seen my dad dance like that before. I told him he just had to show my mom all those new steps. They hadn't danced together in a long time. There was a guitar in the den and Etienne brought it out and played a sad French song and Antoinette sang. She has a beautiful voice and everyone wanted her to sing more, but she said she only knew sad songs and she didn't want to spoil the party. My dad slept on the couch in the living room. He could have slept in Bernie's old room, but he said he'd rather take the couch. I didn't blame him. After everyone else went to bed Grandma stayed up and talked to him for a long time. I stayed awake until she came to bed and she told me that she had never been happier in her whole life.

The next morning we had a great breakfast and then we had to leave for the ferry. I wanted to cry but Antoinette told me that she and Etienne would be staying for the wedding so I would be seeing them again in a week or two. I was still sad because I knew everyone else would be leaving soon and I might not see them again.

I know that this experience is one that will stay in my mind forever. I am going to have a good life no matter what because of the things I have learned from these people. I think I will someday marry Etienne. I know that sounds like a dumb thing to say at my age, but I can't imagine being with anyone else. I am a lucky girl. I hope I can get a new dress for the wedding, grandma and grandpa's that is.

ADRIAN

I don't have much to add to what everyone else has said. My life has been so wonderful. Oh, I have often wished that Clive would have lived longer and that we could have shared our old age, but I know I'll see him someday. I mourned his death and grieved for him in my own way, but that it is just part of living and I can honestly say that I accepted that grief as part of the whole package and never have I wasted a day in self-pity. I have had lives where I lived in fear and pain and I know what a waste of precious time that is.

When my dear father died I cried for a week. One night Clive and I were lying in bed and I was crying and he turned to me and said, "Go ahead and have your tears. Your father was a wonderful man and I miss him too, but when I die I don't want you to let yourself suffer like this. You get one day to cry your eyes out and then I expect you to get up and do something useful". That is exactly what I did. The day after he died I loaded up his horse and delivered it to a neighbor boy who had been very close to Clive. The boy loved horses and his parents couldn't afford to buy him one. The next day I ordered feed and hay to be delivered on a regular basis and had it billed to me. Keeping Clive alive in that boy's mind was the best therapy I could have given myself. April needs me. She is struggling and I can and will be there for her. The farm is a wonderful idea for both of us and I look forward to raising my pigs.

Etienne has carved himself a place in my heart forever. He is a fearless young man and that alone will carry him through anything he will face in the future. He and his mother are going to live a healthier and happier life from now on. I can already see Antoinette beginning to bloom again and I can't wait to hear what they decide to do next.

As for Sam, let me just say that he hung in there and got the girl. and brought a lot of happiness to a lot of people in the process. Amanda once said he was almost like an Eagle Scout. Well he finally got his badge.

If there is anything I would like you to take away from the stories we have shared with you, it is to live and love fully, without fear. If you can do that, everything else will fall into place. You won't be troubled by anger and hatred. Those pesky deadly sins will find no place in your life and you will be an inspiration to others. I want to stress this above all to women because you are the people who teach love, inspire trust and have the innate ability to influence through gentle persuasion, one person at a time. Others who serve as leaders and role models need the help of the gentler sex to remind them of their mission from God. I am not saying that women cannot be leaders and they certainly are role models, but I firmly believe that God gave women a special gift. It is our ability and willingness to serve our families, our communities and our God unselfishly in all the seemingly small arenas of life without demanding fame and power. The order and subtle guidance this provides is what brings civility to a chaotic world. Too many women are denying themselves the honor of serving in this role. They strive to be more like men in order to gain the power that they perceive as being superior to that of their mothers. It doesn't work. Over time, the structure that keeps families and communities together erodes and we lose some of the connection that God intended us to have with him and each other. Of course I don't mean that women should be passive little doormats. That would be a waste of a great deal of talent. What I am saying is that, for those who enter the world outside of the home, use fully the skills that you use at home to accomplish your goals. Lead by example. Don't allow rationalization of improper behavior. Be fair, but firm. Give praise and credit where it is due and nurturing and direction where it is needed. Punish offenders and remove those who will not learn to be part of the organization so that you don't have to make ridiculous and ineffective rules and laws to include those who perform their duties well. Show courage in your decisions, but make your decisions based on knowledge, fairness and sound judgment, not the hot button of the day. Negotiate but don't make "deals". Demonstrate and demand integrity in all you do and all you supervise. In other words, take the principles that guide you in caring for your family and community to the workplace and be incorruptible and steadfast. Don't worry about the person who acquires more wealth or power than you do through unscrupulous means and don't give in to their tactics. You may not achieve fame and fortune, but whatever you gain will be real and yours to keep and share with others.

It would be a sad world without the strength and courage that men possess, but the virtues and gifts that God gave women are just as powerful if they are properly applied. So whether you are a man or a woman, know what God expects of you and then do it. Use all of the wisdom and love your soul possesses. You can't use up love. The more you use it, the more it grows.

JENNY

Who would have thought two months ago that I would be going to Scotland with a man that I have known less than a month, and Alfie would be going to his new life in San Francisco! Yet, I am not the least bit scared. This life has not always been easy, but I don't regret one minute because it all fit together to bring me to this point. I couldn't have dreamed up a better man for me than John. It's silly, but I even enjoy the fact that he is taller than me.

He has led a "restrained" life as have I, but we are both ready to go out there and enjoy the world. I'm going to have some real challenges building a career in Scotland, but I'm not worried. John will be my first client and he says he has a kitchen and seven bathrooms that need my immediate attention. I am so excited about working in those old homes and castles that I could pee my pants just thinking about it. John has few friends because he and Meaghan isolated themselves to protect their secret about Andrew's death. We will make our own friends together and I'm trusting that we will have visitors from this part of the world as well.

It's funny. With all the wisdom and knowledge from so many lives that we have shared here, I have to say that I learned the most from Sam with Bernie as a close second. Sam, because of the love and devotion he has shown to Amanda and Samantha and the generosity of his gift to the rest of us. Oh sure, he would say that he had ulterior motives in bringing us together, but that doesn't account for his constant concern for our comfort and wellbeing, which was well beyond that required to make this journey a success. Then of course, there is the added benefit of having shared the experience with Serena and her magic kitchen.

Bernie is a close second because of the example he set as one who denied himself love and lived a life of fear and rejection of his gift. Bernie was not an evil person, he was a void in the universe of mankind. This showed me that evil does not have to be present for there to be destructive influences. Bernie generated hate and revulsion by his failure to see the beauty in the world and his refusal to believe that he could create anything worthwhile in his life. I believe his mistake was so disastrous to his soul that in the end, when

Bernie realized what he had done, God showed him mercy and granted him his death so that his soul could be rejuvenated before it was totally destroyed. From this I learned two things. First is that our souls can become brittle if we don't care for them and second that God loves us unconditionally and will shower us with his grace if we ask for it.

I once drove through a neighborhood with tree lined streets and expensive homes. It could have been so beautiful were it not that all the homes looked alike and all were painted in taupe, tan, or light gray. The homes were landscaped with the same shrubs in the same locations and even the numbers on the houses matched. People paid a lot of money to live there, but that neighborhood did not feel like it was alive. I wondered if I could awaken the soul of even one street by sneaking in and painting one of the houses a nice butter yellow with pure white trim and a red door, maybe plant some bright colored zinnias by the porch. That neighborhood is how I visualize souls that are languishing instead of growing. Then along comes one thriving soul and pretty soon one or two other souls get a new paint job and some bright flowers. They look so inviting that other souls join the parade and voila, you have a whole new scene, one that invites you to join. That is the reason we are given the memories. We are to be that first yellow house. Maybe in a past life we were one of the gray houses and a yellow house brought us to life and it is now our turn to carry it forward. I want to be the yellow house and John says he will be the red door. Sam is a yellow house without even knowing it. Everyone at Sam's place is a different color with different landscaping and it has been my joy to visit this neighborhood. If your soul needs a paint job, look one of us up, we are easy to find. Just put your lips together and smile.

AMANDA

During the days after Bernie's death, everyone was preparing to leave for their new lives. Once the coroner released the results of his investigation, Sam accompanied Bernie's body to Seattle for cremation and to claim the ashes. The rest of us were given the task of preparing a memorial ceremony for Bernie. Glen stepped up to take the lead in that project. Sam did not want to keep the urn with Bernie's ashes and we had been unable to locate any living relative. We didn't even try to find a friend since none of us could imagine that he had one. Glen promised to find an alternative to Sam's salon as the final resting place for the urn.

Before he left with Bernie's body for Seattle, Sam received a mysterious phone call. He took the call in the den with the door closed and refused to tell me or anyone except Glen about the caller. All he said was that when he returned from Seattle, he would have a big surprise for us. Glen took great pleasure in being the only one who knew what was going on. He even refused to tell Kate. I feigned indifference.

When Sam returned two days later he was accompanied by a stranger. Serena and I were in the kitchen working on dinner. Sam crept into the room and grabbed me from behind. I jumped out of my skin and Sam was still laughing when I came face to face with the mysterious stranger. He looked exactly like Jack Nicholson. I expected him to come out with "Honeyyyyy, I'm hooooome". He had that same grin and one eyebrow raised so high it almost joined his scalp. He was wearing black slacks and a black turtleneck sweater. I searched my memory bank to see if this was someone from our past that I should recognize, but I came up blank. Just then, Antoinette entered the room and shrieked as she ran into the stranger's arms. Etienne heard her and hurried into the room as fast as his chair could carry him. Spotting the stranger he wheeled over and stretched his arms toward the man. Antoinette turned to me and introduced the man as Father Karl.

He had called Sam to find out how Antoinette and Etienne were faring and Sam had invited him to come and see for himself. They arranged the pickup in Seattle while Sam was conducting his Bernie business. Sam grinned from ear to ear as Antoinette ran to him and gave him a hug and several kisses. It was wonderful to see her so animated.

As each person entered the room, their first reaction was the same as mine. Father Karl looked so much like Jack Nicholson that it took a second or two to realize that it wasn't the great actor in the flesh. The second reaction was always a nervous laugh as Etienne or Antoinette made the introductions. Glen was especially gregarious in order to play up his role in the scheme. Kate rolled her eyes and told him to go get his new best friend's luggage.

Father Karl was not at all hesitant to occupy Bernie's old room. Sam had already filled him in on the details of Bernie's life and, to the best of our knowledge, his death. Father Karl laughed and said that if he ran into Bernie's ghost, he would perform an exorcism. Sam announced that Father Karl would perform Bernie's memorial service and Glen stated that he had found the perfect resting place for Bernie's remains. The service was to take place at ten a.m. the next day.

Father Karl participated fully in our happy hour, making a large dent in the bottle of Jameson's Irish whiskey that Sam had brought back from Seattle. He regaled the group with hilarious stories of the trials and travails of a parish priest. No one mentioned Glen's story about Father Paul. We weren't sure if his sense of humor would extend that far. Etienne and Antoinette were glowing and I realized that Father Karl and John were the closest thing to a family that they had, and Sam had managed to get them all in the same room at the same time, still another of his miracles.

Dinner consisted of glazed pork chops with an apricot compote, curried rice with shitake mushrooms and pine nuts, broiled asparagus, a radicchio salad with citrus balsamic dressing, and Serena's best key lime pie. Antoinette ate like a lumberjack and drank four glasses of sauvignon blanc. She was a little more than tipsy and revealed herself as a bit of a clown. We were all dazzled by the change in her and no one was more pleased than Father Karl. He had led us in prayer before dinner and referred to us as "God's little mysteries", indicating that he had long ago given up making a judgment regarding our beliefs as they pertained to his church. His prayer included thanks to God for renewing Antoinette's life and for the joy He had brought Etienne through Sam' generosity and love. Sam was embarrassed.

Later that evening Sam asked me if it was OK if Father Karl performed our marriage ceremony. I loved the idea. Antoinette and Etienne were overjoyed that he would be able to spend a couple of weeks or more with them. Father Karl had not taken a vacation in five years and he said that he couldn't think of anywhere he would rather spend his rest period. Of course this added any extra discipline Sam and I might have needed to behave ourselves until after we were married. The rest of the evening was spent in storytelling. Father Karl listened attentively as Adrian told of a life in which she was an actress in a traveling opera company in Italy. April remembered herself as an orphan who lived her entire life waiting to be adopted. She died of pneumonia at the age of seventeen. Before retiring he spent over an hour talking with Jenny to help him form the words for the memorial service.

The next morning was cold and rainy as Glen led us to the site he had planned for the memorial service. We followed the same trail we take to Sam's boat and we hadn't gone far before I realized what he had in mind. We were heading to that large rock that Sam, for some strange reason, salutes whenever he walks by. That is where Jenny told Bernie about the life they had shared as Horace and Luther/Lucy and where Bernie began his transformation from a troubled, dark, hopeless soul into whatever he has become. That spot marks the beginning of the end and the beginning of the beginning for Bernie. Glen had brought a small, narrow shovel and he and Alfie took turns digging a hole under the rock big enough to accommodate the urn and protect it from the elements and predators. We were sharing several umbrellas but were still miserably cold and wet, yet none of us wanted to leave. Finally, the urn was nestled under the rock and the soil was replaced and packed tightly over it.

Father Karl stepped forward. He held a large cross as he spoke to the rock. I looked at Sam and I could see that he was strained, but I couldn't tell at first what the problem was. Then I realized that he was trying with all his might not to laugh. I prayed, "Oh please dear God, don't let him start laughing because if he does, I will too. Neither of us means any disrespect. It just sometimes happens to me when I am in a somber or emotional setting and Sam is the one who bails me out. If you let Sam laugh, we are both doomed. Please God, make him stop!" My prayer worked, but only to a certain degree. We were able to camouflage but not conceal. We took turns turning our backs to accommodate a fake cough. The others were polite enough to pretend they didn't know what was happening, but the service, which lasted only about ten minutes, seemed like an eternity to me. The second it was over and we were returning to the house, the urge to laugh passed. What was that all about?

My opinion of Bernie took longer to change than it did for some of the others. The day he died, I saw no reason to mourn for anything but the life he had wasted. However, listening to some of the others over the past few days, I guess my heart has softened and I can honestly believe that Bernie will become a better soul, but it's going to take a lot of work from whatever forces are given the job of leading him. I am now able to pray for him and mean it!

This is the last you will hear from me. I'll leave the rest of the story to Sam and anyone else who wants to jump in. Just know that the rest of my life will be dedicated to living in the present with those I love. I have always had Sam's love and that could have been enough if I had been less fearful. My memories, good and bad, will always be with me, but they will no longer take me away from the enjoyment and enrichment of this life. Samantha has already acquired the knowledge that it took me fifty years to gain and I suspect that long after Sam and I are gone, she will have Etienne to keep her soul strong. To add to my joy, Alex really "gets it" now. I can thank Sam, Adrian, and even Bernie for that.

The night of Bernie's funeral I had a strange dream. I know it was a dream and not a memory, but the dream was about Isaac. You remember that Isaac was the trapper in Lily's life that brought Jeremy back to her and loved and protected her for all those years. In my dream I was back in my condo sitting in my favorite chair when I saw Isaac lying on his side on my couch with his head propped up on his hand. He was smiling at me and I wasn't at all surprised to see him there. He sat up suddenly and reached over and took both my hands and said "I have always wanted you to be happy and now I can see that you have everything you need, but I'll always be there for you". Then he disappeared. I awoke with a warm glow-not a hot flash-a real glow. After that I slept beautifully, as I have ever since.

SAM

Amanda and I are preparing to leave the island and return to Seattle. We will be making the trip on the boat and leaving the Escalade here for the time being for Etienne and Antoinette's use. One by one, or should I say two by two, everyone has left except Father Karl and the two of them. Antoinette took me by surprise when she asked if she and Etienne could stay on for a couple of months. I spoke with Patrick and he said that he would not need the house until after the first of the year and he would be glad to have someone staying there. Needless to say, Samantha is overjoyed at the prospect of making more visits and it is already planned that they will join us and Alex and Tiffany for the holidays. Antoinette said that they need this time to decide where they are going to live and to let Etienne's leg finish healing. I have a feeling I know how this is going to play out. At least I can hope.

Once everyone else left, Serena ended her employment with us and began making the changes she had planned for the kite shop. Amanda and Antoinette spent a couple of days helping her clean the place out and I did some much needed repairs to the plumbing and wiring and installed some better lighting. The place looks fabulous and smells even better with her fresh baked pastries, incense, candles and herbal teas. She is installing four booths, where people can sit and enjoy her refreshments while they assemble their kites. She also is bringing in a line of umbrellas and rain gear. I always did find it amazing that there was not one place on the island where you could buy an umbrella: This on an island where it rains half the year, if not more. Another development, Serena is going on a date with Etienne's doctor. She confided in Amanda that this will be her first real date. She has had many men friends, but no romance in her life. I can tell you that the changes in her appearance are nothing compared to the change in her view of herself. She is a sweet, wonderful, fearless winner. She has already agreed to accompany Etienne and Antoinette for the holiday visits, so our departure is less painful where she is concerned.

Amanda and Antoinette have been doing all the cooking since Serena left and they have us all on a pretty strict diet. They both are great cooks so we have enjoyable meals that don't result in added bulk, but I do miss those desserts. We have also given up the happy hour and are settling for a little wine with dinner, although Father Karl and I have partaken in an occasional sip or two of Jameson's.

Our wedding ceremony was short and sweet, very sweet. Alex, Tiffany and Samantha came the day of and spent that night so that they could enjoy the wedding dinner which was lovingly prepared and served by Serena and Antoinette. Also present was the inevitable Thelma. She was a model of grace and propriety before and during the ceremony and she managed to stay perfectly sober until dinnertime. It only took her one bottle of my finest pinot noir to work up the courage to embrace me and apologize for all those years of abuse. I believed she was sincere so it wasn't hard to accept her apology and tell her that she will always have a place in our lives. The fact that she brought me a check for fifty thousand dollars to repay her loan helped a lot. She and Serena had a lot of fun that night, but it was clear that Antoinette wanted nothing to do with her. The French have long memories and strong loyalties.

For the wedding Amanda wore the same dress she wore on Adrian's birthday and I managed to get my suit pressed and a new shirt and tie. Etienne was our photographer and he did a fine job of capturing the spirit of the day. We had promised to e-mail everyone pictures and he volunteered to take care of that as well. Father Karl performed a very traditional ceremony and everyone except Amanda cried. She got a little teary but said she would be damned if she was going to have crescent roll eyes at her wedding dinner. She carried a bouquet of purple and white mums, those being the only flowers available on the island at this time of year, and she looked beautiful and happy. I looked very handsome if I do say so myself. I can't think of any moment in my life that meant more to me.

Throughout the ceremony Etienne was working in his notebook, only by then I knew what he was doing. As each of the members of our group left he had presented them with a beautiful charcoal sketch of themselves. He is a gifted artist along with all his other skills. The amazing part was that in the background behind each sketch were very faint sketches of the characters, as he saw them, from their former lives. He even did a sketch of Bernie which he presented to me. He caught Bernie perfectly and you can see the faint images of Lucy and Luther with Horace Spencer barely visible looking on from a distance. As he presented the sketches to each person, I could see in their faces that these would be treasured possessions. I looked forward to the sketch of our wedding and the fun Amanda and I would have in selecting the place where it would be displayed. It will mean more to us than anything a professional photographer could provide. The sketch he did of Amanda had Lorretta and Lily in the background and I fell in love with the both of them too. That sketch he gave to me instead of Amanda and said it was mine to keep. Amanda liked that idea.

Amanda and I are going to wait until after the holidays to decide where we are going to live. We will be staying at her condo until then because it would be too hard to move all of

Amanda's clothes to the boat. We are thinking about building a home in the country. Amanda loves to garden and I am never happier than when I'm operating a large piece of equipment. I am taking a real interest in Kubota tractors. If we do that I am going to get a couple of dogs. One will definitely be a border collie like Camille and I am thinking about a blue heeler as the second. Of course I'll have to have a horse and one for Amanda and Samantha, maybe an extra one for when Etienne comes to visit. He should have one of his own. I wonder if Antoinette likes horses. Maybe I'll dig up old Bernie's ashes and give him a real plot somewhere off and away from the house. I'll see what my wife thinks about that.

The last thing I want to say to you is that I hope the stories we have shared with you have given you some food for thought. Whatever may be troubling you in your lives can be overcome. You don't have to wait for some rich guy to pull you off to an island for a few weeks. You just have to decide to face your fears and have faith that there is a reason and a plan for whatever comes your way. Struggle is that part of our lives that gives us the opportunity to grow our souls, or sink into self-pity and despair. Do you want to be a Bernie? I doubt it. Perhaps you can create your own "do over" right here in this life. Our minds and bodies may be flawed, but a little faith and a lot of courage can build a fearless soul.

BERNIE

You probably thought you had heard the last from me, but I insist on having the last word. Sam and Jenny were right. I was granted the opportunity to just slip out of my "Bernie body", but I have also been told that this is my last chance. You see, I am an old soul and therefore should be farther along than I am. I should be more like Adrian or Glen, two other old souls, but I keep messing up.

I am in that "in between" world now and it looks like I will be here for a long time. When I arrived I was surrounded by love, but I can't say that I sensed the joy that April described. It is clear that I have been a disappointment and I have a lot to prove before I will be let loose on the world again.

I am being shown my Bernie life, one bad choice at a time, and it is painful and frankly, pretty embarrassing. The mentor I have been assigned has a good sense of humor which makes this process a little easier, but believe me, I don't ever want to go through this again. My mentor told me that the only reason I am getting another chance is because I did finally "get it" and because my plea to be released so I could start again was so sincere and heartfelt.

If I had not found Sam's website on the internet I would have spent the rest of my life in my bitter pity party, poisoning the air wherever I went and, when I died, that would have been the end of me. I wish I could tell you what that means, but I still don't know what happens if we are "ended" and I don't intend to find out. Sam Merrick was my savior aided by Jenny and the rest of the group. I hope my presence didn't harm anyone or hamper their exploration too much. Maybe they were able to learn from my bad example.

You don't have to feel bad for me, if by some chance you were inclined to do so. In spite of my grueling schedule of self-evaluation, this is a wonderful place. I will spend some time with my mentor and then I will be sent to a place where I will be alone to rest and rejuvenate. I use words like time and place, but here time means nothing and place is a state of mind. It's hard to describe, but I can tell you that you do want to come here so do the best you can with your life. The harder you work, the better the experience.

My mentor told me to call him Buck. Now you and I know that isn't his real name, but he said I wouldn't understand his real name if I heard it and he has always wanted a name that reflects strength. Anyhow, Buck has had many lives and in between those lives he gets to act as a mentor for others while his own soul is resting. He said it took him many lifetimes to be elevated to that trusted position. He likes to share the experiences of the other souls he has mentored with me. There is no privacy here. Everyone knows everything about everyone else so he is not violating some man-made code by doing so. Besides, there are no lawyers here so he can't be sued. At first it made me very uncomfortable that all of my flaws and failings were out there for all to see, but now I have come to realize how free we become if we don't have to hide behind a façade. There is no longer any need for fear of exposure. Besides, there is nothing here but love and healing forgiveness so I have come to see this transparency as the gift it is.

I was telling Buck about how fortunate I felt to be given another chance and he told me that I was right to feel that way because I sure as hell wasn't in a class with some of the other souls he has helped. He told me about one very old soul in particular that had been a hero in every life he had been given. This guy had been through many wars and had always been the one who would throw himself on a grenade to save others. He had always loved with his whole heart even though he seldom got the girl he was after. He always put the happiness and well-being of those he loved ahead of his own. There was one life where he was a trapper in Wyoming leading a group of pioneers from the East to their new homes on the frontier. He fell in love with a woman whose husband got mixed up with a pack of wolves and he took care of the man until he could bring him back to his wife. He could have done otherwise and had a chance at spending his life with this woman himself, but he put her happiness ahead of his and did the right thing. Then he stayed with them and loved and protected her for the rest of her life without ever letting her know how he felt. I recognized the story. Buck confirmed that the man's name was Isaac and the woman was Lily. Buck said he enjoyed working with that soul more than any other and that he actually felt a little sad when it went on to another life. I asked Buck if he knew who was carrying Isaac's soul now. He didn't answer at first, but looked at me as if I should already know the answer. I did. His name is Sam Merrick.

The end? NEVER!

CPSIA information can be obtained at www.ICGtesting.com
Printed in the USA
LVOW07s0538281014

410740LV00002B/8/P